Praise for *Crossings*

A Jenny Lawson Book Club Pick and Indie Next Pick

"I don't know where to begin with this book: literally. It is a complex tapestry woven across time and space, a story that flows across decades and oceans and circles back again. It's a Möbius strip, a puzzle for the eye and the mind, a dream with architecture. Moving and inspiring and haunting—a reading experience that will stay with me." —Charles Yu, National Book Award–winning author of *Interior Chinatown*

"Romance, mystery, history, and magical invention dance across centuries in an impressive debut novel. Landragin layers historical fiction, metafiction, mystery, fantasy, myth, and romance in a way that might remind readers of such books as *Cloud Atlas, Life After Life, The Time Traveler's Wife*—or even Dan Brown's conspiracy-based adventures, albeit with more elegant prose. Landragin carries off the whole handsomely written enterprise with panache." —*Kirkus Reviews* (starred review)

"This novel is outstanding for its sheer inventiveness. The alternative ordering of chapters creates a tension that heightens the awareness of the interlocking aspects of time and space, while deft writing seduces the reader in a complex tale of pursuit, denial, and retribution moving from past to future. Highly recommended." —*Library Journal* (starred review)

"An exquisite novel. My initial melancholy rage at not having written it myself swiftly transformed into blissful gratitude that it exists at all, and that I am lucky enough to read it. Sure to be one of the biggest literary events of the year." —Sam J. Miller, Nebula Award–winning author of *Blackfish City*

"A high-concept speculative adventure novel executed with intelligence and grace . . . An invigorating puzzle of a book that reads like a complete, intricate work of genre-defying fiction."
—*Vulture*

"A sparkling debut. Landragin's seductive literary romp shines as a celebration of the act of storytelling." —*Publishers Weekly*

"Alex Landragin has created something entirely original."
—*Shelf Awareness*

"*Crossings* is playful, obsessive, romantic, intelligent, and wholly absorbing, with fascinations enough for a whole shelf of novels. I followed its alternate sequence rather than its conventional one, and reading it I had the unusual—for me maybe even unprecedented—sense, no matter where I was in the page count, that I was always occupying its exact center. Like its characters, I was never sure how close I was to the beginning of the story, how close to the end, which gave it an aura of inexhaustibility. It's a book that feels not endless but endlessly replenishable." —Kevin Brockmeier, *New York Times* bestselling author of *The Brief History of the Dead*

"Netflix would do well to option it immediately."
—*The New York Times Book Review*

"Alex Landragin's *Crossings* is a delightfully engaging tale: an epic love story, a gripping thriller, a playful puzzle box. Landragin is a confident and ambitious storyteller, and his debut novel is a joy to read." —Scott Smith, *New York Times* bestselling author of *The Ruins*

CROSSINGS

{Consisting of three manuscripts}

THE EDUCATION OF A MONSTER

CITY OF GHOSTS

TALES OF THE ALBATROSS

ST. MARTIN'S GRIFFIN
NEW YORK

Published in the United States by St. Martin's Griffin,
an imprint of St. Martin's Publishing Group

CROSSINGS. Copyright © 2019 by Alex Landragin. All rights reserved.
Printed in the United States of America. For information, address
St. Martin's Publishing Group, 120 Broadway, New York, NY 10271.

www.stmartins.com

The quotation on page 261 is taken from page 34 of
The Hours by Michael Cunningham (Farrar, Straus and Giroux, 1998).

The Library of Congress has cataloged the hardcover edition as follows:

Names: Landragin, Alex, author.
Title: Crossings : consisting of three manuscripts : The education of a
    monster : City of ghosts : Tales of the albatross.
Description: First U.S. edition. | New York : St. Martin's Press, 2020. |
    "Originally published in Australia by Picador, Pan MacMillan
    Australia Pty Ltd"—Title page verso.
Identifiers: LCCN 2019059177 | ISBN 9781250259042 (hardcover) |
    ISBN 9781250259059 (ebook)
Classification: LCC PR9619.4.L3563 C76 2020 | DDC 823/.92—dc23
LC record available at https://lccn.loc.gov/2019059177

ISBN 978-1-250-79672-1 (trade paperback)

Our books may be purchased in bulk for promotional, educational,
or business use. Please contact your local bookseller or the Macmillan Corporate
and Premium Sales Department at 1-800-221-7945, extension 5442,
or by email at MacmillanSpecialMarkets@macmillan.com.

Originally published in Australia by Picador, Pan MacMillan Australia Pty Ltd

First St. Martin's Griffin Edition: 2021

10 9 8 7 6 5 4 3 2 1

To the baroness

If you set out in this world, better be born seven times.

Attila József

CONTENTS

ooooo

Preface

I DIDN'T WRITE this book. I stole it.

Several summers ago, I received a call in my workshop on Rue des Bernardins from the noted bibliophile and book collector Beattie Ellingham. She wished to have me bind a loose-leaf manuscript that she described as the pride of her collection. There were no constraints of time or money, she said, but there was a condition, to which I agreed: I was not to read its contents. The manuscript was, in her estimation, priceless and I was to bind it accordingly. We agreed that it would be bound in what is called the Cosway style, in doublure, framed with pearls, using materials that she would provide.

I'd known Beattie Ellingham all my life. She was one of the Philadelphia Ellinghams. She'd married into the Belgian aristocracy but, having been widowed early, reverted to her maiden name and never remarried. She divided her time between her apartment on the Boulevard Haussmann and her estate in Belgium. Privately and as a term of affection, my wife and I referred to her as the Baroness, although there was in fact nothing remotely pompous or ceremonial about her. The Baroness was my oldest and most loyal client, as she had been for my father before I inherited the bindery. In the course of a long collector's life, she'd assembled one of the finest private libraries in existence of material pertaining to Charles Baudelaire.

She was more than a collector; even the word *bibliophile* did not quite do her justice. She was an obsessive. She lavished on her books the same doting affection other members of her class reserve for horses and wine. She accorded as much importance to a book's binding as to its contents. To her, bookbinding was an art, and a bookbinder an artist almost the equal of the writer. A well-crafted, bespoke binding, she liked to say, is the finest compliment a book can be paid. Whenever I undertook one of her commissions, the Baroness would visit my studio, keeping an interested eye on proceedings without interfering. For her, it was a pleasure to witness a rare book given a second lease of life in an equally rare binding. And as her collection was intended only for her private pleasure, and her fortune inexhaustible, she liked to indulge her whims to the fullest extent of the law, and even, on occasion, beyond it. Previously, I'd bound a rare Arabic edition of *Le Spleen de Paris* in leather made from the skin of a black panther, and an illustrated underground edition of the banned poems of *Les Fleurs du mal* in alligator skin with inlays of water python.

Three days after her call, the manuscript was delivered by a young fellow on a scooter. He didn't remove his helmet, which muffled his voice and obscured his face. He handed me a package containing the manuscript and the leather with which to bind it. I immediately placed it in a safety deposit box I keep above the workshop.

There are many decisions to be made when binding a book, over and above the choice of binding material. The inlays, onlays, gilding, embossing, stitching, stamping, endpapers, ex libris, boards, frontispiece, edges, headband, glue, joints, marbling, slipcase, the title page—all these were choices about which the Baroness, for all the trust she invested in me, liked to be consulted before any work could begin. That evening, I opened the package to inspect it. Seven lustrous pearls tumbled out of their black velvet purse. The enclosed leather was dyed coral-red. The ivory miniature was not, as is traditionally the case with Cosway-style binding, a portrait, but a stylized illustration in black ink of an open eye. Finally, I took in hand the manuscript itself. Even when specifically instructed not to read it, the most scrupulous bookbinder cannot help but accidentally glimpse certain words or phrases. In this case, the handwritten title leaped out at me: *Crossings*. Underneath the title was a long jumble of figures, also handwritten, seemingly without any bearing on the manuscript. It consisted of what appeared to be three separate documents, all written by hand in French, although one of them was significantly older than the other two and written in a different hand. The manuscript appeared to have had an eventful existence: many of the pages were creased, folded over or mottled with damp, and the paper itself was yellowing and pungent with the chocolatey, nutty aroma that old paper exhales as it decays.

It took me a week to call the Baroness, a little longer than usual, and when I finally did so a man's voice I didn't recognize answered the telephone and informed me she'd very recently passed away, peacefully, in her sleep. When I inquired about the funeral, I was told it had taken place only the day before, at her Belgian estate. The news so surprised me that I forgot to ask what to do about the manuscript.

The book-collecting fraternity is a small circle, and news travels fast. Two days later, as I was walking by the river along the Quai de la Tournelle, I ran into Morgane Rambouillet, a riverside *bouquiniste* who specializes in nineteenth-century romances and who I knew had counted the Baroness among her regulars. She was beside herself with excitement. According to Rambouillet, the Baroness had not died in her sleep at all. She had been murdered, and moreover her body had been found with its eyeballs missing. I shuddered when I heard this, remembering the illustrated ivory miniature that had arrived with the manuscript a week and a half earlier. I hurried home to investigate the matter online. The obituary in *Le Monde* repeated the version of events I'd been given over the telephone—a peaceful, somnolent death—while *Le Figaro's* obituary glossed over the circumstances of death altogether. The only mention of the Baroness's grisly demise was in a short report in the Belgian newspaper *L'Echo*, published the day after the incident. To an untrained eye, it seemed as if the details surrounding the Baroness's death had been hushed up.

For days afterward, my wife and I discussed the matter. What haunted me, no less than the murder of one of the last grandes dames of Paris, was the fate of those two gray agate wonders, remarked upon by all those who'd known her—her eyes. My father had told me that, in her youth, though not especially pretty, Beattie Ellingham had passed as a great beauty thanks to those eyes. They were the wellspring of her charm, perhaps even the key to her destiny. Her marriage to the Baron de Croÿ had turned out unhappily, but her eyes never lost their sparkling, feline quality.

My wife, always more practical than I, considered it perfectly understandable that I'd been lied to on the telephone. "They have to think of the family's reputation," she said. "They're not going to tell every random stranger who happens to call that she was mutilated and murdered." We concluded that the Baroness must have been mixed up in some shady book business. Rare books can bring out the worst in people.

Naturally, this led us to the same thought, one almost too awful to contemplate: could the murder of the Baroness be connected somehow with the manuscript now lying in my safety deposit box?

I waited, over the following weeks, for instructions from the estate—whether to go ahead with the commission or to return it to its new owner, whoever that might be. But I never heard from anyone. If I didn't volunteer the information that it was in my safekeeping, it was not entirely out of self-interest, but also from dread. Obviously, I didn't wish to visit upon my own family the fate that had befallen the Baroness. There was only one person in the world, other than my wife, who might know where it was: the man who'd delivered it—and I hadn't so much as seen his face. I wasn't even sure it had been a man. Given the value of the package, I was confident the estate would eventually contact me, and so I left the manuscript unbound.

Several months passed before I finally accepted the possibility that no one would be coming in search of it. It had, by accident, fallen into my lap. I decided the Baroness's request no longer applied. Now that it belonged to me, even if provisionally, I was free to read it. In one fevered sitting, on a winter's night so cold ice was forming on the Seine, I read all three of the manuscript's stories in the order in which I'd found them. The first of them, "The Education of a Monster," appears to be a short story written by Charles Baudelaire, although no other record of such a story exists anywhere other than a brief note in the poet's journal. The handwriting, however, seems authentic, even if the story itself does not, for reasons that will become clear to the reader. The second story, "City of Ghosts," is a kind of noir thriller set in Paris in 1940, seemingly narrated by Walter Benjamin, in which "The Education of a Monster" plays a pivotal role. The third story, "Tales of the Albatross," is the strangest of the three: it seems to be the autobiography of a kind of deathless enchantress.

And so, having read the story, working alone in a soft dawn light, I set about binding it. In the end, I chose a conventional, nondescript binding, using a horse leather the French call "skin of sorrow," in cardinal red. I had no doubt in my mind that it was valuable, perhaps even priceless, as the Baroness had contended. But the circumstances in which it had come to me suggested the manuscript should not draw undue attention to itself.

Once it was bound, my wife also read it. Upon seeing the jumble of figures scrawled on the first page, however, she immediately guessed that they were in fact an alternative page sequence, which we dubbed the Baroness sequence. She, too, read the manuscript, but following this alternative sequence. Having finished it, she urged me to re-read it the same way. To my astonishment, I encountered an altogether different book, not so much a collection of stories as a single novel—and no ordinary novel either. But the book was already bound and, given its antiquity and fragility, we decided that *Crossings* should remain in the order in which I'd received it—the state in which you also find it, dear reader. You will have to choose for yourself whether you wish to read it as a collection of loosely connected stories or as a single novel.

The circumstances of the death of the writer Walter Benjamin (born in Berlin, Germany, in 1892; died in Portbou, Spain, in 1940) are well known. Having fled Paris in mid-June—possibly the same day German troops occupied the city—Benjamin spent two months in Lourdes, a pilgrimage town in the Pyrenees, before making his way to Marseille to try to secure a passage to America. When this failed, he returned to the Pyrenees in mid-September, joining a small group of Jewish Germans hoping to make an illegal border crossing into Spain.

Reaching the fishing village of Portbou on September 26, the group was initially refused entry into the country. Benjamin, his heart failing and knowing he was wanted by the Nazis, was told he would be forcibly returned to France the next day. That night, in a hotel room, he swallowed a lethal dose of morphine. The following day, the others in his group were inexplicably granted entry into Spain after all.

After the war, rumors began to circulate of a manuscript Benjamin was carrying with him at the time of his death that had subsequently vanished. According to a witness who made the border crossing with him, Benjamin had been carrying a leather satchel (his only luggage) over the mountain. When asked what was in it, he'd replied that it contained a manuscript he valued more highly than his own life. As Benjamin's postwar reputation grew, so did speculation about the manuscript and its contents.

I cannot, in good conscience, claim that this book is the lost manuscript of Walter Benjamin. Its provenance is too uncertain, its contents too fantastic. But it *purports* to be just that—and nothing in it that is verifiable contradicts the claim. Let us proceed on the assumption that it is, in fact, what it appears to be. It cannot be described as anything other than a *novel*. We know Benjamin was a literary scholar, and that he even anonymously co-wrote a detective novel. We know that his French was impeccable, and certainly up to the task. All the same, to publish the manuscript under his name would be unconscionable. And so, for lack of another name—perhaps also, if I am honest, out of a booklover's vanity—I decided to publish it under my own name, with the caveat that takes the form of this preface. Strictly speaking, I am but the adopted parent of this foundling—still, there are no genetic tests for manuscripts. If the ethics of my decision are suspect, I am confident I at least stand on solid legal ground. As it is now more than seventy years since Benjamin's passing, the book (if it is indeed authentic) is, under French law, beyond the reach of the Benjamin estate.

I am convinced the Baroness never intended to publish her manuscript: she wanted it bound for her own private pleasure. While the story of how *Crossings* came to be published—and why, and its history—must be reserved for another occasion, publishing it was not a decision taken lightly. For reasons of provenance alone, I don't expect its publication to be uncontroversial, at least in the remoter corners of academia or bibliophilia. Having come to know it intimately, I believe there are at least seven ways *Crossings* may be interpreted: as an imagined story—an anonymous work, therefore, of *fiction*; as an elaborate joke, prank, or puzzle inexplicably fabricated by Benjamin himself; as a hoax or forgery concocted by an unknown third party; as the delusions of a man in declining health and under overwhelming psychic pressure; as a complex and subterranean allegory or fable; as some kind of enigmatic code to an unknown recipient; or as thinly veiled memoir. I am by now too close to this tale to have a dispassionate view. I must have entertained each of these possibilities at least once, and some of them several times, and still I am undecided.

Note to the Reader

As related in the preface, this book can be read in two ways: conventionally (that is, from first page to last) or by following the Baroness sequence. Those reading the Baroness sequence will find, at the end of each section, a page number in curly brackets (such as that below this note) indicating which page to turn to next. Readers of the Baroness sequence will thus begin the novel on page 150. For reference, the Baroness sequence's pagination order is outlined below. Readers who decide to read the novel in the conventional manner need only turn the page.

Baroness sequence pagination:

150–39–157–53–1–175–71–11–206–23–87–226–
31–257–103–308–124–352–141–154

{150}

The Education of a Monster

A Disgraceful Episode

As I write these words, it occurs to me that I have never known a tale to be so *beyond belief* as that which I am about to relate to you, dear girl. Yet nothing I have written has ever been so true. Paradox, all is paradox. Perhaps I have taken leave of my senses once and for all. You see, as a youth, I contracted the pox, no doubt from Jeanne Duval. This scourge is known, in old age, to drive its victims to madness, so that they know not the difference between the real and the unreal. I live in the permanent shadow of my impending lunacy. But as you will learn, it is not the only way in which Jeanne haunts me still. Indeed, if I am writing to you at all, it is because of Jeanne.

We are not strangers, you and I. I am the gentleman you met this afternoon in the Church of Saint-Loup, accompanied by Madame Édmonde. Your name is Mathilde. You are a sullen, bovine sixteen-year-old girl. Despite the assurances of the nuns who discharged you into Madame Édmonde's care, you can barely read. Admittedly, you recognize the letters of the alphabet, but that can hardly be called reading. You can scribble your name, but that can hardly be called writing. Still, I trust that Madame Édmonde knows what she is doing. I have no choice.

As you know, I am a poet. I am forty-three years old, though I appear much older, due to many years of deprivation. Success, at least of the worldly variety, has hitherto eluded me, despite the excellence of my verse. In April last year, in poor health and low spirits, I left Paris, where I had lived almost all my life, determined to see out the rest of my days in Brussels as an exile. I had somehow convinced myself that I had better prospects here. I was following in the footsteps of my publisher and dear friend Auguste Poulet-Malassis, who had left Paris hoping to make some money by publishing pornography—the Belgian censor is less prudish than his French counterpart—and smuggling it into France. I arrived filled with an élan I had not known since my youth.

Upon my arrival, I rented a room in an old, decrepit hotel called the Grand Miroir on the sole basis that I liked its strange and poetic name. It had little else to recommend it. I asked for the cheapest room. It was on the uppermost floor, up three flights of a tortuously winding staircase. There was a small bed with a mattress of old damp straw, a tattered divan, a rickety writing desk, a stove that emitted more smoke than heat, and a chest of drawers. I was, at least, able to observe through a solitary window the clouds drifting across the sky, above the cityscape of rooftops and chimneys. It was one of my few remaining consolations. As long as I have a glimpse of sky, I can tolerate almost any hardship.

I had hoped my self-imposed exile would bring an end to the daily humiliations of my Parisian existence. In fact, my prospects in Brussels were no better than anywhere else. I was soon beset by the same trials and tribulations that had dogged me before: cold, damp, penury, sickness, and calumny. I have been unable to keep up with my expenses and the only reason the proprietors, Monsieur and Madame Lepage, have allowed me to remain is the hope that, should I die, they might be paid their due out of my estate—with interest, of course. They not only hope for my death, they are counting on its imminence.

The evening on which this tale begins, early last month—that month being March of 1865—I had just dined at Madame Hugo's. Madame Hugo has always been unfailingly kind to me despite my occasional fits of distemper. Like me, her husband is in exile, but he lives in comfort in Guernsey with his mistress, playing the part of the national hero.

His wife shares a large bourgeois house on Rue de l'Astronomie with her son and his family. A little colony of Parisians has formed in Brussels lately, despite its backwardness. We have taken flight from Napoleon's grand-nephew and his overzealous prelates. As Auguste was also invited to dine at Madame Hugo's, he met me at the hotel and we walked there together, as we had many times before, arm in arm in case one of us should trip on the paving stones—the streets here are in a lamentable condition. As we walked, complaining about Belgium as we habitually did, I felt the wetness of the paving stones ooze into my shoes through holes that had opened up in the soles, which for lack of money I had not had repaired. As we neared the Hugo residence, Auguste urged me to guard against my usual outbursts of slander and to preserve my honor, and his too, which was linked to mine by friendship.

The maid, Odette, opened the door and ushered us in to the light and warmth. A consoling odor of roasted meats pervaded the house. There were eight of us in attendance that evening. Other than Auguste and myself, Madame Hugo, her son and his wife, there was a trio of young ladies whose names I instantly forgot. I kissed my hostess's hand with an exaggerated bow. Wine was served in the drawing room—bad wine, of course, in tiny glasses. When we took our seats, I lowered my head and devoted my attention to the soup—an excellent consommé. All around me I heard a literary conversation begin, which I studiously avoided joining. I was concerned solely with the spooning of the soup into my mouth. I did not touch the bread, knowing it would be moist, soft, and burned, as is all bread in this country.

As much as I tried to keep my mind on this simple task, however, it strayed near and far according to its own desires. I heard one of the three ladies ask me my opinion of Belgium. Auguste interrupted and attempted to steer the conversation in another direction, but another of the three demoiselles repeated the question not a minute later, by chance at the very moment there was no more consommé left in my bowl.

This time I could not resist the temptation. I paused to gather my thoughts as the maid removed my soup plate and replaced it immediately (as is the custom here) with a plate of the ubiquitous parboiled beef. Auguste's face was crumpled in a supplicating expression. I ignored it. "Where do I begin?" I began, wiping my mouth with my napkin and studying the faces of the three ladies before me. "For one thing, in this country, people's faces are ill formed and pale. Their jaws are strangely built and display a menacing imbecility. At every level, people are lazy and slow. Happiness here is an accident of imitation. Almost everyone wears a pince-nez or is a hunchback. The physiognomy of the inhabitants is shapeless and flabby. The typical Belgian is part monkey and part mollusc. He is thoughtless and heavy, easy to oppress but impossible to crush. He hates to laugh but will do so to make you think he's understood you. Beauty is despised, as is the life of the mind. Non-conformism is a heinous crime. Dancing consists of jumping up and down in silence. No one speaks Latin or Greek, poetry and literature are loathed, and people study only to become engineers and bankers. The landscapes are like the women: fat, buxom, humid, and somber. Life is insipid. Cigars, vegetables, flowers, fruits, cooking, eyes, hair—everything is bland, sad, tasteless, and drowsy. The dogs are the only creatures who are truly alive."

Other than some uneasy laughter emanating from one end of the table, my provocations elicited only silence.

"As for Brussels," I continued, "there is nothing sadder than a city without a river. Every city, every country, has its own odor. Paris smells of sour cabbage, Cape Town of sheep. There are tropical islands that smell of sandalwood, musk, or coconut oil. Russia smells of leather, Lyon of charcoal. The Orient, in general, smells of musk and carrion. By contrast, Brussels smells of black soap. The hotel rooms, the beds, the towels, the footpaths—everything smells of black soap. The buildings have balconies but one never sees anyone on them. The only sign of life is shopkeepers cleaning their shopfronts, which seems to be a national obsession, even when it is pouring with rain."

"Charles, please," I heard Auguste mumble.

"The difference between Paris and Brussels is that in Paris one is permitted to visit a brothel but not to read about it. In Brussels, it is precisely the contrary. It's a small town, teeming with jealousy and slander. As a result of indolence and impotence, the people take inordinate interest in the affairs of others—and pleasure in their misfortunes. The streets, though lifeless, are somehow noisier than Parisian streets, on account of the irregular paving, the poorly constructed buildings, the narrowness of the public thoroughfares, the savage and immoderate local accent, the prevailing rudeness, the constant whistling and the barking of dogs. The shops have no window displays. Dawdling, so dear to people endowed with imagination, is impossible—there's nothing to see, and the paths are unnavigable. Everything but the rent is expensive. Wine is a curiosity, drunk not for the taste but out of vanity and conformity, to ape the French. As for the food, everything is parboiled, never roasted, and smothered in rancid butter. The vegetables are execrable. The Belgian cook's idea of seasoning is limited to salt."

I paused. My diatribe was garnering some nervous chuckles and an occasional tut-tutting from Madame Hugo. The three ladies in front of me seemed unsure of how they should react—whether this was a performance intended to amuse or injure. Once again I heard a distant plea from Auguste: "Charles, please stop this nonsense." But when in this sort of mood, I cannot help myself.

"There are no women in this country. No women and no love—no gallantry among the males and no modesty among the females. The women are physically comparable to sheep, pale and yellow-haired, with enormous, tallow legs—not to mention the horrors of their ankles. They appear unable to smile, due no doubt to some congenital muscular recalcitrance and the structure of their teeth and jaws—"

"Enough!" This time it was Charles Hugo who interjected, throwing his chair back as he rose to his feet, his face scarlet, his clenched fists visibly trembling with rage. "I will not have my guests humiliated thus!" He threw his napkin on his plate and strode out of the room, which was left in a frosty quiet. The three ladies were blushing crimson, and two of them had tears in their eyes.

"Charles," said Auguste, "please, let us take our leave."

Auguste offered to accompany me to the Grand Miroir. I expected him to berate me for once again humiliating the both of us with my antics, but instead he packed tobacco into his pipe and smoked it quietly as we walked arm in arm over cobblestones rendered slick by the foggy evening. My nerves were soothed by the closeness of my friend, the fragrance of the burning tobacco, and the night's icy stillness.

As we walked, I put my free hand, tingling with cold, into my coat pocket and felt it rub against soft, thick paper. I stopped and took it out and held it up to the light of a gas lamp. It was a note for no less than one hundred francs, presumably slipped into my pocket by Madame Hugo as we were bidding each other farewell. I was delighted: I would be able to buy more laudanum in the morning. I suggested we go to a tavern and have a drink to warm ourselves. Auguste stopped walking and considered me with an odd look on his face, a look at once loving and sorrowful. "No, my friend," he said, "I think I'll go home to my wife and children." *Home. Wife. Children.* The words cut me to the quick. If only I was worthy of uttering such a simple phrase. He embraced me and walked away without another word, huddled over in cold and worry. As his silhouette retreated and faded into the dim fog, I saw for the first time the extent to which he, too, was a defeated man, this lifelong friend of mine, my publisher and protector, my staunchest ally and closest confidant. It was evident that he had, without my even noticing it, perhaps without even noticing it himself, joined me among the ranks of the vanquished. There is a mysterious alchemy that overtakes a man when he tastes the bitterness of one of life's definitive routs: a shrinking and a stooping, a seeping away of vital energies, a realization that the best is behind him. While I had been prophesying my own demise my whole life, anticipating it, relishing the foretaste of it, his defeat was still new and unfamiliar to him. His palate was not yet habituated to its flavor. Worse still, I was partly to blame. He'd lost a small fortune publishing my poems, defending them in court when the censor deemed several among them on the subject of sapphic love to be indecent, and then pulping the lot when the trial was lost. As his silhouette slinked away in the pale lamplight of that frigid Brussels night, even the hat on his head seemed smaller, and his shoulders disappeared under the scarf he'd wrapped around his neck.

With Auguste gone, I headed down the Rue des Paroissiens in the direction of the Grand Miroir, turning my collar up against the drizzle. The streets were empty and silent, except for the sigh of burning gas in the lamps and an occasional flurry of footsteps behind me. I slipped on a paving stone and landed with both feet in water up to my ankles.

As I turned a corner to face the railway station, wading miserably through one ankle-deep puddle after another, I heard the echo of a stately carriage in a nearby street ahead of me. It turned the corner and was suddenly careening toward me. In my rush to remove myself from its path, my left ankle twisted on a protruding paving stone and, thrown off balance, I landed face-first in the slush with the two horses bearing down on me. Intending to dive toward the gutter, I was getting back to my feet when a wheel collided with my right shoulder, throwing me askance once more and spinning me around, so that I landed—this time on my back—in yet another puddle. Needless to say, the carriage continued on its way, turning left into Rue des Colonies, the driver in all likelihood oblivious to the fact that he had just now bowled over, and very nearly finished off, the greatest lyric poet of the age.

Lying on my back in the filth, icy water seeping through my coat, I was convinced my life was finally nearing its pitiable conclusion. It occurred to me that I ought to have jumped in the other direction, *under* the horses rather than away from them. As I lay there in that puddle, on those slick paving stones, in that strange city, on that icy evening, all my hopes extinguished, I found the prospect of my imminent demise unexpectedly consoling. In the cold and the damp, I began to shiver with a violence that would not be brought into abeyance. Presently the pain of my injuries began to recede, the wild beating of my heart slowed and my breathing became less frantic. I realized I would not be dying there and then. My accursed existence would continue, at least for now. At the dawning of this thought, I began to scream, abusing that tenacity of life that seems to override every wiser instinct. And once I had begun, I continued, wholeheartedly cursing, stringing beads of curses together to make garlands of curses, which I hurled at Victor Hugo and Madame Hugo, at her sons and her guests. I cursed the Grand Miroir and Brussels and Belgium and the Belgians. I cursed the King of Belgium and for good measure I cursed the Emperor of France. I cursed men and women, mankind and womankind too. I cursed poetry and literature and art and love, and when I had finished cursing all those things I cursed life and God Himself. And it was while I was cursing God that I noticed, standing above me, the silhouette of a man's body, wearing a round hat and a cape. A gaunt whiskered face leaned down to study me closer. "Are you in pain, monsieur?"

"I hardly know," I said, "but it seems I cannot raise myself."

"Here," he said, "let me help you to your feet." He bent down and put his gloved hands behind my shoulders and under my arms. He smelled of black soap. "On the count of three," he said, "*un, deux, trois.*" I was lifted to my feet and the stranger released his grip slowly so that I might bear the weight of my body. I felt a sharp pain in my left ankle and let out a strangled cry. The stranger had to catch me to stop me from falling again. "You are injured, sir, and your wounds must be treated. Allow me to take you back to my mistress's quarters so that you may receive the rest and medical attention you require."

Naturally, my first inclination was to refuse him, to insist on continuing to the tavern. But a wave of weariness descended upon me, and all I wanted to do was sleep. "Yes," I said, swaying on my feet until I sank into his arms, "rest and attention. That is precisely what I need."

☞ *{175}*

A Touching Reunion

EVER SINCE I WAS a young man, I have been prone to bouts of a kind of nocturnal dementia, awoken by the terrors of my dreams, finding myself sitting upright in the dark, my entire body moist with perspiration. As soon as I open my eyes, the offending dream invariably retreats, leaving only the subtlest traces—the white sand of a distant tropic, a great volcano, a storm-tossed sea, overripe flowers, a ship under full sail . . . And, above all, eyes. Eyes the color of obsidian, eyes I have dreamed of so often I can see them with perfect clarity even when I am awake. Normally this occurs while sleeping in my own bed and, quickly recognizing my familiar surrounds, I can pull myself together, light a candle, perhaps open a book or write until I am lulled back into the arms of Morpheus. In a bygone time, I would have found Jeanne lying beside me, her beguiling black eyes open, awoken by my commotion, and she would have asked me what I had dreamed, and once I'd told her, she would have interpreted my visions according to some far-fetched, pagan mythology of her own devising, in which she and I were the reincarnated souls of an ancient bird-god, until I would once again sink into sleep.

And so it was on this particular night that I was startled awake by another nightmare. Only now that I had long since abandoned her there was no Jeanne to console me. The bed in which I found myself was unknown to me. Rather than the lump of damp straw I slept on at the Grand Miroir, this was a four-posted Medici bed with a finely carved oak frame canopied with swathes of purple and gold silk brocade. The mattress was the highest and softest I've known. The mellow light of an oil lamp revealed an aristocratic boudoir. The ceiling was coffered in gold, and in every corner of the room crimson camellias burst from Oriental vases. I heard the spit and crackle of embers glowing in a hearth on the other side of the room. It took me some time, my head misted by an opiate fog, to remember the chain of events that had led me here: a collision with a coach's wheel, lying in a puddle on a cobblestoned street, and then the unexpected succor of a stranger.

I tried rolling over and was struck by a cluster of pains: one in my head, one in my back, another in my right hip, and, most acutely of all, a throbbing pain in my left ankle. Slowly, I attempted to stand, but the discomfort sat me back on my haunches. I tried again, and eventually my feet found a pair of woolen slippers. I limped across the room, where on a velvet divan was laid a vermilion gown brocaded with arabesques. My effects were nowhere to be seen. I hobbled to the window and pulled back the heavy satin curtains. I had presumed it was early morning, but I was dazzled by the light of a sunny day after snowfall. I was in a room on the ground floor of a manor house, either in the country or on the city's outskirts. I looked over a courtyard garden hibernating under the cover of snow. While my room was adorned with the most dazzling colors, the outside world was a daguerreotype of black and white.

In a corner of the room, beside the divan, was a writing table with a pen, an inkwell, a polished brass bell, and several leaves of *papier japon*. The uppermost leaf had a note scrawled on it. I slumped into the chair and read it: *Monsieur, I trust you have rested well. Giacomo is waiting to assist you. You may summon him by ringing the bell. Madame Édmonde.*

Moments after I'd followed the letter-writer's instructions, the door creaked open. Into the room floated a large silver tray followed by its deliverer, a butler whose whiskered face was as still as a death mask. It was the stranger who had saved me the previous evening.

The best domestics have an almost magical ability to divine their master's wishes, and Giacomo returned moments after I'd finished my coffee to guide me to an adjoining room with a bath. He helped me bathe, shaved me, and, once I had dried myself, dressed me in clothes of the finest quality: the kind of suit one might have tailored at Staub or d'Humann, a shirt and cravat from Boivin, a tie-pin from Janinch, and a cane from Verdier, with a solid silver handle in the shape of a duck's head. Once, as a young dandy, I would have been proud to wear such finery. Now, in my syphilitic autumn, I felt like a doll dressed for some maudlin carnival.

Thus, seated before the fireplace in my costume, I meditated upon this turn of events for some time before Giacomo reappeared to announce that dinner was served. He eased me into a chair on wheels and pushed me down a long, sparkling hallway to a dining room where, at opposite ends of a long table, two places were set. "Madame Édmonde begs the pardon of monsieur," Giacomo said dryly. "She has been unexpectedly detained and will join monsieur as soon as possible. In the meantime, she begs that you begin dining without delay."

I ate, as if I had not eaten in days, all kinds of roasted meats, cheeses and jams, toffees and tarts, washed down with fine wine, coffee, and brandy. The dining room was decorated even more garishly than my bedroom—ribbons of gilding on the walls, the ceiling divided into lozenge panels, intricate parquet floor, a marble fireplace, and more camellias in every corner. The windows looked out onto the same courtyard I'd observed from my bedroom, and the walls were almost covered over with fine paintings depicting various maritime and colonial scenes.

Finally, as I smoked a cigar, Giacomo announced the arrival of Madame Édmonde. He opened the doors at the end of the room and the slender shape of a young woman wearing a sumptuous black dress appeared. Pinned to the crown of thick braids that adorned her head was a veil of dark tulle that masked her face. I tried to stand but a shot of pain in my ankle cut my gallantry short. She approached the table hesitantly, almost shyly. There was a subtle, feline grace about her movements, set to the rustle of the velvet of her dress. She approached until she stood directly before me. "Please, monsieur, remain seated," she said. Her voice was hushed, as if coming from a much greater distance than where she stood. "I am given to understand you are pained, and at any rate, I do not stand for excessive formality."

Giacomo helped her into the seat at the opposite end of the table. She asked if I had eaten my fill; I assured her I had, and thanked her for her hospitality. My clothes, she said, were being laundered. I asked after my fob watch. "It was shattered," she replied. "It has been sent to a watchmaker to be repaired."

"If you will pardon my forwardness, madame," I began, "I am brimming with curiosity. Who are you?"

"My name is Madame Édmonde de Bressy."

"De Bressy . . . Your name is unfamiliar to me."

"That is of no consequence."

"Why are you lavishing such generosity upon a complete stranger?"

"You are not a complete stranger."

"Do we know each other?"

"In a manner of speaking."

"I do not recall having ever met a Madame Édmonde, or even a Mademoiselle Édmonde."

"That does not alter the fact that we have had occasion to know each other, in a distant past."

"Perhaps," I said, "if you reveal your face I will remember."

"I assure you it will make no difference at all," she replied, but all the same she raised her hands to her veil and lifted it, pulling it back over her head, revealing a face that was hideously disfigured, closer in resemblance to the face of a monster encountered in a dream than that of a man or woman. Among the living, the only faces I have seen that could compare are in the daguerreotypes that were fashionable in Paris years ago, and which can still be found from time to time in the stalls of the riverside bouquinistes, depicting the deformed countenances of certain unfortunates residing in the Salpêtrière hospital. It was as if some demon had pulled her eyes down toward the floor and simultaneously lifted the nose upward and to the right. Her mouth was diagonally distended. The skin of her face appeared to have been ravaged by flames in its lower part, and her chin was inverted. As it was already nearing dusk, she was illuminated by candlelight, and its shadows accentuated the unnatural walnutty crevices of her face.

I knew not what to say, and a silence as thick as snow descended upon us. It was Madame Édmonde who broke it. "You may take every advantage of my hospitality for as long as you wish," she said, lowering her veil. "You are not a prisoner here. You may come and go. You are welcome to stay as long as you like, to leave whenever you like—now, tomorrow, or next week. When you decide to leave, you will be provided with a carriage and driven to your hotel." *Your hotel*, I noted, without interrupting her. She knew far more of me than I of her. "If you choose to stay," she continued, "I will unveil every mystery about myself that you wish. But if you should choose to return to your lodgings tonight, I have only one thing to say to you."

"And what is that, pray tell?"

She sat in perfect stillness. Somehow I felt her eyes fixed on me, even though they were hidden behind her veil. "Monsieur, listen carefully to what I have to tell you. All the stories Jeanne Duval told you are true—every last one. They were not fantasies. They were not hallucinations. They were not inventions, fabrications, or lies. She was no lunatic, hysteric, or Scheherazade. She was not a ghost or a ghoul. She was a teller of the truth. And you would do well to heed it." With the utmost grace and dignity, Madame Édmonde stood and, bidding me a good night, walked off toward the doorway.

I was, at first, lost for words, but I managed to blurt out one final question before she disappeared. "How is it that you know of this—of Jeanne, of me, of what occurred between us?"

My host stopped at the threshold of the room, still turned away from me, and replied, "I shouldn't have to explain. You already know."

And then she was gone, leaving me to return to my apartment with the help of Giacomo. For all the laudanum I swallowed, I could not sleep that night, but was plunged into a labyrinth of memories that, since my departure from Paris, I'd done my best to forget. Now, they returned with such force that I feared they might consume me altogether.

The following morning, I was woken by a nightmare. I rang for Giacomo, who once again assisted me to rise from bed, bathe, and dress. He pushed me in my chair on wheels to a deserted drawing room and poured me a cup of tea. This room was furnished in mahogany and velvet, and as exuberantly decorated as the dining room of the previous evening. Outside, yesterday's snow was beginning to melt in the late winter sunshine. I sat in my armchair, sipping my tea, excited by the prospect of seeing Madame Édmonde.

When she arrived several minutes later, she was, once again, veiled. Her dress was as dark and sumptuous as the previous evening's. As we bade each other good morning, she sat on an armchair beside mine, still moving with that satin grace I'd noticed before. Giacomo poured her a cup of tea. I noted how her veil was a source of power, for it made it impossible to discern precisely where her gaze was aimed. My desire to observe my host was due not to morbid curiosity but to the fervid meditations of the previous, sleepless night. With that veil, such observation was impossible.

It was only when Giacomo had retired from the room that she resumed the conversation. "Are you feeling better, Monsieur Baudelaire?"

"Decidedly not. I barely slept and can hardly move without the assistance of your manservant."

"What, pray, was the cause of your insomnia? Is the bed not to your liking?"

"My restlessness had nothing to do with the bed, which is in fact the most comfortable I have ever known. Rather, it was the riddle you posed me yesterday."

"It was less of a riddle and more a statement of fact."

"It was a riddle, and I spent the entire night seeking its answer."

"Then I fear you wasted your time. The riddle is its own answer."

I felt a sudden wave of ill temper wash over me, a lifelong habit that has worsened with age. I let it pass before continuing. "You said everything Jeanne ever told me was true. Surely not *everything*?"

"I said all of her stories were true. Jeanne was not incapable of lying, but about certain things her word was her honor."

"If you know all you claim, you also know how fantastic her stories were."

"I am aware of their nature."

"Jeanne believed in the transmigration of souls."

"Yes. She called it *crossing*."

"And yet you insist her stories are true."

"Evidently."

"You will excuse me if I ask you for proof of your knowledge."

Madame Édmonde sighed. "Where to begin? Shall I tell you about Koahu and Alula, and how they loved one another? Or about the island of Oaeetee, the chief Otahu, and the sage Fetu? Shall I tell you about the *Solide*, its captain Marchand, the surgeon Roblet, and the sailor Joubert?"

I was in disbelief. "What about the albatross? What do you know of that?"

I had the distinct impression that, with that question, I had managed to launch an arrow of my own through her veil. Her head drooped down. "Ah, yes. The albatross. You mean the story of the owl and the tern." Her head lifted again.

I could not hide my astonishment. "How is it that you are so familiar with these tales?"

"Oh, Charles, if I tell you, will you not react with your customary disdain?"

"Jeanne's stories were a child's fairy tales—a lunatic's *delusions*!" I said, thumping an armrest with a clenched fist.

Madame Édmonde remained perfectly still until she finally said, in almost a whisper, "Do you remember the last occasion you saw Jeanne?"

"How can I forget?"

"How many people have you told about it?"

"No one." How could I have told anyone? I was too ashamed.

"If I told you, now, would that be sufficient proof?"

I nodded. "Yes. I suppose it would." And yet I didn't want to hear.

"You had just awoken from one of your nightmares. Jeanne began to console you, as she had done throughout the years. But that morning you would not be consoled. Her tales had long since ceased to comfort you. And on this occasion you were especially inconsolable." Madame Édmonde paused. "Do you remember how you responded?"

I nodded shamefully. "Yes," I murmured, "I'm afraid I do."

"You lost your temper. You told her she was a hysteric, that you could have her locked up, that if she did not stop her nonsense you would have her committed to the Salpêtrière."

I hung my head. It was all true.

"Of course, it wasn't the first time you'd lost your temper. But this occasion was different, wasn't it?"

"Yes," I groaned. "Yes, it was."

"And what made it different was that you took out your belt and you began whipping me."

I opened my mouth, as if by reflex, to both protest and defend myself, but caught between the two reflexes I could only stammer, unable to find the words for the task.

"You tore the dress from my back, and you whipped me, over and over, until the skin was streaked with blood. And do you remember what you said?"

"No, please don't . . ."

"You said you were whipping me like the slave I was, like the slave I would always be . . ."

"Enough!" I cried. Despite my injuries, I sprang from my seat and, cane in hand, limped over to the window that overlooked the courtyard. The pain in my heart now rendered me oblivious to that of my ankle. "You want me to believe that you are Jeanne?" I looked back at her, but no reply emanated from behind the veil. "How can such a thing be possible? It contravenes the fundamental laws of nature—of science and physics. I simply cannot accept the notion that the woman who is speaking to me right now was once another woman, one I knew intimately, the woman with whom I shared the best and worst moments of my life. It is utter nonsense—the worst kind of flim-flammery."

"You who are a poet, do you not see that the power of the crossing is within every human soul? Whenever you look another person in the eyes, do you not feel within the pit of your stomach a kind of forward yearning so powerful that it frightens you? Do we not avert our gazes in polite society precisely because of the vertigo that comes from looking into the eyes of another? And isn't that vertigo not so much the fear of crossing as the fear of the desire to cross? Are not our souls constantly reaching out toward the other, striving for the freedom of the crossing?"

"And now you dare suggest that this ability, altogether too strange to believe, is available to any poor fool?"

"Yes, it is within us all, only it takes many years of training to undertake it, and many more to master it. It should begin early, as early as possible, as a child learns to walk and speak. Once that moment is past, it is almost impossible to learn. But the *potential* to cross lies within every single human being."

I turned back to face the woman whose voice seemed to be floating to me not from across a room but from across an ocean.

"The knowledge of the crossing has all but disappeared," she continued. "And yet, in classical times, it was known to many peoples. The myths and legends have survived—all those stories of metamorphosis are vestiges of a time when the practice of crossing was commonplace."

"Stop, I cannot bear any more of this nonsense!" I turned away again to regain my composure. "Madame Édmonde, my sanity is barely hanging by a thread as it is. Do you wish me to slip into madness once and for all?"

"Charles, you used to call me your Scheherazade. Do you remember what it was that Scheherazade did?"

"She told the king a story every night to stop him from executing her, as he had all his previous brides."

"The difference between Scheherazade and me is that my stories were not intended to save my life but to save *yours*. To prepare you for your next crossing."

"You misunderstand me. I am not afraid of death. In fact, I long for it."

"Charles, you cannot die. You must return with me."

"Return where?"

"To the island."

At the mention of the word "island," my vision blurred and I felt a hot teardrop inexplicably creep down my cheek. I approached Édmonde and slowly lowered myself down beside her. Her bearing was so still it was impossible to divine what she was feeling behind her veil. "Oh, Jeanne," I whispered, taking Édmonde's hand in mine and kissing it, "how I have missed you! There is not a day that goes by . . ."

"Charles, please," she whispered, withdrawing her hand. "I am no longer Jeanne. I am Édmonde."

I reached for her veil and lifted it slowly. Before me was revealed that hideous face I'd seen the previous evening. Had an old Flemish master painted the visage of Death itself, he would scarcely have found a better model. Yet I did not feel the revulsion that had taken ahold of me before, but instead detected the stirrings of an old affection.

"I was Jeanne once," spoke those blighted, shriveled lips. "I was beautiful once. But I am beautiful no longer. In my ugliness I have discovered my freedom. And now I am offering you yours. I have come to Brussels specifically for this task. I have rented these lodgings with the sole task of finding you and offering you another crossing. Believe me, Charles, believe and trust me. I will arrange another crossing for you. A crossing with someone who is young and strong. Then, together, we will return to the island. And somehow, we will find a way to repair the damage we have done."

☞ {206}

A Suitable Candidate

HAVING RETURNED TO the Grand Miroir, I did not hear again from Madame Édmonde for some days. This was how she had intended it. "Continue your life as before," she had impressed upon me as we discussed our plans. "Draw as little attention to yourself as possible. Let no one suspect you have had a change of fortune." Giacomo gave me my old clothes and shoes back—laundered and mended—and I left the manor as I had entered it, only a little cleaner and plumper.

Édmonde had taken it upon herself to find a candidate for a crossing. Before we parted, she encouraged me to consider crossing with a young woman, arguing it would be easier to find a suitable candidate. But I was against the idea. What man in his right mind would choose to be a woman?

My return to the Grand Miroir caused a commotion from the landlord Lepage and his wife. Evidently, they'd decided I'd vanished without paying my bills. I gave them twenty francs to ease their worries—Édmonde had given me a little money, advising me to spend it cautiously—but not so much as to raise their suspicions.

My instructions were strict. In preparation for what was to come, I was to write down everything I knew about the crossing, everything she had told me as well as everything Jeanne had told me. "This way, after the next crossing,"

Édmonde had explained, "you will have all the proof you need regarding who you are and where you have come from, so that if we should be separated again you need not spend a whole lifetime piecing together the clues scrambled in your nightmares." And so, on Édmonde's fine *papier japon*, I began writing the story you are reading, beginning with the dinner at Madame Hugo's and the accident that followed it, my rescue by a stranger, and finally my encounter with Édmonde. I wrote constantly, obsessively, writing and rewriting, as is a poet's wont, burning the drafts in the stove to prevent the landlady from reading them. In days gone by, I might have protested at the absurdity of the notion of crossing from one body into another, and even now I was assailed by doubts. But passing as I was through the valley of the shadow of death, I surrendered myself completely to it. I was certain that Édmonde's reminiscences of Jeanne constituted incontrovertible proof that what she was saying, however ludicrous, was true. The chance to live again, in a youthful body, the chance to escape the clutches of penury, insanity, and mortality, and perhaps above all the chance to redeem myself for my past failures—all of these taken together added up to a temptation I could not—perhaps even should not—resist.

I settled back into my hermetic life. I spent my days in bed, writing. After a few days, I began to fear I would never hear from Édmonde again. I considered returning to the manor where she'd lodged me, but I realized I had no idea of how to find it on my own. When her letter finally arrived, more than a week after we'd parted, it was on plain paper, with no letterhead or return address. The envelope appeared to have been tampered with, as if opened with the aid of steam and resealed. The landlord, I suspected, hoping to find money inside. Édmonde had thought of this: we'd agreed to write to each other in a kind of code, impenetrable to outsiders.

Dear Charles, her note read,

Forgive me that this letter has taken rather longer to reach you than I would have wished. I am making every effort to find the person matching your description. Even under normal circumstances, arranging such a meeting would prove troublesome, but my physiognomic impediment only adds to the difficulty. You asked me to find an able-bodied youth with literary talent. I have made my tour of the city's universities and seminaries and have unearthed no such personage. I shall now venture further out, into the provinces and towns, and shall write to you as soon as I have found a candidate. Please remain patient and hopeful. Yours, etc.

Three days later, Édmonde's next missive arrived. It, too, betrayed signs of having been opened illicitly. *Take the nine o'clock train to Charleroi on Tuesday. I will meet you there.*

Standing beside the ticket counter at the village railway station, Édmonde, veiled as always, appeared to be the dark center of the revolving world, impervious to the noisy, smoky hubbub that overtakes a railway station in the moments after a train's arrival. But when she spotted me limping toward her (I was still walking with a cane), she sprang into action. She took me by the arm and led me outside, through the clatter of horses, buggies, and drivers, to the village coffee house. "His name is Fernand Roux," she said. "He is exactly what you asked for—young, educated, from a family of clerics. He is healthy, afflicted neither by the pox nor by consumption. And he is a seminarian. After his ordination, he wants to travel to the colonies to convert the natives."

"What does he know of our intent?"

"Only that your soul needs saving," she replied. "Which is not untrue." We entered the coffee house. Édmonde looked about a moment and, still gripping my forearm, started off in the direction of a young man sitting alone at a wooden table. The youth was so gaunt and angular in appearance he reminded me less of a man and more of a praying mantis, with a wispy beard and longish hair carefully arranged to fall over one eye. On account of his unusual height, he had adopted a permanent stooped posture and seemed to be folded into his chair rather than seated upon it. "Bonjour, Monsieur Roux. Allow me to introduce you to my friend, Monsieur Baudelaire."

Roux stood and suddenly towered above me. My eyes reached only his shoulders. We bowed our heads and shook hands. His was clammy and insipid. There was a heavy pause for a moment as I found my kerchief and wiped the hand the seminarian had just held. "Madame Édmonde tells me you are in need of spiritual counsel," the young man finally said, in a high, nasally voice that, I suspected, was intended to sound urbane.

"Quite," I replied, and we fell back into an involuntary silence. I looked helplessly across to my co-conspirator but, as her face was veiled, found no clue of how to proceed. "And you are pursuing religious studies?"

"Why, certainly, I am resolved to serve God's mission in the tropics—life among the savages of the Congo, saving the souls of the cannibals, bringing them into the light of Christ and so forth." He began to describe to me, in a pinched, precious tone, the righteous future that lay before him. The impression his discourse made was not so much of vocation but of vanity, and yet he was completely unaware of his effect. As I listened to him, I began to consider the possibility of inhabiting that elongated body, of speaking in that whine, of using those spindly, spidery fingers for every task, of stooping my head every time I had to pass through a door. The thought of it was not a pleasant one. Would I, in the new body, comb my hair the same way? Would I speak with the same insufferable tone? If I retained no memory of my previous existences, and I entered such a body, what kind of fate was it that I was condemning myself to? He, in turn, was completely unaware of the fate that would befall him, were we to execute our designs. He would cross into my body, which teetered on the edge of permanent decrepitude. Such a fate was hardly better than mine. The thought of crossing with the seminarian seemed suddenly obscene.

"Charles?" I heard Édmonde's voice. The youth had stopped talking and must have asked me a question, which, lost as I was in my meditations, I had not heard. I affected a toothache and begged my leave.

When Madame Édmonde joined me outside moments later, I was leaning against the wall of the coffee house, deeply troubled. Once more she took me by the arm and we began walking back in the direction of the railway station. "What is the matter, Charles? Are you displeased with the fruit of my labors?"

"The man is a simpleton, there's no question about it. The thought of a life in that body is unbearable. But there are other considerations: if we were to cross, his soul would die in the misery of my body and, as contemptible as he is, I cannot consent to that, especially if it were to happen without his knowing it. It would feel too much like theft. I would rather undertake no crossing at all, and die and be done with it."

We entered the station's waiting room and Édmonde helped ease me onto a seat. "Charles, you stipulated a man, and not just any man, but a healthy, educated man. Can you conceive how difficult it is to persuade such a person to take seriously the idea that a crossing might be possible? And even if it were done, to then convince him to give his body away, especially for one that is ill and frail? There is not a man in all of Europe who would agree to such a thing." Even from behind her veil, I could sense Édmonde's ire radiating from her. "If you are now insisting that you will only cross with someone know-ingly, you have made my task almost impossible. For who will believe such a story? It took you more than twenty years to believe me."

"I cannot agree to it."

"Very well," Édmonde sighed, "I will find someone who wishes for death. But Charles, I beseech you, the streets abound with young women in despair, women whose circum-stances are so straitened that to them death seems preferable to life. Think on it."

We parted in disagreement.

On my return voyage to Brussels that same evening, I was at first alone in my compartment. With Édmonde's words still ringing in my ears, the pain of my neuralgia flared as never before. I swallowed an entire bottle of laudanum to dull the aches and entered into euphoric somnolence. When the train stopped at Genappe, two young women entered the compart-ment. They appeared to be sisters. Upon their entrance, they greeted me by saying, in French, "Good evening, Father."

It was not the first time in my life I had been mistaken for a man of the cloth, no doubt on account of my gloomy visage and dark vestments. The two demoiselles sat opposite me and retreated into each other, speaking Flemish. Because I was invisible to them, they were behaving quite naturally. I watched them discreetly, so as not to diminish the spontaneity of their comportment. I sat so that I appeared to be looking out the window at the passing pastures, but as it was dark there was little to see, other than the reflection of the illuminated interior of the compartment. I fixed my attention on the reflection of the two women in the glass and listened to that strange language, which always reminded me of the gurgling of a stream. I studied their femininity—their voices, their movements, the clothes they wore, the intimacy they enjoyed. Surrounded by women every day, I have nonetheless never ceased to be astonished by their strangeness. What is it like, I wondered, to be a woman? What is it like to be able to conceive life? I'd always flattered myself that, as a literary man, I had the imaginative wherewithal to answer the question poetically—and that poetry was my only available means of answering the question. But could writing alone cross the gulf that separates men and women? For the first time in my life I was willing to admit that I doubted it, and from that admission sprang a succession of thoughts that led me, by the time the train arrived in Brussels, to a conclusion diametrically opposed to the opinion I'd held when it had left Charleroi. If a crossing was indeed possible, what did I have to lose by exploring that other manifestation of the great human duality? Woman. Womanhood. Observing those sisters, I was for the first time intrigued by the possibility of such a crossing—by the thought of no longer being imprisoned by the tomb of manhood—the freedom, the release from that dungeon of violence, ambition, and lust! The only person I'd known whose life had been more difficult than mine was Jeanne—and I had contributed mightily to its hardship. I decided I could justify refusing womanhood on no moral grounds other than cowardice.

☞ {87}

An Unsuitable Candidate

As I waited for Édmonde's next missive, I continued—between bouts of neuralgia, when I was too debilitated by laudanum to even pick up my pen—to write the words you have been reading. Despite the pain I was suffering, I felt a kind of ecstatic serenity that was hitherto unknown to me. My nightmares, which had tortured me throughout my life, were no longer a tribulation. They were replaced by dreams that were at once lucid and consoling. My body and my soul were detaching from each other. The one was racked with pain, dying, while the other was beginning to look forward to its next journey.

Édmonde had advised me to avoid all visitors, for fear that I would betray our plans. But when Auguste knocked unexpectedly on my door one morning I could not turn him away, knowing it was perhaps the last time I would see him. He entered, saw me lying in bed weakened with pain and laudanum, and frowned.

"Are you unwell?"

"Oh, it is nothing new, my friend," I replied. "Simply the neuralgia that has plagued me all these years."

"Do you have enough laudanum?"

I smiled and nodded drowsily.

He wandered over to the writing table where sheafs of

paper were spread, the ones you are reading at this moment, and began to cast an eye over them.

"What's this?" he asked. He took the title page. "A story? 'The Education of a Monster.'"

I somehow managed to rise from my bed and take the page from his hand, gathering all the pages together and slipping them into a drawer. "It's not ready."

"Have you started writing again?"

"I have, but no one can read it." He eyed me curiously. "Not until it's finished."

Auguste's eyes narrowed. "What's the matter, Charles? You're not usually so timid about your work."

I slumped back onto my bed while he sat in the only chair in the room. "Nothing is the matter, I assure you. I will show you in due course and you will be very impressed. Long have you urged me to write stories. I have taken your advice. This one is sure to change our fortunes."

He smiled a little sadly. He'd heard this kind of talk before. "I'm very glad to hear it, Charles."

I could not bear to see him one last time without bidding him adieu. "I . . . I am about to go on a journey, Auguste." I could not disguise a tremor in my voice.

"Where to?"

I hadn't considered that. Where was I traveling to? "The tropics."

"Whatever for?"

"I've been wanting to go for many years, as you know."

I could see that my friend did not believe me, but was indulging me as if I had finally taken leave of my senses. "I see," he said. "And when will you be leaving?"

"Any day now."

"I'm sorry to hear that. Did you come into some money?"

Ah, money. I hadn't considered that either. "Yes—my mother. She sent me some money recently. I will be traveling by train to Rotterdam, and from there to the Indies."

"Well, you must come to dinner before you leave, say good-bye to the family."

"Yes, with pleasure."

Auguste stood again. "I suppose I should be on my way." He cleared his throat. "Come for dinner tomorrow night."

"I shall, my friend, thank you." I was very sorry to see him go.

Left once more to my own devices, I hauled myself to my feet, took the papers out of the drawer, and set to work again, writing in my bed, surrounded by papers and empty bottles, which was how I woke the following morning, to knocking at my door and the landlady's voice calling my name. "A letter has arrived for you," she said as she came in with a platter containing coffee, bread, and an envelope. She began to fuss about the mess, but I sent her away. The letter was from Édmonde, and, as before, it showed signs of having been opened before delivery. I contemplated giving Madame Lepage a few choice words demanding my privacy be respected before remembering my arrears and deciding against it. When she had left, I tore the envelope open.

Dear Monsieur Baudelaire,

Please forgive the delay in sending you this letter. I have been undertaking the mission we discussed. Until today, my efforts had come to nought, but I can finally declare that I have made the acquaintance of a suitable candidate. I will meet you tomorrow afternoon at the railway station in Namur. The train leaves Brussels at a quarter past ten o'clock.

I did not go to Auguste's for dinner that night. Instead, I sent a note explaining I was feeling a little unwell and would visit the following evening. But I did not keep that rendezvous either. Rather, the following day, under a cool gray northern sky, I left the Grand Miroir with no luggage other than a satchel containing this story, a pen, a small bottle of ink, several bottles of laudanum, and a little money. I hailed a buggy and told the driver to take me to the railway station.

The Church of Saint-Loup, where I was to meet my next body, is a sinister and elegant marvel, with an interior embroidered with black and pink and silver. Having met me at the station—standing on the platform like a funereal hourglass—Édmonde brought me to the church, telling me nothing of the person I was about to meet other than she was a young woman who had been fully informed of what was about to happen.

There was a girl of no more than sixteen sitting on the front pew. She turned around as we approached her. It was, of course, you. You were exceedingly plain, wearing a white headscarf and a convent dress. There was something at once defeated and ill-tempered about your expression, as if you had borne the brunt of many beatings. Your complexion was pale and your hair the color of straw; your only coloring was the pink tinge to your cheeks, which gave you the appearance of being in a state of constant embarrassment. You rose to your feet, biting your bottom lip anxiously.

"Charles," said Édmonde, "this is Mathilde Roeg." You curtsied. "Mathilde, this is Monsieur Baudelaire, the gentleman I have told you about."

"Pleased to meet you, sir, *crénom!*" you said as you curtsied again. I immediately noticed, with a shiver, the low, lilting tones of a Belgian working-class accent, punctuated with that ridiculous exclamation, *crénom*.

"Likewise, I'm sure," I said, bowing my head. "I understand Madame Édmonde has explained to you the nature of our affair. Do you have any questions?"

"No, sir." That lisp was most comical. "The lady told me what's what, *crénom*! You want to look in my eyes for a few minutes, and then the lady will take me away with her and I will live a life of luxury."

I wondered if, despite Édmonde's explanation, you hadn't fully grasped the proposal that had been made to you. "Are you sure that's what you want?"

"Yes, *crénom*! I don't mind at all. Men have all kinds of strange appetites."

"Can you read and write?"

"Yes, sir! The nuns taught me good, sir, *crénom*!"

"Reading, writing, and religion, no doubt," I sighed. I took a piece of paper out of my trouser pocket, unfolded it, and handed it to you. "Can you read this out to me?"

You looked at it for some moments as if it were in a foreign language before hesitantly beginning to read, the tinge on your cheeks blushing an ever deeper shade of red as you stumbled over the longer, unfamiliar words:

To amuse themselves, the men of a sailing crew often
Capture albatrosses, those great birds of the ocean,
Who follow, indolent travel companions,
The ship gliding across the sea's bitter chasms.

Poor girl, you stumbled on the poem's title, and it only got worse from there. "Stop, I beseech you!" I cried, before you were midway through your labors. "You are strangling my words!" I snatched the paper from your hands and rubbed my forehead to dull the pain that had shot through the blanket of laudanum. "Thank you, child, that's quite enough."

"*Crénom*, I didn't understand a thing. What is it, then?"

"A poem," I snarled. "Do you even know what such a thing is?"

"Of course I do. Sister Bernadette had us learn one by heart, about Jesus. But why would you write one about a bird? What is an albatross, anyway?"

"It's a kind of big seagull," said Édmonde. "Thank you, Mathilde, you did very well. Why don't you go wait for us outside and we'll call you in again very soon."

You nodded, curtsied again, and shuffled off toward the church's main entrance. You had barely left when I erupted. "Impossible! Simply impossible! Charmless, witless, allergic to poetry, and she can barely string a sentence together. That accent is dreadful, not to mention the profanity. *Crénom, crénom!* She's insufferable."

"It's a truncation of *sacré nom*. Surely, being a poet, you appreciate the sentiment. 'Holy word.'"

My entire body was quivering like a violin. "I know perfectly well what it means. It's not the point. The point is that not only is the girl hideous to contemplate, she doesn't even have a sense of beauty. And what is a woman without beauty?" As soon as I had uttered the phrase, I realized I had committed a cruelty.

Édmonde sat beside me and took my hands. "My dear Charles, do you think I have never asked myself the same question?" I looked up at her. She had lifted her veil. The ugliness of her face was once again on full display, mocking my suffering and the anger it had spawned. "All I am asking you to do is live. And all she wants to do is die. She has told me herself."

"Why?"

"Because she's pregnant—and not for the first time. She had to give the first child away to the nuns, which is where I found her—imprisoned in a convent laundry. She didn't even get a chance to hold her child before it was taken away. Since then, she has been riven with despair, and tried to kill herself more than once. The same thing will happen this time. But since it is her second time she will now be sent to a workhouse. Her child will grow up in an orphanage. She doesn't want that. She wants her child to grow up lacking for nothing."

"How did you get her out of the convent?"

"I told the prioress that I was seeking to raise up in society a fallen girl, that I would train her and educate her to eventually become my personal secretary. The prioress believes Mathilde is a lost cause, to which I replied that a lost cause is exactly what I'm seeking."

"And what have you told her about the nature of the crossing?"

"Everything."

It is ten minutes to two o'clock in the morning. I am lying in a bed in an upstairs room of Namur's only inn, exhausted, barely able to hold my pen, surrounded by empty bottles of laudanum and sheets of paper upon which I have scrawled by candlelight the last of this, the finest and truest tale I have ever recounted. Édmonde is in the next room. We will meet with you tomorrow at the same splendid church where we met today. Édmonde reassures me that I am able to cross, that the power is in me even if I can't remember. All I have to do, she says, is look into your eyes for a few minutes. Soon enough, a feeling of frothy joy will overtake us, she says, and the crossing will take place naturally, effortlessly. If, when we meet tomorrow, nothing of the sort happens, then I will simply have been deceived by a prankster or a lunatic. But if a crossing does take place, if events do transpire as Édmonde has foretold, then this story will stand as the testimony of it, so that if all you remember of your previous lives is in your dreams, then this story will serve you, dear girl, as both reminiscence and evidence of the man you once were.

Charles Baudelaire, Namur, Belgium,
Thursday, April 15, 1865

☞ {257}

City of Ghosts

The Cemetery

SHE STOOD IN front of the poet's grave, smoking a cigarette, lost in her thoughts, in the Montparnasse cemetery. It was a brilliant May afternoon in Paris—not today's Paris, vanquished and humiliated, but the city as it once was, only a short time ago but already far distant and forever lost. She wore a black silk dress printed with blooms of red hibiscus. The skin of her bare arms was golden, her raven-black hair curled into a chignon. It was nearly closing time, I remember. I was walking past her along the cemetery alley, headed for my apartment. I glanced at her without slowing—although perhaps, if it is at all possible, there was a flicker of hesitation, a hint of desire, a fleeting urge to stop, to approach her, to ask why she was standing there in front of this particular grave, a grave I myself had stood before many times, on this sunny and too-warm weekday afternoon in May. The sky was a dazzling and pure azure. My tie was loosened and my jacket slung over my shoulder. The grave she was standing before was that of

Charles Baudelaire, the poet to whom I had, in a way, devoted the best years of my life.

It was Monday, May 27, 1940—not even four months ago, and yet it might as well be many years, an age, an epoch. Seventeen days earlier, after keeping the world in suspense for nine months, the Germans had finally launched their invasion of Belgium and France, sending their tanks through the Ardennes forests, circumventing the famous Maginot Line, crossing the Meuse River before the French could destroy the bridges—or had the French defense been sabotaged by traitors, as many believed? In a little over two weeks, the Germans had pinned the armies of three nations back against the English Channel. Boulogne and Calais were cut off, and Dunkirk was next.

I had stopped reading and listening to the news. I should not have been there to begin with, in that graveyard. I should have already left Paris. I was a refugee, after all, a Jew, an ex-German. My papers were not in order. They were substitute papers. The nearer the Germans advanced, the more danger I was in. For several weeks, a black suitcase had stood upright behind the entrance door of my apartment, a reminder that I ought to go, to vanish. But one wearies of vanishing acts. I couldn't bring myself to leave. I tried not to think about it. I was in a state of denial, preoccupied more with the past than the present. For years, I had been working on a book that remained unfinished. It gave me an excuse to stay, to keep wandering these streets I knew so well, forever dawdling, in secret communion with the phantoms of the past, ready to join their ranks, to become another spectral presence in this city of ghosts. If that was not enough, there was no shortage of other, more mundane excuses: the imminent arrival of a telegram, an application for a visa, a request for a letter of recommendation, the chaos at the railway stations. And at the very moment when there could be no more excuses, I was about to be granted another, in the form of this woman. She would, for a time, be my alibi, my reason to stay, to surrender to the city and be swallowed into it, once and for all.

After the declaration of war the previous September, the city's libraries and museums were closed, their collections packed away in crates and sent to storehouses in the country, as were the artworks and artifacts in the museums, leaving the palaces of art and learning standing darkly empty, like, in certain ports, hulks that have been stripped of their fittings and are permanently moored. I'd spent the last several years burrowing into those libraries, writing a book about this city, a neverending book in a constant state of expansion, a book that grew faster than it could be written. Now that the libraries were closed, I began to contemplate the possibility that my book would never be published.

And so, stripped of my work, I began to live a kind of floating life, setting out every day for long walks in my adopted city, the city I'd come to know and love more than the city of my birth, which I knew I would never see again. The war did not come straightaway, of course. By day, during those nine months, the gears of the great machine of Paris continued to grind as they always had. The signs of war were subtle: bread rations at bakeries and restaurants, blue shade-cloth covering the streetlights, dry fountains, sandbags piled around statues and buildings, posters on billboard hoardings with the latest ministerial diktats. Those who could returned to their villages or, in the affluent western neighborhoods, to their country estates. Those who stayed behind—those, that is, with no-where else to go—seemed, after nightfall, infected by a fever of pleasure-seeking. The ten o'clock curfew was not enforced, and the indigo darkness served only to heighten the sense of the carnivalesque. Despite the dimness, rarely had the café terraces been so crowded, the brothel mattresses squeaked with such abandon, or the wooden floors of the *bals-musettes* trembled so lustfully with the thump of dancing heels.

I walked endlessly, in those nine months, all over the city, through neighborhoods new and old, opulent and threadbare, and even, occasionally, through the makeshift slums of the Zone, where the city walls had stood until only a generation ago, and out into the bedraggled suburbs. In the hush of early morning, the mist that laced the streets might have been mistaken for ghosts risen from the catacombs under my feet, piled floor to ceiling with the bones of millions of the city's dearly departed.

My walks would lead me more often than not to the river, that quicksilver vein that curves across the city's breast, with its twin islands—the Île de la Cité and the Île Saint-Louis—as its centerpieces. I liked to amble along, fossicking through the green bookstalls that have lined the Seine for centuries, manned by the bouquinistes, those riverside booksellers who tend doggedly to their modest treasures in sun and rain. If there was a glue that held together the sheafs of my existence during those months of the *drôle de guerre*, it was that cheap printer's paste used in the manufacture of railway-station paperbacks, which dries and cracks prematurely, shedding the pages it binds as an animal sheds its winter fur. For when I was not walking the streets of the city, I read pulp novels bought several at a time from the bouquinistes. I raced through them in the evenings, lying on my bed in my little apartment, avoiding the propaganda on the radio and in the newspapers as much as I could. There was something consoling about these jigsaw-puzzle stories, steeped in melancholy, seesawing pleasantly between the familiar and the new, in which criminals and detectives faced off against one another in lurid intrigues of passion, revenge, and misanthropy. Each one was an expert inquiry into the byzantine machinations of the French police, the same machine I myself was so keen to avoid.

I was a fugitive at a time when there was an oversupply of fugitives. After the declaration of war, all Germans, even ex-Germans, had been required to hand themselves in to the police. We were dispatched to makeshift internment camps in the countryside. I'd spent most of the previous winter sleeping on a concrete floor in a school gymnasium in a desolate corner of Normandy, surrounded by Germans. All my adult life I'd suffered from night terrors, and so in the camp I slept during the day and stayed up at night, smoking and playing cards with the insomniacs, for fear of waking the entire dormitory with my screams. Finally, when it was clear there'd be no winter invasion, we were released. Now that the Wehrmacht had finally invaded, German expatriates were once again ordered to surrender themselves. But this time I was determined not to give myself up so easily.

The key to staying out of reach of the secret police was to go out walking at dawn. For some reason, the Sûreté Nationale conducted its round-ups before breakfast. I also resolved to avoid speaking to strangers for fear that my accent would betray me, thus depriving myself of one of life's great pleasures. There is no hiding an accent. No amount of effort or care or practice can ever rid one of it. Outside my circle of friends, every sound that came from my mouth was a possible self-betrayal as a *boche*, a *chleuh*, a *fridolin*. Two friends lived in my building on Rue Dombasle: Arthur, a Hungarian journalist, and Fritz, a surgeon I knew from Berlin who now earned his living performing illegal abortions. For a price, the landlady was prepared to overlook certain discrepancies in our paperwork. We played poker together on Saturday nights. Sometimes I would have coffee in one of the cafés where German émigrés gathered to swap fragments of information. It was tempting to believe that, with enough of these scraps, one might weave a kind of protective blanket around oneself, but the information was unreliable, and these dens swarmed with spies and informants.

Often, at the end of my long walks, I would return to my apartment through the Montparnasse cemetery. It was an island of tranquility in an ocean of chaos. Here, I was beyond danger's reach, as if I'd stepped out, for a moment, of the city's hall of mirrors. I was a giant in a miniature city. The graves, grand or simple, tended or abandoned, depending on the fortunes of those buried inside them, were miniature buildings that lined its miniature avenues. From the main entrance on Boulevard Quinet, I'd turn right into the Avenue du Boulevard, past the old Israelite section (the cemetery's ghetto), and turn left into the Avenue de l'Ouest, where, buried in the family crypt a little way up the incline between the mother he loved too much and the stepfather he loathed, lay Charles Baudelaire. There were always flowers on the tombstone left by the poet's admirers, as well as little notes: a few lines from one of his poems, or an original poem imitating his style, opening a trapdoor into a secret universe of longing. I'd continue walking uphill along the Avenue de l'Ouest to the rear cemetery wall, re-entering the tumult of the city through a narrow gate in the corner.

As for the woman standing in front of Baudelaire's grave, she was, for now at least, still a stranger. But it wasn't the first time I'd seen her. The first time had been the previous winter, soon after my return from the camp, when she'd been wrapped up in a great double-breasted coat. The second time had been only weeks before, when the linden trees were budding. And now on this third occasion, standing motionless in exactly the same place, in exactly the same pose, at exactly the same time of day, puffs of blue-gray smoke drifting away in the golden light. Everything about her suggested a tightly wound, fiercely protected stillness. Deep within herself, she seemed unaware of the existence of anything except the grave before her—oblivious to passersby, oblivious to the twittering of birds and rumble of distant traffic, oblivious even to what loomed overhead, a steep bank of violet clouds crowned by an aureole of sunlight.

I passed near enough to detect a faint scent of sandalwood and continued up the incline without stopping. Other than the two of us, the cemetery was empty. There were no funeral processions, no bereaved family members paying their respects, no sightseers or pilgrims in search of resident illuminati, not even a gardener tending to the plants. The emptiness brought out the secret heartbreak that lurked in every direction. *Love is fleeting, regret is eternal,* read the inscription on one of the tombstones. Midway between the grave and the rear gate, I turned to see if she was still there. She hadn't moved. When I reached the gate, I took another look over my shoulder. She was gone. I stopped and, after a flicker of hesitation, turned back, determined to follow her.

In between gravestones, I caught a glimpse of hibiscus: she dashed toward the center of the cemetery, down the Avenue Transversale. We must have made a strange sight, she slinking between gravestones, I trotting along the parallel path by the cemetery's back wall further up the hill, stooping behind a crypt every now and then to peer through the marble forest between us. But the cemetery was otherwise deserted, and there were no witnesses to this curious dance.

I had to hurry to keep up with her. I kept my head down, catching another red and black flash of her from afar. She darted to the next crypt and looked about her as if checking to see if she'd been followed. Pursuing women in this manner was not something I had ever done before. Why now? Curiosity, of course. Perhaps also out of the anxious boredom of those days. But I remember realizing I was enjoying myself. She scurried across the circular clearing at the center of the cemetery, where an angel stands disconsolate on a plinth inscribed with the word *Memory*, and disappeared behind a thicket of headstones. I stopped and surveyed the scene. No sign of her. I approached the place I'd last seen her, where the Avenue de l'Est meets the Avenue Transversale. Still no sign of her. She'd disappeared. I scanned all around, my heart thudding in my chest, my eyes squinting in the sun's glare. I hadn't been to this part of the cemetery before. On my left stood a marker of mottled gray and pink marble. Engraved in gold leaf on the plinth were the words *La Société Baudelaire*, below which were the following names:

Édmonde Duchesne de Bressy, 1845–1900, founder and president
Lucien Roeg, 1866–1900, secretary
Hippolyte Balthazar, 1876–1917, secretary
Aristide Artopoulos, 1872–1923, president

I felt a presence behind me and heard the click of the catch of a gun being released. I turned and there she was, the woman I'd been following, pointing a small gun at my chest.

"Who are you?" we both asked in unison, then stood glowering at each other in silence. The hand that held the gun trembled slightly. The features of her face, the face of an elegant Asiatic woman in her forties, were unadorned and severe.

"Why are you following me?" she asked. "What do you want from me?" She, too, spoke with an accent. The music of her speech, the rhythms of it, were organized differently, but I could not say precisely how. Being a foreigner means not just speaking with a foreigner's accent, but being unable to recognize the accents of others.

"I saw you standing in front of Baudelaire's grave and . . ." She didn't react. I felt as if I were dreaming the situation rather than living it. "I, too, admire him." She appeared very fierce and very fragile at once. "I've seen you before, and I was curious . . ." Realizing I was not making much sense, I turned my attention to the weapon pointed at me—a Remington derringer, a popular choice for a certain kind of lady. Only my adversary did not appear to be that kind of lady. She did not seem accustomed to brandishing a weapon. She held it with both hands, its barrel wavering a little, and had she fired it she may have needed to shut her eyes to do so. "You look as if you've never shot a gun in your life."

"Don't tempt me. What is your name?"

"My name is—" But I stopped. Since the start of the war, I'd made it a rule not to give out my name unless it was strictly necessary. A Jewish name, combined with a German accent—at times like this, such things lead to trouble. "I'm a . . ." But this tack suddenly seemed just as hopeless. What was I, in fact? In the shadow of war, to be a writer seemed the most frivolous, absurd thing possible. But if I was not a writer, what was I? An ex-German, a Jew, an exile, a bachelor, a scholar, a flâneur, a drifter, a failure—all these were equally true and untrue. "I'm an admirer of Baudelaire. That's why I was following you. I took you for a kindred spirit."

"You couldn't be further from the truth. I am most decidedly not a kindred spirit."

We heard a whistle from a distance. Behind the woman, a groundskeeper turned into the alley further down the hill and walked in our direction. "Don't turn around," I said, "but there is a *gardien* approaching us."

The woman tucked her firearm into a pocket in the side of her dress.

"Monsieur, madame," said the *gardien*, "you heard the whistle. I'm afraid it's closing time."

"Yes, of course," I said, mumbling to hide my accent. I pointed in the direction of the rear gate. "This way?"

"That's right. I'm on the way there myself, to lock up. I'll see you out."

The woman took me by the arm and uttered the two words I least expected to hear: "Come, darling." As we walked, she held her face against my shoulder, as if wishing to keep it out of the groundskeeper's sight. So starved for affection was I that, despite the circumstances, I found myself enjoying this simulation of it.

We marched up the incline toward the rear gate when, from above to our left, we heard the rumble of rolling thunder in the clear blue sky. The woman kept her face averted. Seconds later, a wail of air raid sirens came from every direction for the first time since the start of the invasion.

"*Oh là là!*" said the groundskeeper. "Those boches always pick the worst moment!" He ushered us out of the gate, locking himself in, and wished us not the customary *bonne soirée* but *bon courage*, before trotting away. I seized the opportunity to reach into the woman's pocket and took her derringer.

"Hey!" she said, slapping me on the cheek. "Give it back or I'll scream."

"I doubt anyone will be particularly interested," I said, throwing the gun over the cemetery wall, "given the circumstances." From behind us, another whistle. A policeman in a black cape was in the middle of the next intersection, waving his white gloves frantically to and fro. "He's pointing us to the nearest shelter."

I took the woman by the hand and we began to run, with sirens wailing around us. We came to a stop in the middle of the intersection, where the traffic policeman was directing us toward a corner bistro. Some ran in that direction, others stood about on the street or on balconies above it, looking skyward, staring at the heavens as if observing an astronomical phenomenon. Outside the bistro, a man in a white armband and a helmet from the previous war was urging people inside. We made our way in and through a throng of bodies and wicker chairs to a trapdoor behind the counter, out of which poked the top rungs of a stepladder. The atmosphere was congenial: some patrons, interrupted during their aperitif, were still holding their glasses, and one even tried to descend the ladder single-handed until the shelter warden lost his patience. He stood at the top of the ladder with a hand-rolled cigarette suspended between his lips, his helmet tilted at a rakish angle, holding glasses and purses and shoes while people disappeared into the cellar. "Come along," he repeated, "there's room for everyone." And then, bending down into the void, he yelled, "Make room down there!"

The woman went first. When she let go of my hand I realized I'd been holding it since we began running. Once underground, we were jostled into a corner, pushed together ever closer by the arrival of each newcomer, the last of whom was the traffic policeman who had waved us in. Several more people were left outside, complaining loudly, while the warden urged them to seek another shelter. A sense of improvisation pervaded the entire scene: there were no chairs, so everyone had to stand, including a one-legged veteran of the last war. The walls were lined with shelves bearing wheels of cheese and racks loaded with dusty bottles of wines and spirits. Hams and sausages were suspended from above. The bistro owner stood on a box in the corner, hands on hips, eyeing the room for thieves.

The trapdoor was lowered, plunging us into a gloom barely relieved by a single naked bulb buzzing overhead. There must have been forty or fifty people squeezed together in that cellar. My companion was pressed up against me, her hair brushing the stubble of my chin. The sirens outside stopped their wailing and the room was engulfed by a heart-pounding silence as everyone listened for the sound of the destruction that was surely about to rain down from the heavens. I wondered if, by the time we emerged from our hiding place, the Paris we knew would still exist. But then, I thought, if the building above us was bombed we'd be buried alive.

I felt her body tremble like a captive bird and put my arms around her, not to embrace her but to push back against the weight of human bodies crushing us both. My nostrils were stinging with the smell of the sweat of the crowd and my shirt was sticky. My heart thumped wildly—there it was, that sharp stab of pain with every heartbeat, the premonition of my mortality. I had pills for this pain, pills I never took. Her cheek was pressed against my chest. I was frightened too, but I'd been frightened so long fear had become a part of me, twisting its way around and through me like a vine, sustained by the same sap that kept the rest of me alive.

There was a click of the lid of a cigarette lighter. Someone on the far side of the room said, "I really need to smoke. I'm claustrophobic." I smelled burning tobacco. The trembling of the woman in my arms became more violent. Her whole body was shivering. Between the silence and the crush and the smells of meats, cheeses, sweat, and tobacco, I felt my own rising tide of panic: beads of sweat trickled down my neck and back. My heart was beating ever faster, my breathing was short, a migraine was building behind my eyes. With all my senses lunging upward and beyond the cellar for a sign of what was happening outside, of what was to be our fate, I lost all notion of time's passage. I began to imagine that we would never emerge from this cellar, that we would all die in it under a mountain of debris. I thought of Rotterdam: it had taken only four days for the Nazis to reduce Europe's greatest port to rubble. "I need to get out of here," I whispered, more to myself than anyone else. I felt her arms tighten around my waist. Somehow, that modest sensation dislodged something inside me, and the panic that had threatened to drown me began to subside.

As the minutes dragged on, there was only silence from above. Paris, it seemed, had been granted a stay of execution. The sirens started up again, a sign that the raid was over and we were free to go. The warden climbed the ladder and the trapdoor swung open. Fresh air and cool evening light washed over us. More cigarettes were lit and the gathering burst into a dozen simultaneous conversations. People waited their turn to climb the ladder. Some of them remained to talk and drink in the bistro, others lingered outside on the street under a golden sky. They chatted, promised to meet again for a drink, shook hands, and wished each other good luck.

As we neared the stepladder the woman from the cemetery started climbing before me. I was about to follow her, but I ceded my place to an elderly gentleman waiting beside me. By the time I emerged above ground in the bistro, the woman was gone. I rushed out and caught a glimpse of red hibiscus on black silk on the other side of the street. She was already half a block away, running with her shoes in her hands. I set off after her. It felt good to run after our brief and anxious imprisonment. And I didn't want to let her vanish. She'd helped me somehow, down there in the cellar, without even knowing it.

I caught up with her at the back gate of the cemetery, where she was gripping the grilles, shaking them as if they might miraculously open. But the lock would not be cajoled and the woman turned and collapsed against it, slumping to her haunches and burying her face in her hands. I approached her. "What's the matter?" I asked, bending down onto one knee and touching her on the shoulder.

She looked at me as if for the first time, eyes sparkling with tears. "I have nowhere to go."

☞ *{157}*

The Apartment

I WOKE TO find two coal-black eyes looking back into mine. The woman from the cemetery. The back of her fingers were stroking my stubbled cheek and she was murmuring something reassuring.

"You had a nightmare," she said.

"Was I screaming?"

She nodded.

"I'm sorry."

"That's all right. You warned me."

"I did?"

"You told me you have nightmares every night."

"Yes, so I did."

A full ashtray, two dirty glasses, and an empty bottle of calvados on the table. In the dull light of the bedside lamp, my one-room apartment was plunged into a deep, middle-of-the-night silence. I recalled inviting her to spend the night. I was in the armchair. She'd been sleeping in my bed in her black silk dress. I remembered the events that had brought her here—the cemetery, the raid, the shelter. I was surprised she'd accepted the offer. She'd told me her name: Madeleine.

She gave me a sidelong glance. "What were you dreaming about?"

"Oh, a jumble of things. I have a few recurring nightmares.

They always seem to take place in the past. This one was on one of those old-fashioned three-masted sailing ships. I was the ship's surgeon, and had to saw off a man's arm with nothing more to numb the patient's pain than alcohol and laudanum. That's one I only get every now and then. There are others. In some, I'm on a tropical island. In others, I'm a woman raising a child during the Prussian siege, or Baudelaire, believe it or not, living an impoverished life with Jeanne Duval. The one element that seems to recur above all is . . ." I paused, somewhat embarrassed by what I was saying.

Madeleine, who had been about to light a cigarette, froze and looked at me with a curious expression, engrossed and terrified at once. The match's flame lit her face in a soft orange glow. "What?" she asked.

"Eyes."

She lit the cigarette and leaned forward. "What kind of eyes?"

"All kinds, in all colors, on all kinds of faces. All my dreams seem to end with me looking into the eyes of someone, and every time I get to that point I wake up screaming."

"Why do you scream?"

"I have no idea."

"And your accent," she said. "Are you German?"

"Yes. I'm from Berlin."

She bit her lower lip and looked away, holding the cigarette with trembling hands and puffing nervously. She was, for a moment, entirely alone, withdrawn into herself as if unaware of my presence.

After a minute or two she stood and sauntered over to my bookshelf, crammed with books. "What do you do?"

"I'm a writer."

"I see you have a great many books about Baudelaire." She picked up *Les Fleurs du mal*. She smiled, curling up one side of her mouth almost imperceptibly. "Which is your favorite poem of his?"

"That's a hard question to answer. There are so many. Perhaps 'To a Passerby.'"

With her forefinger running over the spines of the books, she recited, from memory, "*Fugitive beauty, in whose gaze I was suddenly reborn . . .*"

"*Will I see you again only in eternity?*"

She gave me a searching look from across the room, as if not knowing quite what to make of me. "Interesting choice."

"And yours?" I asked.

"'The Albatross.'"

"*The Poet is the prince of clouds, the storm-clouds haunting and the archer mocking . . .*"

"*But exiled on earth amid the crowds, his great wings prevent him from walking.*" She gave me that little smile again. "He stole that poem."

"Stole it? From whom?"

"From me." She turned back to the shelf and studied the books with her head tilted at an angle. "I gave him the idea. I told him the tale of the albatross, and he turned it into a poem."

"You knew him?" The notion was absurd, of course, but it was a pleasure to indulge her fantasy.

"Yes. Not in this body, of course. In another."

"Whose?"

"Jeanne's."

"I don't quite follow," I said, as it began to dawn on me that she was serious. "Do you mean Jeanne Duval? His mistress?"

Madeleine sauntered to the bed and lay back on the mattress.

"I was his mistress," she sighed. "His mistress, his slave, his torment—and, for a while at least, I was also his muse." She snorted. "*Muse*—how I detest that word. Charles was a thief. He stole from everyone—money, poems, books, love, you name it. Of course, he had talent. But his greatest talent was for theft."

Perhaps, at any other time, I would have reacted to these signs of delusion differently. I might have been more guarded. I might have gently shepherded Madeleine through the night and then out of my life. But, at that moment, her fancies seemed harmless compared to the great tide of madness consuming the outside world. "How is that possible?" I asked.

She shot me a piercing glance. "It *is* possible, that's all that matters." She sat up on one elbow and looked at me. Despite what she was saying, I found myself enjoying the sensation of her gaze. "When did they begin, these nightmares of yours?" she asked.

"When I was a young man, just before the last war. When I was maybe nineteen or twenty."

"What caused them?"

"I can't remember."

"Surely something happened around that time. They couldn't have just started by themselves, caused by nothing in particular. Were you sick? Did you have an accident? Maybe you were in the war?"

"No, it was before that. Only I can't remember."

"Think back carefully."

"I'm trying, but I can't . . ."

"Can I ask you a question that may seem a little strange?" she asked. I nodded. "Have you ever been hypnotized? Has anyone ever asked you to look them in their eyes? Not just a passing glance, but to really look, for several minutes?"

"Never."

"Are you sure? No hypnotist, no magician, no woman you loved who asked you to look them in the eyes? Even just for fun? Try to remember."

"Not that I can recall—although . . ." At that moment, a memory returned to me for the first time in many years. "When I was a young man, I visited Paris for two weeks in the summer of 1913, when Paris still dazzled. I had an encounter that seemed nothing more than an amusing anecdote, one of those stories that young people like to tell when they return home from their travels as a sign of the worldliness they have acquired. Paris back then was still a walled city. Cars were a curiosity. Horses and trolleys ruled the streets, and a pedestrian could still walk down the middle of a boulevard without being run over. I thought everything about the city was enchanting. I liked to browse the bouquinistes' stalls and then find a café somewhere in the Latin Quarter where I could read and observe the passing crowd.

"One such afternoon, I noticed, among the men in frock coats and hats and the ladies in long white dresses, a stout elderly woman pushing a small cart on wheels, bent over almost at right angles, walking in my direction with a slow, waddling gait. I was drawn to her as soon as she appeared from a block away. I studied her approach, stopping at the café terraces and offering her wares to the patrons until she was shooed away by a waiter. When a customer took some semblance of an interest in what she was selling, as if in accordance with some unwritten code, the waiter would leave her to her commerce. She was an unforgettable sight. Her body was twisted forward with age, her fingers were gnarled and her face seemed no less wrinkled than a walnut shell. Even in the bright summer sunshine, her clothes were colorless rags. But her expression was cheerful. She was one of those old women whose demeanor has naturally withered into a permanent beam of light. As she drew closer, I noticed her lips were in constant motion, as if she were murmuring something intended only for herself, which is not an uncommon sight in any city. Finally she neared the terrace where I was sitting and caught my eye. 'Would you like a book, sir?' she asked. She had an accent, but I couldn't pick it. Perhaps, I thought, she's a foreigner like me. A waiter saw her from inside the café and rushed out, barking at her to leave the customers alone. I waved him away.

"She was a book peddler, a rare sight even in those days, although it had once been the noblest of street professions. By 1913, however, book peddlers had almost disappeared. I wanted to pay her my respects, to help her in some way, the kind of gesture tourists are fond of. I beckoned to her to bring her cart of secondhand books closer. As she did, I heard her reciting, in a lilting accent, like an incantation uttered so often it's become a reflex: 'Adventure stories, crime stories, ghost tales, tales of love and romance, books new and old from near and far, only two francs!' She continued the recitative as she opened the cart's cover to let me browse her selection. It was outdated and eccentric. Like her, the books were relics of a bygone era. At first glance, she had nothing I wished to read, but all the same I asked her for a recommendation. 'They're all good, monsieur, the finest of the age. Two francs each, or six for ten.' She continued to recite her incantation in a low voice, as I cast another look over the sorry selection and picked up a book at random. 'How's this one?' I asked. 'I wouldn't know,' she replied, 'for to be perfectly honest with you, monsieur, I'm not much of a reader.' She burst into a fit of wheezy laughter cut short by consumptive coughs, whose residue she expertly spat onto the pavement. 'Not of books, at any rate,' she added. 'Time, monsieur,' she continued, although I'd said nothing. 'I read time. The future as well as the past. I am an expert in the ancient arts of remembering what has been and foretelling what is yet to be. And all for just two francs.'

"The waiter shot the woman a contemptuous glance. 'How about it, sir? Who would not want to know what surprises fate has in store for us? Only two francs.' I took two coins from my pocket and gave them to her, holding out my hand with palm turned skyward. 'Begging your pardon, sir,' she said, 'but I don't read palms. I read eyes.' I told her I'd never heard of such a thing. 'Oh, it is a noble art that comes to us from ancient times. No doubt, sir, you will have heard the expression that the eyes are the window to the soul. I have mastered the technique.' She drew closer. 'May I look?' I nodded. 'I ask only that you look into my eyes, and stay still. Do not look away. Do not speak. Do not allow yourself to be distracted—by the crowd, by the waiter, by anyone. I need only look into your eyes for three or four minutes, and then all will be revealed.'

"I don't know how or why, but I must have passed out. When I came to, I was surrounded by a circle of onlookers. One man was leaning over me, holding my hand, talking to me, although I could barely make out what he was saying. My head was heavy and foggy, as if it had just been struck or woken from a long, narcotic sleep. The book peddler was opposite me, slumped back in her chair, her eyes wide open in terror, her mouth opening and closing, like a fish just hooked from the sea. The waiter appeared, asking what had happened. Two of the onlookers began talking at once, describing what they'd just witnessed—that we'd been looking at each other in silence when we both began convulsing for a short time, and then fainted. The waiter leaned over the woman and began shaking her by the shoulders. She was awake but barely aware of her surroundings. 'You'd better get out of here before the police arrive,' he told her. 'I've a good mind to have you arrested.' He turned to me and began apologizing profusely."

I paused, searching for words to describe the strangeness of the memory, until now so long obscured. Madeleine's gaze was fixed on me unwaveringly. "And then?" she whispered, almost reverentially.

"I was, for some moments, completely mystified about everything—who I was, where I was, how I had come to be there. My surroundings had not changed. Rather, it was inside me that everything had changed. *What is my name?* I wondered, and my name suddenly appeared to me. *Where am I?* I wondered, and the word *Paris* rose to the surface of my mind. *Where am I from?* Suddenly *Berlin* appeared. Who was this woman splayed on a chair before me? A book peddler who'd offered to read my fortune. And so on, a gush of memories surfacing one after the other, all in the space of a moment.

"A policeman arrived in his képi and black cloak. The waiter launched into a complaint about the book peddler, how something ought to be done, that it was bad for business, just look at the state of this young German fellow, and all for what? In a display of anger, the waiter kicked the woman's cart, tipping it over on its side so that books were spilled across the pavement and passersby had to step around them. One of the onlookers said the woman was a necromancer, and that I had been mesmerized. The policeman asked me if, indeed, this is what had happened. In my stupefied state, I could barely manage a nod, but when he asked if I wished to file a complaint, I shook my head. Did I wish to be taken to the hospital? 'No,' I said,

'I'll be fine.' I stood awkwardly and fell back again into my chair, raising a gasp among the onlookers. I was suddenly convinced I was in some kind of unknown danger, that I must distance myself from the scene. I took a coin from my pocket and pressed it into the waiter's hand. 'Please,' I said, looking to the policeman and the onlookers, 'go about your business, everything is as it should be.' The small crowd dispersed, and I turned to the woman before me, helping her to stand. She swayed uncertainly on her feet a little. I held her hand until she steadied, then picked up her cart and began gathering the fallen books. With one arm clasped around her waist to help her walk and the other pushing her cart, I made my way from the café toward a nearby bench. I lowered her gently. Her eyes were open but she seemed barely aware of her surroundings. I had no money to call for a doctor or ambulance. In my confused state, I was powerless to help her any further. I left her there, on the bench, beside her cart of books, her mouth opening and closing mutely, as if wishing to ask a question but not sure of what question to ask.

"I can't remember how, but I made my way back to my hotel room and went to sleep. I slept almost a full day, only waking the following afternoon. When I went down to the hotel lobby, the concierge asked me if I was feeling better. Apparently I had screamed so loudly in my sleep that the staff had knocked several times at my door, and had even resorted to entering the room at one point. I had told them, when they had woken me, that there was nothing the matter, that they needn't worry. I had no recollection of this middle-of-the-night interruption. I suppose this must have been the beginning of the nightmares. They've continued just about every night ever since."

My story had a curious effect on Madeleine. When it ended, she looked down at the empty space in front of her for some time, plunged in thought. I studied her face, lit by the glow of the bedside lamp.

"We've met before," she said.

"Where?"

She flashed a sad little smile. "You won't remember."

"A long time ago? In another life, perhaps?"

"It was."

"Was it in Berlin? Were we at university together? I think I'd remember. There weren't many women students back then."

"No, it was in Paris." She lit a cigarette with a trembling hand. "Other places too. But there's no point talking about it."

"No, no, now that you've brought it up I must solve the mystery. It seems you can remember the occasion, and I cannot. But perhaps if you give me a clue . . ."

She was leaning back on the mattress, looking down at one hand, which skimmed back and forth across the duvet. "Can I tell you a story instead?"

"Will it answer my question?"

"Perhaps." And she began telling me the tale of the albatross.

Until only two or three generations ago, there existed, in Paris as throughout the world, people who earned a living of sorts as storytellers. In taverns and coffee houses, around banquet tables and campfires, people gathered to listen to their tales, tales the storytellers recited with great skill, perfected and elaborated over years and decades. Sometimes their stories rhymed or were sung. Sometimes they lasted several days, weeks, or months. Each night, people would crowd around the storyteller, eagerly awaiting the next installment. Mechanical printing ended the era of the storyteller, just as radio or cinema or some other wonder yet to be invented may one day end the era of printing. But to hear Madeleine tell her story was to be magically transported back to that era. Everything about the way she told it was mesmerizing. Her diction was low and precise, obliging me to lean in to capture every word, but her voice dipped and soared according to its own music. She kept her facial expressions and physical gestures to a minimum at first, but as her story progressed so were its twists and turns enacted by her body. As for the story itself, it was breathtaking. The tale of the albatross was the myth of two young lovers, a young woman called Alula and a young man—a mere boy, really—called Koahu, who lived on a faraway island, and of their exile. I have since committed it to paper, writing everything of it I can remember—but mine is a pale imitation. There are a great many details I cannot recall, for one thing, and for another I cannot tell the story the way it was told to me. I can scarcely reconstruct the circumstances of its telling—the nocturnal silence of the city outside, the soft light of the bedside lamp, the curlicues of blue smoke rising from the glowing end of a cigarette, the scent of sandalwood.

Sometimes now, when I can't sleep for worry or boredom or both, I like to play a game with myself. I try to pin down the exact moment I fell in love with Madeleine. I am quite certain that when she began her story, I was not in love with her, or at least I hadn't realized I was in love with her. I hadn't fallen in love for years. I considered myself inoculated against it. But by the time she had told me her story—which was only her first story, the first of many—something had changed inside me:

I was unexpectedly, reluctantly, wholly in love, not just any love but a consuming love, an unwanted love, an inconvenient love, the kind of love that a man wants to be cured of, that makes a man feel ashamed of himself, only the more he denies it the more entangled he becomes, like one of those nautical knots that tightens with every pull. It felt like an infection, a sudden illness, in which everything is at once the same as it was before and yet transformed. Being in love is a kind of hypnosis and, as any hypnotist will tell you, to be hypnotized one must secretly want to be hypnotized, so secretly that one doesn't even know it. Falling in love is an act of involuntary will.

Perhaps it was Madeleine's story I fell in love with, more than Madeleine herself. Perhaps the spectrum of love is broader than we think, and it is possible to fall in love with a story, or a song, or a film or painting, the way one falls in love with another person, only one assumes it is the storyteller one is in love with, the singer, the actor or artist, because the thought hasn't occurred to us that it is possible to fall in love with a thing. I knew her story was a fiction, but I believed it all the same. Our passions seem unable to distinguish between the real and the imaginary. But as much as I was enchanted by her story, I never considered it anything other than a story—a marvelous story, granted, perhaps one of the most marvelous stories I'd ever heard, but just a story. Madeleine, on the other hand, seemed wholly convinced that the story she was telling was not only true, but that it had happened to her, and by implication also to me. She believed these stories the way others believe in the signs of the zodiac. This was completely new to me. I had never before fallen in love with someone who held beliefs so different from my own. But there are a great many beliefs in common currency that are less credible than Madeleine's were, and the mysteries of love do not require the complete alignment of convictions. I was drawn to her despite these differences, and I couldn't understand why. That is a riddle I am still trying to solve.

When her story, or at least what would turn out to be its first installment, was done, I blinked as if waking from a dream. Through the cracks in the shutters, I could see the first blush of sunrise. Madeleine was already half asleep. "We have to go."

We walked toward the river in silence. The streets were an especially delicate, limpid blue, and their stillness was enlivened only by the occasional errand boy or delivery man, here a staggering drunk, there a woman of the night returning home at the end of her work. The bakeries were open, as were the workers' cafés, their windows crossed with brown adhesive tape in case of bombardment, but the rest of the shops were shuttered, some with the ever more common sign: *Closed until further notice*. Pedestrians walked about carrying their boxed gas masks. By the time we got to the river, the sun had just risen above the rooftops. We walked along Quai Voltaire. Diamonds of light sparkled on the water and through the leaves of the riverside trees. We passed the green bookstalls of the bouquinistes, their tin lids fastened overnight with great iron locks.

As we walked, we heard a rumble disrupt the morning stillness from further upriver. As we neared the Place Saint-Michel, we saw the Pont Saint-Michel was clogged with cars, lorries, tractors, horses, and oxen, each piled high with furniture and mattresses. Evacuees, haggard and exhausted, escaping the German advance for southern safety. Some were on bicycles, others pushed carts, wheelbarrows, and prams. Their vehicles had northern and Belgian license-plate numbers. The mattresses that crowned their vehicles were intended to protect them in case of strafing by Stukas. Street urchins nipped at their heels, selling newspapers, water, *choucroûte,* and hot chicory. Along the Boulevard Saint-Michel, the crowds in the cafés and restaurants spilled over into the streets. These signs of imminent invasion did nothing to dull the glow of intense happiness I felt walking arm in arm with Madeleine. They had the opposite effect: they burnished it. They gave it a counterpoint and a purpose.

I felt Madeleine squeeze my arm. "We must go back to the cemetery."

"Why?"

"My gun."

At the Pont Neuf we turned right into the Rue Dauphine, where calm was restored. Away from the tumult of the southbound boulevards, the streets were empty. We turned into the Boulevard Mazarine, crossed the Boulevard Saint-Germain, and continued onto the Rue de l'Odéon. The echo of our footfalls bounced off the surrounding walls, plastered here and there with posters demanding *Silence! The enemy is listening.* We stopped to look in the window at Shakespeare and Co. The shop was closed, but a cat was reclining on a shelf, blinking contentedly among the books on display, its ginger tail twitching. Adrienne and Sylvia were stirring upstairs, I imagined, among those who refused to leave Paris. In a couple of hours they would open the store as usual. The store of the antiquarian bookseller Jacquenet was a little further up the street. We stopped to look there too. My attention was taken by an advertisement pasted on the window. It was a notice of an auction that was to take place the following week at the Hôtel Drouot.

"What is it?" asked Madeleine. She craned her neck forward and mouthed the words as she read them, before stopping and looking at me with eyes wide.

ANTIQUE & MODERN
——BOOKS——
ORIGINAL EDITIONS BY MODERN AUTHORS, MANY PERSONALLY SIGNED BY THE AUTHOR

Including several works printed on Rare Papers

ILLUSTRATED BOOKS
SIGNED MANUSCRIPTS & LETTERS

Previously unpublished novella by
Ch. Baudelaire—Fine assortment of works by
Stéphane Mallarmé—Lithography by Daumier

*Diverse collections, several works in English
from a collection of Prestige*

—— AUCTION ——

HÔTEL DROUOT—ROOM 10
MONDAY, 3 JUNE 1940, AT 2 P^m

M. Robert BIGNON, Auctioneer, 12, avenue de l'Opéra—
M. JACQUENET, expert Advisor at the Tribunal de Commerce,
10 rue de l'Odéon—(where catalogues are available to the public)

EXHIBITION BEFORE THE AUCTION FROM 1.30PM TO 2PM

The books can be viewed until Friday, 31 May at the
Librairie Jacquenet, 10, rue de l'Odéon

❖

"It can't be," she said, leaning against the glass, her hands shielding the sides of her face as she scanned the interior of the store. "And yet . . ." She gasped, drawing back and putting her hands to her mouth. "There," she said, pointing to a table on the other side of the window, upon which were a number of volumes on display stands. "There on the right, the small volume. Do you see it?"

"Yes." It looked innocuous enough—a slim volume bound in dark red leather. I studied it at length. The title and author's name were embossed on the cover for all to see: *The Education of a Monster, Ch. Baudelaire.*

"I can't believe it," said Madeleine, but when I asked her what she couldn't believe, she didn't reply. Instead, she fell into a silence that continued until we reached the cemetery.

The previous afternoon, as the air raid sirens wailed, I had flung the derringer over the cemetery wall into the back section of the cemetery, which, like the older Israelite section on the other side, is reserved for Jews. Here, the family crypts are covered in stones and engraved with names like Cahn and Meyerbeer. This was where we now headed, scouring the weeds between the plots until I found the gun lying atop a grave. I opened the bullet chamber. It was empty. I was standing there, gun in hand, when Madeleine suddenly approached, wrapped her arms around my neck and kissed me languidly on the mouth. "Drop the gun into my pocket," she whispered into my ear. I folded my arms around her waist and, kissing her, did as she asked. At that moment, an old groundskeeper holding a rake and a shovel sauntered by, whistling tunelessly. When he saw us, he changed direction and wandered off. Madeleine pulled her head back and looked at me as if trying to memorize my face. Her dark eyes were so near mine I could see my reflection.

"I'm sorry," she murmured, pulling away and blushing. "I forgot myself." My heart beating wildly, I pulled her back and kissed her again.

We set off, hand in hand, toward the exit we'd passed through the previous evening, which already seemed a distant age. On Rue Froidevaux, Madeleine stopped before a Morris column to read a government ordinance:

EXPATRIATE GERMANS LIVING IN FRANCE

You must report immediately to the nearest police station. Bring no more than one bag containing your daily essentials. Disobedience of this order will incur the maximum penalty.

By order of the Ministry of the Interior, 18 May 1940.

"You must leave," she said. "You can't turn yourself in."

"I know, but where would I go? My papers aren't in order. I can't leave France. I don't have an exit visa. I don't have money."

"How does one get an exit visa?"

"You apply at the Ministry of the Interior. But my application would be denied. I don't have a release certificate from the internment camp. They let us go without them so that we wouldn't be granted exit visas. That way we can't leave." I gave Madeleine a fatalistic smile. "I'm like you. I have nowhere to go."

She curled her arms around my neck, closed her eyes, and kissed me again. Even if at that moment I had been magically wired the money I had been waiting for and granted every piece of paper I needed—a release certificate, an exit visa, a real passport (not the Schengen substitute that served only to mark me out as a dubious exile), a ship's boarding pass, a Portuguese transit visa, an American entrance visa—I doubt I would have gone anywhere.

☞ *{1}*

The Auction House

MADELEINE AND I NEVER discussed how long she would stay. She just did. To me, every moment we were together was a gift, a stay of execution. Ambushed by love, I succumbed to it without thought to my survival. It was a love devoted entirely to the present, without a tomorrow, and thus entirely of its time. I should have been at the railway station with my black suitcase, camping out on the platforms with the crowds, waiting for a place on a train headed south. Only I didn't want to go.

The writers, artists, publishers, intellectuals, and other natural enemies of the Nazis, in those last few weeks of the Third Republic, adhered to two opposing schools of thought about how best to survive: there were those who opted to leave and those who preferred to stay. To leave—provided one had the wherewithal—was to abandon an entire life, to embrace exile, to choose to be cut off from everything that was familiar, to risk destitution. And yet to stay was to risk, once the Germans arrived, internment, interrogation, torture, even death. Every time I saw someone I knew, when I bumped into Arthur or Fritz on the stairwell, for instance, or a friend in the street, or if I came across the postman or my landlady, we discussed the matter: stay or go? Go or stay? I was in the remain camp. I felt I was faced with two different kinds of suicide, and in the face of this choice, my decision felt arbitrary and therefore inconsequential. I couldn't bear the thought of leaving my adopted city. I was too old to adopt another. And, in any case, if worst came to worst, I had sixty-four capsules of morphine, enough to kill a horse. They'd accompanied me everywhere since I'd left Germany seven years ago. Death would be easy. Painless. Blissful, even.

But now, having met Madeleine, I found my thoughts on the matter changing. I was still in favor of staying, only now it was because I wanted to, not out of despondency and torpor. Over the following week, we spent most of our time in the apartment, or walking the streets of Paris like tourists, living on cheap red wine from Languedoc, Salomé cigarettes, and rationed bread, in a state of profound contentment. The little world we spontaneously created between us felt more real than the outside world, which at any rate was falling apart. The greatest of our pleasures, in that time, was to tell each other stories. Madeleine overcame my natural reserve by peppering me with questions about my childhood, travels, the people I'd known, the books I'd read, and, above all, my dreams. Madeleine's stories were of an altogether different nature: she continued recounting the tale of the albatross, a story that spanned generations and continents. Her stories never lasted more than an hour or two, with occasional questions from me to illuminate some obscurity or clarify some uncertainty, before her energies withered and she began to apologize, saying she could go no further, she was spent. She would curl up, lay her head on my shoulder or my chest, and fall asleep. She was like a cat that way, asleep more often than she was awake. While she slept I would take out my gray notebook and write down everything I'd just heard. I didn't want to forget a single detail, and yet, even so soon after the telling, there were so many I could already not recall.

And a curious thing—I stopped waking in fright at night. Within days of meeting her, I noticed I'd slept through the night for the third time in a row. With the end of my night-mares, a great and ancient burden was lifted from me.

The only thorn in the happiness we shared was Madeleine's fixation with the auction of the Baudelaire manuscript the fol-lowing Monday. She was desperate to acquire it or, rather, for me to acquire it on her behalf. Of course, I wanted to see the Baudelaire manuscript for myself. I wanted to touch it, to hold it, to read it, if possible, in part if not in whole. I was a biblio-phile, and as such I had obsessions of my own. Chief among them, coinciding neatly with Madeleine's, was Charles Baude-laire. A new story by the great poet—the idea made my heart beat faster. I peppered Madeleine for specifics about it, and she indulged me by describing it in loving detail: a story in four parts, told in the first person. She'd even memorized the first sentence. She made me write it down so I could check it at the auction: *As I write these words, it occurs to me that I have never known a tale to be so beyond belief as that which I am about to relate to you, dear girl.* I would attend the auction, alone, and buy the manuscript on her behalf. Why alone? She wouldn't say, other than that all would be revealed in time. How would I pay for it? Again, she wouldn't say—money seemed to be al-most an abstraction to her. She seemed to think that, if all else failed, I could simply steal the thing.

It was when Madeleine was making no sense at all that I loved her the most. From the start, she suspected I didn't take her tales as seriously as she did, and when she sensed her words were bumping up against a wall of incredulity her lips would quiver with hurt and her dark eyes glisten with tears, but she never lost her conviction or her composure. I must simply trust her, she kept saying, and so I did, or at least I pretended to. To disbelieve Madeleine was to risk losing her; to believe her was to risk losing myself. And so I devised a way of loving her without being ashamed of myself: I believed and disbelieved her at one and the same time.

The only time we were apart was in the evenings. Paris was not the glittering jewel it had been before the declaration of war. A dusk-to-dawn blackout meant the city of light was plunged into darkness. That was when Madeleine, who lolled about indolently during the day wearing one of my shirts, would spring to life, put on her black silk dress with red hibiscus, apply mascara to her lashes and red lipstick to her lips, and disappear without explanation. Again, I found this feline quality deeply seductive. When I asked where she was going, she kissed me tenderly and told me it was best I didn't know, but that she would be back, in the early hours of the morning, and that I shouldn't wait up for her. But I couldn't help myself. I would stay up awaiting her return, unable to read or write or do anything other than pace to and fro in my room, in agonies of worry. Eventually, I would go to bed and close my eyes, mind whirring, until in the wee hours the door would creak open and she would slink in, smelling of cigarette smoke and alcohol, undress, and curl herself up beside me. She was small, and our bodies were a perfect fit, even for a single mattress. At sunrise I would wake and there she would be, sitting in the armchair, naked, reading Baudelaire, smoking a Salomé, the contours of her body streaked with rays of sunlight, and, seeing me awake, she would recite what she was reading.

Come, handsome cat, come on my flaming heart lie;
Sheathe the claws of your paw,
And let me plunge into your handsome eyes,
Where metal and agate alloy.

Then we would head out into the streets for our morning walk.

The German war machine rolled on, delaying its arrival in Paris by picking off the remnants of the French and British armies, cornered against the English Channel. The southbound traffic on the boulevards thickened, the traffic in the other streets thinned, and every day more shops were shuttered.

The following Saturday afternoon, Arthur knocked on my door. Madeleine was dozing on my bed, so I stepped out onto the landing. I presumed he wanted to inquire about our traditional Saturday-evening poker party, which had entirely slipped my mind, but instead he told me he was leaving. His well-heeled English girlfriend had managed to buy a car and they were driving down to Bordeaux. "There's room for you too, if you want to join us."

"I don't want to leave."

"The French have pretty much capitulated, you are aware of that, aren't you?" he said, seizing me by the arm. "The Germans will be here in a week or two."

I hesitated, feeling foolish for throwing away this lifeline, an opportunity for which so many others would have willingly paid a fortune. "I'm not ready."

"I see," he said, momentarily downcast before perking up again and slapping me on the shoulder. "Well, we'll see each other again sometime, I'm sure." We shook hands and he was gone, dashing down the steps three at a time. I went back into the apartment to see Madeleine, lying on my bed, turn her head sleepily in my direction.

"Who was that?" she asked.

I crossed the room, sat on the side of the bed and squeezed her hand. "No one."

That day and the next, she finished recounting the tale of the albatross. The nearer she was to the conclusion of her story, the harder it was to ignore the chasm of belief that divided us. The saga's denouement was a first-rate paranoid delusion, in which Madeleine's fantasies were so thoroughly entangled with the real world that it was hard to imagine her ever extricating herself from the web. She seemed to believe that Gabrielle Chanel, better known as Coco, a high-society dressmaker who lived at the Ritz Hotel, was also President of the Baudelaire Society, and that the two of them were enmeshed in a decades-old rivalry. She was convinced Chanel wanted her killed, and that the auction of the Baudelaire manuscript was somehow a part of her plot, with the manuscript as the lure that would entrap her. By the time she finished her story, I was so concerned by what I'd heard I couldn't return her gaze. She must have sensed my despair.

"Why don't we try it?" she said.

"Try what?"

"Crossing."

I gave a heavy sigh. "I don't think that would be wise."

"Why not?"

I'd never challenged her about her beliefs—what purpose

would it have served? There were worse—she wasn't a Fascist, after all. I had friends who believed in a god, in an afterlife, or in Stalinism—why couldn't I tolerate Madeleine's beliefs?

"Well, for one thing, I don't think you'd want to end up in this body." I pointed to myself. "I'd clearly be the one with the most to gain, but it wouldn't be fair on you."

She let out one of her long, throaty chuckles. "I don't want to end up in your body either. We would cross back."

"That's possible?"

"Of course. I would see to it."

"I thought crossing was a one-way affair."

"Most of the time, for me, it is. But there's more than one kind of crossing. There's the blind crossing, where afterward you have no idea what just happened. Then there's the wakeful crossing, where we cross in such a way that at each moment you are wholly aware of everything that is happening."

She was beginning to frighten me. "I'm not sure it's a good idea."

"Are you worried about ending up a woman?" she teased.

"I would have no problem being a woman."

"That's what you think." She smiled and tilted her head a little. "So what do you say?"

For days now, I'd been wrestling with this, until now, hypothetical dilemma. On the one hand, I figured a failed crossing might pull her back to reality, but on the other I worried she might not be able to handle it if her elaborate fantasy-world was exposed as a fraud, that she would react badly and I might never see her again. But at that moment I decided the charade could not continue a moment longer, and that were I to refuse her invitation I would be complicit in her delusion. We were both lying on the bed. I had my head propped up on a pillow while Madeleine lay on her back. We locked eyes. I couldn't help but feel a little appalled that I had allowed myself to do this, but within a few moments I felt my body begin to tingle all over with pleasure. This, Madeleine had told me, was the first stirring of the soul, which all people naturally feel when looking into the eyes of another. She believed the ability to cross was latent in everyone, only the teaching of it had been lost. This, she claimed, was why looking someone in the eye was such a powerful, and occasionally dangerous, act, because even the untrained soul stirs when gazes meet. Now, staring into her eyes, I preferred to think of it simply as love. What sorrows had she endured in her life, I wondered, a life about which, for all her stories, I still knew very little? I thought of her as one of those people defeated by hardship and solitude who conduct one-sided conversations on the street, loudly berating someone who exists only in their imagination. And so, looking into her eyes, tingling all over with pleasure, I was all at once flooded with tenderness for this woman, and for her woundedness. Her tales were merely a cover, a disguise, a front. Underneath them was a deeply, perhaps irretrievably, mislaid soul. The sadness of it overwhelmed me, and the image of her blurred, and I looked away.

"What's the matter?" she asked.

"I'm distracted. I was thinking about the auction tomorrow."

Later that evening, Madeleine dressed and left the apartment as always. Before leaving, she gave me an exceptionally tender kiss. I thought she was trying to repair the unspoken rift that had emerged between us, but the next morning, when I woke and noticed she wasn't lying beside me, I understood what it had really meant. She'd been saying goodbye. But she'd left me a gift. Lying on the bedside table was her derringer.

I don't intend to recreate the agonies I suffered that morning. Suffice it to say I didn't leave the apartment for my usual morning walk, and in the throes of anguish I lost all sense of time. I had to hurry to the Hôtel Drouot on the other side of the river, carrying 873 francs in notes and coins—the sum total of my funds—which jangled ostentatiously in my trouser pockets, taking the Métro instead of walking, as I preferred to do, because round-ups were easier to avoid above ground than under it. The second-class compartment was lightly sprinkled with passengers, as if it were a Sunday rather than a Monday.

Stepping through the arched corner entrance of the Hôtel Drouot, I entered a hushed, red-carpeted, high-ceilinged world that whispered promises of aesthetic pleasures. I'd attended many auctions here, always as a spectator. Each time I visited this elegant bazaar of all that is precious and exquisite, I felt a familiar heady rush. Room 10 was located up the stairs. There were barely a dozen people in the large room, including the auctioneer, Bignon, and his assistants, waiting glumly for the clock on the wall to strike two o'clock so the auction could begin. Bignon stood on his podium wielding his gavel like a judge, dressed in a fine dark suit, thinly disguising his contempt at the dismal turnout: a few middle-aged onlookers, peppering the empty seats alone or in small clusters.

I'd wanted to arrive early. It was the custom, before an auction, for the items listed in the catalog to be displayed for inspection. There was only one item of interest to me, but as I didn't wish to draw attention to myself, I feigned interest in several others. I flicked through a first edition of Mallarmé and pretended to study some Daumier lithographs before turning my attention to the object of my real desire, the red leather-bound notebook lying open on a bed of blue velvet: *The Education of a Monster, Ch. Baudelaire.* I had to put on a pair of white cotton gloves to handle it. The manuscript had been bound in *peau de chagrin*, with gold-leaf embossing on the spine and cover. Inside, the yellowing pages were filled with the distinctive curlicue of the poet's own handwriting. I read the first few lines and my heart began to palpitate with that excitement known only to collectors when they are within reach of a rare, once-in-a-lifetime prize: *As I write these words, it occurs to me that I have never known a tale to be so beyond belief* (these two words were underlined) *as that which I am about to relate to you, dear girl.* Exactly as Madeleine had remembered—word for word. I read on. *Yet nothing I have written has ever been so true. Paradox, all is paradox.* I skipped ahead a few pages and found the dinner party scene, exactly as described. So Madeleine had not been imagining things. She was intimately familiar with the manuscript. I continued turning the pages, reviewing the chapter headings—"A Disgraceful Episode," "A Touching Reunion," and so on, just as she had described. Just then, chimes began to echo throughout the building as dozens of clocks waiting to be auctioned in adjoining rooms rang the hour all at once.

"I'm sorry, sir, the auction is about to begin." I looked up. A man in a sky-blue frock and white gloves was reaching for the book—one of the auctioneer's assistants. If I pocketed the book and ran out of the room, I calculated, I'd never get away with it. Instead, I would end up in prison, no place to be when the Germans arrived. So I handed the book back to the assistant and found a seat. Suddenly I desired that book with my entire being, as if all the love I had felt for Madeleine was now transferred to the object before me, as if somehow Madeleine had *become* that book. But what chance did I stand with 873 measly francs to my name? Under normal circumstances, a manuscript of this rarity would not be cheap. Perhaps the invasion had chased away the serious collectors who would normally have dropped a small fortune, without a second thought, on such a rarity. In any case, if I were, by some stroke of luck, to snare the jewel, my destitution would be a small price to pay.

The auction began with a brief introduction by Bignon, after which he started up his consoling, monotonal patter, reminiscent of a priest's Latinate incantations. Against this stream of rapturous descriptions and figures hopping ever upward, like goats up a mountainside, three assistants buzzed to and fro, ferrying and displaying each item in turn, keeping a meticulous record of its commercial destiny. But for all their efforts, a discernible torpor presided over the occasion. Bignon's voice betrayed little enthusiasm. The bidding was sporadic and many of the objects were passed in.

"Now we come to the last item in the catalog, undoubtedly the drawcard of today's proceedings," said Bignon as one of the assistants proffered the Baudelaire manuscript as an altar boy would the Eucharist. "More than a mere curio, this is a work of genuine rarity and literary significance: a short story, previously unknown, written in Baudelaire's own hand. The handwriting has been authenticated by the expert appraiser Monsieur Jacquenet. It appears to have been written at the end of Baudelaire's life, in the style of Edgar Allan Poe, of whom Baudelaire was, as we know, the first French admirer and finest translator. The reserve price is two thousand francs."

My stomach sank. I was already out of the running. There

were no bids, however, so I thought I might still stand a chance. Bignon's face was stoic. He repeated the price, gavel hovering in the air, and all seemed lost until he spied something—a raised finger belonging to the old man standing by himself in the row in front of me—and the fall of the hammer was postponed another moment as Bignon's voice barked, "We have two thousand. Do I hear two thousand, two hundred and fifty?" I studied my competitor jealously: he was hatless and bald, grizzled and bent forward, dressed despite the weather in an outmoded, shapeless trench coat. His profile was vaguely familiar—I must have seen his face before—but where? There was another lull and another last-second bid. Again I looked around for the culprit: this time my attention fell on a thick-necked man in an expensive-looking suit at the back of the room. The two bidders continued the rally two or three more times before the old man's tenacity carried the day and the man in the suit relented. The gavel struck the lectern at last, marking the manuscript's sale, the auction's end, and my own abject failure.

I followed the successful bidder in the trench coat to the front of the room, where the purchasers had gathered to settle their accounts and collect their trophies. I overheard him spell out his name to one of the auctioneer's assistants: V-E-N-N-E-T. The Baudelaire manuscript was the only item he'd purchased. When he turned toward me, I saw his full face for the first time, and again sensed an untraceable recognition.

One of the assistants tapped me on the shoulder. "Do you have something to collect?"

I shook my head.

"In that case, please make way for the buyers."

I went to the back of the room and smoked a Salomé while

I waited for Vennet. Where had I seen that face before? An image of a riverside bookstall down by the wine market came to mind. Was he a bouquiniste? Having put the manuscript in a brown leather satchel, Vennet left the auction room. From a distance, I followed him as he descended the stairs and exited the building. He set off in the direction of the Rue de la Grange Batelière. I noticed, walking a short distance behind, that he was also being followed by not one but two separate men: the thick-necked fellow in the expensive suit who'd bid against him during the auction and another man, thin and bespectacled, wearing a gray homburg hat, whom I hadn't previously noticed. From what Madeleine had told me, I'd expected one pursuant—an employee of the Baudelaire Society—but not two. When the bookseller turned right into the Passage Jouffroy, his two pursuants quickened their steps and also disappeared into the arcade.

Against the cool, blue shade of the street, the interior was dazzling. Sunlight streamed in through the glass roof, ricocheting off the pale mosaic floor and the display windows of the shops lining both sides of the arcade. Unaware he was being tailed by three men, Vennet had gone into an antiquarian bookstore. The two other men were pretending, not very convincingly, to study the displays of nearby shops. I stepped into the shop where Vennet was talking to the bookseller, showing off the manuscript he'd just purchased. Remembering what Madeleine had told me, I realized he was in some kind of danger, although I couldn't say precisely what kind. I wanted to warn him without revealing myself. Speaking to him was out of the question, on account of my accent, so I took my notebook and pencil out of my shirt pocket and scribbled a note: *You are being followed by two men. Your life may be in peril. Hide the manuscript and watch out for yourself.* I tore the paper from the notebook, folded it, tapped Vennet on the shoulder and handed it to him without uttering a word, face averted. I didn't wait to see his reaction—as he opened the note, I slipped out of the bookshop, hiding my face from the two men with my hat, then turned and began to run.

Behind me, I heard Vennet stumble out of the shop and yell, "Hey! Hey there! What is the meaning of this?" I continued running, the coins in my pocket jangling like a tambourine as I did, to such an extent that I had to hold my hands against my thighs to keep them quiet. I darted across the Boulevard Montmartre and into the Passage des Panoramas, without looking behind me to check if I was being pursued. I weaved around some window-shoppers, ducked left into the Galerie des Variétés, and left again, up a narrow stairwell, three steps at a time until I reached a door at the top. I entered a softly lit room where a stout woman in her fifties sat smoking from an opera-length cigarette holder behind a Second Empire desk.

"Bonjour, Madame Yolande," I wheezed, puffing, my every heartbeat the thrust of a dagger in my chest. "I'm glad to see you're still open, despite everything."

"Bonjour, monsieur, good to see you again," replied the madame. "We've never been busier. Is everything all right?"

"Yes, yes," I panted, "all is well." I bent forward to catch my breath. "I just . . . ran into someone . . . I didn't want to see."

"Have you brought trouble with you? You know we don't like trouble."

"No trouble, madame, no trouble at all . . . Room twelve, please."

"Room twelve is Simone's room, monsieur. As you know, Simone sees customers by appointment only, without exception."

"Simone, yes, of course, it slipped my mind, my apologies. What about Room Eleven?"

"Room Eleven is Paulette. Is it Paulette you wish to see?"

"Yes, Paulette. Thank you." Madame Yolande looked me up and down with narrowed eyes before shrugging her shoulders and handing me a key. I paid the usual sum, adding a tip for the madame. In return, she gave me the slightest hint of a smile, signaling that while she disapproved of my behavior, I could count on her discretion.

Crouching so that I wouldn't be seen from below, I made my way down a corridor with doors to the rooms on the left and windows on the right overlooking the arcade. I opened the door to Room 11 and stepped into a consoling hush. I left the door slightly ajar and peered through it onto proceedings downstairs.

"Bonjour, monsieur," I heard Paulette say from over my shoulder. "I haven't seen you in such a long time."

"Bonjour, bonjour, dear Paulette," I replied, still peering through the gap in the door. The arcade below was as still as a postcard. There was no sign of Vennet or his pursuers, only a lady choosing a magazine at the newspaper kiosk and some youths inspecting a tobacconist's window. I closed the door and locked it, turning around to face Paulette. She was reclining on an uncovered bed with one raised knee, wearing only a black negligee, silk stockings, and a great deal of makeup. A brocaded lamp glowed in a corner and from an old phonograph player warbled a violin and a guitar. The room smelled of perfume and hashish. "Pardon the subterfuge," I said, taking off my jacket and hat and placing them on a stool by the phonograph player. Approaching the bed and sitting on its edge, I reached out and brushed the dyed blonde hair from Paulette's face to better see those blue-gray eyes of hers, which had so bewitched me once upon a time. Now they had no effect at all.

"What can I do for you today?" she asked.

"Just keep me company."

"I see. Nothing more?"

"If someone knocks at the door, I shall kiss you. But otherwise, just keep me company."

She reached beside her and took up a pack of cards. "In my experience, nothing soothes a troubled heart better than a game of double solitaire."

"I know it well."

☞ *{11}*

The Palace of Justice

When I returned to the apartment that evening, I half expected Madeleine to have returned somehow, to be lounging on my bed, wearing one of my shirts, smoking a Salomé. Instead, its emptiness struck me like a blow to the stomach. I thought I could detect a faint aroma of sandalwood, and I sniffed various things—the pillow, the sheets, a towel—in search of a more tangible sense of her presence. I wanted to tell her that she had been right, that the auction had gone exactly as she had foretold, that I had done what she had instructed me to do, that I ought not to have doubted her. But I could only speak to the Madeleine in my mind. That imaginary Madeleine was very much alive—I found myself talking aloud to her, continuing our long conversations—but there would be no touching her, caressing her, holding her. I had a feeling that, this time, she wouldn't be back. At least she had left me a keepsake to remember her by.

I stroked the cold, metallic contours of the derringer as if they were Madeleine's own flesh. I knew exactly why she'd left it behind. We'd talked about it. She was asking me to do something on her behalf, something unconscionable. She wanted me to commit a crime—to murder someone, to be precise. And not just anyone; she had asked me to murder Coco Chanel. There was no point asking why, it was all part of her paranoia—otherwise known as the tale of the albatross. Of course, there was no question of my doing it. Even had I wanted to, where would I find bullets for a derringer?

A letter had arrived by pneumatic tube and been slipped under my door. It was from Fritz, who had spent several nights camping on a platform at the Gare de Lyon in the hope of securing a seat on a southbound train. He'd bought two tickets for a train leaving the following morning, and the second ticket was mine if I wanted it. But there was never any question of taking up the invitation. I was too deeply involved in this affair with Madeleine and the manuscript.

I spent a sleepless night, haunted by memories, and dawn came as a relief.

On my habitual morning walk, I went to the station, skirting the Montparnasse cemetery, which had yet to open. The memory of our meeting—barely more than a week ago, and yet already an age—was almost too painful to bear. The Gare de Lyon was swarming with unhappy, disheveled Parisians, many of whom had been here for days, hoping to leave before the arrival of the Germans. When I found Fritz he was standing in a long, unmoving queue, waiting to board a steam train—even decommissioned steam locomotives had been brought out of retirement for the exodus. All around, entire families were splayed on the ground, surrounded by their baggage and possessions—umbrellas, flower pots, chickens, coffee-makers, birdcages, sheets, curtains—awaiting their turn to leave on the next train, or the one after that. I saw Fritz from a distance, but we didn't speak until we were quite close, so as not to be overheard speaking German in public and denounced. "Where's your suitcase?" he asked. I told him

I couldn't leave, that he should give the spare ticket to someone else. He looked at me in disbelief. "Why?"

I looked helplessly at my old friend. "I'm still waiting for
my American friends to wire me money."

"I can lend you money, if that's all it is. Have them wire it
to Marseille."

"There's something else, a manuscript." Listening to myself,
I realized how foolish my words must seem to him. I didn't
want to mention Madeleine, whom he hadn't met, and this
reluctance bothered me. Was I ashamed of her—or of myself?

"A manuscript!" He couldn't help but smile and shake
his head. "You're going to risk your life for a manuscript!"
I shrugged, as if to say, there's nothing to be done, I can't go.
He nodded sadly. "I see," he said. "Well, if you change your
mind, go to Marseille, it's your best chance of getting out of
France alive. Leave a message for me at the Hôtel Splendide."
There was a youth standing alone nearby in a cap and long
shorts, looking forlorn. Fritz offered him the ticket and the
boy lit up with happiness. We smoked cigarettes together until
a whistle blew and the line began to move. One by one, people
entered the carriages and hauled their suitcases aboard. The
train vanished in a cloud of smoke and steam.

I left the railway station and walked toward the river and
the Île Saint-Louis, then across the Île de la Cité to the Quai
Malaquais. Despite the circumstances, some of the booksellers
were opening their stalls, setting up their wares, tending to
shelves, gossiping among themselves, smoking. Were it not for
the evacuees streaming across the Pont Saint-Michel on their
carts and lorries, it might have been any ordinary, sunny day.
At the corner of the bridge, I recognized the pear-shaped

figure of the bookseller Lanoizelée, wearing his customary round glasses and black beret. I'd been a customer of his for years; we trusted each other. We exchanged nods and said bonjour. I flicked through the detective novels on his shelves. I'd read most of them, some of them several times, but all the same I found a couple I thought I could bear to read again. "By the way," I said, as if it was of no particular consequence, "have you heard of a bouquiniste called Vennet?"

"Vennet? Yes, he's down on the Quai de la Tournelle, near the wine market. Sells vintage lithographs to tourists with a side trade in antique pornography. Are you after some racy pictures?" He showed me an illustration of a dark-skinned woman wearing only a boa constrictor. "Look at this—look at the detail. A real work of art." I shook my head with a smile. "Maybe next time," he said.

"There may not be a next time."

"Oh, there's always a next time."

I continued walking upriver toward the Quai de la Tournelle. Away from the southbound boulevards, the sunshine and pre-invasion quiet lent every scene a summer holiday tone. Near the wine market, I found a woman in her sixties smoking a pipe. She sold romance novels.

"I'm looking for Vennet's stall."

"It's just here," she said, pointing to the next stall. It was locked shut.

"Do you know where I might find him?"

"He's a popular man. You're the second person to have asked after him." She puffed on her pipe.

"Was the other guy big, thick neck, nice suit?"

"No, he was thin, pencil mustache, homburg hat. Came

looking for Vennet yesterday afternoon." A flash of panic shot through me. I was a day late.

"Where can I find Vennet? I'm afraid he might be in some trouble."

She looked me up and down, sizing me up. My accent, I thought. I took a twenty-franc note out of my pocket and gave it to her. "He was closed yesterday too, but he came around as I was closing up. He seemed flustered, but I didn't ask why. I don't like to pry."

"What did he do?"

Again she paused. I gave her another twenty francs. "He opened up the stall, rummaged around for a minute, then locked it up and left. He barely said a word, which is unlike him. He's normally the talkative type."

"Did you tell the other guy this?"

"He didn't ask."

"What *did* he ask?"

"He wanted to know where Vennet lives."

"And where's that?"

She looked at me without replying, puffing calmly on her pipe.

"Where does Vennet live, madame? His life may depend on the answer."

"You're German, aren't you?" she eventually spat.

I took all the notes and coins I had in my pocket and gave them to her.

The address the old woman gave me was in the Faubourg Saint-Marcel, one of the city's most hard-pressed neighborhoods. For centuries it had reeked with the stench of the tanneries that lined both sides of the Bièvre, the little stream that had since been covered over but still flowed under the streets, past the Jardin des Plantes and into the Seine. The neighborhood had long been condemned as insalubrious, and what hadn't already been demolished was slated for the wrecking ball. But all that was forgotten in the light of the noonday sun. It was lunchtime and the narrow streets teemed with children—at least, those too old to have been sent to the country—immersed in countless self-devised intrigues. They seemed unworried by the impending invasion. Their parents had no country homes to flee to, and they would simply have to make do as they had always done. As I wandered in search of Vennet's apartment, the heat, the interplay of sun and shadow, the white waves of bleached linen suspended overhead, the smell of frying onions from open windows, all combined dizzyingly with less tangible things—my worries, my sorrows, my fears—so that, more than once, I had to stop and put my hand against a wall to regain my composure.

Having found Vennet's building, I groped my way up four flights of stairs in near total darkness, lighting matches to view the names written beside the doors. When I found Vennet's place I knocked without reply. I tried turning the handle and the door swung open. I stood at the threshold for a moment before stepping inside. All was stuffy, gloomy—the smell of cigarettes and a human body. It was a single room much like my own, with a kitchenette in one corner. The curtain of the only window was drawn. Against every wall, stacks of books were piled waist-high. The middle of the room was strewn with more books, as if piles of them had been ransacked or knocked over in a struggle. I felt like King Kong standing in the middle of a ruined metropolis of books. There was a bed by the window with a body lying on the thin mattress, turned away from the door. I called out Vennet's name but there was no response. Crossing the room with careful steps, I reached the other side, threw back the curtain and opened the window, breathing in the fresh air with the relief of a drowning man.

I went to Vennet's side, called his name and shook him gently. The bed hadn't been slept in. His body, lying on its side, was cool. He was fully dressed, in the same clothes he'd worn the previous day, minus the trench coat. He wasn't breathing. In fact, rigor mortis had set in and at his chest his shirt was soaked in congealed blood. Blood had trickled through the thin mattress and formed a little pool of crimson under the bed. There were traces of blood on the floor, and a jet of it had squirted across the room as far as the opposite wall. I turned my attention to Vennet's face. Where the eyes ought to have been were two voids underscored by tentacles of dried blood. His eyeballs had been removed. I turned away, stomach heaving, leaning against a wall to regain my composure. I thought of Madeleine. She'd warned me about this.

I heard a rustle behind me. I spun around to see, standing in the doorway, the thin, bespectacled man in the gray homburg hat I'd seen the previous day. "Looking for someone?" he said.

"I found him."

"He doesn't look in great shape." The man stepped over some books and into the apartment. "I've seen you somewhere before."

"The auction, yesterday."

"Ah yes, and afterward in the Passage Jouffroy. What did you say to Vennet that alarmed him so?"

"I gave him a warning."

"You told him his life was in danger," he said. "Rather prescient, wouldn't you say?"

"A lucky guess," I replied.

"Who are you and how did you come to be muddled in this business?"

"Who wants to know?"

"Commissaire Georges-Victor Massu of the Police Judiciaire."

"You're from the Quai des Orfèvres?"

"Indeed. Do you know it?"

"Only from pulp novels."

"That's a pity. They don't do it justice. It really is worth a visit. In fact, why don't we go there now? I have a car waiting outside." He stood to one side of the doorway and beckoned to me. "You know," said Massu, "they say you haven't really seen Paris until you've seen the Quai des Orfèvres."

"Who says that?"

"Everyone and no one."

The black Citroën rattled across the paving stones of the Pont Saint-Michel, over the mercurial waters of the Seine flowing darkly below, through the stream of cars and carts fleeing southward. Beside me, Massu hummed tunelessly to himself. Meanwhile, I was nauseously remembering the cadaver I'd just seen, and Madeleine too. For Vennet's murder corroborated the most improbable of Madeleine's delusions: that someone at the Baudelaire Society—Coco Chanel, no less, or some hired proxy—was killing people, and gouging out their eyes, as part of some ancient vendetta between them that I could never quite understand. And if Madeleine's tales were true, I was suddenly neck-deep in a sordid affair that

I barely understood, in a city where I was persona non grata. What was worse, I was now in the hands of the police, the very people I most needed to avoid. Luckily, I'd left the derringer hidden in my apartment.

The police car lurched left onto the Quai des Orfèvres, swerving through an arched entranceway and heaving to a stop in the courtyard of the Palais de Justice, headquarters of the Police Judiciaire, which investigated all of Paris's homicides. In the middle of the courtyard a large fire was burning while several men stood by with trolleys. One of the men was stoking the fire, and from the shade of the early afternoon sparks rose into the patch of blue sky above. I was led inside, through a gloomy maze of corridors and stairwells to a room where I was fingerprinted and photographed. My notebook was confiscated. Then I was marched across the building, up more stairs to the top floor, through a commotion of voices, typewriters, and ringing telephones, and instructed to wait outside an office marked *Brigade spéciale N° 1*. Occasionally someone would enter or leave the office, and I would catch glimpses of a large smoky room filled with desks facing each other, each with a typewriter on it. Men milled about purposefully, or sat at one of the desks, typing with two fingers. There was a smell of burning paper mixed with tobacco and body odor. I must have sat there for an hour or two, fretting at this unexpected turn of events, smoking Salomés while my heart thudded painfully in my chest. Now that I was a guest of the judicial police, my main goal was to avoid ending up in the hands of the secret police. I was counting on the famous interdepartmental hostility of the French police. With any luck, I thought, I might still walk out of here a free man.

Finally I was ushered into a room labeled *Bureau du*

Commissaire, a smallish office with a solitary porthole window overlooking the river and the Latin Quarter. There were shelves on three sides half filled with folders, which two men were loading up on trolleys to transport to another location. Massu was standing, leaning over his desk. His hair was neatly combed, the homburg hanging from a stand in the corner. He didn't look up when I came in, but gestured for me to approach while instructing the other men to leave us. Pictures of Vennet's apartment were fanned out on the desk in front of him. It had been photographed from every possible angle. There were shots of Vennet's body, lying fully dressed on the bed in the fetal pose in which I'd found him. There was one photograph so gruesome I had to look away: a shot of his eyeless face.

Massu must have noticed me flinch. "Once seen, never forgotten," he said. "Note the minimal bleeding from the eyes. No laceration of the epidermis inside or around the sockets. Eye injuries don't bleed much, as a rule, but there is evidence of abrasion around the neck"—he pointed with his index finger—"indicating the victim's head was immobilized. What does that tell you?"

"That he was alive when his eyes were gouged?"

"Precisely. The poor man was tortured." Massu sat down in his deskchair and began stroking his chin. "But why?" I had no reply. He took a manila folder out of a drawer, opened it, and began scanning its contents with a raised eyebrow, emitting a series of staccato grunts. He seemed the kind of man who was never rattled, whose mind was always turning, whose slight smile disappeared rarely. "Tell me, monsieur," he said, "what were you doing at the auction yesterday?"

"I was interested in the Baudelaire manuscript. I'm a writer, and something of a Baudelaire scholar."

"Why did you follow Vennet afterward?"

"I happened to be walking behind him after the auction and saw that he was being followed by two people, one of whom was you, of course, although I didn't know you were a policeman. But the other one was the man he'd beaten to the prize. It seemed suspicious to me. When I saw that he was in the bookshop, I went in to warn him that he was being followed."

"After you fled the scene, Vennet took your advice and gave us the slip. So I was unable to protect him, which was why I was there in the first place. By the time I tracked him down he was already dead. So, in a way, if it wasn't for your interference, Vennet might still be alive. Then, wonder of wonders, you turn up the following day at the scene of the crime. How does that happen?"

"I didn't murder Vennet, which is what you seem to be implying."

"I know. We checked your file. According to our records, you have lived in Paris only seven years. The origins of this crime are much older. Whether you know it or not, monsieur, you have stumbled upon one of the oldest cases of multiple homicide in the history of this marvelous city. And I believe you may be able to help us."

"I will do whatever I can."

Massu gave one of his little philosophical smiles. "Tell me, monsieur, how did you get tangled up in this mess? You shouldn't even be in Paris."

"I'm wondering that myself."

"Have you seen the manuscript?"

"Yes, yesterday at the auction."

"What did you make of it?"

"Well, I only looked at it for a few minutes, but nothing

I saw suggested it was a fake. The handwriting appears to be Baudelaire's, the paper stock seems old enough."

"Have you read it?"

"I didn't get time. I skimmed over the beginning—again, nothing appeared inauthentic."

"I read it last week, at Jacquenet's bookshop. I'd been waiting to read it for eighteen years. Let me tell you what is in it—this may interest you, not just as a scholar but as a human being. It is not a work of fiction. Baudelaire has written it as himself. It tells the story of his preparation for a transformation of the most unusual variety."

Just as Madeleine described, I thought to myself. Much as I wanted to hear what Massu knew, I also intuitively felt compelled to keep everything I knew about Madeleine to myself. "A transformation?"

"Metempsychosis, monsieur—are you familiar with the term?"

"Of course, the transmigration of souls after death."

"Precisely," said Massu. "Except that what Baudelaire seems to allude to in this story is a transference of souls that occurs before death."

"I see." Massu was studying me closely. "Sounds like fiction to me."

"Normally, I would tend to agree with you. But this case, which incidentally dates back at least eighteen years, blurs the lines between the real and the fictional. What do you know of the Baudelaire Society, or of its president, Madame Gabrielle Chanel?"

I'd been rather hoping he wouldn't mention Chanel. By doing so, he'd made it impossible to keep pretending that Madeleine's stories were delusions. Still, I thought, better to keep all this to myself. "Until recently, I'd never heard of the Society," I replied. "The woman's name rings a bell."

"Let me fill you in. The Baudelaire Society is a relic of a bygone era, when literary associations were fashionable. At its height in the 1900s, it was considered the most prestigious such association in Paris, and therefore the world. In 1923, its presidency passed to Gabrielle Chanel, a young high-society seamstress. She is now the wealthiest woman in France, and is better known as Coco. Surely you've heard the name?" I nodded. Massu paused, as if weighing up what to say next. "Do you know what that smell is, monsieur? It is the smell of burning paper. You will have noticed, upon your arrival, a fire in the courtyard below. Currently, in the courtyards of government buildings all over Paris, paperwork is being burned. Entire archives are going up in flames. This is all the information anyone needs to gauge how the defense of the republic is proceeding. And knowing this would naturally lead you to wonder why, at a time like this, an overworked police commissioner should take such a personal interest in a case about a murdered bouquiniste. But this is no ordinary case. Vennet is the third victim I know of to have had their eyes removed when they were killed, and each time the Baudelaire manuscript was involved. The first was in 1922. I was a neighborhood policeman assigned to assist the investigation. The victim was an antiquarian bookseller. His eye sockets were empty, his eyeballs never found. When I interviewed the widow, she mentioned that her husband had been commissioned by a new client to sell a manuscript on consignment: a previously unknown story by Baudelaire. The manuscript had vanished. The client turned out to have been the Baudelaire Society. I went to pay the Society a visit—it is headquartered in a *hôtel particulier* on the Île Saint-Louis. The president at the time was Aristide Artopoulos. Strange fellow—he claimed to have no recollection of the book, or of the bookseller. Eventually the suspicion of guilt fell on the bookseller's brother-in-law, a brutal alcoholic who owed the victim some money. He was charged, found guilty, and guillotined. I attended the execution—it was in the early morning, outside the prison on Boulevard Arago, and I remember thinking that the wrong man was being executed. But such is police life, and I put the matter out of my mind.

"A decade passed, during which time I rose through the ranks to deputy commissioner. Shortly after New Year in 1931, a suburban policeman called in a murdered body one morning, adding that the corpse was missing its eyeballs. When I heard this, my thoughts immediately returned to the bookseller, all those years previously. The victim's papers were still on him—he was a Belgian industrialist and notorious playboy. He owned a superb library on the subject of his beloved Belgium. He'd told his friends at the Jockey Club the evening before his death that he was in Paris to purchase, for a handsome sum, a story written in Baudelaire's own hand during his exile in Brussels. After dinner, he'd gone to the Chabanais, a high-class brothel in the second arrondissement where he was a regular. He left the Chabanais at four in the morning but never made it back to the Hôtel George V, where he was staying. His body was found in the Bois de Vincennes by two kids the following morning.

"The story made a bit of a splash in the papers before it was hushed up. Suspicions fell on a taxi driver with a gambling problem who'd picked up our Belgian outside the brothel. But I wasn't satisfied. I sifted through the evidence and recognized an address scribbled in his notebook—17 Quai d'Anjou. The address of the Baudelaire Society. So I paid it another visit. By this time, Artopoulos was gone. Instead, it was presided over by a woman, one whose name was familiar to me: Coco Chanel. She'd known the man socially, she said, but knew nothing of his death other than what had been printed in the dailies.

"The taxi driver was found guilty and he, too, was guillotined at dawn on Boulevard Arago, and once again I attended the execution. I was convinced that another miscarriage of justice had occurred—only I had no evidence. I decided to delve into the archives, looking for murders that had involved the gouging out of the victims' eyes. I found several. Hippolyte Balthazar, a psychologist who worked in the military asylum at the Salpêtrière hospital, was murdered in 1917. Balthazar, it turned out, had been a prominent member of the Baudelaire Society for seventeen years. Encouraged, I looked even further back. In 1900, on a train from Nantes to Paris, Édmonde de Bressy, founder of the Baudelaire Society, and Lucien Roeg, its secretary, were both found dead in their cabins, their eyes gouged out. In the same year, Gaspard Leducq, a captain in the merchant navy, was murdered in Le Havre, eyes also removed. He had been an employee of a shipping company owned by the Artopoulos dynasty. All of these homicides remain unsolved.

"Vennet's death confirms my intuition: someone out there is killing people associated with the Baudelaire manuscript, and by removing the victims' eyes they are doing it conspicuously, as if they want the murders to be noticed, to be connected. The common thread that links them is the Baudelaire Society. Which poses an interesting question: can a literary institution be guilty of the crime of murder?" Massu rose from his seat and walked over to the window. The water in the river below continued its dark, restless flow. "That is why, monsieur, we are not holding you here as a suspect: you've only lived in Paris since 1933. But you may be able to help us find the culprit. Perhaps it is the other man who was tailing Vennet yesterday."

"The one in the tailored suit?"

"Precisely. I'd like you to find out his connection to the Baudelaire Society. Perhaps you could pay Madame Chanel a visit."

"How do you suggest I do that?"

"That is up to you. But you would be appropriately rewarded."

"I see. You want me to become an *indicateur*."

"A time-honored tradition. You are at last becoming a true Parisian."

"Just as I was thinking of leaving. What's in it for me?"

"Name your price," said Massu.

"An exit visa."

"For the right information, it can be arranged." His smile disappeared for an instant. "But the information would have to be very useful indeed." He went to the door and opened it, signaling it was time for me to leave. "You would basically have to solve the mystery on our behalf. We are very stretched, as you can see."

The interview was at an end. I stood and we shook hands. I was almost out the door when I remembered my notebook. It contained all the notes I'd made of Madeleine's stories. "And my notebook? May I have it back?"

"Ah, the notebook. For now, we shall keep it—as a security deposit, if you like. Good day, monsieur."

☞ {226}

The Baudelaire Society

I WANDERED HOME slowly in the afternoon sun. Commissaire Massu's story had left me in a daze. Even without referring to my notebook, it was clear that somehow his story and Madeleine's dovetailed almost exactly—to such a degree, in fact, that they'd both asked me to run the same errand on their behalf. It seemed there would be no avoiding a rendezvous with Madame Chanel.

In the lobby of my apartment building I ran into the concierge, Madame Barbier, shuffling envelopes.

"The Germans may be coming but the bills must be paid all the same," she said, speaking in the old country way, rolling her r's. She approached me with a worried look. "What are you still doing here? Don't you know it's all over?"

I held up the copy of *Le Temps* I'd just bought. "The English are sending more troops, apparently, and the Americans may enter the war at any moment."

"Well," she huffed, "you're quite the optimist. I don't believe a word of it. It's a veritable nightmare. When I think of my poor Jeannot . . ." Her son was a conscript. She lifted a crate by her feet and carried it to the building's entranceway, where her husband was packing their belongings onto an old Peugeot. "We're going to my aunt's place in Vichy. There'll be no trouble there. You should leave too, if you know what's good for you."

Inside my front door, the black suitcase was waiting for me like a faithful hound. But instead of picking it up and leaving, as I ought to have done, I lay down on my bed and started reading the newspaper. The headlines were upbeat, it was true, but reading in between the lines there was no denying Madame Barbier was right. The situation was worsening: Belgium routed, the French army outmaneuvered, and the British evacuating at Dunkirk. The government itself was leaving Paris for the relative safety of Tours. By concentrating on a total military victory in the north, I calculated, the Germans had delayed their arrival in Paris by a few more days. That, I figured, gave me just enough time. I wanted to get to the bottom of this affair—if there was indeed a bottom to get to. And if my plans went awry, there was always the morphine.

The next day, I sent a letter by pneumatic tube to the Baudelaire Society on the Quai d'Anjou, signing it with Arthur's name and apartment number.

Paris, Wednesday, June 5, 1940

Dear Madame Chanel,
I recently acquired a previously unpublished work by Charles Baudelaire, a story entitled "The Education of a Monster." The work is of enormous literary significance and prestige. I cannot guarantee its safekeeping in these troubled times. Given that the libraries are all closed, I would be grateful if the Baudelaire Society would consider accepting it with a view to assuring its preservation. As for obvious reasons I do not wish to send you the manuscript in the post, I am happy

to bring it to the Society and give it to you in person at your
earliest convenience.
Cordially, Arthur Koestler

I had no idea if Chanel had already recovered the manuscript from Vennet, but either way, I was betting she would
take the bait. It wasn't much of a plan, hardly better than a
derringer without bullets, but it was all I had. I was racked by
anxiety and doubt, excoriating myself for my foolishness, but
once the letter was sent there was no going back. My motiva-
tions were several, each of them slight when considered alone
but constituting an irrefutable argument when combined. First
of all, I coveted the Baudelaire manuscript, and I figured I still
had a chance of acquiring it. As a reader of crime novels, I had
an interest in solving Vennet's murder. I figured that if there
was half a chance of acquiring the exit visa Massu had dangled
before me, I might as well take it. But above all I wanted to
verify Madeleine's story, and visiting the Baudelaire Society
was my best chance at certainty.

The reply finally arrived Friday around noon. When I heard
the familiar tinkle of the postman's bell, I raced downstairs,
found the blue envelope, and tore it open: I was invited to meet
Chanel at the Society headquarters the following Monday afternoon. I would have to wait another three whole days! What if
the Germans were to arrive before then?

The weekend weather was summery and joyous. I continued to head out for walks at daybreak, wisps of mist drifting through the streets and across the river. Paris, in its state
of suspended animation, was lovelier than ever. On Saturday,
couples ambled arm in arm along the quays, here and there
fishermen cast their rods into the river, and the bouquinistes

tended to their stalls. All of these scenes were tinged with nostalgia, as if they already belonged to the past, while I began to seriously consider, for the first time, a future beyond the here and now: leaving Paris, making my way somehow to America or Argentina, starting again, making a new life. In every such snapshot of the life to come I was not alone—Madeleine was there by my side.

On Sunday, I woke to the sound of distant artillery fire coming from the east. All at once, the previous day's idyll was forgotten and in the streets Parisians hauled suitcases to the nearest Métro station. I too ventured out, lumbered with notebooks and papers wrapped in string, to visit my librarian friend Georges. Weeks earlier he'd agreed to hide the book I'd been writing for so many years, a book that would now have to remain unfinished, at least for as long as the war continued. But it would survive in its hiding place, the archives of the Bibliothèque Nationale. It gives me a shiver of pleasure to know a piece of me is still there.

On my way home, I dropped in at the Café de Flore, which was full of writers and artists who'd gathered to speculate on the latest developments, as the radio wasn't to be trusted. I ran into Tristan Tzara, who advised me to go straight to the nearest train station. Of course, I had no intention of following his advice. Passing the Montparnasse station on the way home, I noticed Republican Guards separating men fighting for train tickets in the forecourt.

Between my painfully thumping heart and the rumble of distant artillery, I slept little that night.

At noon on Monday, with Madeleine's derringer in my jacket pocket, a leather satchel slung around my shoulder and a newspaper in hand, I took a seat on a shaded bench at the far western corner of the Île Saint-Louis. From here, I could survey everything happening on the cobblestoned street that ran along the riverbank, including anyone entering or leaving the Baudelaire Society. I'd brought the newspaper to hide behind, but after scanning the headlines—Reynaud's latest appeal to Roosevelt, four spies executed, reports of poisoned milk—I folded it away.

The Baudelaire Society's headquarters was the Hôtel de Lauzun, formerly known as the Hôtel Pimodan, where Baudelaire and Jeanne Duval had lived together, when she was his muse and he her protector and they were, in their own fashion, in love. Beneath and around me the river flowed silently, while above, in a slight breeze, the leaves of a willow whispered their secret language. The rumble in the east was constant now, putting the lie to the warm, dappled sunshine.

Shortly before two o'clock, a gleaming burgundy Delahaye cabriolet pulled up in front of the Baudelaire Society. The thick-necked man I'd seen at the Hôtel Drouot the previous week jumped out from behind the steering wheel and opened the rear passenger door. A lithe woman in a black dress emerged and disappeared into the building. She was too far away to make out her face, but even from this distance it could be no one other than Chanel.

Half an hour later, at the agreed time, with my right hand wrapped around the derringer in my pocket, I rang the bell at the Society's entrance. It was opened by the same besuited thug I'd seen before who, if he was at all surprised to see me, didn't betray it. Ushered into the entrance hall, I felt like I'd stepped into a recurring dream. The marbled staircase with curved cast-iron palings, the damask drapes, the frayed oriental rugs strewn over the mosaic floor tiles, the chandeliers, the mahogany furniture—it was a kind of museum dedicated to the moth-eaten pomp of the Second Empire. I was led down a corridor to an anteroom where I was instructed to await Madame Chanel's arrival. The sense of déjà vu continued: every object—the velvet confidante on which I sat, the brocaded floor lamp beside me, the rug on which my feet rested, the Delacroix lithographs in gilded frames hanging on the walls—prompted chimes of recognition and dread.

The valet reappeared and announced that Madame Chanel would receive me. I followed him into the library, where two leather armchairs faced each other across a wide mahogany writing desk. Three of the four walls were entirely covered with books. I cast an eye over them. One wall was given over to every edition ever published of Baudelaire's work, including in foreign languages. The other shelves were devoted to the secondary literature—books about Baudelaire: biographies, memoirs, criticism. All the volumes were uniformly bound in the same red *peau de chagrin*, with gold-leaf embossing, that had covered the Baudelaire manuscript at the auction. So about this, too, Madeleine had been right: "The Education of a Monster" had been in the Society library all along. Why was the Society going to such lengths to retrieve a book it had just sold at auction? The only possible explanation was Madeleine's.

To be unable to trust one's own mind is a rare and unenviable terror. And this was now the condition that took hold of me. All these corroborations of Madeleine's stories were eroding the pillars upon which had rested, for four and a half decades, my sense of what was real and what was not. Trying to pull myself together, I continued my tour of the room. Hanging between two windows was a framed, tea-colored chart of the world, not as it is but as it had been known a century or more ago. Someone had drawn a line that curved from one side of the map to the other, tracing a circumnavigation of the globe that had started and ended in Marseille and included a stop in the Pacific, on an island too small for the cartographer to record, but which the holder of the pencil had marked and named as Oaeetee. Below the map, on a stand, stood a scale-model replica of a three-masted sailing ship called the *Solide*, sailing under a French tricolor flag—not the blue, white, and red flag that was approved in 1794 but the red, white, and blue flag introduced in 1790, shortly after the Revolution. The model's craftsmanship was first-rate. The maker had reproduced everything, every sail and rope, down to the officers and crew. Some were climbing the rigging, others keeping lookout, and one was manning the wheel. A circle of men was gathered on the main deck, where a sailor was tied to the bulwark and—I leaned forward to better study the scene depicted—being flogged. His back was expertly striated with waxy scarlet streaks, while another crewman was standing near him with a whip in his hand. Again, everything was exactly as Madeleine had described. Between the books, the map and the model ship, not to mention the events that had led me here, this was the moment of my complete persuasion, my conversion, my Damascus moment. If I could have slipped out of the building then and there, without even speaking to Chanel, I would have gladly done so, even at the cost of finding the manuscript, for I now had the answer to my most pressing question: Madeleine's story was verified. There was no longer any need to meet Chanel. But it was at that very instant that I heard the clipped steps of a woman in high heels approaching from the corridor outside. The door opened and Chanel entered the room in a puff of rhythm, perfume and light, approaching me with a smile that vanished as suddenly as it had appeared. Her hand was glacial to the touch.

"A relic of the Society's founder," she said without introducing herself, looking down at the model ship with a frown. "A bit of an eyesore, really. I'm of a mind to donate it to some provincial museum somewhere and be rid of it." She set off in the direction of a liquor cabinet camouflaged among the bookshelves. "Something to drink?"

"Bisquit Dubouché. You have a fine library. Who's your binder—Meunier? Lortic?"

Chanel shook her head with a smile as she poured. "Guess again."

I approached the nearest shelf, taking a book at random, examining the leather, the embossing, the filigree. "This is very fine work, reminiscent of Marius Michel, though more modern. There's an artist's temperament at play here." I opened the book and held one of the pages open against the light of the windows. "My guess is . . ." And there it was, a spectral fingerprint: the binder's watermark. "No, it can't be. The expense alone . . ." But the quality of the work was beyond question. "Can it be that this entire library was bound by Legrain?"

Chanel approached me holding two glasses, one of which she handed to me, holding my eye as she did so. It was unsettling, locking gazes with this woman. She was no longer young, but an awesome power emanated from her, elegant and flinty at once, animated by a restless energy that could easily be mistaken for youth, and was even, perhaps, preferable to it. "Using lacquers by Jean Dunand," she confirmed with a half-smile, sitting on the edge of the writing table. "Now you understand the value of the full collection. When I took the reins of the Society, I had it entirely rebound, to give it an aesthetic unity Baudelaire himself would have been proud of. It's the finest collection of its type in the world. These volumes are for the sole and exclusive use of the Society's members. There are books here of which there exists only one copy." Her eyes sparkled proudly.

"Don't you think outsiders also ought to be able to read them?"

"Not at all." She smiled. "Now, to the matter at hand. Do you have the manuscript?"

So I'd gambled well: she had not managed to retrieve the manuscript from Vennet. It was still out there, somewhere, hidden by the old man before he was killed. And now my purpose was clear: I had to get out of here alive and find it.

"I don't."

Chanel blinked. "Then why are you wasting my time?" she said, almost growling.

"Until only a couple of weeks ago, that manuscript was here, nestled among all the other Baudelaire originals on that wall, bound by Legrain, like everything else." I'd based my gambit on what Madeleine had told me, although I had no way of knowing if my arrow would hit its mark. Chanel looked at me with all the inscrutability of a casino habitué. She raised her hand, presumably to reach for the bell on the desk to call the valet. I plunged mine into my pocket and pulled out Madeleine's derringer, pointing it in her direction. "I suggest you don't ring that bell." My heart lurched into another painful, stabbing gallop. Chanel took a sip of brandy, narrowing her eyes and studying me as if sizing me up for the first time. But she didn't say anything. If her silence was calculated to be unnerving, it worked. But I'd long since passed the point of no return. "Why would you sell a manuscript, only to go to such lengths to retrieve it after it was sold?"

She did not reply, but smoked her cigarette calmly, keeping her gaze on me the entire time. I felt foolish, an impostor, playing a role for which I was ill suited. But, receiving no satisfaction, I decided I could only press on. "Why would you murder the man who bought it?" Again, no reply. To make matters worse, I was now blushing. The silence dragged out so long that I couldn't bear it another second. "I think I know why. You thought you could take advantage of the impending invasion to try to tempt Madeleine out of her lair. And perhaps, if things had turned out a little differently, it might have worked."

Finally, a response: Chanel smiled—a sly, barely perceptible smile. At the time, I couldn't understand it. After all, she didn't know that my derringer contained no bullets. "Ah, Madeleine," she said. "Madeleine Pernety—or perhaps you know her as Madeleine Blanc. I should have known she would be mixed up in this. She *is* a most charming creature, isn't she? So easy to fall in love with. Of course, as you can imagine, you're not the first. You are neither the first to have fallen for her, nor the first to have been duped by her. If her story is convincing, it's only because she's rehearsed it so often. And sadly you are certainly not the first to have agreed to commit a crime punishable by death on her behalf. For what we are dealing with is a sadly deluded, and very dangerous, mind. Although I have been a victim of her delusions for a long time now—for as long, indeed, as I have been president of this Society—I am also aware that there are other victims. And among those victims are the men who fall in love with her.

"Madeleine is a woman obsessed. She is very good at recognizing obsession in others. And it's easy to mistake her obsession for love, especially when one is craving it oneself. How long have you known her? I'd wager a few weeks at most. Am I right?"

Having just committed the sin of saying too much, I opted to say nothing at all.

"Your silence speaks volumes. Have you considered the possibility that Madeleine planned everything from the beginning? Or did you think you met by coincidence, like real lovers? A Baudelaire scholar meets a woman who promises him a rare prize—no, two prizes: her heart and a rare manuscript, days before its auction. That's quite a coincidence, wouldn't you say?" She looked me directly in the eye. "Did she tell you you were Baudelaire in a past life? That she was Jeanne Duval?"

I was determined to say nothing. She smiled again, leaning back and drawing on her cigarette.

"Monsieur, I have been shadowed by Madeleine for almost two decades, so I should know a thing or two about her ways. In your own small way you are also a victim of that woman's insanity. But at least we still have the privilege of being alive. Several others have not been so lucky."

She took a sip of her drink. Again, I resisted the temptation to speak, which is easy to do when one is holding a gun at someone. I found myself admiring Chanel's aplomb.

"Consider this," she continued, moving around the writing table and sitting in the leather chair on the other side. "Consider what she is asking you to believe. She contends that it is possible for the soul of a human being to cross from one body into another. Monsieur, I don't know you but I can only assume you are an intelligent man. I assume from your accent that you are German, probably Jewish. In your circumstances, it should not astonish you if your reason is taken hostage by an attractive woman. Being a German Jew at this place and time, you may be excused an old man's folly. So I cannot hold a grudge against you, even though you are pointing a gun at me. Instead, I wish to appeal to your intellect. I am quite sure I can persuade you I have a rational explanation for everything that Madeleine has told you. You see, she was a member of the Society when I first joined it in 1921. She'd been a member for some years, rising to the position of secretary when Aristide Artopoulos was its president. Naturally, she assumed she was the heir apparent. Instead, when I joined, Artopoulos decided the Society would be better off with me as its president. In retrospect, it is clear that Madeleine was already lost in her fantasies—lost to reason and logic—even before my arrival, only it wasn't apparent at the time.

"You see, Madeleine's psyche is deeply scarred. She was a nurse during the war, and it destroyed her. Shellshock. She was one of those survivors of that terrible conflict who appear well but are secretly diseased, only her disease is one of the mind. Perhaps it was Baudelaire's madness that drew her to him. And of all his writings, she identified most with 'The Education of a Monster.'

"At some point, no doubt driven by a kind of primal guilt complex, she fused her own identity with that of the Édmonde de Bressy character described in the manuscript. And over time, she developed this elaborate backstory, piecing together fragments from a variety of sources, even the model ship you were studying when I entered the room. She became so entangled in these inventions of hers that she eventually decided, when Artopoulos accorded me the presidency, that I was her ancient rival, hell-bent not only on her destruction but on that of the entire world. Thankfully, at this point, she did not have a firearm, or my life might have ended then and there.

"So she quit—well, more accurately, she vanished, never to be seen again, taking the manuscript with her. And every now and then, she manages to coax some unsuspecting lover into doing her bidding, hoping that somehow she will be rid of me and will finally reclaim her rightful position as president of the Baudelaire Society."

She rang the bell for the valet and stood. Suddenly I was glad the bullet chamber was empty. Had it not been, I would have found myself torn: in awakening my doubts about Madeleine's sanity, Chanel had led me to question my own.

"Monsieur, you can put your gun away, you will not need it today. I guarantee you your safety. Out of pity. For you are nothing more than an innocent dupe. My advice to you is to leave Paris immediately. The Germans will be here in less than a week and they will come looking for you, I promise you. In different circumstances, I would send for the police right now. You are an unfortunate, but today you can consider yourself lucky. There are more pressing matters to attend to. Good day, monsieur. And good luck." And with that she crushed what remained of her cigarette into an ashtray and walked out of the room as if she didn't have another second to spare.

I did not put my gun away, as Chanel had ordered me to do. I kept that gun in my hand until Chanel's man ushered me out of the building, my heart beating painfully, and even once I was alone on the street I put it in my pocket but kept my grip intact in case I was being followed. I walked along the Quais d'Anjou and de Bourbon, turned the corner and began walking toward the cathedral—slowly at first, deep in thought. Occasionally, one's illusions are stripped away so suddenly that the mind is left spinning like a top. So it was on this occasion. What, precisely, had that meeting achieved? I'd arrived seeking certainty, one way or the other; within minutes, I'd settled on one kind of certainty, only for that certainty to be summarily demolished. I was no closer to solving the mystery of Vennet's murder—nor that of Madeleine's disappearance. And as for the manuscript, all I could be certain of was that the Baudelaire Society did not have it. I had been thoroughly outfoxed. That part of me that had always been ashamed of the thought of being in love with Madeleine was screaming at the part of me that still loved her, *I told you so!*

In the maelstrom of my mind, I tried reconstructing the events of the previous fortnight. Could it really be that Madeleine had chosen me as the target of her elaborate scheme? Had she deliberately led me to Jacquenet's bookstore to entice me into her murderous game? Or had it been more intuitive, less calculated than that, the spell she cast over me? Whatever the explanation, how could I have fallen for it so completely? And if her love was counterfeit, why was my heart still aching?

I realized I needed to retrieve my black suitcase and leave Paris as quickly as possible. But to do that, I would need some help. With the rumble of the approaching conflict behind me, I walked hurriedly across the Pont Saint-Louis and the cathedral garden, past the cathedral, its windows hidden by sandbags, and across the empty square, cutting through the stream of southbound boulevard traffic, now peppered with military trucks and soldiers on foot also fleeing the onslaught, toward the Quai des Orfèvres. At the entrance gate of the Palais de Justice, a line of men were carrying boxes from the offices onto a barge. I asked the guard to see Massu but, after he'd made a call, he told me to come back the following morning. When I insisted on seeing Massu right away, the guard threatened to have me arrested.

I crossed the river and headed homeward down the Rue Danton. Away from the Boulevard Saint-Michel, the streets were so quiet my steps echoed against nearby buildings. Shafts of golden light, speckled with flakes of dancing ash, pierced the afternoon shade, and the air smelled of burning paper.

When I neared my building on Rue Dombasle, Chanel's Delahaye cabriolet was parked around the corner. There was no one in it. Thankfully, I'd signed my letter to Chanel with Arthur's name and apartment number, directly above mine. At the foot of the stairs, I listened for noises. Nothing. I looked up. No sign of a human presence. There was no point being surreptitious, I decided—the staircase creaked—I must walk as any other man would normally walk. Only now I found myself asking, how do men normally walk? Feigning normalcy, I climbed the steps to my apartment and entered it. Knowing Chanel's henchman would be listening, I left the door unlocked. I took off my shoes and, moving as quietly as I could, heart throbbing, I took my black suitcase, my papers, and what little money I had and left, descending the steps two at a time, suitcase, shoes, and all. I ran in my socks down Rue Dombasle, turned right at the Rue de Vaugirard and down the steps of the entrance to the Métro.

I spent the rest of the afternoon underground, mind whirring, shuttling between near-empty second-class carriages, making sure I wasn't being followed, until I emerged at the Gare de l'Est around dusk. The sunset was a glorious affair that made a mockery of human intrigue. I knew of a sordid little workers' hotel overlooking the canal where a German refugee might find a bed without having to show any identity papers. Other than two bored young prostitutes, it appeared to be empty.

I climbed upstairs to the room I'd been given and collapsed on the thin mattress. The walls were damp and the plumbing gurgled and dripped, but at least I could hide here and plan my next move.

My room was on the third floor, overlooking the canal. Unable to sleep, I sat on the windowsill, staring at the crescent moon, listening to the rumble of the distant artillery and watching the flashes of light over the eastern horizon. In the darkness of the blackout, the stars sparkled on the water's surface as brightly as they shone up above. I smoked one cigarette after another, going over the day's events as if I were watching a film. There was no doubt about it: I'd been mesmerized by a master hypnotist—but who was the hypnotist, Madeleine or Chanel?

There were two things in particular that perplexed me: that sly, subtle smile that had appeared on Chanel's face when I mentioned Madeleine, and the fact that she'd sent her man to Arthur's apartment after the meeting. It took me half a pack of Salomés to figure out the puzzle, and when the answer finally came to me, I cursed myself. I'd made a grave tactical error. I ought never to have referred to Madeleine. Until I did, Chanel had not known what to say. It was only at the mention of Madeleine that Chanel had spoken. What would she have said had I not mentioned Madeleine—had I not given the game away? I would never know. But the fact that she had sent her man to find me after the meeting was itself a kind of clue. Of course, I'd pointed a gun at her, but had she been innocently aggrieved, she need only have called the police. The fact that she hadn't suggested she had something to hide.

It wasn't much to go on, but love thrives on ephemera: hunches, gut feelings, obscure clues are all the fuel it needs.

Whenever the fragile fabric of a lover's fantasy is undone by reality, all it takes is the merest hint of hope and its threads start knitting together again. Combined with what I'd seen—the manuscript, the scale model of the sailing ship, what Massu had told me—the memory of that smile punctured the certainty of Chanel's argument. It introduced the element of doubt. And that faint glimmer of doubt was all that was required for the screaming voice of shame in me to subside, and for that other voice, the voice that hoped, that loved Madeleine, that spoke to her even now that she was gone, to make itself heard again. My first mistake had been to lose hope—to look away from Madeleine's eyes at the very moment when I could have settled the question once and for all: were her stories true or not? Smoking Salomés in the darkness, there was nothing I wanted more than to find her again, to look into her eyes and discover their secret.

I woke from fitful sleep in a cloud of smoky light. The sky was smeared with an inexplicable orange fog and my nostrils stung with the smell of petrol. I checked out of the hotel and walked with my suitcase toward the Palais de Justice. Everyone on the streets was walking south carrying luggage. I'd done what Massu had asked, and even if I hadn't learned anything of use to him, he owed me my notebook, at the very least, and perhaps I could still cajole a favor out of him.

The guard at the gate called for the Brigade Spéciale, then nodded me inside. Another guard searched me and confiscated my derringer. I was escorted to Massu's office and found him on the telephone, stroking his mustache while listening to the voice at the other end of the line. There was a pile of blankets on the floor in a corner where he must have slept, and my notebook was lying open on his desk. He gestured to me to take a seat. "Very well, *mon général*. Consider it done." He hung up and looked at me with a resigned expression. "The government has evaporated. Shops are being looted. The army is now in charge. And the Germans are only forty kilometers away. We expect their arrival any day now. Paris will be declared an open city."

"Why?"

"Because there is no point defending it, it's already lost," he said.

"What is the orange fog?" I asked.

"The army is setting the petrol reserves on fire as it retreats." He took my notebook in his hands, licking his index finger each time he turned the page. "Things are about to get very dangerous for you, monsieur."

"They took my gun," I said.

"You don't have a license for it. Technically, we could have you arrested." He looked at me with a raised eyebrow.

"I'm a German—you could have me arrested for that too."

"True. But what would it achieve? Your compatriots will be here soon enough. Thankfully for you, the gun was empty. Given the circumstances, we can let that go."

"Will it be returned to me when I leave?"

"Monsieur, please, be reasonable." He looked back at the notebook. "So this is what you write?"

"They're notes for a book I hope to publish some day."

"What is Shéhérazade?"

I wasn't sure if he was being serious. "She's a character in the *Arabian Nights*."

Massu blinked. "I see. Why is her name written in your notebook?" He held the notebook up for my scrutiny, opened to the last of the written pages. There, in handwriting other than mine, was scrawled the word *Shéhérazade*.

"I've never seen it before. Perhaps you wrote it."

"Now why would I do that?" He examined the word. "The *Arabian Nights*, you say."

"Yes, it's a medieval story cycle, in which the heroine marries a murderous king and saves her own life by telling him tales."

"Is that so?" Massu drummed his fingers on his chin.

It could only be Madeleine who had written that word in my notebook before she vanished, but I had no idea why. I didn't want to repeat the previous day's mistake and mention her to Massu. I didn't know what, if anything, he knew of her. The notes I'd written were incomplete. Her name didn't appear in its pages. The conclusion to Madeleine's tales—her own story, recounted to me the very day of her disappearance—was still unwritten. For now, it existed only in my head. After she'd gone, I hadn't had the heart to so much as open the notebook, let alone write in it, which was why I hadn't seen the clue she had left me.

Massu was waiting for me to say something. Fortunately, life had taught me the value of a poker face in a crisis. "It must have been written by my neighbor Arthur, during our last poker party. He suggested it as the title of a book I'm writing."

"Looks like a woman's handwriting to me."

"Arthur is Hungarian. Perhaps it's a Hungarian's handwriting."

"Where is this Arthur?"

"I believe he's currently in Bordeaux."

"Pity," said Massu. "Although that's where you should be."

"Perhaps it's not too late to leave."

"The railway stations are crammed with crowds of people who agree with you."

"I thought we had a deal."

"Did you see Chanel?"

"I did."

"What did you learn?"

"She doesn't have it."

"What?"

"The manuscript."

"Monsieur, I'm a detective, not a scholar. I'm not interested in a manuscript. I'm interested in solving a series of murders."

"Ah, well, I'm afraid I learned nothing of any use to you about all that."

Massu sighed. "Well, your incompetence as an informer is more than compensated for by what I read in your notebook." He slid it across the desk.

"They're just fairy tales," I said, stuffing the notebook into my jacket pocket.

"Oh, I doubt that. But tell me something. The story finishes during the last war. What has happened since? How does the tale of the albatross end?"

"I don't know," I replied. "I haven't figured out the ending."

"Well, if you do, please let me know. So that I can do what I can to protect whoever this Shéhérazade might be."

"She's not real. She's a chimera. What about protecting me? I'm real. And you promised me an exit visa."

"You haven't been very helpful, I'm afraid. And anyway the rules of the game have changed. I can't help you. I no longer have the authority. The army is in charge now." He raised that eyebrow again, and added a half-smile. "But I will have my secretary draw up a *laissez-passer* and a ticket on the night train to Marseille for you, leaving the Gare de Lyon at eight o'clock tonight." He picked up the telephone receiver on his desk and instructed someone to prepare the documents. At the end of the call, Massu stood and gestured to the door. "Marseille is your best bet. Ships are still sailing out."

"Not without an exit visa."

"I'm sure you can arrange a crossing in Marseille." I studied Massu's face, twinkling with irony behind that ridiculous little mustache. Here was a man who seemed to take amusement in the messiness of life—as close to a definition of happiness as I know. He walked me to the door and opened it for me.

"Oh, one last thing," he added. "Shéhérazade is also the name of a nightclub near Pigalle." Before I could say anything else, he shook my hand. "Goodbye, monsieur, and bon voyage."

I heard him chuckle as the door clicked shut.

{308}

The Shéhérazade

"WELCOME TO THE SHÉHÉRAZADE!" boomed the old door-
man from behind his silvery walrus mustache. He was the
only sign of life on the otherwise darkened street. His Russian accent ricocheted off the paving stones and the walls of
nearby buildings as he swung open the door to the nightclub.
I stepped inside and down a flight of stairs into an Oriental
fantasy world—part seraglio, part Aladdin's cave—of arches,
grottos, and drapes. A pall of tobacco smoke lent the light of
the Arabian lamps an exotic haze. A solitary couple swayed on
the dancefloor while on stage a gypsy band played, fronted by
a singer in a long sequinned dress who waved her arms about
in an approximation of languor.

"J'attendrai
le jour et
la nuit,
J'attendrai toujours
ton retour . . ."

She was accompanied by two guitarists and a double bass
player. I removed my hat, sat at the bar, and ordered a calvados. This place had been fashionable once, I thought, looking
around—in the heady years after the last war, the war to end
all wars. When the calvados arrived I tipped the barman well
and said, "I'm looking for Madeleine Blanc."

"Never heard of her."

"Sure you have. Oriental features, beautiful, in her forties. Any idea how I can get in touch with her?"

"Who's asking?"

"Koahu."

The barman stuck his head behind a swinging door for a moment and then attended to another customer. I settled down to drinking my calvados and watching the band. The waiters, dressed in Cossack uniforms, buzzed from table to table, under the watchful eye of the Russian maître d'hôtel.

"J'attendrai,
car l'oiseau qui s'enfuit
vient chercher l'oubli
dans son nid . . ."

While I waited, I sifted through the events of the day. After leaving the Palais de Justice, I'd walked down to the Quai de la Tournelle in search of Vennet's stall. All the bouquinistes on this stretch of the river were closed. Having found Vennet's stall, I inspected it from every angle. Like all the others, it was made of crate-wood and painted with forest green oil. It did not appear to have been forced open. I fondled the brass lock. I would need a hacksaw or, better still, a boltcutter, only where would I find one? By now, most shops and banks were closed. I made my way to the Métro with my suitcase. The carriages were emptier than ever. The effect was ghostly. I alighted at Pigalle, where the cafés and bars along the Boulevard de Clichy were shuttered. There were no tourists. I had little idea of where to find the nightclub, so I had to overcome my resistance to speaking with strangers. I approached two policemen who were plastering bills on a Morris column that usually advertised cabaret shows.

PARIS HAS BEEN DECLARED AN OPEN CITY

The military governor requests the population to abstain
from all acts of hostility and expects it to maintain the
calm and dignity necessitated by the circumstances.

By order, General H. Dentz, military governor

Mustering all my courage, I asked them where I might
find the Cabaret Shéhérazade. They looked me up and down a
moment—admittedly I must have been an odd sight, with my
German accent and black suitcase, as if I were the vanguard
of a different Wehrmacht from the one they were expecting.
A day or two ago, I thought, they would have arrested me.
But instead they pointed down the Rue Pigalle. A little while
later—around noon, I guessed (the bells of the churches were
not tolling)—I dropped my suitcase in front of a doorway and
knocked. There was no response. According to a small sign by
the entrance, the nightclub only opened at eight in the evening, which was exactly the time my train was due to leave.
I sat on my suitcase, fished a Salomé from my pocket and lit it.
It seemed I would have to choose between finding Madeleine
again and leaving Paris for the relative safety of the south.
I could almost hear Massu's ironic chuckle. Had he put me in
this position by design, as a sadistic practical joke or punishment for not being more helpful? I would never know. But
between love and liberty, there was no doubt which I would
choose. I made my way back to the hotel I'd stayed in the previous night and rented my room again. I spent the afternoon
there, napping, smoking, rereading my notes, until evening,
when I struck out again to find the Shéhérazade.

*"Le temps passe et court
en battant tristement
dans mon coeur si lourd.
Et pourtant, j'attendrai
ton retour."*

At the song's conclusion, the patrons took a moment from their drinking, smoking, gossiping, and giggling to applaud half-heartedly. The singer bowed her head in acknowledgment. A waitress approached her and whispered something in her ear. They both looked in my direction. The band followed the singer off stage, behind a red velvet curtain, and a few minutes later the singer re-emerged. She came to sit beside me at the bar. "Two more of those," she said to the barman, pointing at my empty glass. She turned to me. "Were you followed?"

"No. I mean, I don't think so."

"Did you come from your apartment?"

"I haven't been to my apartment since yesterday. I'm staying in a hotel by the canal."

"Are you signed in under your own name?"

"Of course not. I wasn't born yesterday."

"Good. All the same, I can't take you to Madeleine tonight, it's too dangerous."

"I'm sure the police have better things to think about."

"Perhaps. But then there's also Chanel's people."

"How is she? Where is she?"

"She's been waiting. She expected you sooner."

"Why did she go?"

"You should ask her that. In my opinion it was because you didn't believe her."

"I changed my mind."

"She was counting on that." The singer paused and gazed

into her drink. "I, on the other hand, was hoping for the contrary. You will forgive a little jealousy on my part—we are rivals, you see. She didn't tell you that, did she?"

"No," I said.

"Ah, evidently Madeleine is not as trustworthy a storyteller as you might have imagined. And, believe me, I have been a far more faithful servant to her than you. But you . . ." A bitter expression stole across her heavily made-up face. "You are Koahu. You will always hold a special place in her heart." She threw the rest of the calvados down her throat. "Never mind. There are more important matters to consider than our own sordid little romances. Did you see Chanel?"

"Yes."

"And?"

"It all checked out."

"Did you do what Madeleine asked?"

"What with? I had no bullets."

The singer cursed under her breath. "Do you have the manuscript, at least?"

"No. But I know where it is. All I need is a boltcutter."

She took a long breath. "Very well, I'll organize to have someone take you to her. But not tonight. Tomorrow morning at ten. At Saint-Eustache, the church behind Les Halles. An old widow will be praying in the front pew. Kneel down in the pew directly behind her. When she leaves, follow her. From a distance. She'll take you to Madeleine. And you'll get your boltcutter. Whatever you do, don't go back to your apartment. You can't be too cautious. Chanel has enormous power, and anyone left in Paris right now is suspect, even these old White Russians here tonight." She glanced around the room at the nightclub patrons, who were drinking and smoking as if invasion were a banality. "They'll be volunteers in the Germans' welcoming committee. They've seen a lot worse than this. They're all hoping Hitler will invade Russia next and return their family estates to them." She looked back at me with an expression of crushing sadness. "Tomorrow morning, when you go to Saint-Eustache, make sure you're not being followed." She stood. "Madeleine won't leave with you, you know, if that's what you're hoping. She must stay here. In a strange way even she doesn't understand, she must stay close to Chanel." She shot me a glance that struck like a dagger. "She loves you, but she doesn't *need* you. Not anymore." She turned. "Drinks are on me," she said to the barman, and without saying goodbye, she strode back to the stage, hips swaying, just as the other musicians emerged from behind the red velvet curtain and took up their instruments. She curled her hands around the microphone and began to sing. No one seemed to notice, let alone care. I finished my drink and left.

Another night in the hotel. I spent it in a fitful sleep, eyes closed but mind spinning like a motor. I woke famished—I hadn't eaten since the previous morning. I headed out with my suitcase to find some food, into another morning of golden fog laced with the sting of petroleum. The rumble of distant artillery was louder than the previous evening's. Outside the locked gate of the Gare de l'Est, an old toothless woman sold me a boiled potato, ungarnished. A vendor standing nearby was selling a newspaper I'd never seen before, *L'Édition parisienne de guerre*. I bought a copy. Retreat, panic—finally the headlines were coinciding with reality. It was almost eight o'clock—two hours until my appointment.

I walked down a hushed Boulevard de Strasbourg, rendered

sepia by the smoke; it was as if I'd stepped into a Marville daguerreotype. Remembering the singer's words of the previous night, I looked around to see if I was being followed. A figure in a black hat and cape, possibly a priest, was half a block behind me. I turned left into the Passage du Désir as far as the Rue du Faubourg Saint-Martin. Every shop was locked and shuttered. I turned south again as far as the Passage Brady. The man in the black cape was nowhere to be seen. It occurred to me that I might thread together all the arcades on the way to Saint-Eustache—a good way to kill time and shake a tail.

I crossed the street diagonally into the Passage de l'Industrie and looked over my shoulder; my heart skipped a beat. There, stepping into the Passage Brady, was the figure in black. Was it just coincidence? I waited to see if he would reappear, but there was no further sign of him. I hurried on, left into the Rue du Faubourg Saint-Denis, left again into the Passage du Prado, following its rightward turn until I emerged next to the Porte Saint-Denis, where the walls of the old city had stood in the time of Louis XIV. I pressed onward, sweating now in the morning heat, shoulders aching from carrying my suitcase, threading together the Passages Lemoine and Ponceau, dedicated almost entirely to Jewish textile merchants; next was Passage du Caire, the longest of them all; I turned back at Réaumur to Passage Basfour and Passage de la Trinité, hardly arcades so much as back alleys with their usual ammoniac stench; down to the neighborly Passage de l'Ancre; and finally through the stately Passages du Bourg l'Abbé and du Grand-Cerf, two of the finest arcades in the city, more luminous than ever in the golden light streaming through their glass roofs. The few passersby I came across seemed dumbstruck, walking as if underwater.

At the approach of ten o'clock I made my way to Saint-

Eustache, quite sure that, if I'd been followed by the man in black, I had by now long since lost him. The mid-morning heat was becoming oppressive. It would soon rain. I stepped into the church as into a great cool grotto. Its interior was more somber than usual. The recesses of the stained-glass windows had been filled in with sandbags to guard against a bombardment that had never come. Flickering candles were the only light, and it took a few moments to adjust. I approached the altar. Every little sound, every footfall, echoed in the silence. Finally I spotted the widow, dressed in black weeds, her face veiled, kneeling in prayer in the front pew. I slumped into the pew behind her, overcome by exhaustion. A headache was sprouting behind my eyes. After a few moments, the widow stood and left the church. As I stepped outside, the sunlight blinded me. I took my suitcase and followed her from a discreet distance toward the slums of Beaubourg. She turned into Rue Quincampoix and then into an *antiquaire* on the corner. The shop's shutters were drawn almost completely shut. The jiggle of a bell above the door announced my entrance. In the shadows at the back of the shop, I saw an open doorway and a stairwell behind it. I climbed it to the first floor into a room as full of antiques as the shop below. There was no sign of the widow. I thought I'd been left alone until I heard the rustle of a body beside mine. I turned and there was the widow, lifting her veil to reveal the face it had hidden, the face of Madeleine. She approached me without saying a word, curled her arms around my neck and kissed me with trembling lips.

"I'd given up on ever seeing you again," she said.

"Why did you leave?" I said, kissing her neck, drinking in the scent of sandalwood.

"Because you didn't believe me."

"Do I need to believe you to love you?"

"Yes," she said. "Yes, darling. You must."

We spent several hours lying side by side on an antique divan in the upper room of that little antique store, among Savonnerie carpets, Louis XV clocks, Pompeiian lamps, armchairs resting on feet of bronze sphinxes, porcelain *japonaiseries* encased behind pearwood vitrines, and candelabras that on closer inspection turned out to be coiled snakes.

"I want to try again," I said.

"What?"

"Crossing."

Madeleine hesitated. "You want certainty. You want to be free of doubt. But even if we cross, it won't be enough. You'll never be certain. It's in your nature to doubt."

"I need to try. I need to be sure."

"Not yet. You need to rest. Your mind is racing. You'll get distracted."

"How can I sleep when you are here beside me?"

"Here's how," she said, and kissed me again.

I opened my eyes and there she was, lying next to me on the divan with one leg curled across my body, her head propped up on an elbow, looking down at my face, stroking my cheek with the back of her fingers. Other than a lamp lit in a corner of the room, it was dark.

"What happened?"

"You fell asleep."

"Why didn't you wake me up?"

"I tried, but you were so tired, you wouldn't be woken."

"What time is it?"

She looked up. There were several clocks in the room. "Four." She lowered her head onto my chest.

"So why is it so dark?"

"It's four in the morning. Thursday morning."

"Four in the morning! How long was I asleep?"

"Eleven, maybe twelve hours."

"Well, at least I wasn't woken by a nightmare." I stroked her hair for a while until she raised her head.

"I want you to look into my eyes without getting distracted," she said. "Do you think you can manage that?" I nodded, searching out her lips to kiss. "That means no kissing," she smiled, pulling her head away.

"All right."

"All that is required is the willing suspension of disbelief."

There was something in her gaze that had not been there previously, a kind of openness. I returned it without equivocation, keeping my eyes locked on hers until they were the only thing I saw, those bottomless wells of love and sadness. We held that gaze without moving or speaking, losing all sense of time. Gradually, I began to feel germinating in me a tingle of joy that continued to blossom, spreading over my entire being until I felt myself starting to dissolve like an aspirin effervescing in a glass of water, as if every part of me that was solid matter was dissipating into the air, only instead of becoming nothing I was becoming something else, something rarefied and euphoric, pure existence. Every time my mind wavered, every time doubt threatened to puncture the precarious perfection of the moment, I nudged it back into that space of pure existence. At the very instant I seemed to have finally passed through the threshold of that purity, it began to recede, or perhaps it was I who began to recede, moving back into corporeality, contracting, solidifying, materializing, until I was once again peering into a pair of eyes, only they weren't the dark eyes I'd been looking into moments ago but the ocean-gray eyes I'd been staring at in the mirror all my life. It was my own face I was now looking into, my own eyes, and this face of mine was looking back at me. This face leaned toward me and I felt my own lips, which were no longer my lips but another's, brushing against my new lips, embracing with this new mouth, and the stubble of that other face, which was after all my own stubble, bristled against my soft new skin. The moistness of my old tongue flickered against that of my new tongue. Both bodies, the former and the current, the old and the new, took up that familiar rhythm, the gift and receipt of love, except that nothing was familiar, every sensation was novel and strange. I felt a presence entering me where once I would have entered. Tendrils of shuddering pleasure extended throughout this new body of mine from one end to the other, over and again, as we explored the limits of our bodies, until the body that had been mine for so long came to the natural resolution of its efforts and collapsed upon me, and deep inside I felt it release the expression of itself. We lay next to each other for some time, breaths intermingling, lulled into blissful rest, the light coming through the shuttered window brightening as a new day dawned. Then, looking into each other's eyes again, we began the journey in the opposite direction.

When we had returned to the point of departure, Madeleine roused herself and sat up. "Now you know how it's done," she said, slipping on my shirt just as she had in my apartment. She walked to the window and swung the shutters open, letting in a waft of cool morning air. She leaned out and studied the sky. "It's going to rain." She turned and took the packet of cigarettes, lighting one.

"Why am I able to remember everything?"

"Because I made sure of it."

"Can I do that?"

She sighed. "No. I wish you could. But you can't. That's why you need to write all of this down. You need proof. Evidence. Will you do that?"

I nodded.

"Promise?"

"I promise."

"You must be hungry," she said. "You haven't eaten since yesterday morning." She disappeared for a moment, and naturally my first thought, upon being alone, was to wonder at what had just occurred. Something had happened—of that there was no doubt. I was even willing to call it a crossing. But what precisely was it? Had I been tricked somehow—or had I tricked myself? Was it possible for a mind to deceive itself thus? To be so malleable, so suggestible? I sighed. Madeleine had been right: I had my answer, but—just as she'd foretold—it wasn't enough: my doubts were still niggling away at me, pushing me to know more, to understand, to be sure. But about love she had been wrong. I didn't need to believe her to love her. I loved her now more than ever. That was an illusion about which I had not a shred of doubt.

She returned with a glass of water and a bowl full of black cherries. "It was all they were selling at the market." I drank the water all at once and began devouring the cherries, the sweet dark juice exploding in my mouth with every bite.

"What happened with Chanel?"

"I went to see her," I said between mouthfuls, "just as you asked. I couldn't . . ."

"I know."

"I had her, in a room, with the gun in my hand . . ." I raised my hand as if it were holding a gun. "But a gun without a bullet . . ." My fingers squeezed an imaginary trigger.

"I know." She looked away. "Where's the gun now?"

"Massu has it."

"Who's that?"

"He's with the police—the Brigade Spéciale at the Quai des Orfèvres. He knows about Chanel. He's been keeping an eye on her for years. And he knows the tale of the albatross— although don't worry, he doesn't know anything about you. But he could be a friend for you, if you ever need one. It's always useful to have a policeman for a friend. Just tell him I sent you. Tell him you know how the story ends."

"I will."

"And the nightclub?" I asked.

"What about it?"

"Is that where you went, every night, when we were together?"

"Yes. I worked there. Lately it has become too dangerous."

"And the singer—do you love her?"

Right on cue, there was a knock at the door downstairs— two loud knocks followed by three softer, quicker ones. Madeleine rushed to the window and leaned out. "That's her now." She scurried down the stairs and opened the door. I heard the two of them murmur a few minutes before Madeleine returned alone, holding a boltcutter. She went to an armoire, pulled open a drawer, and took out a bundle of banknotes.

"There's a train departing the Gare d'Austerlitz in a little under an hour," she said, approaching me and pressing the money and boltcutter into my hands. "If we hurry we can make it."

We walked through a drifting golden fog toward the Île de la Cité. The rumble of battle was very near now, punctuated by the occasional explosions of suburban petrol depots. Along the way we saw stray dogs and cats, freed by their fleeing owners and scrounging for food. We even saw a cow that must have wandered into town from the suburbs in search of pasture. At the Quai de la Tournelle, we stopped at Vennet's bookstall. While Madeleine stood watch, I took the boltcutter. I was about to clamp its jaws around the lock when from around a corner appeared a mounted Republican Guard. Madeleine slid between me and the boltcutter, threw her arms around my neck and kissed me until the horse had passed, as if Paris were still a city where two lovers might embrace by the river. With my arms reaching around her, I squeezed the handles of the boltcutter and felt the lock give way. When the mounted policeman had disappeared, we opened the green wooden lid of the stall.

There it was, the leather satchel Vennet had been carrying as he ambled away from the auction house toward his own demise, not so long ago. I looked inside and gushed with relief to see the slim red leather volume with the words embossed in gold: *The Education of a Monster, Ch. Baudelaire.* We set off again in the direction of the station.

As we reached the Gare d'Austerlitz, the first drops of rain fell from the orange sky. The station's entrance gate was locked, and refugees were camped on the pavement. Taking a train ticket out of her purse, Madeleine spoke to a guard, who opened the gate for us. Inside, there were few people and even fewer signs of the tumult that, until yesterday, had reigned for weeks here. The only clue to that time of panic was the litter strewn across the lobby: a stray sock, a teaspoon, cigarette butts, a sheet of yellowing newsprint flapping in the breeze. It would be swept up before the end of the day and every trace of the great exodus would soon be erased. We walked past shuttered ticket counters onto a concourse strewn with more such detritus. Under the roof above, several canaries and parakeets were flying to and fro, enjoying the freedom granted by their departing owners. And on the furthest platform a locomotive to which several carriages were attached was hissing. I lunged forward, one hand carrying my suitcase, the other hand holding Madeleine's, but then I felt her slip away. I turned to her. She was wearing the same dress she'd worn when we first met—the black one with the prints of red hibiscus.

"What's the matter?"

"You have to go without me," she said. "I can't leave Paris."

"But I can't leave without you."

"For you to remain would be suicide. But I must stay."

I remembered the singer's words at the nightclub. "Does this have something to do with . . . ?" I couldn't finish the sentence.

"With Chanel? Of course. I must stay close to her. I am responsible for her, in a way. I have to follow her, watch her. I have to make sure she doesn't do any more harm."

"You've done everything you can."

"And it hasn't been enough. I have to finish what I started. It's my duty. To make up for breaking the Law. She's . . . my twin, my destiny."

"I can't leave you behind."

"You *must*. You must get away. You must write down everything you know about crossing—everything I've told you, everything you've lived through yourself, and the manuscript too, you must include that. Make a book, a book about the crossing, a book that will remind you of who you are when you have forgotten. Once you've done that, you must make a crossing yourself. Then, when the war is over, when Paris is free once more, come find me. I'll be waiting."

She who had been so close to me only moments ago was now unreachably far away. Perhaps sensing my despair, Madeleine closed her eyes, threw her arms around my neck, and kissed me repeatedly on my lips, my cheeks, my neck. "Promise me you'll write it all down. Promise me you won't forget."

"I promise," I said, in between kisses that tasted of sandalwood. I remembered something I'd been meaning to tell her. "There's something you ought to know about Chanel—she knows your name."

"How do you know?"

"She let it slip when we spoke."

"Did you tell her?"

"Of course not."

"What about your name?"

"As far as she knows, my name is Arthur Koestler."

"Who's that?"

"My old neighbor." Madeleine nodded. I looked at her, drinking in her face, her mouth, her eyes. "When will I see you again?"

"If not in this life, then in the next." We kissed one last, lingering time, until the shriek of a locomotive whistle shattered our union. She pulled back and her eyes were brimming over with tears. "You must go," she said, as I took a handkerchief from my jacket pocket and wiped her eyes dry.

"Where will I find you?"

"In the cemetery, darling. I'll be visiting Baudelaire's grave every day, waiting for you."

The locomotive shrieked again. I looked around. The platform was deserted other than a conductor waving at us to hurry. We ran to the furthest platform, the only stragglers, and reached it just as the train shuddered to life and began to creep forward. I stepped onto the railing with my black suitcase in hand and the leather satchel slung over my shoulder and turned to wave goodbye. She stood perfectly still, with her hands clasped in front of her. I waved until she was no more than a smudge of black and red in the distance, and then, reluctantly, I turned to go inside.

The train was only half full. Most of the passengers were well-dressed men—government officials, I suspected, railways administrators, perhaps, maybe some diplomats from countries hostile to the Germans, no doubt a sprinkling of spies among them, and a few of their wives, all making a last-minute exit on the last train to leave a free Paris. I did not speak to anyone for fear of betraying my accent. As the train made its way through the southern suburbs, the dusty window was streaked with thick, oily orange raindrops.

☞ *{352}*

140

The Hotel Room

FOR THE NEXT day and night, the train advanced southward in fits and starts, hurtling forward for an hour or two, then inexplicably grinding to a stop at some tiny village or junction in the middle of fields. We were not strafed or bombed, and the journey had an air of unreality about it, as if I'd fallen asleep and was dreaming of a train journey in a landscape mysteriously emptied of people. It was only when we clattered through Nevers that I realized we were headed into the center of the country. All day and night, we continued in this stop-start way. Under the crescent moon, the train traversed high plateaus, and I could see miles into the distance over somnolent countryside. The thrum of the engine, the swaying of the carriages, and the ricochets of the tracks rocked me to sleep and back again several times. We passed villages I'd never heard of, forlorn little places with poetic names like Montluçon and Ussel, Brive-la-Gaillarde and Figeac. By sunrise the following morning we entered the outskirts of Toulouse, where many of the passengers alighted, but a porter told me through the window that the train was continuing south to Lourdes, in the mountains near Spain, and I remained on board. It was a place of pilgrimage, so I reasoned the locals would be more accommodating than most.

Lourdes was filled to bursting with refugees and Catholic

pilgrims glowing with religious fervor. They'd come from far and wide to pray for France. I found a vacant room with a little writing desk on the second floor of a boarding house. From the window, I could see the spire of the basilica and the mountains. Within days of my arrival, the newspapers and radio announced that France was to be divided in two: there would be an occupied zone in the north and west, while the south and east would be a neutral zone governed from Vichy, that wedding-cake spa resort that would henceforth be the capital of the new puppet regime. I thought of my old concierge Madame Barbier and her husband, who'd gone there to flee the Germans, only now to find themselves surrounded by them. At the cinema, a newsreel showed footage of Hitler touring Paris alongside Albert Speer and others. The streets were sprinkled with people cheering hesitantly for the camera. Hitler stood on the Eiffel Tower and surveyed his new dominion. I had to look away.

I spent my days writing. I wrote everything that had happened to me since I'd first met Madeleine in the cemetery only weeks before and I transcribed my notes of her stories. It was a way of both remembering her and forgetting her. I avoided the company of others for fear of attracting attention to myself. Mornings, I wrote or visited the post office, the town hall, or the police station, applying for a travel permit to go overland to Spain or by rail to Marseille.

Afternoons, I wandered through the gloomy hills behind the town or down to the grounds of the basilica, where legions of sick and infirm pilgrims gathered, many in wheelchairs pushed by nuns, to drink the spring waters they believed would miraculously cure them. I avoided the news and the intrigues of my fellow émigrés. Every newspaper was a summons, every radio broadcast the news of fateful tidings, every knock at the door a policeman sent to arrest me.

In late August I was finally granted permission to travel by train to Marseille. A short distance from the terminus, I alighted the train to avoid a police check. I trudged across the scraggy limestone hills with my black suitcase and the satchel containing the manuscript until I came to an incline overlooking the city. It stretched out before me in the early morning light, cradled between white mountains and a turquoise sea. I walked on into town and caught a streetcar to the port, greeted by the city's familiar perfume: oil, urine, and printer's ink. Turned away from every hotel on the harbor, I scoured the backstreets and alleyways until I found a room in a dingy hotel overlooking the Cours Belsunce.

Marseille was a hive of deserters, outcasts, artists, philosophers, and criminals. Arrivals swelled daily. No raid, no decree, no threat of internment could keep them from coming. They came because it was the last French port from which ships were still sailing. The city was the bottleneck through which all had to pass. Conversations invariably revolved around the same themes: passports, visas, travel permits, bonds, port authority stamps, certificates, currencies, and lists. Each one of these themes had endless variations: real, substitute, and counterfeit passports; entry, exit, and transit visas; refugee, customs, health, and discharge certificates; old, new, and counterfeit currencies; police lists, passenger lists, prefectural lists. Everyone guarded their papers as if their lives depended on them, which was indeed the case, and all the while the authorities invented cleverer ways to sort, classify, register, and stamp us like sheep in an abattoir. One spent hours in a café hoping for some morsel of useful information, but rumors flew about so wildly it was impossible to distinguish truth from fiction. A whole day could be spent in a waiting room, the air thick with exhaustion, only for someone behind a counter to tell you to return the next day, the next week, or even, as August came around and government offices began to close for the summer holidays, the next month. Applicants would fill out endless forms, whisper among themselves, doze, or rehearse their stories for their interviews. A single slip-up—eleven photographs instead of twelve, for instance—and the entire chain of documents, each one with its own expiry date, could unravel.

At the Hôtel Splendide I found Fritz standing in the lobby one morning soon after my arrival and, though it had only been a couple of months since I'd last seen him at the station in Paris, we hugged as if reuniting after a long estrangement. Fritz told me Arthur was also in town, and the three of us went for a drink. It was a non-alcohol day, according to the wartime regulations, but the bartender added some schnapps to our chicory coffees.

"Whatever happened to that girlfriend of yours?" asked Arthur.

"She decided to stay in Paris," I replied.

"Ah," they both said, nodding their heads knowingly, and she was never mentioned again. Such stories were common.

Fritz and I were in the same boat: he was unable to procure an exit visa. Without permission to leave France, every other jewel—a Portuguese transit visa, an American entry visa— was worthless. Arthur had had all kinds of adventures since leaving Paris. His English girlfriend had managed to board a ship leaving Bordeaux for Portsmouth. Between them, they filled me in on the rumored fates of various friends and acquaintances: one had left for America, another had committed suicide by swallowing veronal in Paris, another still slit his wrists in a prison camp near Avignon. One poor fellow swallowed strychnine, and another disappeared from a camp in Savoy and hadn't been heard of since.

Poised precariously between hope and despair, we settled into our temporary lives as the world we'd known became unrecognizable to us. The newspapers and radio became infected by a new kind of language. In the name of national renewal, they preached the virtues of collaboration and authoritarianism, the corruption of trade unions and treacherousness of the Jews. As France's humiliation was deemed to be a moral failure, the remedy would be a moral revolution. The windows of Jewish shops were smashed. The words *liberté, égalité, fraternité*, which had recently adorned the entrances of state buildings, were replaced with a new trinity: *work, family, fatherland*. Labor camps became mandatory: every nineteen-year-old boy would have to work six months in a camp. Monthly food rations were reduced to a pound of sugar, half a pound of pasta, three and a half ounces of rice, four ounces of soap, and seven ounces of fats. It was impossible to put a telephone call through to Paris or send a letter there. Packs of officials roamed the streets day and night, throwing anyone they considered suspicious in prison. Without money for a bribe or a lawyer, anyone snaffled in one of these roundups was destined for a camp.

The American delegation at the Splendide granted me an American visa, but my efforts to procure an exit visa met with disappointment at every turn. I needed a certain stamp, and I didn't have the certificate required to obtain it. I went through the motions all the same, hoping to be the beneficiary of an error, an oversight, an act of mercy. I joined the throngs waiting from morning to night at the Bureau des Étrangers.

When, after a month, I received the final, definitive refusal, I staggered from the préfecture and wandered aimlessly until I reached the waterfront of the Old Port, entering a bistro simply to escape the blinding sun. I ordered oysters out of grief. They were one of the few things that were not rationed.

Even at night, the city glowed with a desert heat. Sundays, when the cafés and bars would close and the streets fell into somnolence, were the hardest to endure. The only relief from the heat was to swim in the clear, cold water off the rocks at the little port of Malmousque, one of us looking out for thieves at all times.

In desperation, Arthur and I tried disguising ourselves as sailors and boarding a ship. But our pasty skin betrayed us as the landlubbers we were and, when challenged for our merchant sailors' tickets, the ruse was unmasked. We were lucky not to be reported to the police. Soon after, Arthur managed to get all his papers together; he left on a Thursday morning on a boat bound for Lisbon. Fritz and I went to see him off at the pier. "If anything happens to you, have you got something?" I asked. He shook his head. I gave him half of my morphine tablets. He skipped up the gangplank and, minutes later, the ship drifted away from its berth with a blast of its foghorn, in a cloud of fumes.

Madeleine was never far from my thoughts. Sometimes I would lie in bed at night, unable to sleep, thinking of her in her many guises, mulling over the riddles she'd posed. Remembering her last words, in my idle hours I would sit at a table in a café or at the rickety desk in my hotel room and I would write. The writing held me together. Over several weeks, I wrote out in full the stories she'd told me, trying to recreate the magic of that precious handful of days and nights we'd spent together. It was my way of being close to her. When I was done, I decided to keep writing. This time, I wrote *my* story, *this* story, which is after all only a humble story of a brief affair, one of countless such stories, of no consequence to anyone, perhaps, other than me.

After a month in Marseille, I ran out of options. All the doors had been closed. Unable to leave by sea, I decided to make my way to Portugal over land. The Spanish government had not yet closed the border to refugees from France and I had a Portuguese transit visa. I learned the wife of a friend was smuggling refugees across the border. In Lisbon, I hoped to board a ship bound for America.

I secured a travel permit to Perpignan. At the appointed hour, Fritz, who was still hoping to make it out on a boat, came to see me off on the overnight train from the Gare Saint-Charles. We climbed the hundred and four steps of the grand stairway that lead to the station. I was, as usual, carrying my black suitcase, which contained this manuscript. We farewelled each other, hugged, wished each other luck, made vague plans for a reunion in some indeterminate place at some indeterminate time. Then he turned around and walked the steps back down the hill, disappearing into the crowd. Another friend, another farewell. I wasn't sure how many more I could take.

I traveled to Perpignan with the photographer Henny Gurland and her son Joseph. From there, we traveled on a local train to Port-Vendres and met up with a fresh-faced young German woman called Lisa Fittko, who had taken it upon herself to guide people across the border. She said she would take us over the mountains to Spain on a track dubbed the

Lister route, after a Republican officer who, with his men, had made his own escape, in the opposite direction, only a few years earlier. The two of us would do a trial run, she said, as she had yet to traverse the track herself. Together, we went to speak with the local mayor, who was sympathetic. He told us where to go and advised us to leave at dawn with the grape pickers. I knew I would be spending the night up there in the mountains.

It was still dark when Lisa knocked at my hotel room door, but I was waiting for her, fully dressed and ready to go. We joined the throng of grape harvesters climbing the trail leading up to the vines in the foothills behind the village. They gave us bread, cheese, and watered wine for breakfast. Soon enough, the track steepened in the dawn light and, as the sun finally appeared, we left the pickers to their harvest and kept climbing. As feared, my heart was barely up to the task of hauling a suitcase across a mountain. It was beating fast and each contraction was a spasm of pain. For every ten minutes of walking, I had to rest a minute. Lisa was most patient. Our slow progress afforded us the luxury of admiring the views. The world was bathed in a warm, golden glow. A steep bank of late summer clouds was gathering in the south. Behind us, France stretched out in splendor, and the white-fringed shore of the Golfe de Lion curved away to the northeast.

At times, the track seemed to peter out into nothing. Lisa would walk ahead and call out when she had located it once more. We finally reached the ridge of the mountain in the late afternoon. This was the border. We could clearly see the track that led down into Spain, to the border town of Portbou. As expected, there was no question of my going back to Port-Vendres. Lisa gave me her jacket to keep me warm and, with a wave of her hand, commenced the return to town to fetch the others. I watched her until she disappeared from sight and lit a Salomé to calm my nerves. The sun was already sinking in the west, the shadow of the mountains stretching out across the world. Once the sun was gone, the sky turned its various shades of blue, green, and pink. I spent a frigid night sheltering as best I could in a small copse of little pines, shivering with cold, straddling the border, wondering at the width of that invisible line between two countries. A border is nothing but a fiction—only one that holds the power of life and death over countless people. Still shivering, I wrote in the moonlight to pass the time. I was edging ever closer to finishing the story I had tasked myself with writing. When the moon set, it became too dark to write, so I sat there, contemplating the stars overhead to take my mind off the cold. As fatigue finally took over, they seemed to take the shape of an albatross, wings outstretched across the sky, curving from one horizon to the other.

{154}

THIS IS WHERE the story ends: at this writing desk, on this wobbly chair, in this damp hotel room, with its smell of countless men, their cigarettes and ointments and sorrows. The naked lightbulb above is buzzing. On the wall in front of me is a framed black-and-white picture of Franco, a balding man with a neat mustache wearing an overcoat with a fur collar. His expression is of calm certainty. Above the iron bedstead hangs a wooden crucifix.

I woke on the mountaintop this morning in a pre-dawn light and waited for Lisa and the others to meet me. An hour or so later I spotted them in the foothills: Lisa, Henny, and Joseph. It was mid-morning by the time they arrived, bringing bread, cheese, sausages, and water. After eating, we finally crossed the border into Spain and began the slow descent to Portbou. For the first time in weeks, I felt a stirring of hope. It didn't last very long. We made our way to the police station, where we were promptly arrested.

We are late by a single day. Had we arrived yesterday, we would have encountered no obstacle. But only yesterday new orders were received from Madrid: all refugees arriving from France without a French exit visa are to be deported, even if they have transit visas for Spain and Portugal, even if they have entry visas for America, visas that have cost them immeasurable time and effort and money. As of yesterday it doesn't matter how many stamps there are in your passport if it doesn't have the one stamp that allows you to leave the country that doesn't want you.

Tomorrow we will be escorted back to the border and handed over to the French authorities. All our efforts have been in vain. I will be thrown into a prison cell while my name is cross-referenced against innumerable lists, and eventually I'll be sent to a camp.

The others in the group are being held in adjoining rooms. There are two men guarding us in the corridor outside—boys, really, foot soldiers of the Guardia Civil. The mayor has sent the village doctor to check us, although one wonders why, as tomorrow we will be sent to a place where our health can only suffer. The doctor is very young, possibly a recent graduate starting off his career in the provinces. As soon as he entered the room, toting his medicine bag, I sensed a certain contempt. It was in the sharpness of his movements, the curl of his lips, the curtness of his speech. I was writing when the door swung open without a knock, writing these very words (*The others in the group are being held,* and so on). When he saw what I was doing, he asked me in French why I was writing—not *what* but *why*.

"Because there is nothing else to do," I replied.

He approached the table and picked up the piece of paper I'd been writing on—this very piece of paper you are reading. "What's this?"

"A novel."

"You're writing a novel!" He scanned the words. "What's it about, this novel of yours?"

I pictured Madeleine's eyes. "I suppose, above all, it's about love."

"Love!" He smiled. "A romance novel!" He shot me a scornful look. "You are a foolish man, *señor*." He lowered himself so that his face was directly opposite mine, only inches away. "A foolish Jew," he added very slowly. I had nothing to say in reply. What can you say to such a person? "How can you waste your time like this, given the circumstances? Don't you realize you're going to die?"

"What else can I do?"

"Something! Anything!" he exclaimed, thumping the table. He took a stethoscope from his bag and put its rubber ends in his ears. "The time for novels is through, old man. This is a time for action."

"*Common sense tells us that the things of the earth exist only a little,*" I recited as I unbuttoned my shirt, "*and that true reality is only in dreams.*"

I felt the icy sting of the stethoscope on my chest. "What nonsense," said the doctor.

"They're Baudelaire's words. They're just as true now as they were when they were written, almost a century ago."

"You're an incorrigible Jew with a very sick heart. One more shock will do you in. You're best off forgetting that romance novel of yours. It is useless to you." He returned his stethoscope to his bag and took out a pump for testing blood pressure.

"I have thirty-two capsules of morphine in my jacket pocket. I intend to swallow them all, here, tonight. In your professional opinion, will it be a sufficient quantity to kill me?"

He did not seem shocked by the question. Rather, he considered it for a moment before replying. "Not immediately. You'll lose consciousness first, maybe twenty minutes or half an hour after ingestion. But you won't die for several hours."

He noted my blood pressure and put the pump back in the bag. "The nuisance of it is that they'll send for me again in the morning when they find your body." He closed the bag and paused. "Of course, I'd be more than happy to supervise the process, make sure everything goes smoothly. That way I won't have to come back tomorrow." My physician, I suspected, was a sadist, inwardly drooling at the opportunity to witness my death. "And I've never had the opportunity to observe the physiological effects of morphine overdose at first hand."

"In that case, I'll go ahead and take the pills now."

"Wait," he said. "I have to check on the other Jews in your group. If it's all the same to you, I'd rather you wait until I've returned. I'll bring a glass and a pitcher of water. It helps. I'll be back in just a few minutes. Agreed?"

"Yes, I'll wait. While you're gone, I'll finish writing my book."

That snarl again. "Make sure it has a happy ending, like all good romance novels!" He stood, took his bag, and opened the door. Before closing it, he turned and, lifting a cautionary finger, added, "Don't swallow a thing until I return."

"No chance of that, doctor," I murmured after he'd closed the door.

{39}

I'M SCRIBBLING THIS note in the hotel room while I wait for the doctor to return, anxious to finish this story before he reappears and I can begin swallowing the morphine I've carried for so long for just such an occasion. Yes, this is where it all ends. I'm very close now, I can feel it. These words will be my last. They will be the ending to this book. Of course, the prospect of an ending makes me anxious. My ailing heart is beating quicker than it ought. I think of Madeleine and my heart weeps and is consoled at once. The end of one story is merely the beginning of another.

Don't swallow a thing until I return, he said. Rest assured, doctor, that I will follow your advice. I've noticed something about you. At a time when no one dares look anyone in the eye, you do so brazenly, with the certainty that your time has come, that your ideas have carried the day. So when you reappear, I will invite you to take a seat on the chair opposite mine. On my lap I will be holding this manuscript. When you are seated, I will give it to you and ask you to hold it while I take the morphine. Then, pills in one hand and glass of water in the other, I will swallow them calmly one by one. And as I wait for death to take hold, I will ask you a question.

"Doctor," I will say, "will you grant a dying man one last wish?"

"It depends on the wish," you will say.

"Oh," I'll say, "this wish is the simplest anyone has ever asked for. You won't even have to get out of your chair."

"Very well, what is it?"

"I would like you to look me straight in the eyes and tell me exactly why it is that you hate me so."

THE END

Tales of the Albatross

Alula

Born circa 1771
First crossing 1791
Second crossing circa 1840
Died circa 1840

My name is Alula. I am the one who remembers. Your name is Koahu. You are the one who forgets. You were my beloved once, all those lifetimes ago. I loved you the way the seashell loves the sea: when people put their ears to my mouth it was your song they heard. I loved you the way the sand loves the water: always receiving you with hushed pleasure. I loved you the way thunder rolls through the night, the way butterflies attend to the flower, the way the moon follows the sun. Since childhood, we had longed for nothing—you, Koahu, and I, Alula—other than to be united, although we belonged to rival bloodlines that would not be conjoined by the Law. I was older than you, a fully initiated woman, a master of the crossing. You were barely a man, still a student of the crossing, but you were more interested in other pleasures: laughing, singing, dancing. Each animal on our island had its own dance, and you knew them all. I was a scholar, and you were a dancer.

You were the first to see it. Do you remember? You must have dreamed about it a thousand times since. We were lying together on the grass, in the shade of a hibiscus tree on the hill between the village and the sea. It was where we went whenever we wished to be alone together. The morning sea was calm, the sky was still, and a dappled sun played on your skin. I was looking so closely into your eyes, I could see my reflection in them. Then something caught your attention, and you looked away. You cast your gaze behind me and out onto the sea. In one motion, you narrowed your eyes, creased your eyebrows, and the smile on your lips vanished. Oh, that moment when everything changed. Do you dream about it still? It lasted no more than a second, but it marked the end of our happiness.

You jumped to your feet. I turned to look in the direction in which you were pointing. I saw it and sat up with a start. It was a wonder to behold, drifting cloud-like on the water, shattering in a single moment our every notion of the universe and all it contained. My heart fairly leaped out of my chest at the sight of it. As you watched in silence, drinking in that most miraculous sight, I covered my eyes for a moment, for I could not be sure that what I was seeing wasn't a dream. After a moment, I lowered my hands and looked once more; it was still there, floating on the becalmed water like an island of miracles. We were in such a state of wonder at the sight of it, our eyes could not look enough. I decided we should tell the others. I took your hand but you would not be moved. I pulled again and you told me to go without you. I ran back to the village while you stayed there on that hilltop overlooking the water.

I went to our chief, Otahu, and described what we had seen, you and I, out on the hilltop. He listened carefully and, when I'd finished, looked down at the ground and considered what he'd heard. He bade me follow him as he sought out our sage, Fetu, and had me repeat what I'd told him. Fetu also listened carefully, and stroked his beard, which he did whenever he was considering a delicate matter. Then Fetu and Otahu spoke to each other in murmurs. Otahu took the horn that hung around his neck and blew it to call all the people to council. When the people had gathered together to hear, I was once again asked to describe what I'd seen.

"The boat," I told them, "is like one of our own, with masts and sails, but as if made for giants to sail in. Upon it, three great trees are fastened, the one in the middle being the tallest, as high as any tree on our island, but straightened and stripped of all leaves, twigs, and branches. Only the trunks remain, as well as three straight boughs, fastened crosswise to each. Sails of cloth are attached to them, but greater in size and number than our own, each one wide enough to hold within it one of our pirogues. There are so many of these sails fastened to the masts that, rather than calling them sails, one might imagine them a flock of great, captive birds, paler than the sun, the largest of them in the middle and the smaller ones on the outer branches, with their enormous wings outstretched and fastened by a tangled web of threads, pressing the birds into the service of the wind. These great wings, unfurled, drive the boat forth just as the sails of our own pirogues do, only without oars."

When I told the people this, they asked me to take them

to where I'd seen the boat. I led them to the hilltop, where you were still standing, entranced, in the same place I'd left you. The people marveled at the sight of the ship floating in the distance. The flock of great birds perched upon its branches was gone, and it drifted still and naked on the water.

We waited for Otahu to speak. "We will honor them as our guests and invite them to a feast," he said.

Then Fetu, the sage, spoke: "The Law speaks of all things," he said, "even of this. It tells us to welcome these strangers but to remain wary of them. These boats carry not gods but people like us. Their tongue, their dress, their ways—everything about them is strange to us. We know not what they seek, nor what they bring. Though these men are strangers to us, they are not strangers to the Law, which sees all and knows all. At the feast, I will cross with their chief to learn his designs." Fetu finished his discourse with the usual incantation: "Our highest duty is to the Law, and above all else the Law demands this of us: *There can be no crossing without a return crossing.*"

The Law was our most prized possession, our most sacred jewel. It did not belong to us; we belonged to it. The Law gave life and took it away. All depended on it, all sprang from it, all returned to it. Studying the Law was my greatest joy, and I was Fetu's favorite student. I sat by his side at all the feasts and ceremonies. He devoted more of his time to me than to any other, teaching the Law's highest, most secret aspects.

The Law's greatest gift was the crossing. To look into the eyes of another, to sense the stirring of one's soul, to be transported into the body of the other and dwell therein until the time came for the return crossing—this was the treasure the Law had bestowed upon us. Our teachings taught the crossing, our songs praised the crossing, our dances acclaimed the crossing. The Law forbade all tattoos except those of eyes. With every crossing, another eye would be etched into our skin, until our very bodies became hymns exalting the crossing.

We spent our entire childhoods learning the crossing. We learned there were three different kinds. The first, a crossing between two initiates, is the easiest, although many years of training are necessary to achieve it. The second, requiring years more practice, is a crossing between an initiate and a novice, after which the latter is left in an unknowing state. This is called a blind crossing. The third and highest form of crossing is the wakeful crossing: it too takes place between an initiate and a novice, only once it is complete the novice can remember everything about it. This kind of crossing takes a lifetime to master.

Of all the Law's commandments, the greatest was this: *There can be no crossing without a return crossing.* All must return. The Law was clear: to break it would bring about the destruction of the world. Only a sage could cross without returning, for the sake of the Law's preservation, so that it might be passed on undiminished. When the time came and the sage felt death approaching, parents would bring their youths to him, hoping their own child would be chosen to be the inheritor. Great honor and influence came to the family of a child chosen to cross with the sage. The family of the designated youth would ask the best stonemason to carve a statue to mark the occasion. At the appointed time, a ceremony would be held during which the youth and the sage would sit before each other, looking into each other's eyes, and the spirit of the sage would pass into the body of the youth, while the spirit of the youth would cross into the body of the sage.

When the crossing was complete, the inheritor would plunge the sacred whalebone knife into the heart of the old sage, and gouge out his eyes. The sage's remains would be buried and the carved statue placed upon the burial site. Thus there was only one among us who was deathless. All others must die. So spoke the Law.

Fetu had decided that, when the time came for his last crossing, I would be his successor. And so, when that time came, my own soul would pass into his body, and his into mine. I would become Fetu and, for the sake of the Law, the body I had only just vacated would kill the body I had only just entered.

About love the Law was all-knowing and all-powerful. Only the elders could unite a woman and a man. If a man and a woman should desire a union forbidden by the elders, the Law was clear: the lovers must leave the island and sail the currents and winds eastward, and find another island, and begin a new life there, with a new Law. So it was that our own island had been settled by our two ancestors, young lovers whose union, on another island to the west, had been forbidden.

Sometimes we spoke of eloping, you and I, of sailing east and finding a new island, our own island. But when we were not together our resolve weakened. As much as we wanted each other, we didn't have the courage for the sufferings of exile.

We saw the strangers lower a small pirogue from their ship, and fill it with men, and begin rowing to shore. We descended the hill to the beach and awaited them. We studied the newcomers, in their stiff, brightly colored clothes and hats, and noted how strange everything was about them. They looked wherever and at whomever they pleased, without fear, even though their spears were short and thick and blunt. Did they not know the teachings of the Law about where to look, at whom, and in what manner?

They gathered together on the beach and their chief spoke in a strange tongue, and the others raised their spears, and thunder and lightning exploded from the ends of their spears and into the clear blue sky. Their chief tied a stone leaf etched with strange markings to a tree, and finally they approached us, bearing beads, coins, nails, and mirrors, which they held out to us, smiling at us, placing their gifts into our hands. Of course, we didn't know what these things were and we studied them and were awed by their strangeness. Their chief issued orders that the others followed, but there was a second one among them who did not labor, instead gathering leaves and plants and putting them in a bag, as if harvesting medicines as Fetu did. He marveled at our tattoos. Meanwhile, other strangers were sent to a stream carrying empty barrels, which they filled with water, and carried back to their pirogue.

As I watched them, I was also watching you, Koahu, how drawn to them you were, how easily you communicated with them, despite the strangeness of their tongue, with your eyes and face and arms. Your quick wit, your smile, the way you moved—all were tools with which you bridged the differences between you and the strangers. And your eyes, those eyes I had gazed into so often, now betrayed no other desire than for the foreigners and their strangeness, which you found full of wonder and delight. You admired their brazenness, for you yourself were born brazen.

With your body, with the expressions on your face and the

movements of your hands, you somehow made yourself understood to them. Through you, Otahu invited them to feast with us that evening.

Throughout the day, the strangers were near us or among us. Some of them spent the day filling their barrels with water or hunting for wild pigs and fowl. Others repaired sails on the beach. Their medicine man collected plants and examined our tattoos. Otahu had warned us to keep our distance, and this most of us did, although we kept a watchful eye on them. I helped prepare the feast, but I was watching as often as I could all the same. Whether from near or from afar, we drank in their presence, we studied their strangeness, we observed everything we could about them, noting every last detail, so that, when they were gone, we might feast on our memories of them. Several among us approached them, especially the children, especially you. You helped them wheel their barrels to and from the stream. You helped point them in the direction of the pigs and the fowl.

The feast was held after nightfall, in the glow of a full moon, in a clearing within earshot of the water. Two great fires burned for light. Otahu wore his ritual cloak of carmine feathers and Fetu wore his ritual cloak of white feathers. They sat side by side. I sat by Fetu's side, as his favorite. A score of the most senior of the people sat in the circle—I was the youngest—and about ten of the strangers. Others stood or sat nearby, watching the proceedings or talking among themselves. Then everyone in the circle was served kava, which caused the strangers, upon drinking the liquid, to grimace with such distaste that we laughed. Otahu made a speech, extolling the virtues of the strangers, and the honor they did us with their visit. Then you stepped into the circle and stood between the two fires. The front half of your body was painted with white stripes and adorned with clusters of white albatross feathers. The back half of your body was streaked with lines of gray and clusters of gray albatross feathers. Slowly you spread your arms and, singing the songs that went with it, you began to perform our most sacred dance, the dance that related how our people had come into being: the Dance of the Albatross.

In the old days, two young lovers from rival bloodlines had been exiled from their homeland far away to the northwest. Back then, people could assume the form of the animals for which they had been named, a skill that was later lost. In order to make their journey into exile, the two lovers took the form of the birds whose names they carried. The woman took the form of Pueo, the owl after which she was named. The man took the form of the bird after which he was named, Para, the white tern. Together, the two set off across the ocean. Para the tern darted ahead of Pueo the owl. The island from which they had been banished was barely out of sight before Para began to tire. By the time Pueo caught up with him, Para was floating on the water, dying. "I want to go back," he said. "I'd rather die in my homeland, at the hands of my own people, than drown at sea."

"We no longer have a homeland," Pueo told him. "If you are tired, I will carry you in my claws. We will both spread our wings and beat them in unison, and that way we will traverse the great distances of the ocean without tiring." She picked him up from the water, taking care not to wound him with her talons. When they spread their wings and began beating them together, they became one bird, the greatest of birds: Toroa, the wandering albatross. This is why the albatross is gray from above and white from below, and why it is so clumsy when it walks upon the land. And so, as one, the two lovers wandered the skies over the oceans, from island to island, for a thousand years. As one, they learned to drink from the sea by separating the salt from the sea water and expelling it in their tears. They were turned away from every island they went to. Finally they found an island that was the shell of a giant sea turtle that had run aground on a coral reef. No one lived on this island. Here, they assumed their human forms again and named their new home Toroa'eetee, which means "Home of the Wandering Albatross." Over time, this was shortened to Oaeetee. The albatross became our totem. We used its bones for hooks and spear tips, and its feathers, symbols of peace, we wore in our ceremonies.

Everyone watched you dance and sing the story of Pueo and Para, admiring how with your arms, your back, your legs, your face, you brought to life each of these two birds. Simply by turning your body around you switched from bird to bird, and thus, flickering with firelight, you were able to tell the story of each of the two birds at one and the same time. When you were finished, the strangers did a most unusual thing: they began to clap their hands together. This was a gesture we only ever used to express anger at our children, but it appeared that the strangers used it as a sign of appreciation. This caused us to laugh, and the strangers in turn also laughed, although not exactly understanding why. When the dancing was done, the children stepped into the circle, carrying great leaves laden with food, and went from person to person, serving an abundance of roasted meats, fowl, fish, and breadfruit. As at all feasts, the meat of the albatross was also served, cooked in its own fat, but only to the visitors and the most senior men and women in the circle, as was the custom.

The chief of the strangers was seated opposite Fetu. When all had eaten and drunk their fill, Fetu looked across the circle at him with a smile of such kindness and charm that the stranger looked back without reserve. They continued to hold one another's gaze in this manner for some time. I knew exactly what was happening inside them both, that pleasant sensation that overtakes one in the throes of a crossing, that giddiness, that feeling that one is dissolving into the air, that one is filling up with stars. How I wished I was in Fetu's place, that *I* could cross with the stranger and explore his mind and heart and soul at will. Fetu was such a high master of the crossing that it was soon complete, and I knew the soul of the strangers' chief was now in the body sitting beside me, fully aware of himself, looking around with the unfamiliarity of one who has only just crossed for the first time. Otahu, who was seated on the other side of Fetu, leaned over to speak to him.

"It is a great honor," said Otahu, "for us to receive you, and it is an even greater honor that you do us in making a crossing with our sage, Fetu." Though Otahu was speaking in our language, the stranger in Fetu's body understood him.

"By what witchcraft is this possible?" asked the stranger.

"It's no witchcraft," replied Otahu, "but a gift from the gods that, of the many islands in our ocean, has been lost by all those who possessed it—all, that is, but my people. We have protected and perfected it, so that we may all possess the gift."

"And what do you call it?"

"We call it the crossing," said Otahu. "Fetu is the greatest master of it among us. Only he is capable of the highest level of the crossing, the one you are currently experiencing: a crossing with a novice, in which the novice can converse in the new body, without losing his sense of himself, as you are doing with me. To perfect this kind of crossing takes lifetimes of discipline and devotion."

Otahu asked the stranger his name. "My name is Captain Étienne Marchand. The name of my ship is the *Solide*. We come from a faraway place called France."

Each of these words Otahu repeated like an incantation: *Marchand, Solide, France.*

"And how far is this island, France?"

"It isn't an island," replied Marchand-in-Fetu, "but one place among many, one great island divided many times over, called Europe. It is so far away that it has taken us many months to reach you, and it will take us many more months to return home." Otahu and I were astonished at this revelation. "And what is the name of this island?" Marchand-in-Fetu asked, but all at once his face appeared startled. "How strange," he said. "No sooner had I asked the question than its answer naturally occurred to me—*Oaeetee*. How is this possible?"

"While you are in the body of Fetu," Otahu replied, "his memories and his knowledge are available to you, just as—while he is in your body—your memories and knowledge are available to him."

"I see. And the drink—you call it kava. Is the kava the cause of the crossing?"

Otahu laughed. "The kava is for celebration, but it isn't necessary for the purpose of crossing. The art of crossing must be learned. It takes many years. All our children receive training in it, although not all are equally gifted." Otahu took Fetu's right hand as an expression of friendship. "But tell me, friend, why have you come here? What are your intentions?"

"My country is exceedingly cold. We are on our way to islands far to the north of here, to barter for animal skins, and trade them when we return home, and by this means become prosperous."

"You have come a long way, and sacrificed much. What are your intentions relating to Oaeetee, friend?"

"Everything we need, we must carry on our boat. But fresh water spoils. Meat goes bad. We were in need of water and food, and thanks to your generosity we have all the water and food we can now carry. We thank you for your welcome, and now that we have taken our fill of your hospitality, we will leave you tonight in peace, as we still have far to travel."

"And what is the object you tied to the tree at the cove this morning when you arrived?"

"It's a message to my countrymen," the stranger replied, "to indicate to them that we found friends here."

"Is it a magical object, that speaks?"

"No, there are drawings upon it that my countrymen can interpret."

"And you—you will not return?"

"No, for it has taken too long to come this far, and it will be almost two years before we return home."

Otahu was astonished. "But your countrymen, they will come later?"

"Perhaps, when they learn about Oaeetee, they may wish to visit the island for themselves."

"When will this be?"

"I cannot say. It may take many years, for it is an arduous journey."

"In that case, we will pass on the memory of your visit to our children, and they to theirs, until your countrymen return, at which time they will be welcomed as friends." Otahu smiled. "And your fire-sticks, what purpose do they serve?"

"We call them *muskets*, and they are our weapons, which we use in battle."

As Otahu spoke with Marchand-in-Fetu, on the other side of the circle, Fetu-in-Marchand was deep in discussion with the strangers' medicine man.

"And Fetu," asked the man sitting beside me, "is he now in my body?"

"Yes, he is visiting your mind and your body, just as you are visiting his," said Otahu, gesturing toward the other side of the circle. "He is conversing with your countryman, just as you are conversing with his."

"That countryman is our medicine man, Roblet."

"Roblet," Otahu repeated. "Fetu will be very pleased, because he is our medicine man, and the keeper of the crossing." At that moment, Fetu-in-Marchand looked in our direction to signal it was time to make the return crossing, which the Law required of all. Otahu squeezed the hand of Marchand-in-Fetu. "Friend," he said by way of farewell, "I wish you well in your journey."

The gazes of the two men met once again. Looking at each other thus, each underwent the same process as before, which is to say the dissolution of the bodily union followed by its restitution in the other body, so that each man found himself entered once more into his own body and his own mind, with no difference in sensation. None of the other strangers seemed to have noticed anything even slightly out of the ordinary.

"I have learned much," said Fetu, upon his return to his own body.

"And the stranger?" asked Otahu.

"The return crossing went well. He will remember nothing of it."

Otahu grunted his approval. On the other side of the circle, the surgeon Roblet, who had been seated beside Marchand, keenly observing all that was happening about him, stood and left the circle. I saw him approach you, Koahu, and speak with you. With his hands, he signaled that he wished to study your eyes, beckoning to you with smiles and friendly gestures. From my place in the circle, separated from you by the flickering lights of the fires, I could barely make out what was happening in the darkness. I stood and approached you. I saw Roblet lean over you and look into your eyes, while another stranger held up a flame and yet another stood nearby, holding his musket. I was the only one among our people to notice this turn of events, for Fetu and Otahu were immersed in a conversation, and the others in the circle were enjoying the revelry. You, Koahu, allowed Roblet to look into your eyes, and you in turn looked into his, for such a long period that I began to fret. As much as I wanted to hear what Fetu was telling Otahu about what he had learned during his crossing, there was danger in what I saw taking place between you and Roblet. Despite the prohibition on crossing with the strangers, I knew a crossing was about to take place between the two of you. Your curiosity was too powerful, as was the surgeon's. I approached you discreetly, keeping to the shadows. This was the moment I ought to have intervened, I realize now, before anything happened, but I hesitated, and hid behind nearby shrubs.

I witnessed the fateful moment with my own two eyes. Of what can I be certain? Only that I heard you cry out in a panic. A last-minute doubt, perhaps? Too late—a shiver passed through your body, while the surgeon slumped to the ground. I came rushing out from my hiding place to try to stop what was happening, but my sudden panicked appearance startled the men holding you—holding the body that had, until just now, *been* you. They let go of your body to attend to Roblet's, which now lay on the ground. I ran to catch you, but you lost your balance, you teetered, you stumbled, you fell upon Roblet. One of the strangers, perhaps fearing you were attacking Roblet, took his musket and pointed it at you. It exploded with thunder and lightning, and its lightning bolt shattered your body open. As the noise subsided, you staggered back into my arms.

Your eyes were still open, but when they met mine there was nothing of you in them. Where your stomach had been, that stomach upon which I'd so often rested my head—where that stomach had been was now a spill of blood streaming over your honeyed skin and dripping into the sand. The mouth I had kissed so often was gasping with shallow, desperate breaths, racked with pain. Worst of all, there was no recognition in your eyes. The body I held was your body, but it wasn't you. I know it now just as I knew it then. There'd been a crossing—of that I was certain. You were in the surgeon's body, which was now surrounded by the newcomers. Had I not been so certain of it I would have gladly crossed with you then and there, so that I might suffer instead of you.

More strangers left the feast and rushed to the scene. They were shouting and brandishing their muskets. They began to drag Roblet's body away, in the direction of the beach. As they moved, they aimed their muskets at the people, so that all kept their distance and waited for the strangers to retreat.

I've played that moment over and again in my mind ever since, trying to remember it in every possible detail. It's an exercise in futility: the more I try to pin down the truth, the more evasive it becomes. Did you mean to cross? Did you want it? Did you desire it? I didn't even think you capable of it, not with a stranger. Your initiation was still incomplete, your technique imperfect. But a crossing occurred, of that I am certain, fueled by the surgeon's curiosity and your own wanderlust. The alternative would be too terrible to contemplate—the alternative would be that you actually did die that night, after all, and that everything that has happened since has been in vain.

There are occasions when one is seized by a terror so great, the heart suddenly sees further than it has ever seen, and the mind is granted an unexpected cunning. This was such an occasion. In the ensuing panic, I disappeared into the brush, found the path to the beach, and ran there like a hurricane wind. There, slumped against a boat the strangers had rowed to shore, was a sailor who seemed oblivious to the distant commotion I had just fled. I approached him and saw that he was drunk. I slowed my breath, smiling at him, touching him tenderly and pointing to the parts of myself men consider desirable. He was wary, at first, and disbelieving, no doubt having heard the musket shot earlier, but the temptation was more than he could resist and, as there were no more shots to be heard, he relented, and allowed himself to be disarmed by my advances. He placed his musket in the boat and let me circle my arms around his neck and kiss him lustfully on the mouth.

I led him by the hand to a secluded spot behind a dune, in the full glow of the moon. I unclothed him as if I could wait not a minute more to satiate my desire. He was but a young man, shy and clumsy at first, and in his eagerness he seemed not to hear the party of outraged strangers as they reached the beach, carrying Roblet's body. Perhaps he thought he could have his way with me and still reach them in good time, or perhaps he had no intention of joining them but wished to remain among us on the island. At any rate, he was drunk, and completion eluded him. The strangers embarked upon the boat and rowed away from shore. Twice, in the throes of our embrace, as I swayed my hips above him and felt him inside me, he closed his eyes with the pleasure of it. Twice I had to prize them open with my fingers. I took his face in my hands and held it still so that our gaze would meet. With only the light of the moon to see each other, crossing was no easy task, but the youth eventually understood what was being asked of him and was most compliant. His eyes met mine, and did not stray.

The crossing occurred just as I felt the first shivers of his pleasure.

☞ {53}

Pierre Joubert

Born 1771
First crossing 1791
Second crossing 1825
Date of death unknown

THE EYES I WAS now looking into were the same eyes I had looked through only moments ago: the dark eyes of an island woman. They now returned my gaze with an expression of bewilderment. I'd just seen a very similar expression on Koahu's face, and I would come to see it over and again: the stupor of a soul that has just been ripped unknowingly and without warning from its moorings—a blind crossing. The unknowing soul awakens in the new body in a state of shock, unaware of what has just occurred.

I withdrew from my embrace with Alula with a pang of sadness that I was leaving my body behind. I rose to my feet and ran to the water. In the moonlight, the beach was deserted, the longboat nowhere to be seen. From the ship I heard a whistle I recognized as the bosun's and the muffled sound of men's voices barking orders. I threw myself into the water and began to swim, but while, in my previous body, swimming was something I had always done without a second thought, I now discovered that this new body could barely float, let alone move forward in the water. I had, there and then, to teach myself how, using all the memories of a previous life. They were barely sufficient to the task. It was slow and difficult going, all thrashing and gasping for air. Water seeped up my nostrils and left them stinging. Still, I did not sink, and before long I was past the surf and making progress.

The closer I swam to the ship, the more I feared I would be left behind. In the confusion and flailing movement, I heard the thud of canvas unfurling and the crackle of sails filling with air. This, despite my exhaustion, excited my endeavor. I was closer to the ship now than to the shore, and all but spent. Should I not make it aboard, it would be the end, for I hadn't enough life in me to make it back to shore. I cried out with all my might, which only slowed me down the more. The ship had just begun to move forward when I heard the lookout's cry and those two blessed words, *Man overboard!* Moments later, the slap of a rope hit the water. I was exhausted. I clung to it desperately while a trio of sailors hauled me up and over the bulwark. I lay on my back on the deck amidships, gasping for breath. Orders were still being barked and men dashed to and fro as the sails were set to the desired trim. I was paid no mind, other than by my friend Brice who, in passing, said, "I thought you couldn't swim, you devil!" and the bosun Icard, who muttered, "I hope she was worth it, boy, because you will pay for her with your blood, make no mistake."

The ship's course now set, the frenzy on the upper deck quietened. Once the beating of my heart slowed I raised myself onto my elbows. My first thought was to find you, but you were nowhere to be seen. Another whistle blew and the men of the larboard watch began descending into the hatchways, one after the other. Before I could join them, Icard took me before

Captain Marchand, who asked why I had deserted my station. I invented a lie but to little effect. He turned his back on me. "You'll get what's coming to you at noon," he mumbled wearily.

At that moment my punishment was of no consequence. I went below deck and found my hammock and stretched it out in its usual place, hauling myself into it without changing out of my wet clothes. Compounding the weariness of my body was the dizziness of my mind, swimming with novelty and strangeness. Upon crossing into a new body, one takes up the course of a new life, scrambling, at first, to master the mechanism. One is like a weaver who has just sat down at a strange loom, upon which is a carpet already half spun with an unfamiliar weave. Yarns of different colors are already threaded through the spools. One must trust that the skill to continue weaving the carpet is embedded within the very muscles of the fingers, and that the correct sequence will arise of its own accord at precisely the moment it is needed.

Surrounded as I was by strangeness—the strangeness of my body, of the clothes I wore, of my surrounds—sleep eluded me. I lay in my hammock listening to the creaking of the ship and the snoring of the crew, watching slivers of moonlight creep back and forth across the boards with the motion of the water. My mind was beset by questions. What had I done? I'd broken the Law—and why? For your sake, Koahu—impulsively, unthinkingly. And then, from the other end of the ship I heard a man's voice in the masters' quarters screaming as if struck by a mighty blow.

Shortly before dawn, the quartermaster woke the midshipmen and the mates while the bosun stood at the main hatchway and barked instructions. "All hands! Larboard watch ahoy!" Shortly after, I smelled charcoal smoke as the cook lit a fire in the galley. For a moment I was at a loss as to what to do, but like an automaton my body stirred into action, storing my hammock, taking a holystone from the hold, climbing the hatchway, and setting to polishing the deck and flemishing the lines. Everything felt habitual and unhabitual at once. At eight o'clock, the bosun's mate piped breakfast. Most of the crew had slept poorly and were hungover, and we ate our miserable stew of rotten oatmeal in silence.

I looked out for you—for the new you, in the body of the strangers' sage. But I now remembered, without any effort on my part, that the strangers were not strangers but French, and that the medicine man was a surgeon, and his name was Roblet. And so the memories of my new body came to me in this way, naturally and of their own accord, like bubbles to the water's surface.

At eleven, Icard called all hands on deck and the captain addressed the crew. Finally I saw you, standing among the masters on the quarterdeck. Your eyes darted here and there, as if, unsure of your surrounds, you wished to draw as little attention to yourself as possible, while observing proceedings closely for clues as to how to behave. Captain Marchand issued orders that three men were to be flogged as a result of the events of the previous day: twelve lashes for the helmsman Bonicard for drunkenness; twelve for Roussetty—the man who had shot you—for the reckless discharge of his firearm; while I was to receive twenty-four lashes for my disobedience and desertion of my station. As he spoke, Icard and two sailors rigged a grating for the flogging. I was to be last.

First Bonicard had the flesh on his back flayed by the cat-o'-nine-tails. Then it was Roussetty's turn. The crew watched on silently with a combination of horror, sympathy, amusement, and boredom—the sight was clearly no novelty to them. Then I was called forth. I removed my shirt and the bosun's mate, Infernet, strapped my wrists to the grating and walked back several paces with the whip in his hand. The first lash landed upon my back, and could hardly have inflicted more pain than had I been slashed with a knife. It was followed by another, and another, each more terrible than the last. Icard counted aloud as each blow flailed my skin. I fainted for the first time at the eleventh stroke, and several times thereafter. Each time I fainted I was revived with a bucket of sea water that served only to excite my afflictions. Afterward I had to be carried down the hatch, while a man followed me with a mop and bucket to wipe away all trace of blood.

I was hauled to the sick bay and laid upon my stomach on the surgeon's table, whereupon I fainted once again. At the next seizure of pain I opened my eyes—and there you were, mere inches away from me, tending to my wounds with a cloth in one hand and a bottle of spirits in the other. You moved slowly, tentatively, as if every movement you were making was for the first time. I recognized the same hesitation in myself. Reynier, the surgeon's mate, stood by your side, looking at you quizzically, sensing all was not right with you. He could not know what I knew: that, not knowing what to do, you were waiting for the impulse to come to you from somewhere unknown, that in your hesitation you were searching for some intuition of what to do next. You were listening to your new body, waiting for the memories of what to do to come to you, one at a time: take the rag, dab it with spirits, press it gently upon the wound, and though it hurts the man, undoubtedly, it cleanses him too.

I continued to sink in and out of sleep, each time awakened by the throes of suffering my wounds inflicted upon me. You bent over me, alleviating my pains by adding to them, aided by Reynier, who sensed your uncertainty and gently suggested the techniques as were normally used in such situations. In my pain, I was consoled by your nearness. When you brought a cup of water mixed with spirits to my lips and told me to drink, I took comfort in your touch.

"Koahu," I whispered in the old language through my veil of agony. You seemed not to have heard me. "Koahu," I repeated in our language, "it's me, Alula." I thought I saw you freeze for just an instant, and glance at me, before you resumed your activity. "Koahu, I saw what happened with the medicine man," I said. "I followed you. I crossed too." The words came out with great effort, as the new mouth was unaccustomed to making such sounds.

You put your hand on my forehead. "Speaking in tongues," you said in the new language, "hallucinations, but thankfully no fever."

"Koahu," I repeated, "can you not hear me? It is I, Alula, I have followed you, can you not understand?"

"Reynier," you said, again speaking the new language, "go tell the bosun Joubert is to be relieved of duty for two days. He needs rest. Work would only finish him off." Once more you put the cup to my lips to drink. "Do not fear, your suffering is a commonplace thing. Flogging is cruel and stupid and utterly futile, serving only to break men and to set them against their masters." You cradled my hands in your own and I began to weep. To relieve my torment, you gave me laudanum to drink. Unable to sleep on my back in a hammock, I fell into a fitful slumber right there on the surgical table, lying on my stomach. You settled into a chair beside me, to spend the night keeping vigil over your patient. I was woken in the middle of the night by your screams.

My wounds healed quickly enough. Before long I was back at my post, standing on lookout high among the sails, where I could meditate at my leisure upon recent events. The *Solide* continued to be carried by the trade winds into the fogs of the north Pacific. But from a distance, every night, I heard you calling out in your tormented sleep. The nightly hullabaloo you raised soon began to stoke the flames of superstition in the crew. Sailors sleep poorly even in the most placid sea, and are in the habit of stewing on their grievances like a cook stirring his soup. These nocturnal disturbances became a favorite topic of conversation among the more conspiratorially minded, who gathered together below decks, whispering at first and later declaring their speculations boldly to all who would listen: the doctor had been possessed, they said, that night on the island, by the spirit of the dead boy.

I avoided the idle gossip and wild speculations, though they were truer than any reasonable man might have imagined. I had speculations of my own to confirm. I could not understand what had happened. To begin with, I'd been certain that you had made a crossing. But in denying me you had planted in me the seed of a doubt, a seed that found fertile ground. Was I all alone on this boat? Had I left the island for no good purpose? Had I desecrated the Law in error? My intent had been to follow and protect you, to help you return to the island, to uphold the Law and our love, but now it appeared that in trying to honor the Law I had only succeeded in desecrating it. This thought tormented me.

I sighted, from my lookout one morning, an island in the west, my heart thudding with joy at the thought that we might have miraculously returned to the island so recently left behind—but the island was one of those known as the Sandwich Islands. We did not stop or even deviate from our northerly course, for this archipelago was already well explored and the captain was anxious to arrive at our destination before the northern autumn, when conditions for sailing become anything but pacific.

The day after this sighting, I saw an albatross that had set its course to that of the ship, eyeing, no doubt, the school of pilot fish following in our wake. The crew, much perturbed by the nightly screams emanating from the doctor's quarters, were delighted at the omen. The albatross continued to follow us for three days, gliding overhead hour after hour, waiting for the cook to throw his kitchen scraps overboard and for the pilot fish to rise to the surface to feast on them. Then it would dive to the water to eat its fill. At night, it would perch atop the foremast and rest there. On the third day it flew off, taking with it the little glimmer of happiness it had brought us.

The *Solide* continued to sail north across the ocean. I tried to mind my own affairs, attending to my chores and keeping lookout at my post. I became accustomed to my new body. It was, for the most part, an easy body to inhabit. Though Joubert was but twenty years old, he had been at sea more than half his life. Before that, he had lived the life of a street urchin in Toulon. I loved the freedom and the rigors of the sailor's life. The freedoms of port life, on the other hand, I could not abide: I had inherited a taste for rum, a cunning mind, and a vindictive temper to match. I bore bitter grudges that I could never let die. I was the most loyal of friends, but in the role of foe, the merest unresolved slight might become, in the shadows of my heart, a lifelong vendetta bearing little resemblance to the modesty of its origin.

I never stopped seeking out a way to speak with you directly—in vain. This was no straightforward thing, for I was but an ordinary seaman and you a master. Other than in illness and injury, a ship's surgeon has scant opportunity to commune with the crew. Oft-times I doubted such an opportunity would ever come. My old friend Brice noted the sullenness into which I had fallen, barely guessing its true cause, and began to badger me about it. Although I had little tolerance for such banter, and told him so, still he continued, often alluding to it at the mess table. One night, as we chewed without appetite on our biscuit dipped in foul brackish water, Brice addressed me with tender-hearted exasperation. "What's taken hold of you, Joubert? Ever since you cavorted with that savage you've been acting strangely. Are you in love? Are you afflicted with some malady of the loins?" I felt a rising tide of rage so strong I launched myself at him with a view to landing a blow that would shatter his jaw and quit his badgering. Thankfully I missed, for I would have been flogged once more and might not have survived another ordeal. But my only friend was lost to me, and for the rest of the voyage I never passed over an occasion to slight him.

In the heavy fogs of autumn, we sighted land once more,

and a cheer went up among the weary crew. We had come to our destination, the islands of the Alexander Archipelago. The aim of our expedition was to purchase furs from the natives, which we would take to Macau to sell to the Chinese. At each landing, we made it known that we wished to trade their skins of beaver, seal, otter, bear, elk, and wolf in exchange for guns, iron nails, knives, blankets, and spirits. But on each occasion we learned that all their best furs had been sold to another ship only weeks before, leaving us a meager assortment of second-rate merchandise. Our luck was no better in the Queen Charlotte Islands. And so, with winter approaching and our commerce left greatly in want, we set sail for China, hoping there to sell what furs we had procured. By the time we departed Alaska, a wintry pall was set in across the sky and the ocean had become stroppy and cruel.

I barely said a word to you over the next few weeks, but I thought of you constantly. A crossing is a perilous venture. Each one is slightly different. Some crossings fare better than others, and no two crossings are the same. You had been young, not yet fully initiated. Then there was the musket shot. Perhaps it had interrupted the crossing somehow, cutting it short. And now, though you seemed to remember nothing of your previous life, every night you were racked with nightmares. What was left of you? I longed to speak to you at greater length, but for now I could only bide my time and watch you from afar. With the passage of time you shed your hesitations and became more assured in your work. The memories buried within you of your craft were retrieved by the demands placed upon you, the knowledge returning not all at once but in a drip, one remembrance at a time. Perhaps, I reasoned, your memories of your other, previous life would return to you in a similar way.

There is many an idle hour when a ship is at open sea. A man's mind, in such slackness, can twist upon itself like old rope. So a sailor devises all kinds of ways to amuse himself, with cards and dice, with song and dance, with the telling of stories and jokes, with the whittling of driftwood and the knotting of lines, and the inventing of designs with which to adorn his body. Since our passage through the South Seas, tattoos had become something of an obsession among masters and seamen alike. Before the crossing Joubert had been esteemed as the finest aboard for his drawings on paper and skin. It was no strange thing for a seaman to approach me asking that I draw a sea monster upon his back, or the name of his sweetheart upon his shoulder. But on occasion a man would come with no specific drawing in mind, simply the desire to feel the satisfying prick of the needle piercing his skin. Whenever I was left at liberty to draw whatever I fancied, I liked to tattoo upon their skin the figure of an eye, such as the eyes that were tattooed on the skins of my island people. After I'd drawn several of them, these tattoos became admired among the crew as a memento of our circumnavigation, only the second such expedition by a French vessel. Even some of the masters came to me, requesting that I ink the design into their skin. Such is the superstitious tendency of a sailor's soul, they believed that this tattoo was an omen of good fortune.

On a calm Sunday afternoon, as we neared the coast of Formosa after an especially wrathful storm had besieged the ship for two days, I was in the hold, inking the image of a whale on Mozoly's back by the light of a porthole, when you approached us. You paused to observe my technique, as if I were undertaking a medical procedure. You asked questions of me. You watched me dab the needle in the ink and sink it deep into Mozoly's skin. You explained how the needle penetrated the skin's outer layers and went so deep as to set the ink permanently upon the body. Mozoly hid his discomfort, with the pride of a veteran sailor. Once the picture was done, he walked away sore but with a smile, to display his new adornment to his shipmates. You asked if I might draw one of my tattoos on the back of your shoulder. An eye? No, you said, the Virgin Mary. You admitted having prayed to her during the storm, promising her that if the ship were spared you would have her image engraved on your person.

When Mozoly was gone, you removed your shirt and sat on a chair before me at an angle so that your shoulder was directly before me. I dipped the needle into the India ink and began puncturing your skin with holes of blue. When a man is having his skin tattooed, it takes him some time to become accustomed to the sting of the needle. Once habituated, he learns to ignore the sensation, even to enjoy it. "Tell me, doctor," I said when I sensed that you were used to the pain, "for some time you have been greatly tormented in your sleep. I have heard your afflictions—we all have. What are these nightmares that torture you so?"

"I admit," you replied, "it is irksome for me to know that I make such a din. The dreams themselves are strange and confused. Oftentimes I cannot remember anything of them, and if I do it is but a glimpse. They seem to take place on that island where the boy was shot."

"Koahu," I said. "The boy's name was Koahu."

"Koahu," you repeated. "I cannot get this Koahu out of my head."

"Perhaps," I said as I dipped the needle once more into the ink and then plunged it into the skin of your shoulder, trying to be as gentle as possible, "perhaps there is a reason for this."

"The reason is surely nothing more than guilt. But it was an accident. How can I be guilty if it was an accident?"

"Perhaps it is more than guilt." I continued my work as I spoke: needle in ink, perforation of skin, stain of midnight blue. "Perhaps if you think back to that moment you will remember something that might help you understand what happened. Perhaps it is not guilt that bothers you but something else—something unusual, something perhaps miraculous in its nature."

You were looking ahead now, into the darkness of the hold. "I am a surgeon. I have seen many a corpse. Many a man has died in my care, some even in my arms. And yet the memory of that boy haunts me still."

"Perhaps it is more than a memory that haunts you, doctor. Have you not considered the possibility . . ." I began, and paused, waiting for the words to come.

"What possibility?"

"The possibility that the boy—the boy . . ." I knew not how to continue, so I pushed a needle into you, only in my nervous state I plunged it too deep. You flinched. I removed the needle, but blood had begun to seep from the puncture.

"I thought you knew what you were doing!" you snapped.

"Forgive me," I said, wiping your skin clear of the scarlet drop. "I ought to leech the wound."

"Wait, I beseech you, I'm almost done. It won't happen again."

"If you talked less perhaps you would work better. And such idle talk! Such futile conjecture!"

In silence, I resumed dipping the needle in the ink and puncturing your skin. The auspiciousness of the moment had passed, and yet I was so close to my goal that I could not stop now. "What I am trying to suggest," I continued, as calmly as I could, "is that perhaps the cause of your nightly torment is that . . . you are not who you think you are. Or rather, you are *more* than you realize. Perhaps, on the island, you divined something about the customs of the natives. Perhaps your curiosity led to an exchange of some sort, completely unexpected, an exchange of souls—do you see what I am trying to say? Perhaps Koahu is *in* you. Perhaps he *is* you." The drawing was finished. I poured sea water upon it to cleanse it and cool the reddened skin. I had not drawn the Virgin Mary, as you had asked. I'd drawn an eye, the finest eye I had ever drawn. I knew you would be enraged, that there would be consequences, but I wanted that eye to be there whenever you espied a reflection of yourself. For as long as you were alive in that body, that eye would be there, returning your gaze in the mirror's reflection, reminding you of our conversation. I gave you a looking-glass to hold, and held up a second one so that you could see the reflection of it.

"What have you done?" you said, your face aghast. "Where is the Virgin I asked for? Why have you drawn that terrible pagan symbol?"

"As a reminder of who you are," I said, determined to impose my message upon you. "That boy *is* you. *You* are *the boy.* I saw you cross, I saw it all with my own eyes, and I, too, crossed, for I could not let you cross on your own." You said nothing, yet I felt a hardening in you. You had become perfectly still. "I am Alula. I am the one who loves you. I followed you. I crossed too. I'm here with you." You stood and took your shirt and slung it over your shoulders with your back turned to me. The moment was over, I could tell, but I could not stop. I could not stop until I had told you everything you needed to know. "Something happened in the crossing, something went wrong. You can't remember, or perhaps you can only remember it in your dreams. But this is who you are: you are Koahu, never forget that. You have crossed once, and you must cross again. The Law says there can be no crossing without a return crossing. I am Alula, and I will never abandon you." Still you said nothing, but only continued to button your shirt. "We must return to the island before it is too late."

It was once your shirt was buttoned that you turned to me and, voice trembling, declared, "You will be punished for this, Joubert, mark my words. You are a madman and a fool, and you have humiliated the very man who saved your life."

Then you walked away into the darkness without so much as a backward glance.

Later that day, the bosun Icard approached me. "What did you say to Roblet?" he asked.

"Nothing of consequence."

"Whatever it was, he's complained to the captain. You're not to speak to him again. If you do, you will be flogged—and this time Roblet won't be there to tend to your wounds."

Our luck only worsened in Macao. Just weeks before our arrival, the Emperor of China had granted the Russians a monopoly on the fur trade. After a fruitless month spent repairing the ship, with second-rate furs moldering in the hold and tempers faring no better above deck, we continued our course toward the French colony of Isle de France, off the east coast of Africa. We moored in Port Louis for eleven weeks, waiting out the worst of the summer storms, and while the sailors caroused in the portside taverns and brothels, I was melancholic all the while, for I took what I saw on this island—the poverty, the sickness, the slavery—as a premonition of the fate of our own. In that time, I barely saw you. You were with the masters, guests of the colonial officials and plantation owners, attending balls and luncheons in their estates in the surrounding hills.

We set sail once more at the end of the storm season, and it wasn't until Isle de France was little more than a smudge of blue ink on the horizon that I noticed your absence. I went looking for you in the sick bay below decks but I found only Reynier.

"Roblet?" he said. "He decided to stay in Isle de France. They were in great want of a surgeon. Perhaps I can help you?"

I turned away from him, masking any hint of my heart's sorrow. I climbed down into the hold to sit among the rats and foul water, for at least here I could be alone and allow my heart to grieve in peace. When the bosun's whistle blew soon after for the changing of the watch, I somehow took hold of my senses and climbed the ropes to the crow's nest. I cannot say how I climbed those ropes without falling—for falling is what I wished for. I wanted to break my neck, I wanted to drown, I wanted to be swallowed by a whale. But my body acted in defiance of my heart. I climbed the rope-ladder and I stood upon that platform, looking out upon the sea and the sky.

It was dusk. The ship sailed sou'-southwest toward a tropical sun sinking into the ocean. It would have been as nothing to imitate that golden orb, to leap from my perch high on the mizzen mast and disappear into the water, leaving me to sink into my own everlasting night. My absence, most likely, would not have been noticed until the ship was long gone. Behind me, still within view but by now no more than a drop the size of the head of a pin between an infinite sea and an infinite sky, was Isle de France, the island we had left that very morning. Even though I could still see it with my own eyes, it was already as unreachable as if it had been on the other side of the world. I watched it until it was nothing more than an illusion of the eyes. Still I watched it, until the futility of the task impressed itself upon me: it was gone, and so were you.

The ship sailed onward. In the twilight, the evening star shone steady and true. One more time I wondered, should I let myself fall? Should I surrender to the longing for oblivion? The sea seemed to beckon to me, promising unending peace. But I did not succumb to its call. Instead, I made a vow. I cannot say to whom I made it, whether it was to me or you, to the gods above, or simply to the evening star shining in sweet solitude in the blushing sky ahead. To whom or what I cannot truly say, but I made a vow. And I did not fall.

By the time, weeks later, we finally arrived in Marseille, I immediately set about seeking a return passage to the island by way of Isle de France. It was already more than a year since we had left Oaeetee. In stifling August heat, I trawled the dens of the Vieux Port, visiting the offices of the shipping agents in search of a ship bound for the South Seas. When I told them where I wished to travel, some laughed at my foolishness while others gave me looks of contempt or pity. There were, I learned, no ships sailing to such places. The *Solide*'s expedition had been the first voyage to those parts to have ever sailed from this port, and it had stripped its investors of their fortune. By now, what's more, all of France was gripped by revolution. The seeds of republicanism had sprouted all over Europe, and the continent's monarchs were mobilizing for war. Voyages of discovery, which had seized the public imagination for a generation, were now of little interest to the fledgling republic. If I wanted to travel to the remotest parts of that ocean, I was told, I should join a ship trading in furs or sandalwood or the oil of the sperm whale, as such vessels sailed the globe in search of their merchandise, and sometimes ventured as far as the South Seas.

But before I could return I had to find you again. I hatched a plan that would take me to Isle de France, where I might find you, convince you to come with me, and together we would find postings upon a ship bound for the Indies, then another bound for the Spice Islands, and another for Formosa, and thus by and by we would sail once more the oceanic waters of our home. I thought it might take me several months to find you, and perhaps several years before returning to the island. Whenever such thoughts entered my mind, I would be cast into despair, and only the most resolute determinations kept me from becoming altogether unmoored: what did it matter, I told myself, if it should take ten years or twelve, or even twenty years, for us to return? The only thing that mattered was that we should arrive, after all, and restitute the Law that our actions had offended.

Once more I took up the life of the sailor. I found a passage to Isle de France and searched for you there. I asked in all the taverns of Port Louis after the surgeon Roblet. I learned that only weeks earlier you had joined a ship bound for Coromandel, and thus I contrived a posting aboard a ship bound for that Indian colony. Once there, I learned that you had taken a position aboard a ship bound for Malabar.

And so began the years of searching: a dozen years chasing rumors of you from port to port, crisscrossing oceans and seas, asking in taverns and coffee houses after the surgeon Roblet, moving from table to table, sailor to sailor, asking the same questions over and over, so that my pursuit of you became my regimen, my raison d'être, my life. Countless times I engaged in the same conversation, and countless times I met the same reply: "What is his description?" To this I had no special answer. In body, you were a man of no uncommon height and weight, with blue eyes and dark hair like so many of our compatriots, and no discernible deformities. You were possessed of both your eyes and ears; your nose and mouth were neither large nor small, your skin pocked by no illness, and the sum of all your fingers and toes was twenty. I could not say, "He has upon his shoulder a tattoo depicting an eye," for, other than a surgeon's mate, an ordinary seaman would rarely spy a master in a state of undress. But there was one particularity I knew of that would never be forgotten by any man who had sailed with you. And so I would reply, "His description is not special; he is a man like any other. Yet every night in his sleep he suffers such terrors that he is known to scream like the Furies." And thus at every port I went to I would soon find someone who had recently sailed with a man of that description, or who knew someone who had done so, and who would attest with various admixtures of bitterness and pity that the poor bedeviled soul had been relieved of his post at the nearest port, sailors being so thoroughly prone to superstition that such nocturnal behavior had half the crew convinced a great curse had fallen upon them.

As well as being superstitious, sailors are also gifted tellers of tales. As a story passes from mouth to ear, ear to mouth, each teller adds to it some ingredient of his own. So it was not long before I noticed that the tales of you I encountered began to stretch and widen. The first time this happened was on the island of Gorée in Africa. I entered a rum shop and asked after you. One young lad claimed he had sailed on a ship with you the previous year and that you had traveled on to Argentina. Another sailor, an old salt, claimed to have been with you aboard a completely different ship only weeks previously, and that you were now on your way to New South Wales. Such contradictory reports began to occur ever more frequently until I realized that a myth of you had been born, and sailors, as is their wont in the idle hours of drink and card games, had added your story to the book of legends that they carried around in the libraries of their minds—your legend being that of the man of medicine cursed with a spiritual affliction without remedy, the surgeon whose malady was such that no ship would keep him. The greater the legend, the more distant you became. Eventually I felt I was no longer seeking a man but rather shadowing a ghost who was both everywhere and nowhere in particular. The legend of the accursed surgeon continued to grow and over time the stories of you became more vivid and varied. In Montevideo I heard tell of a dwarfish doctor with miraculous healing properties whose demons were so powerful the ship he sailed was cast into a vengeful maelstrom, killing all aboard save the surgeon himself—and the teller of the tale. Then, only months later, in Zanzibar, another sailor—a Moor—told of a doctor seven feet high with a great mane of red hair, whose terrors had proven such a malediction upon a ship bound for Ceylon that it had been becalmed for weeks on end and, by the time another ship had come upon them, all had died of thirst and hunger—all, that is, but the surgeon himself—and the teller of the tale.

And so, in the knowledge that it was one thing to pursue a man and another altogether to pursue a legend, I determined, several years after the dawn of the new century, with France no longer a kingdom or even a republic but a great empire stretching from one end of Europe to the other, to abandon my search for you and to take up another. Over the course of the following years, I sailed upon several ships that plied the furthest reaches of the oceans, ships that traded in fur and sandalwood and whale oil, in the haphazard hope that one such vessel might some day pass near our island, and I might somehow convince the captain to moor there. As the years followed one another, I must have circumnavigated the globe a dozen times, and neared the island on at least two occasions, but never more, at a guess, than within several hundred leagues. The first time was on a passage from Lima to the port of Manila, around the year 1805; the ship having recently moored at Easter Island for fresh water, we continued to sail without pause. The second time was in 1811, on a Nantucket whaler. When the lookout called land nor'-northwest, I watched the captain on the poop deck for his reaction. Again, there was none: the ship did not veer from its northerly direction, in search of the next whale. I was suddenly seized with a sickness to see my island so strong that I rushed to the larboard bulwark for a glimpse of dry land, but from the deck there was no such thing to be seen. I began to climb the rigging in the hope that I might catch sight of it from the crow's nest. The bosun ordered me back to the deck but I pretended I did not hear. At the crow's nest, I explained to the astonished lookout that

I was landsick and wished to lay my eyes on solid ground—such madness is known to every sailor. The lookout explained that what he had taken for land had been nothing more than a dark bank of storm clouds on the horizon. I returned to the deck in a forlorn state only to find the bosun awaiting me. He pronounced a punishment of twelve lashes at next noon watch.

Both times I felt the nearness of it—I recognized the shapes of the sea and the wind, the color of the sky, the smell of the air, the display of the heavens at night. But a seaman's influence on a ship's direction is akin to that of a flea on a dog. The power of setting a ship's course resides solely in the hands of the captain. I would never have that power, for I was an ordinary seaman and my prospects were those of an ordinary seaman. My station in the world of men was to be my destiny.

Years passed. I traveled the length and breadth of every sea and ocean in the world. When I grew too old for work on deck, I cooked in the galley. Eventually, I grew too old even for this. In the spring of 1814, as the French Empire crumbled to dust and its emperor began his first exile, I found myself stranded, whale-like, on an island on the other side of the Atlantic, in Nantucket, Massachusetts. The end of our youth invariably takes us unawares, and I had little intimation, having arrived in that famous port on the whaler *Illumination*, that this would be my last circumnavigation. I spent all summer in Nantucket seeking a berth on another whaler, and on each occasion some long-faced Quaker would reply that his crew was fully accounted for.

I took jobs on other ships, plying shorter routes between ports on the Atlantic coast and the Caribbean. I sank into melancholy. I worked harder than any other sailor and, when

I was not working, I drank. *There can be no crossing without a return crossing.* The phrase hounded me day and night. Now that I was too advanced in age to sail vast distances, what was I to do? How could I return to the island before dying without making another, second crossing? I was trapped—to redeem my first sin, I would have to commit another. It was better to accept that there would be no return. After all, the world had not ended as a result of our betrayals. I began to doubt the Law. Perhaps it had been wrong. Perhaps it had been invented by humans rather than passed down from the gods for the purpose of regulating the traffic of souls, to preserve the order of identity, to prevent the chaos of untrammeled crossings. I began to entertain the idea that there was no consequence to a crossing without a return crossing—only this was no less of a torment than the preceding idea. If it was true, it meant that all my efforts to find you and to return had been in vain. I might as well have thrown myself into the sea after all.

And so, my faith in the Law diminished, the temptation to make another crossing was never far from my thoughts. The first imploring look from some wretched girl in a brothel somewhere, or some shackled boy below decks on a slave ship between Baltimore and New Orleans, and I felt my soul begin to stir. It would have been a trifle to make a crossing with such a girl or a desperate captive, exchanging old age for youth, but it would have been futile, for its effect would have brought me no closer to my destination. Only a crossing with a ship's captain could advance me. I still yearned to return home, but to do so I needed to become a man possessed of the power to set a ship's course. Such an endeavor was easier said than done, for how often does one have the occasion to look such a man in the eye? A ship's captain must be a hard man, not given to prolonged gazing into the eyes of even his wife, let alone one of his crew. To look someone uninterruptedly in the eye for the several minutes it takes to make a crossing is a revelation either of the deepest love or the deepest hatred, and it is the duty of every sailor to earn the love of his captain, and the interest of every captain to withhold it. I never crossed eyes with a captain for more than an instant—to do so any longer would have earned me nothing but trouble.

With age, it became harder to find employment, and sometimes I would find myself in one port or another—Nantucket, Baltimore, Caracas, Havana, or Port-au-Prince—for weeks or months on end. Whenever this happened, I whiled away the hours in various taverns, coffee houses, gambling dens, and brothels, waiting, with a deck of cards marked especially for the purpose, for a ship's captain to sit at my table and take up a party of whist, like the orb spider who spins his nocturnal web and waits patiently in its center for the passing insect, only to dismantle it in the morning. But not once did the spider trap his fly.

The very last days of my life were spent in the port of New Orleans, Louisiana. Having all but surrendered hope of making another crossing, I had just enough money to buy myself a bumboat, and spent my days running small errands for a few coins upriver and down, from town to plantation or plantation to town, between ship and shore, shore and ship, or making river crossings, ferrying people or cargo from one riverbank to the other. By night I drank and played cards, still spinning my nightly web, though more out of a taste for liquor, women, and gambling than any higher purpose.

On a Monday afternoon in July 1825, I was in the back room of an inn playing widow whist for pennies with two other boatmen. It was late in the afternoon and outside a thick summer rain had emptied the streets, with peals of thunder that threatened to crack open the sky itself—a great thunderstorm of the tropics. The clatter of heavy raindrops upon the tin roof was like the applause of an audience in an opera house, making conversation impossible. Throughout the room, glints of droplets trickled through the rusty tin overhead and fell with a thud to the sawdust floor.

In the tumult of the rain, the entrance door opened and in walked a man in a dark woolen suit unsuited to the climes, so soaked through he looked as if he had just stepped out of a river baptism. I did not recognize him, nor, from the looks upon their faces, did my companions. He stood for some time in the entrance, accustoming himself to the darkness, rivulets of water trickling from his sleeves and the hem of his coat. He carried in each hand a leather satchel, which appeared heavy and well traveled, marking him a man of modest means, for a wealthier man would have engaged a porter to carry his luggage, and there would have been more of it.

The stranger continued to stand in the open doorway undaunted by the attention he was attracting, staring out into the empty darkness as if he had just witnessed a spectral apparition. He bore the demeanor not of the sinner, but of a man long and greatly sinned against. He was thin of body, wore a pencil mustache along his upper lip, and a wispy goatee on his chin. His flaxen hair, from under a wide hat, was grown long over his collar. Even wet and bedraggled it was evident that his suit was good, tight fitting, and well cut, such as is only seen in the port of New Orleans among the scions of the upriver plantations or the well-to-do young Yankees lately settled in the city.

Whist being a game best played by a party of four, I was gladdened by the sight of a newcomer to square our triangle. I called out in English to invite him to join us, but he remained mutely standing and looking into the darkness, staring down some great, secret demon. I tried again, in Spanish, with the same effect, and a third time in French. This caused him to flinch, as if startled from a mesmeric episode. He then asked, in the most perfect French, the kind of French rarely heard in these parts, what game we were playing. Widow whist, I replied, although we would prefer a game of Boston if he were willing.

Without another word he sat and we began to play. He played Boston with neither skill nor luck, and gave no indication that he had any interest in winning. He played by rote, more machine than man, paying scant attention to the cards. He had to be constantly prodded and prompted, suggesting that his mind was as distant as his person was near. After the game, as my companions were leaving, he asked them to return his money—he must have lost a dollar or more in a short time—and by way of reply my two friends laughed, judging his request an attempt at humor. Their reaction left him in a state of even greater despondency.

When we were alone, I resolved to satisfy my curiosity about the youth, and asked if he had just seen a phantom, for he had the countenance of a man so confronted. He assured me that he had seen no such thing. It took but little prompting for him to begin—tentatively at first, and then, assisted by a bottle of rum, with gathering confidence—an account of his life, both recent and ancient, of which the following is a summary.

The newcomer's name was Jean-François Feuille. That very afternoon, he told me, he'd waded fully clothed into the muddy waters of the Mississippi with every intention of never returning to shore alive. Once fully submerged, he changed his mind and, after a great struggle, managed to haul himself out of the river despite the pull of the current and the added burden of his sodden woolen suit, which he had worn to prevent this precise eventuality. Thus, he told me morosely, he had proven himself a coward twice over—retreating out of cowardice from committing a coward's act. The young man intrigued me, and I asked him his provenance.

Feuille was the youngest son of a wealthy, ambitious Bordeaux farmer. I told him I was from Toulon and he seemed somewhat uplifted by this compatriotic bond. Although his father had envisaged a career in the priesthood for him, as a child Feuille had instead developed a love for the paintings adorning the walls of his parish church. His father's disapproval only fanned the flames of his ardour, and at the age of sixteen, against the wishes of the paterfamilias, he'd set off for Paris, determined to become an artist. Thanks to a letter of introduction penned by an aristocratic family acquaintance, he'd studied under the tutelage of the master Anne-Louis Girodet de Roussy-Trioson. Feuille, by his own admission, was a devoted and conscientious student but not an especially gifted one, and at the end of his studies he'd spent several fruitless years scrounging an existence in Paris, garnering few commissions of his own.

When word of the successes of certain French portraitists in America began to filter back to France, Feuille resolved to emigrate. He inherited a modest sum after the death of his father, sold all he possessed (which didn't add up to much) and bought a passage to New Orleans, determined to establish himself in the New World. His emigration did not, however, mark the slightest upturn in his fortunes—if anything they worsened. He was afflicted, he complained, by a profound timidity that prevented him from making the acquaintances and friendships required to prosper in his trade. To make matters worse, he had lost a good deal of his inheritance, such as it was, playing cards during his passage across the Atlantic. Upon his arrival he discovered a compatriot, Jean Joseph Vaudechamp, had arrived from France only a month earlier and set himself up in a studio in the city's French quarter. Moreover, unlike himself, Vaudechamp had arrived with a benign temperament and substantial capital: he had placed advertisements in the *Orleans Gazette* boasting of his renown in the royal houses of Europe, and had furnished and decorated his quarters in the style of the artist's studios of Paris, with a divan, vermilion silk-screened wallpaper, ancien régime furnishings, velvet drapery, and, on the walls, a gilt-framed portrait of a plump young woman—his sister, although the astute Vaudechamp hinted to prospective customers that it was, in fact, a noble woman for whom he had suffered an unrequited passion.

Feuille had, in the several weeks since his arrival, spent almost all that remained of his father's wealth and was now on the verge of ruin. All was lost, he said, including his honor, for even if he had the money to make the return passage to France, it would be as a failure.

I'd had occasion, in the course of my life as Joubert, to become acquainted with many unfortunates who had suffered the most accursed fates. None of them had borne their burdens with such lack of grace. I ventured to remark that perhaps not all was lost, that if he so chose he might discern silver linings to the clouds that palled his horizons. No, he continued relentlessly, on the contrary—everything, everything was lost. He was damned, he cried, his head in his hands, cursed and damned, and did not wish to live another day.

As I listened to the painter's tales of woe, I felt welling up within me a most unexpected combination of feelings that I can only describe as envious contempt. What wonders I might do, I thought, in his circumstances, endowed as he was with a young, handsome body, an educated mind, and good standing. As the natural and almost immediate consequence of this sentiment, an idea sprouted that, despite all efforts to banish it, quickly colonized my mind, as if every attempt at suppression merely hastened its triumph. Picture the scene: the two of us alone except for the innkeeper, wiping glasses with a bored look on his face at the far end of the empty room. The thunderstorm now at an end, a brilliant sunshine poured through the inn's small, solitary window.

He was not a ship's captain. He wasn't even a sailor. In fact, he told me, he'd been seasick the entire journey across the Atlantic. But I was suddenly seized with the desire for the very thing he wished to throw away. If he cares not for his life, I thought, I shall care for it in his stead.

At times the best plans come to us fully fledged, as if bestowed from the heavens. So it was on this occasion. I told Feuille all he needed to do to revive his fortunes was to paint a portrait as an advertisement of his powers, which he might subsequently exhibit to attract more customers. It should be a portrait of a remarkable visage, one that would arrest the attention of every passerby with its virtuosity. I offered to commission such a portrait of myself, as I was at the end of my life and wished to have my countenance, such as it was, memorialized. Afterward, he would be welcome to display it in his studio for a time until other commissions were asked of him. At first, he refused my offer—in fact, he evinced a most disagreeable stubbornness. I had to insist upon it several times, and cajole him into accepting, which was only further evidence of his foolishness, for my suggestion was plainly as wise as it was generous. Finally he agreed, although not without a look of doubt upon his face. He suspected me of exploiting him but was not able to divine exactly how. I gave him my winnings from the card game we had just played—some three or four dollars—then twenty dollars more as a guarantee of my sincerity, and so that he might buy any supplies as were necessary for the agreed purpose. We even fixed the date—on the morrow—and the time—two o'clock in the afternoon. I poured two last glasses of rum, emptying the bottle, as a celebration of our agreement.

Then came the moment of inspiration. He raised his glass to his mouth with an avidity that suggested a weakness for liquor. I put my hand on his arm to stop it momentarily from lifting any higher. "The eyes," I said, leaning forward, "are the thing. Render them well and you capture the soul of a man. Render them ill and you have missed him altogether."

He nodded his agreement. "The eyes are at once the most important feature of any face and also the most difficult to paint," he said. My hand was still on his arm. I felt it lifting upward once more but prevented it from doing so. I asked him if he had a preference for painting eyes of a certain color over eyes of another color—did he prefer to paint blue eyes, for instance, or dark eyes? He thought about this a moment and replied that in his experience dark eyes were generally easier to paint than blue or green eyes, for oftentimes they were less variegated, and the tint easier to imitate. Ah, I said, then I shall ensure my eyes are brown tomorrow. Feuille gave a puzzled look and asked me to repeat what I had just said.

"In that case, I shall ensure my eyes are brown tomorrow," I said, "to make it easier for you to paint them."

"But your eyes are blue," he replied.

"They are blue today, but tomorrow they will be brown."

"By what magic will they have changed color from one day to the next?"

"There's no magic in it," I said. "In a short time I can change their color from blue to brown."

This visibly astonished the poor man. "Is this some kind of joke at my expense?"

"Not at all, merely an ability I've possessed from birth, just as some contortionists have the ability to bend themselves backward in two, or others can speak in tongues."

"How is it done?"

"I merely concentrate my mind for three or four minutes and the color is transformed."

"You do this with your eyes closed?"

"Quite the contrary, it can only be done with my eyes wide open."

"Can you demonstrate this to me?"

"Of course," I replied, "I won't say it is a trifle, but it is no great thing. All that is required is the utmost mental concentration. You must look into my eyes without looking away. Shall we try it now?" He nodded vigorously. "Very well," I said, "watch very carefully."

{71}

Jean-François Feuille

Born 1797
First crossing 1825
Second crossing 1838
Date of death unknown

DESPITE THE STING of his temper, there had been something resolute about Joubert: his dogged nature, his dependable body, his old sailor's ways, his indefatigable ethic of work and purpose. It was not so with Feuille. He was a man of feeble spirit and great appetite—a glutton, a squanderer, a *débauché*. If he did not hold grudges, as Joubert did, it was because of his prodigality. Even before the crossing, I had detected a dissipation in him. After it, I could not help but sink into its mire. I now had youth, good looks, education, talent, and even a little social standing, and yet in every other respect the man I was now was the inferior of the man I'd been. Where Joubert was resilient, Feuille was easily discouraged; where Joubert was vivacious, Feuille was sullen; where Joubert made friends, Feuille collected enemies; where Joubert was resourceful, Feuille was incapable and disorganized. Forever after, it was as if the part of me that had crossed over and the part of me that was already there were in constant battle with each other. I found myself the prisoner of impulses I could barely master.

During a crossing, one enters into a body and inherits its capacities and incapacities, its appetites and proclivities. But one also enters into a mind. When I crossed with Feuille, I brought with me all the memories I had accumulated in the course of my previous two lifetimes. I also inherited a corpus of new memories, the memories of this new *me*, all its pleasures and tribulations, its qualities and flaws. How much more frightened of pain was my new host than Joubert had ever been! And how much more in need of pleasure!

The crossing itself, though complete and unimpeded, had been decided upon on the spur of the moment. As soon as it was done a part of me regretted it. There was Joubert in front of me with the same expression of bewilderment in his eyes that I had seen in Alula's: the bewilderment of the ambushed soul—a soul that knows *something* has happened without knowing precisely *what*. For once the crossing has begun, its effects are so strange and pleasant that it is a rare will that is strong enough to resist it. Resistance, after all, is simple: all that is required to prevent a crossing is to look away. But few who have begun a crossing can defy its seductive pleasures. It was sad to look upon the man I had just been, the body in which I had lived for more than three decades, now sitting directly in front of me with that look of shock upon his face. I took all the money in his possession—he was too deep in his stupefaction to murmur a word of protest—then I wished him well and was gone. Knowing exactly how much more money he kept hidden in the skiff he slept in, I went to the river, found his boat, and took the rest.

Almost as soon as I had left that coffee house in New Orleans I realized something was amiss. I had committed a wrong, perhaps even an evil, and try as I might I would never shake the shadow of my guilt. My first crossing had been motivated by my love for you, but the purpose of my second was more nebulous. It did not take long for the enormity of my wrongdoing to take hold. For as long as I was Joubert, there remained the possibility, however remote, that restitution of the Law might still be possible. Now that I was Feuille, there was no such possibility. Now there could never be a return crossing. I had thrown away any chance that the Law might be preserved. It was desecrated now, once and for all, and I was the one who had desecrated it. But—or so I reasoned to myself—a thing can only be broken once. Once broken, it can be broken again and again, and the result is the same.

I forgot about you too, Koahu—or rather I did everything I could to erase you from my mind. I put my convictions at the service of my interests. The Law, I told myself, was merely the superstition of a backward people. A crossing would not—could not—bring about the end of the world. The Law was merely the invention of men, men who sought power and control over others. The Law served only to limit our freedoms. I renounced my faith in it and yielded to all the freedoms within my reach, and in so doing became something terrible to behold: a charming persuader who sought only the satisfaction of his basest desires.

I began touring the cities of the American south, promoting myself as France's finest portraitist, offering the planters, merchants, officers, and other eminences the occasion to have their likeness, and those of their families, their houses, and animals, even their slaves if they so wished, forever memorialized by the application of oil on canvas. Wherever I went, prosperous men would give me foolish amounts of their money to sit in a room with them, their wives, and their daughters for hours and days on end, while in the evenings I would spend their money on women, cards, liquor, and roast meats.

Customarily, a portraitist arrived at the home of his subject with a canvas already painted in all respects save the face. If the subject was female, the canvas would show the figure of a woman in the center, with a large empty space where her face would be. For the standard fee, the background would be an Arcadian scene. For an additional fee, the client might specify the particulars of the portrait. He or she might request a classical or a bucolic scene, or ask that a dog be included in the subject's lap, or that a particular object—a pair of elegant hands, a jewel, an item of clothing—be displayed. Such things were all subject to negotiation, and every particular represented an additional profit for the portraitist.

This was how I met the woman who would become my wife, Hortense Michaux, only daughter of the widower Desire Michaux, owner of the famous Desire plantation of Louisiana. He sauntered into my rented studio in Lafayette one day and said, "I wish to immortalize my daughter." She couldn't travel, he explained, so I would have to displace myself to the Desire plantation, some ninety miles upriver of New Orleans in the Saint James Parish. I would be in want of nothing, he promised, and would be paid twice my usual fee.

I departed New Orleans on a steamboat two days later, in Desire's company. I quickly realized that, as Feuille, I suffered from an especially vicious form of the landlubber's affliction: seasickness. It's a wonder I ever crossed the Atlantic. Desire distracted me from my travails with tales of himself, his primary theme of conversation. He had been born the third in a line of sugarcane planters and married a cousin who died in childbirth. He was a heavy-drinking braggart, unpleasant in every way but one: he loved his only daughter more than anything else in the world.

When I finally met Hortense, on the porch of the master's house, she was sitting down. I was not struck by her beauty so much as an innate, sincere goodness. The chair she sat in had four small wheels at the ends of its legs and handles sticking out of the back of the frame. She had been struck by polio as a child and was unable to walk. I unrolled the canvas I had earlier prepared, a figure of a faceless woman wearing a silk mother-of-pearl evening gown. Hortense, however, insisted that I paint her wheelchair, as she called it, with a scene of the plantation in the background. When I told Desire this would add several days and several scores of dollars to my fee, he said, "Take your time, boy, take your time," and clapped me on the shoulder. "*Pronay votrah toe*," he added in his mangled Acadian French. He was very proud of his ability to speak French, but just about every time he did I nodded and smiled in reply without understanding a word he had said. It mattered little. On such occasions, a nod and a smile were all that was required of me.

The Desire plantation was not one of the biggest in the parish, nor was it one of the smallest. The master's house had cost Desire Michaux forty-eight thousand dollars, and so he was fond of boasting. It was a two-and-a-half-story building with galleries twenty feet broad all around, supported by fluted columns. The stately apartments were fitted with old oak and rosewood and filled with priceless furniture and antique portraits. Hortense, Desire told me, was determined to turn it into a treasure house of art, statuary, and books. It had a library with the latest tomes she ordered from Europe, a music room with a grand piano made in New York, a wine cellar that stocked only French wine, and a dungeon for the punishment of slaves. The lawns between the house and the river levee were planted with magnolias, orange trees, and large, twisting oaks dripping with Spanish moss. Around the main buildings were an assortment of outbuildings: a kitchen, bachelor apartments, a dovecote, stables, a greenhouse where orchids grew, and a cellar to store the great blocks of ice shipped downriver from Canada in the winter. The Desire plantation, boasted its master, was entirely self-sufficient and wanted for nothing.

A grove of cypress trees separated these buildings from the slave quarters, which were organized in four rows of six two-roomed, open-windowed cabins, each of which was shared by two families. At the center of this slave village was a planting of great sycamores growing around a belltower that rang morning, noon, and night, dividing the day into a routine that with the passage of time became as familiar as one's own heartbeat. Beyond the slave quarters was the sugar mill; beyond the mill were the sugarcane fields; and beyond those the impenetrable Louisiana bayou.

It was in the drawing room of the master's house that Hortense and I would meet every morning after breakfast. As I painted, I would tell her stories. I told her stories of a childhood in a family impoverished by the revolution, whereas in fact my father had profited immensely from the turmoil of that generation. I told her stories of my time spent as Napoleon's aide-de-camp during the Hundred Days, how I was there at Waterloo and had seen the Prussians entering Paris, whereas in fact I had, through well-placed connections and counterfeit illness, avoided the military altogether. She had a weakness for blue blood, so I told her stories of painting the portraits of some of Europe's most illustrious grandees by day while carousing with some of the continent's most notorious artists and conspirators by night. All lies. The artists and conspirators with whom I had caroused had labored in near-complete obscurity, penury, and illness. But with her romantic sensibility, Hortense swallowed whole the stories I told her, day after day while I painted, and night after night at the dinner table.

Sometimes it is the plainest who are bravest. On the evening of the last sitting day, which was also the eve of my departure, Hortense gave me a scented envelope as a token of her esteem, suggesting I might read it on my journey back to New Orleans. Of course I opened it as soon as I got back to my quarters. It was a poem about flowers called "Love's Bouquet." It mentioned the pansy, the gardenia, the apple blossom, the bachelor's button, and the forget-me-not. It contrasted the heather and the holly, praised the ivy and the violet over the amaryllis and the passionflower, and finished with the star-of-Bethlehem. I had to consult a book on the subject in the New Orleans library to decipher it. The girl had written me a coded declaration of love. I was only too delighted to feign reciprocity. Somehow, the motherless Hortense had grown to be a tender and amorous soul despite her father's brutish instincts. As delicate as she was plain, an old maid in years when I met her and yet still almost a child at heart, Hortense had developed a stubborn passion for me that her indulgent father could not refuse, despite the antipathy he bore toward all of humanity, other than his daughter, and toward artists in particular. Old Desire, a man who so clung to the manners of the French ancien régime that he still wore buckled shoes and silk stockings, was for all his foolishness not so easily fooled. When he looked at me, he saw a mystery so beneath contempt it did not even require solving. He tolerated me only for Hortense's sake. On the night before our wedding, as we smoked cigars and drank claret together, he told me that his daughter, who had since childhood been of melancholic disposition, had never been happier. He clapped his broad hand on my still slender shoulder and said, "As long as my daughter remains happy, you're welcome at Desire."

At the Desire plantation, the daughter's every wish was indulged. The great majority of her whims sprang from her love of beauty. Hortense loved art more than I did. She herself painted—landscapes of the plantation and its surrounds, which were all extravagantly framed and hung on the walls of the master house. Her style was that of a precocious child: a little skill and complete artlessness. When she played the piano, she was so careful not to make a mistake that she slowed to a near stop for all the difficult passages. When she sang, with much practice she could almost manage to sing in tune. She subscribed to literary journals, which arrived, months out of date, in the post, and from them she memorized long passages of the latest verses by the most notorious French and English poets. After dinner she liked to recite at length verses by such fashionable poets as Lamartine or Byron, or if she was feeling especially bold she might recite one of her own verses, over which she labored with infinite patience. She favored poems about the wonders of the European landscape, landscapes she would never see with her own eyes. Her recitation style veered between the wooden and the floral: here and there, she would stumble or omit a crucial word and, flushing crimson, would reach for her book and flick to the right page so that she might correct herself. Her guests, as gracious toward their host as they were immune to the charms of lyric verse, listened with seemly attention. Daydreaming politely until it was clear the recitation was at an end, they would applaud and liberally praise a blushing Hortense, marveling at her talent and those of Europe's most renowned poets, so that the one seemed indistinguishable from the other. Though I did not love Hortense, it would be untrue to say I loathed her. My attitude was more one of benevolent self-interest. I was, above all, glad to put the life of the traveling portraitist behind me.

The bloom of youth wilts, as is universally known, but beauty lingers longer on some faces than others. A short decade after my crossing, I was no longer the dashing, romantic hero I had affected in my youth. I had done little in the meantime other than indulge myself in every pleasure plantation life can afford an idle man, which are, in the main, eating, drinking, and lording it over the servants. As a result I had become obese. My hair had fallen out in uneven clumps. My skin was blotched with gin blossoms. My teeth, rotting one after the other, were extracted and replaced with teeth of gold. I suffered from the gout, what's more, and was barely able to raise myself from a chair. Hortense spent her days in her wicker chair on wheels, fretting endlessly over my welfare while I parried away her attentions. Between meals, I liked to sip great quantities of rum, mint, and lemonade on the porch in the mottled sunshine, watching the comings and goings of plantation life, and giving myself over completely to poisonous thoughts, until it was time for the next meal.

As the years passed, my thoughts began to circle increasingly around one particular subject: my next crossing. I had already twice desecrated the Law, and on the second occasion passed a point of no return. I was beyond redemption, and yet the world was not destroyed. On the contrary, it appeared as intact as ever. There was, other than the lack of a body, nothing to stop me crossing again. I debated this question endlessly, sitting on the porch, observing, studying, and scheming my escape from the prison-within-a-prison in which I was trapped. I was determined that my next crossing would not be as impulsive as the last. All I needed was to find a suitable body with which to cross, and a means by which to do it.

When I first spied the girl, crossing the yard alongside her mother, a scullery maid called Berthe, she must have been no more than twelve or thirteen years old. I was sitting in my usual position, sipping iced rum, lemonade, and mint. I noticed her reserve, her languid grace, how quiet and imperturbable she was. She was so contained she gave the impression she existed within a soapy bubble that might pop at any moment. Only it never did. The effect of her was thus always slightly miraculous. Having never seen her before, I made inquiries about her. Her name was Jeanne. She had been loaned out to a neighboring plantation for some years. She was lighter of skin than the field slaves, and it was assumed her father was Desire, as there were rumors that Berthe was his favorite. Half-castes were spared the field and worked inside the house.

Now that I had seen her once I began to see her often. Although she never paid me the slightest mind, I made her the object of my fascination. I studied her every movement. She seemed near and far at once, as if she knew everything there was to know and was indifferent to it.

Hortense quickly divined my interest in Jeanne and despised her for it. In spite of my hideous appearance, Hortense's love for me continued to burn, perhaps because it never found its satisfaction. She asked her father to banish the girl from the house but this was a rare whim that Desire did not indulge. He even defended me, calling it proof that I was a red-blooded Frenchman, proof he was glad to have, as he had often doubted my manliness. I denied everything, of course. In truth Hortense had every reason to be jealous, but she mistook the nature of the desire. The bronze glint of the girl's skin, her reserve, her youth—when I looked upon her it was not lust I felt, for my bloated body was no longer capable of such outbursts of passion. It was recognition. She reminded me of myself, of the girl I had once been, lifetimes ago.

For eight months of the year, dinnertime on the Desire plantation—always an elaborate affair—was conducted on the porch. Michaux *père et fille* flaunted their French heritage, and dinner was invariably served in the continental manner, in courses that followed one another rather than all at once, on Limoges crockery, with wines from Bordeaux served in crystal glasses. At such times, seated at the head of a long table opposite Hortense, with Jeanne and other servants hovering nearby, Desire Michaux was irrepressible. He enjoyed an audience, and we were ever faithful to the call, Hortense and I, along with the overseer, Champy, and more often than not several invited guests, either planter families from neighboring estates visiting for a day or two or visitors from downriver staying several days or weeks.

After a drink, Desire was fond of launching into a long disquisition on one of a handful of favorite themes, and no discussion would be entered into. He fancied himself an amateur philosopher, especially regarding the subject of the races—the Negro, the failings thereof, and the advantages servitude brought thereunto. Regarding the full-blood slave, Desire had little to say: the full-blood Negro was beyond human redemption because of the curse of Ham, but could nevertheless receive divine redemption, which depended not on man but on the mercy of God. But was the half-caste subject to the same curse? There were, he admitted, undoubtedly many instances of half-castes in Louisiana who had flourished in their freedom, which indicated that they possessed certain qualities that might, in certain circumstances, approach those of a white man. But was the half-caste capable of human redemption? He would continue on this theme night after night, often alluding directly to one of the half-castes present, including Jeanne, all of whom had been trained to remain perfectly oblivious to the nature of the conversation being conducted by the masters they served. The disquisition always ended with its customary conclusion: that the Negro was better off in his bestial state than burdened with the ennui of the white man's life.

Over the years, by force of repetition, one could follow the course of his argument paying only the slightest attention, and otherwise enjoy a moment of perfect solitude. It was best, when Desire was drunk, to keep one's attention firmly fixed on one's plate. As what was on my plate was my chief delight, I was only too happy to comply. I questioned his racial theories just once and regretted it instantly. He saw my words as a challenge to his unassailable authority. The viciousness of his retort was such that he stopped only when Hortense burst into tears. It was a most unpleasant episode, and I resolved never to provoke another like it. But the seed of defiance was planted in my mind and was watered nightly by Desire's monologues.

Meanwhile, I continued my own, sad metamorphosis into a sight ever ghastlier to behold. I could barely stand to see my reflection in a mirror—and the house was filled with them.

I had a sweet tooth that could never be satisfied, and a sugarcane plantation is no place for a sweet tooth. Subjected to a fatal admixture of gluttony and idleness, my body continued to swell, and my teeth to rot. Every toothache set off a nauseous trip downriver to the dentists of New Orleans, with tearful farewells from Hortense and a procession of servants to navigate the passage of my monstrous body over and around the hazards of the outside world. Eventually, for expediency's sake, my few remaining teeth were removed all at once. By the time I was hauled out of the dentist's office, my jaws were worth several slaves.

Year after year, I observed the girl's metamorphosis into a young woman with a proud, dignified bearing. The resemblance to the young woman I had once been only grew. I watched Jeanne become my double, my likeness, my sister. Of course, she never paid me the slightest attention. Her only acknowledgment of my existence was the minimum necessary for the fulfillment of her duties. I began, in the solitude of my thoughts, to contemplate the prospect of making my next crossing with the slave girl who served me my every meal. But if I was to cross again, I wished to avoid making the same mistake I had made with this one. I was lost, cast adrift here on this Louisiana plantation, and what I yearned for was a new beginning, morally as well as physically. Jeanne became the symbol of the fresh start I craved. And as I did not wish to live a life of slavery, before crossing with her, I would need to procure her freedom.

Obtaining the freedom of a slave was no simple undertaking. I could either buy her myself and free her or organize her escape and expose her to the risk of capture and punishment. In the dungeon under the same house where, nightly, we gathered to eat our fill, recalcitrant slaves were subjected to unspeakable cruelties. I was determined to avoid that fate. However, having no money of my own, I was unable to purchase the girl myself—and even if I had, the act would have caused more problems than it solved. For whenever Jeanne was near, Hortense's gaze blazed in my direction, envious of the attentions I devoted to the girl; all Hortense ever received from me was politeness. Sometimes, when she caught me gazing longingly at Jeanne, she would slip into an uncontrolled rage and, in tears, beg her father to send the girl away. Desire would reply that he had nowhere to send the girl, other than the slave market. "Send her to the slave market, then, Papa!" she would plead, knowing it was the banishment of his own daughter, her half sister, that she was asking of him.

At dinner on the porch one evening in the autumn of 1838, with fireflies flickering softly in the darkness of the garden below and all the world soft and gentle, Desire finally relented after another of Hortense's fits of pique. Jeanne was attending to us impassively as always. She was standing within earshot not a few feet away from him when he announced, "If it makes you happy, I will sell the girl."

Hortense looked up, wide-eyed with happy astonishment. "What did you say, Papa?"

"Jeanne. If it makes you happy, I will send her away."

The news sent me into a panic I was at labors to disguise. Instantly I looked in Jeanne's direction. She did not blink or falter or startle. She betrayed no emotion at all. Desire might have been speaking about some distant stranger. We might just as well have been discussing repairs to the belltower or the price of sugar.

Hortense, by contrast, was delighted. She did not say anything, not wishing to gloat, but all the same she beamed with satisfaction. Finally her triumph was in sight. It had taken her years to persuade her father to sell his half-caste daughter. She now had her wish, and in her mind her responsibility was to accept victory with as good a grace as she could muster. The signs of her happiness were subtle: the liveliness of her eyes, the inflections of her voice, the vivacity of her movements. The pronouncement had been made, and there was to be no more talk of it.

As usual, after the madeira was poured and cigars lit, Hortense picked up the book she had been reading to us nightly. It was a book, she'd assured us, that was much in vogue across Europe. She began reciting, taking it up at the point she had finished the previous night, the scene where Victor Frankenstein climbs the Glacier Montanvert:

"'Alas!'" she read, "'why does man boast of sensibilities superior to those apparent in the brute; it only renders them more necessary beings. If our impulses were confined to hunger, thirst, and desire, we might be nearly free; but now we are moved by every wind that blows and a chance word or scene that that word may convey to us.'"

She continued:

We rest; a dream has power to poison sleep.
We rise; one wand'ring thought pollutes the day.
We feel, conceive, or reason; laugh, or weep,
Embrace fond woe, or cast our cares away:
It is the same; for, be it joy or sorrow,
The path of its departure still is free.
Man's yesterday may ne'er be like his morrow;
Nought may endure but mutability.

Later that evening, as I lumbered past the door of Desire's apartment, I noticed it was slightly ajar. Hearing the murmur of voices, I peered in discreetly and saw Jeanne's mother Berthe kneeling at Desire's lap, beseeching him tearfully not to send Jeanne away. He stroked her hair tenderly. "There, there," he said, "there, there."

At dinner the next evening, with Jeanne and Berthe both attending to us, Desire announced that he had decided to sell Berthe as well as Jeanne. Again, the young Jeanne betrayed no emotion, but her mother picked up the hem of her skirt and scurried away, sobbing. Her inconsolable wailing continued for hours thereafter until, in the middle of the night, Desire's booming voice was heard commanding that she be taken to the dungeon and placed in shackles so that he might sleep in peace.

I knew Hortense would ensure I had no opportunity to approach Jeanne before her departure. My best chance at a crossing would be to devise some plan that would allow me to credibly leave with them. On the eve of their departure for New Orleans in the company of the overseer, Champy, gathering together all the little courage at my disposal, I put my plan into effect: I reluctantly hauled myself to the summit of the grand staircase and, after several minutes of hesitation, abandoned myself to gravity's cruelties in such a way that my front teeth were knocked out in the fall. As blood was gushing out my mouth, and with my golden teeth clutched in my hand, it was decided I would go to New Orleans instead of Champy, have my teeth attended to, and subsequently see to the auction of Jeanne and Berthe at the slave market. I would be gone for a week. I will never forget the stricken look in Hortense's eyes as she kissed me on the cheek. Perhaps she somehow sensed we were saying goodbye.

As I sat with the two women in the buggy that would take me down to the jetty, Desire approached, gave me Jeanne's and Berthe's ownership titles, and said in a whisper that I might sell them separately if the price was better. He turned away without farewelling his daughter—who, as usual, betrayed nothing of her thoughts or feelings—or her mother, whose distress was clearly etched upon her face.

The boat trip to New Orleans took all the rest of that day and a good deal of the next, a bone-shaking, nauseating journey on the steamboat *Phoenix*, whose boiler was too powerful for the boat's frail frame. A terrible tremble shook us throughout the journey. Down the river we rattled, through burning fields of sugarcane, with thick smoke billowing into the sky all around. I spent the entire journey in a fog of laudanum to dull the pain in my mouth, which only made my seasickness worse.

Having arrived in the port of New Orleans, I immediately took two rooms in a hotel by the river and went directly to a shipping agent and asked for two tickets on the next boat to France. A steamboat bound for Marseille was scheduled to leave three days hence, I was told, so I bought two first-class passages there and then. I returned to the hotel and found Jeanne and Berthe locked in the room where I had left them. I reassured them that they would not be sold and showed them the tickets I had just purchased.

We spent the following two days running endless errands in preparation for our journey. I went to the dentist and had my broken gold teeth replaced with new gold teeth, which

I charged to the Desire plantation. Then I hocked an array of precious objects I had stolen from the Desire plantation. I accompanied the mother and daughter to various Creole clothiers, buying dresses and luggage and such provisions as would be needed for their journey, all of which I charged to the Desire plantation. And I bought a small hammer, which I also charged to the Desire plantation. The morning of our departure, we returned to our rooms after breakfast and I told the women the time had come for their escape to freedom. I took all the money Desire had given me and placed it on the table beside the window. I removed my wedding ring, signet ring, and fob watch and did the same. I took my old gold teeth and added them to the loot, piling all these riches together. All this, I said, was theirs, and they were greatly pleased.

"Before I grant you your freedom," I said, "there is one small matter we must attend to, after which you will be free to go." I turned to the mother. "Berthe," I said, "I would like you to leave me alone with your daughter for a short while."

Berthe looked at me pleadingly, tears filling her eyes.

"I insist upon it," I replied. "I cannot let you go until you grant me an hour alone with your daughter. I promise you nothing untoward will occur."

Berthe let out a single sob before regaining her composure. She looked sorrowfully at her daughter, whose eyes returned the look with just as much sorrow.

"Please, Maman," said Jeanne, her voice shaking, "do what monsieur asks." The women embraced and Berthe, with a heavy sigh and tears trailing down her cheeks, left. Jeanne was standing in the middle of the room with an expression that betrayed no feeling. I took my last bottle of laudanum in hand and swallowed its contents.

"Now, Jeanne," I said, sitting on one of two bentwood chairs I'd placed opposite each other, "this is what I would like you to do." I took her by the wrist and dragged her close to me, handing her the hammer I had bought the previous day. "I want you to use this to knock out all of my teeth, making sure you retrieve all of them and let none of them fall down my throat." A look of panic flickered across her face. "Yes, it will hurt, but that is not your concern. I won't get angry at you. I won't punish you. I want you to do it. In fact, I insist on it. Come now." I tilted my face toward her and opened my mouth wide as I had at the dentist two days earlier. If Jeanne had any hesitation, she of course showed nothing of it. She simply gave a little nervous sigh and began hammering. I made such a commotion that Berthe opened the door a little to see what was happening. I waved her away with one grunt and, with another, urged Jeanne to continue. When she was done, she washed the gold teeth in a glass of water without a word and placed them with the other precious things procured thanks to the unwitting generosity of Desire Michaux.

I felt as beaten up as after a flogging, and spent some minutes hunched over, blood drooling from my mouth. Admittedly, I might have made things easier on myself by crossing with Jeanne first, and then chiseling the gold teeth from Feuille's mouth, but I was determined to inflict no needless suffering on the girl, considering that what I was about to do was cruelty enough. It would be a blind crossing, and she would inherit a broken body, but I appeased my conscience with the thought that at least it was the body of a free man, a white man, a wealthy man. It would be assumed that he'd been the victim of a violent robbery.

I could hear Berthe fretting outside. My bloodied mouth was throbbing and swollen and I could not speak, so it was with gestures and grunts that I instructed Jeanne to sit on one of two chairs. Then I locked the door.

{23}

Jeanne Duval

Born 1822
First crossing 1838
Second crossing 1864
Date of death unknown

ON A FROSTY day shortly before Christmas 1864, around noon, there was a knock at my door. I lived, at the time, in a small room I shared with a ragpicker in Batignolles, a dreary worker's suburb outside the Paris city wall. That day I was alone, which, at this advanced stage of my life, was how I spent most of my days, reclining on the bed or on a tattered divan in a corner of the room, reduced to infirmity by the pox. I had, several months earlier, suffered a paralysis of the left side of my body. Such a simple task as answering the door was beyond my capacities.

When the door opened, I saw in the gloom of the landing the silhouettes of two slender women. Entering the room in their wide dresses, they gladdened it like two upturned bouquets, the first of iris purple and the other of lily white. I invited them to be seated on the divan, which they approached hesitantly before accepting the invitation. In the pearl-gray light that entered the room through a single dirty window, I noticed how exquisitely dressed they were. For warmth, they were draped in furs of fox and ermine, which they did not loosen upon entering as, despite the stove, it was barely warmer inside than out. The woman dressed in mauve wore a veil over her face, which she did not raise. The other had a young face of rare beauty, with alabaster skin and great wide turquoise eyes set far apart. Under the little hat she was removing was a mane of chestnut hair, tied in two chignons at the nape of her neck, with ringlets covering her ears. The other's hair was, like her face, hidden by a veil, and when I invited her to remove it she replied most politely that she preferred to leave it on if it was all the same to me.

My visitors introduced themselves. The one dressed in purple who would not remove her veil was Mademoiselle Édmonde, while the pretty one introduced herself as Mademoiselle Adélaïde. They spoke in turns, shyly, hesitantly, almost in whispers, as if overawed by a great occasion. They did not tell me their family names but it was evident, by their demeanor, their dress, their manners, and their speech, that they were of the most rarefied provenance, and that such rooms as the one in which I lived were unknown to them. The demoiselles said they were relieved to have finally found me, as some people believed me already dead, while others claimed I had left Paris for the tropical climes of my birthplace.

"As you can see, I am very much still alive and here," I said. "I'm afraid I only have *tilleul* to offer you." When she saw the difficulty with which I heaved myself from my mattress, Mademoiselle Adélaïde offered to boil the water and prepare the infusion. As she busied herself, I asked Mademoiselle Édmonde why it was they had come. She explained they were readers of Charles Baudelaire, and they wished to meet his muse, the woman who had inspired his greatest poems. Such was their fondness for Charles, in fact, that they had founded a society devoted to his work, which naturally enough they had called the Baudelaire Society. They had written to Charles care of his publisher in Brussels, she said, expressing their admiration for his poems, but they had received no reply. So they had begun making inquiries among his friends—Courbet, Manet, Champfleury, Madame Sabatier, and so on—in an attempt to find me. They had even engaged the services of a private detective for the purpose.

Mademoiselle Édmonde's discourse ended as Mademoiselle Adélaïde approached with her pot of infusion and three cups. I was embarrassed—I did not possess two cups that looked the same, nor saucers on which to place them. But, judging by the smiles on the faces of the young ladies, my cups were of little interest. They beheld me as if I were on display in a museum, saying nothing, waiting for me to respond. I took several small sips from my infusion. "So," I finally said, "Charles has readers?"

"Yes," replied Mademoiselle Édmonde from behind her veil, "although we are more than readers—we are devotees, acolytes, disciples. Though small in number, our devotion has no limits. We are determined to ensure that his work shines forever. We think Monsieur Baudelaire is a great genius."

"Greater than Hugo?"

"Without a doubt."

"So Charles was right." I reached forward stiffly for a lump of sugar.

"Let me help you," said Mademoiselle Édmonde, taking my cup, dropping sugar into it, and stirring.

"What do you desire of me?" I asked.

The two young women looked at each other momentarily

and smiled. "Only to meet you and to learn about you," replied Mademoiselle Édmonde. "Nothing of you is known, other than what is in the poems."

"That is already too much."

"Please," said Mademoiselle Adélaïde, giving me a doleful look with her wide green eyes, "we have gone to great lengths to find you. Tell us about yourself. Tell us your story. We will not betray your confidence. We may even be able to provide assistance, make your remaining days more comfortable."

I thought about this a moment. "Do you know the painting by Courbet known as *The Painter's Studio*?" Mademoiselle Édmonde replied that she had been taken to see it at the Palais du Louvre as a girl, and that many of the figures in it had been friends of her parents. "I'll tell you something about that painting you may not know: I was once in it. I, Jeanne Duval, a mere slave girl who can barely read or write, was portrayed standing among France's most brilliant men—Champfleury, Proudhon, and the others. Charles is also in it, seated at the right of the painting, reading a book. When Courbet first painted it, I was depicted standing by Charles's side. What had I done to deserve this great honor? I had been his muse—his *grande taciturne*, his Black Venus." I sighed as memories I had long fought to smother began to resurface. "And yet, when Charles told me about the painting, I fell into such a fury that the very next day he went to Courbet and told him that I was to be removed from it, erased, painted over. Courbet did what Charles asked, but if you look hard enough, you can still see the trace of my image, hovering like a phantom over Charles's right shoulder as he reads his book." I looked directly at the two women. "That is how I wish to be remembered. As a ghost."

"Don't you desire what you deserve?" asked Mademoiselle Édmonde from behind her veil.

"What is that?"

"Immortality."

"Immortality is a curse."

My two interlocutors were silent for a moment before Mademoiselle Adélaïde asked, in as sweet and imploring a tone as I have heard, "Please, madame, tell us your story."

I had never breathed a word of my life story to anyone other than you, Koahu, but now that I was living in the shadow of death I yielded to the temptation of finally unburdening myself. "Very well," I said. "But I warn you, the telling will take all day. It is a tale full of wonders, many of which you will not believe. You will consider me mad, but your opinion is, I assure you, of no consequence to me. If I say anything to which you wish to object, I pray you keep your outrage to yourself. And you must make me a solemn promise that you will never repeat what I tell you, nor commit it to writing." The women agreed to my terms. After they'd sent their coachman out to bring us cakes and coffee, I began to tell them the tale of the albatross.

I began by telling them about us, Alula and Koahu, and our lives on the island. I related the tale of our crossings with Joubert and Roblet and our subsequent separation. I recounted the crossing with Feuille and Feuille's life on the Desire plantation. Finally, I told them about the crossing with the slave girl Jeanne. The two women sat side by side, holding each other's hands as they listened.

After I'd told them these tales, I requested a pause. I was

not used to such exertions and my head was dizzy. It was midway through the afternoon. The sky would darken in an hour or two. The ladies waited in respectful silence, chewing their cakes and sipping coffee politely, worried that I would revoke the privilege they'd been accorded. But now that I'd begun, I would not be stopped. The tales poured out of me, one after the other, like pearls on a necklace.

I took up my own story in the moments following the crossing with Feuille. When one has crossed into a new body, I explained, there is always a period of familiarization with it—with its history and idiosyncrasies. The manner in which the soul adheres with the new body is never quite the same. What's more, the body's memories do not come all at once. Rather, in the first few hours there is a flood of them, triggered by countless exterior sights, sounds, and smells. Over the next few days, the stream of memories slows so that by the third day they are but a trickle. Some memories are deeply buried and can surface weeks, months, or sometimes years after a crossing.

Having just crossed into the body of this girl in that New Orleans hotel room, I turned to take one last look at my previous body, that of Feuille. He sat directly before me, a ghastly sight, his mouth encrusted with streaks of dried blood, the result of the removal of his gold teeth before the crossing. In his gray-blue eyes a dazed new soul was now blinking timorously in perfect ignorance of what had just occurred. The guilt occasioned by my act of thievery stabbed me into action. I gathered together all our belongings, including the money and gold that would launch us into our next lives, and stepped out into the hallway, where Mother was anxiously waiting. Upon seeing me she burst into tears and hugged me. The sight and touch of her prompted a hailstorm of memories in me so great and vivid I almost fainted. I composed myself and told her not to cry but to rejoice, for now we were free.

During our passage to Marseille, I accustomed myself to my new mind and body, glad to be rid of both the venality and the seasickness I had known as Feuille. And I discovered the extraordinary power that lay in the body of a desirable young woman. As the number of men on board vastly outnumbered the women, many of them directed their attentions toward me with indefatigable zeal. The thought crossed my mind on more than one occasion to make another crossing with one of them, for it would be surely more advantageous to me to be a white-skinned man than a dark-skinned woman, but now that I was once more a woman I did not covet manhood. After Feuille, there was something redemptive about being Jeanne. Although given to episodes of melancholia, she was resilient and composed. The great cruelties she'd already witnessed in her short life had endowed her with an aloofness that acted as a protective shell. And so, as Jeanne, I remained unmoved by the gallantries I was paid. Those men that fell in love with me aboard that steamer were only the first in a long line of those who loved me unrequitedly. I myself have only ever once fallen in love, and it was with you, Koahu. I remained for the most part in our cabin, attending to Mother, who was wretchedly sick the whole voyage and pining for the plantation. I thought it prudent to take a protector, on the rare occasions I ventured out of the cabin, to shield me from the excesses of my most ardent admirers. I chose for the purpose Louis Meyerbeer, a man of business based in Lyon. A middle-aged father of seven, he was garrulous, shrewd, and unfailingly polite. He sat beside me at every meal and offered all kinds of useful counsel about what to do with my newfound liberty. He advised me to travel to Paris, the most extraordinary of cities, he claimed. There, I could cultivate my gifts and use my beauty to advantage, for an attractive woman of talent had better prospects in Paris, he said, than just about anywhere else in the world. I found Louis thoroughly persuasive—the young woman in me yearned to see something of life and society, and as I'd long since abandoned hope of ever finding you again, Koahu, or of finding a means to return to Oaeetee, I decided to take his advice.

Having arrived in Marseille, I found the port no less squalid than when I'd last passed through, as Joubert, more than two decades earlier. And so within days of our arrival in Marseille, with Louis as our chaperone, we traveled upriver by steamer to Lyon. We farewelled Louis there and continued by diligence to Paris, a journey of a little over a week. Although we'd bought tickets for inside the coach, several of our fellow passengers objected to traveling in such close proximity to us, and my mother and I were thus forced to travel on the roof, beside the driver. Everywhere I went, I found myself an object of curiosity. I could attract a crowd solely on the basis of my skin color and my freedom, for slavery had yet to be abolished in the kingdom.

It was no different in Paris, where I could silence entire rooms simply by entering them. The Paris we encountered was not the modern city of wide boulevards, train stations, and gas lighting but a dark, damp, gothic place. This was the old Paris, the Paris of the last King of the French, a more intimate Paris, where the poor lived above the rich, where barefoot children thronged at every corner, where rats roamed the streets, and where rivulets of sewage trickled down twisting alleys. Nights were lit by candles and the stars and moon above. Misery was on constant public display and opulence hid behind the high walls of *hôtels particuliers*. When it rained, the streets would flood and Parisians would retreat into the arcades to inspect the shop windows. On Sundays after church, all over the city, people would gather around a guitar to sing and dance. At such times I was happy, for I remembered how, at the Desire plantation, my people would gather around a banjo on Sunday afternoons, singing and dancing to their own songs, and I felt connected to them, even though so far away.

I was a beautiful young woman of sixteen, and I immediately found myself beset by men. The most gifted among them—ambitious dreamers and schemers, professional and amateur plotters, devourers of words and ideas—had grown up on tales of Napoleonic adventure only to enter, in their maturity, a society that discouraged novelty. Their nostalgia for imperial glories extended to a fashion for dark-skinned beauties. They did not wish to marry me, but considered me an ideal mistress to share among themselves. My admirers helped us find lodgings in a respectable rooming house, paid for my visits to couturiers, milliners, and bootmakers, and for lessons in deportment, singing, and acting. I made progress in every art but one: I could never learn to read or write. These were skills that did not cross from one body to the next. No matter how hard I tried, those black marks dancing upon the page never stilled long enough to allow me to interpret them.

When, four years after arriving in Paris, I first met Charles, we were both at the height of our powers. I was leading a life of ease as the mistress of Gaspard Tournachon, who later came to be known simply as Nadar, doubly famous as a photographer and hot air balloon enthusiast. He was among the most turbulent and magnetic men I'd ever known and thoroughly incapable of containing himself to just one woman. Other than this elegant flaw, he was unfailingly charming and respectful. He had, in a few short months, already begun to tire of me. In readiness, I was looking out for my next benefactor.

I was engaged in a drama troupe at a theater by the Porte Saint-Antoine, going by the stage name Berthe, in honor of my poor mother, who had never recovered from our emigration and had died of loneliness. I was playing a slave girl in a farce designed to amuse and be forgotten as soon as the curtain fell. Afterward, Gaspard came to see me backstage, with Charles trailing in his wake like a raincloud. The three of us went to a tavern on Rue des Lampes. I said little, half listening to the conversation of the men. I noticed Charles was trying to find a way to impress me. He had a high forehead, a weak chin, and eyes like two drops of coffee. What little handsomeness he had was spoiled somewhat by his woundedness, which betrayed itself in his eyes and lips. His face flickered with all kinds of grimaces and his gait was jerky. He spent lavishly on clothes of the finest quality: polished boots, black trousers, a blue workman's blouse that was the fashion at the time, bright, unstarched linen, a red cravat, rose-colored gloves, and a long scarlet boa in chenille, the kind working-class women like to wear. He refused to wear hats, which all men wore as a matter of course, and instead wore his dark hair long, with a faint mustache under his nose and a wisp of beard. To be beautiful and shocking at once was his aim, the aim of every dandy, and Charles was among the finest, most shocking dandies in Paris.

I noticed that he was looking at me with a fascination bordering on the uncouth. Eventually, after he and Gaspard had spoken for a time, he asked me where I was from.

"There's no point asking," said Gaspard, "she won't tell you. She never reveals anything about herself."

"A woman of intrigue," said Charles, a smile curling on his lips. The beam of his gaze narrowed on me. I felt it in my stomach. "But you're not from around here, are you? I can hear it in your accent."

"No," I conceded, "I'm not from around here."

"So where are you from?" he asked. I had never told a soul who I really was or where I was really from. It was better to let their imaginations run wild. "Come now," he cajoled, "why the secrecy? Or would you prefer that I guess? I'm very good at guessing such things. I'm never wrong."

"Is that so?" I asked, feigning interest. "Please, do try."

"Be careful what you wish for," said Gaspard. "Charles is quite the traveler."

"Is that right?" I said.

"Indeed," he continued, turning toward Charles. "You should tell her one of your splendid stories."

Charles wasn't listening. His attention was entirely fixed on me. "Let me guess."

"By all means," I replied.

"But if I guess, you must admit it." I smiled and nodded. He narrowed his eyes and studied me for some time. "There are a number of possibilities—Araby, Sumatra, Haiti, Pondicherry, even Mexico, at a pinch, although perhaps your hair is too wavy for a Mexican."

"I have known Mexicans with wavy hair," Gaspard chimed in.

"It is known to happen," said Charles, "but I don't think any of these is quite right. I think I know exactly where you are from."

"Do tell," I said.

"You're from Mauritius."

"Where's that?"

"It's an island off the east coast of Africa. Until recently it was called Isle de France." I smiled sadly at the memory of it—it was where I'd seen you last. I hadn't known its name had changed. "You give yourself away!" he exclaimed. "Are you impressed?"

"I could not be more impressed. How did you guess?"

"I was there recently," he said, "and as soon as I saw you I was reminded of that island colony. How long did you live there?"

"Oh, I left when I was very young. I remember almost nothing."

"Tell her that story you told the Hashish Smokers' Club at the Pimodan," said Gaspard. He turned to me and winked, as if what I was about to hear was a rare privilege.

"It is rather long," said Charles.

"Go ahead," I said, relieved that the attention had finally turned away from me. "If it is as good a story as Gaspard says, I would be delighted to hear it."

"Very well." He cleared his throat as if preparing to launch into a well-rehearsed discourse. "My stepfather, a military man, intended me to pursue a career in law or to follow him into the foreign service," he began. "But I was an unhappy child, overly prone to solitude and jealous of my mother's love for him. I read insatiably, devouring any and every book I found, but especially literature: novels, short stories, poetry, essays, everything. Around the age of twelve, I began to read a book by Hugo, which a schoolfriend had lent me. I think it was *The Last Day of a Condemned Man*; and then in quick succession

I read everything I could find of his: *Les Orientales, Notre-Dame de Paris, Lucrezia Borgia.* I read anything I could find that Hugo had written. And suddenly I decided that I wished to do nothing with my life other than write. Though I wasn't exactly sure *what* I wanted to write.

"I'm sure my dear father, were he still alive, would have been proud of my decision, but my stepfather was against it. You'll end up poor, bitter, and mad, he predicted. To cure me of my folly, he decided to send me to India. This plan had twin advantages: having gotten rid of me, he would secure the full attention of my beloved mother, for one thing, and for another it would toughen me up and make a man of me—or so he thought. He bought me a passage to Pondicherry on a ship captained by a friend of his, and organized a clerk's position with the colonial administration to be made available for me upon my arrival, despite my complete lack of training and aptitude for such work. I was still young enough to wish to please my stepfather, so I went along with his plans.

"I was seasick the entire way. During one particular storm, as we were rounding the Cape of Good Hope, I was so ill and miserable I contemplated throwing myself over the bulwark and into the roiling maelstrom of the sea. But at that instant I thought of my stepfather, and I realized that he would undoubtedly be gladdened by my death. And so I tightened my grip on the bulwark and survived the storm.

"When we arrived in Port Louis, it was the rainy season. The storm had left our ship damaged and in need of repairs, and I was told that our stay in Mauritius might last two or three weeks. At first I took a room in a decrepit inn near the waterside frequented only by Hindus, Cantonese, and Creoles, but the conditions were so hot and humid, and the state of the hotel so foul, that very soon I determined to go into the hills for respite. Leaving my luggage in the hotel, I packed some bread and wine and Lamartine's *Voyage en Orient*, and set off walking along a road that seemed to lead in the direction of the mountainous hinterland, which in that season is permanently covered in mist and cloud.

"It was raining. Before long I was drenched, as was my book, and I began to reconsider my foray into nature, for which, at any rate, I have no great affection. A short time later I was overtaken by a donkey pulling a cart, and was grateful when it stopped and the driver, sitting under a canvas tarpaulin that was keeping him dry enough to smoke a pipe, asked me what I was doing walking on this road alone in the rain. I was astonished to hear myself being addressed in a perfect, if antique, French, punctuated with old-fashioned pronunciations that would be ridiculed now in France, and tinged with a Provençal accent, even though the old man was tanned the same color as the Creoles. I told him I was marooned on the island and was bound for the mountains to escape the heat of the township. He told me he was traveling into the hills and invited me to ride alongside him.

"I boarded the cart and sat beside the old man. He had a haggard visage, so ancient he resembled one of those tortoises that are said to live seven thousand years. Long wisps of white hair crowned his otherwise bald head. From his jaw grew a long gray beard that reached his navel. The natives of Port Louis were dressed with greater civility than he: his ragged trousers were torn at the knee and his shirt was sleeveless. On his bare shoulder I noticed an old blue-green tattoo of an unblinking eye that had dulled over the years. For all his wildness, the old man spilled over with kindness and bonhomie. I will never forget the sparkle of his eyes. He told me his name was Roblet. He said he'd been born in Marseille. When I asked him his age he said he didn't know what year it was, but he remembered having been born in 1762. I told him it was 1841, and he was therefore seventy-nine years old. He shook his head in disbelief. 'So it has been half a century,' he said, more to himself than to me."

Thankfully Charles was too engrossed in his storytelling to notice the look of astonishment my face must have betrayed at this revelation, despite my prodigious capacity to mask my feelings. I said nothing, but never have I listened with such close attention to anything anyone has ever told me as I did to the remainder of his tale.

"At first we continued into the hills in near silence, my companion puffing on the sweet-smelling tobacco in the bowl of his pipe, which he told me was mixed with hashish. Eventually he asked me how it was I had been stranded on this island, and I told him my tale: I was nineteen years old and bound reluctantly for the French East Indies. I then asked Roblet how he had come to live on this tropical island.

"'My friend,' he said, 'my tale is scarcely believable and, if you allow me to tell it, you will no doubt consider me to have taken leave of my senses.' I denied this, promising him I was a most sympathetic audience. The old man paused and looked at me out of the corner of his eye for a moment, as if taking stock of me. Finally, as the donkey pulled the cart that carried us on the narrow and bumpy path into the mountains, he launched into his chronicle. 'Young man,' he said, 'you who seem so well read, so cultured, so thirsty for knowledge, you are perhaps familiar with the notion of metempsychosis?' I told him I believed it referred to the Oriental belief of the rebirth of the soul after death. He paused and looked somewhere in front of him, although nowhere in particular, as if in a profound meditation. 'Yes,' he said finally, 'that is the Oriental point of view. But it would appear there is another kind of metempsychosis that is not described by the Oriental sages. It is the metempsychosis of the living. I have come across it only once, and according to what you have just told me I now know it to be exactly fifty years ago. I am a surgeon by training, and in my youth I plied my trade in the merchant navy. The incident I am about to relate occurred while sailing the ocean the mapmakers call the Pacific, although it is anything but that. Our ship, the *Solide*, discovered a previously unknown island. The natives of this isle called it Oaeetee. They practiced a strange kind of metempsychosis of the living, if you will, which they called crossing. It is done simply enough, requiring only that two people gaze into each other's eyes for several minutes. While on this island, I looked into the eyes of a boy scarcely younger than you in an effort to discover this rare phenomenon for myself. Afterward, I had no memory of it, other than in my dreams—but what dreams! I should rather call them nightmares. Such were my terrors that I became a pariah on board any ship I sailed. But I was too far changed to return to France, so I decided instead to settle here and dedicate myself to the welfare of the natives and Creoles.'

"'If you cannot remember your metempsychosis,' I asked, 'how can you be sure it ever happened?'

"'Another sailor, a fellow named Joubert, had the same experience as me. Later, he tried to explain what had happened, but I denied him. It was Joubert who engraved this.' Roblet pointed to his tattoo of the eye on his shoulder. 'And while he did so, he told me what had happened. Of course,

I am a child of the Enlightenment, a man of science and reason, trusting only the measurable and verifiable. I thought the poor man mad and avoided him. Soon after, we parted company—right here on this very island. I was glad I would never have to see him again, or consider his tidings. It was only later, after many years of nightly torment, that what I had dismissed as Joubert's lunacy began to assume the dimensions of a truth that beggared belief. And so, for many years now, I have been looking out for Joubert whenever I go into Port Louis for supplies, trusting that he is looking for me. Twice, sometimes thrice a week, I check the lists of names on the registers of the ships. But as I am an old man now, so too must he be, and it is unlikely he is still working the ocean-going vessels. Still, I go to the shipping office and check the registers, waiting patiently.'

"'Waiting for what?' I asked.

"'For him to come find me.'

"Upon hearing the old man's words, an excited shiver ran along my spine, such as one feels when reading a fine novel— one need not believe it to feel it. I asked Roblet if he had ever attempted to make another such crossing, as he called it. 'Oh, I've tried,' he said, 'but I've never been able to convince anyone to look me in the eyes for more than just a brief moment.' I replied that his tale had piqued my curiosity, and told him if the notion was still of interest to him I would be willing to attempt it. Of course, I didn't lend his notions any credence, but all the same I considered myself in pursuit of a fine lark. Roblet seemed delighted by the prospect, clapping my shoulder as if we were suddenly the best of friends. He said his hut was but another hour or two up the road. If I was willing to continue the journey with him we might venture such an undertaking upon our arrival. 'It has none of the luxuries to which a Parisian gentleman would be accustomed, but it is clean, and the roof keeps me dry.'

"A short while thereafter, with the sun setting, we arrived at a crude thatch hut at the foot of the volcano that dominates the island. Here the donkey pulling the cart came to a stop. It was raining, and the verdant jungle that surrounded us was enveloped in a thick gray mist that hushed all but the patter of rain. The old doctor alighted from his seat and carried the boxes of supplies he had purchased in Port Louis into the hut, bidding that I follow him. He lit candles and kindled a fire while I found a place to sit on the earthen floor. I sat, legs crossed, with Roblet sitting likewise directly opposite. He poured two cups of rum and we drank a toast to metempsychosis. 'Are you ready?' he asked. I nodded, nervous with anticipation. He told me all I needed to do was look into his eyes, without looking away, while he would look into mine.

"And so we began. At the beginning, there was a sense of unease, such as one feels whenever one is looking directly into the eyes of another person, especially when that person is a stranger, or almost so. This did not last long, however, and soon enough I began to lose all awareness of my surroundings, so that those eyes, although at an arm's length from me, became the only things I could see. This was followed by a most pleasant sensation, as if the inside of my body was suddenly no longer flesh and blood but a freshly poured glass of champagne, full of bubbles ascending upward and out the top of my head and into the sky. This feeling continued to grow ever lighter and more pleasant, more so than any intoxicant I have known. Wine, hashish, laudanum, even opium do not compare."

Charles paused and looked down at his hands, which were lying clasped together on the table between us.

"When I next opened my eyes, I had been lying on the ground for some time. Roblet was also lying on the ground, not far from me, although I couldn't remember who he was at first. Nor could I remember where I was, or how I had arrived here. When I leaned over the stranger beside me to check if he was sleeping, I noticed that his eyes were open, and he was breathing rapidly, looking up at the ceiling above him with a look of terror in his eyes. 'What happened?' I asked, but instead of answering Roblet simply opened and closed his mouth as if wishing to say something but being unable to do so.

"Slowly, unsteadily, I rose to my feet. I looked out of the hut's solitary window. The world outside was a palette of pre-dawn blue, and a fine mist hovered delicately over the ground. My equilibrium had deserted me—I moved as if drunk. I swallowed some water from a jug. The old man was blinking and panting rapidly. Kneeling, I took him in my arms and laid him down on the nearby bed. I then slowly poured water from a cup into his mouth. As the fire had almost burned itself out, I took some wood from a pile beside the hearth, added it to the embers, stoked and blew on it, and soon enough it was blazing once more. I sat in a rocking chair before the fire and closed my eyes, waking a short time later, wet with sweat, haunted by the vague memory of a nightmare. Roblet was in the exact same position I had left him in, lying on his back on the mattress, staring at the ceiling, wide-eyed, blinking and panting heavily. His lips mouthed words I could not interpret. Once more I gave him water to drink and left the jug beside his bed. Satisfied I could do no more for him, I stepped outside into the morning. At a loss as to what to do, I began walking, taking the same trail that had led me there the previous day.

"I wandered in a daze along the path, descending through lush green hills toward Port Louis, meditating upon the events of the previous day and night. I could not say that I felt like a different person, but nor could I say I felt like the same person who had set off from Port Louis only a day earlier.

"As I plunged deeper and deeper into the woods, surrounded by towering trees, I felt as if everything I saw was with someone else's eyes. The forest I was traversing, for example, had seemed to me only the previous day nothing more than a tiresome cluster of verdant rot. Now it was transformed into a forest of symbols that watched over me familiarly, a kind of living temple whose pillars occasionally whispered some unintelligible word into my ear. Scents, colors, and sounds answered one another like distant echoes melding to form a dark and profound unity, vast as the night. By the time I returned to Port Louis several hours later, I understood what it was that had changed in me. I would not continue my voyage to India. Instead, I would return to Paris, and devote my life to poetry."

Charles's tale was at an end. "And so," I asked, trembling uncomprehendingly at the thought that I might have found you again, and yet straining to hide my excitement, "what do you make of the old man's story?"

"I think the old man was a lunatic, and for a time he charmed me into indulging his lunacy."

"You haven't noticed any changes in you since?"

"The only change I have noticed is indeed the same affliction about which Roblet complained: nightmares. They cause me to wake in the middle of the night, screaming with terror.

But who knows, perhaps my sea voyage caused this, or some mysterious tropical disease, or perhaps the old man himself cursed me with his affliction."

We left the tavern soon after, the three of us, and walked together for a while before Charles left us to return to his apartment on the Île Saint-Louis.

The next day I received an anonymous letter in which there was a poem praising my beauty. I had Gaspard read it out to me. "It could only be Charles," he said. I smiled. "The idea doesn't seem to displease you," he said. I smiled once more. "Are you in love with him?"

"I am incapable of being in love with any man."

"That's a relief. It is one thing to be loved by a poet—indeed it is a fine thing. But it is another thing altogether to be in love with one. If you were in love with him I would forbid you to ever see him again. But if he is in love with you, go to him, my dear, with my blessing."

And so, after some fifty years, we had found each other again, and a new chapter began in our story: seventeen years of life together. In those days, Charles had money, having come into half of his deceased father's estate when he reached his majority. He liked to spend it extravagantly. His fortune was one of those inconvenient sums, somewhere between being large enough to seem inexhaustible to a young man and small enough to worry his elders it would soon be exhausted. He spent impulsively, mostly on art, antiques, and, especially, on me. I was his exotic bird, his creature of display, his most precious jewel. While he was courting me, he set me up in my own apartment, on the Île Saint-Louis. It was a short walk from the Hôtel Pimodan, where he lived, a modest seventeenth-century *hôtel particulier* on the Quai d'Anjou that had been transformed into apartments. It overlooked the river and the Right Bank. A hive of young dandies and wealthy eccentrics resided there. Charles rented a three-room apartment on the top floor, and he began to fill it with rare objects, dubious antiques, and paintings bigger than could possibly fit into his quarters. Eventually, his stepfather was forced to intervene to stop the dissipation of the inheritance. What was left of it was put in trust, and Charles was paid a modest monthly stipend. To anyone else, it would have been more than enough. But modesty was inconceivable to him. The thought of earning money by conventional means—as, one by one, most of his friends began to do—never so much as crossed his mind. He already had a profession: writing, translating, and reading.

To save money, I moved in with Charles. There is nothing more fatal to passion than when two lovers chain themselves together. Constrained by the modesty of his allowance, he began to sell off the objects he had accumulated so wantonly, only to discover that much of it was worthless. Soon enough it became apparent that he could no longer keep up the rent of the Pimodan apartment. We moved out and into another apartment.

Between his stipend, funds his mother sent in reluctant response to his almost-daily letters begging for money, the money my gentlemen admirers gave me, and the credit he accumulated without the slightest intention of repaying, we lived for the next several years constantly on the move from one shabby furnished room to the next. Charles was always dreaming up a new endeavor to make him rich but in practice he had as little talent for making money as for saving it. He would spend it on clothes, wine, hashish, laudanum, and, above all, books, the greatest of his vices.

Having lost you once already, I did not want to lose you a second time. The memory of how Roblet had reacted when I'd told him about his crossing, all those years ago on the ship, still burned inside me. I resolved to be gentle with Charles, not to push him away with what I knew by foisting it upon him, but to lead him gently to the knowledge I wanted to share. This I did by telling him stories when he woke at night, consumed by his habitual horrors. He loved my stories. Among the many nicknames he devised for me—his Black Venus, his black swan, his giantess, his *grande taciturne*—he sometimes called me his Scheherazade. He said I was the most gifted storyteller he'd ever known, and that had I been born a man or an heiress I would have made a fine writer. I wasn't interested in books I couldn't read. I was secretive and prized discretion; for me writing was a kind of illness, and writers contemptible and untrustworthy, for they did not know how to keep their stories to themselves.

My storytelling was a nocturnal activity intended to comfort and console as well as to educate. When he woke screaming and wet with sweat, I would ask Charles what he'd dreamed and I played the part of the interpreter. In this way over the years I was able to tell him about Koahu and Roblet, and Alula and Joubert. For a long time, I avoided mentioning that I was Alula and Joubert, and he Koahu and Roblet. I wanted the idea to be born in him. He listened gratefully to my stories—they were a kind of balm for him, soothing his frayed nerves. But he never took them seriously. He considered them brilliant improvisations, exotic fancies, and nothing more. As for his own story about Roblet, he stopped telling it. Rather, inspired by me, he began improvising stories of his own. In these fabricated tales, he had not returned to France from Mauritius at the earliest opportunity, but had continued to roam the Orient. He invented stories about life at sea, the tropics, travel, exile, and adventure, tales designed to impress the impressionable salons of Paris, many of whose guests had never strayed far from the capital. He lied with relish about his fictional journeys in India, in Ceylon and Sumatra and China, Tahiti and the Sandwich Islands, claiming to have traveled for years and suffered all manner of adventures and deprivations. There was always an enthusiastic gallery for his improvisations, and his audiences hungrily swallowed every preposterous word. Traces of my stories seeped their way into his poems too—an albatross, a tamarind tree, a storm-tossed sea—but how could I hold any of this against him? I saw him as a tragic figure: a man who had forgotten his past and, in forgetting it, had become lost in it. This helped me forgive him his flaws: his lies, his vanities, his inconstancies, his cunning, his rages, and his self-absorption.

Seventeen years passed in this way, seventeen years of making do, moving, fighting, reconciling, separating, reuniting, over and again, never the same and yet always the same. Our life together stumbled on, season after season, year after year, ever more nomadic and desperate. One by one Charles's dreams of literary fame were extinguished—and every defeat sharpened the blade of his bitterness. He made enemies everywhere he went. His poems sold poorly; the one book he ever published was pulped; his journalism paid pittances; his ideas for plays and novels never amounted to anything more than notes scrawled in a notebook. In the meantime, we moved from furnished room to furnished room, boarding house to boarding house—each one slightly more rancid than its predecessor—ever watchful for the next place to stay once the proprietor of our current lodgings began to hound us for our arrears. Every few weeks or months, we found ourselves somewhere else, under another name or another combination of our old names, in perpetual motion, trying to keep a step ahead of creditors and bailiffs, sinking deeper and deeper into the mire of debt and want.

While we were waging our private battles, Paris was changing around us. The old Paris of our youth was being dismantled brick by brick and stone by stone, with pickaxes wielded by swarthy southern workers. The city became a strange and unwelcoming carnival of novelties. Even night was vanquished, as gas lamps were installed along every boulevard and street and the new city of light sparkled as seductively after dark as it did during the day.

Our love was marked by stories, but in time Charles wearied of my tales. Rather than consoling him, they began to exasperate him. Eventually, if he woke in panic in the middle of the night and I tried to soothe him, he would become irritated. Certain subjects, even certain words, became forbidden: island, ship, soul, crossing. At first, out of fear of losing him, I obeyed his will, but later, when I realized that he was already lost to me, I shed my reserve. I became more strident: you are Koahu and I am Alula, I told him time and again, let me prove it to you. When I offered to cross with him, he dismissed me like a parent dismisses a child's inventions. He responded to my provocations with increasingly virulent contempt, his fury heightened by the pox, from which we both suffered, and the great quantities of laudanum he drank for the pain.

Then there were the separations. At first, he would disappear for a few days; later he would go for weeks or months. He took to moving to new lodgings without telling me where he was going. I would seek him out and find him, asking his friends where he was, looking into his favorite coffee shops and taverns, or simply scouring the streets. I couldn't help but remain loyal to him, even in the face of his utter rejection. I felt responsible for him, as if I were his guardian.

So it was fitting that it should be one of my stories that undid us. It occurred on one of those penniless nights when he had not drunk any wine or laudanum, and his temper was greatly frayed. A nightmare woke him. I asked what he had dreamed. He did not wish to tell me. I asked him again and he told me to be silent. "Did you dream of an island?" I asked.

He turned to me with his eyes narrowed hatefully and said, "Say the word again and I shall make you regret it."

"Did you dream of a sailing ship?" For the first time since I had known him, he slapped me. The impact of the slap spun my head, but I would not be quelled. "Did you dream of an island?" He slapped me again. "Did you dream of looking into another man's eyes?" Slap. "Did you dream of a sailing ship?" By now, in a frenzy, Charles took his belt from his trousers and began flailing me as I cowered before him, crouched on the ground, my arms wrapped around my head. But I would not be stopped. He tore the dress from my back and whipped me, cursing me as he did so, calling me a slave. By the time he was done, as warm blood trickled from the welts on my back, Charles collapsed on the divan. I asked him one more time about his dream, but he was spent. It was the first and only time he ever beat me. I rose from the ground and, staggering into the next room, fell onto the bed and fainted. By the time I awoke the next morning he was gone, and this time I did not seek him out.

I found myself bereft, a black woman alone in Paris, no longer in the first bloom of youth, nor even the second. I began working in a hotel in La Chapelle where rooms were let by the hour. There I met a Haitian man who believed he was my brother. I told him he couldn't be my brother, but he insisted he was, and that he loved me with a fraternal love, and wanted to take care of me. He was a ragpicker and invited me to live with him here in Batignolles. Soon after I moved here, Charles went to Brussels, fleeing his creditors and censors and enemies. He wrote to me once. He told me about his plans to publish his banned poems and smuggle them into France. But . of course nothing ever came of it.

Now, I said to Mademoiselle Édmonde and Mademoiselle Adélaïde, my health is failing. I'm partially paralyzed on the left side of my body. The eyesight in my left eye is dimming. I have no clients, and depend entirely on my brother. Otherwise I lie here on this mattress, remembering the past, resigned to never crossing again, resigned to never returning to the island, resigned to whatever end fate has in store for me.

At last my tale was told. By now it was quite dark, the only light in the room that of an oil lamp that burned on a low table between us. The two young ladies stirred from the reverie in which they had spent the afternoon, thanked me for telling my story, and stood to leave. Mademoiselle Adélaïde stoked the embers in the stove and added several lumps of charcoal. Mademoiselle Édmonde opened her purse and left several hundred-franc notes beside the lamp, parrying my meek pro-testations. I thanked them, and apologized for not being able to see them out. They turned to leave, but Mademoiselle Adé-laïde hesitated. She turned back toward me and observed me for an instant. She approached the mattress and sat down on its edge, very near me. She leaned forward and I felt her eyes studying my face, almost drinking it. She raised a hand and a finger lightly traced the outlines of my nose, my cheeks, my lips. Mademoiselle Édmonde, standing behind her, was half turned away, motionless. Mademoiselle Adélaïde leaned for-ward slowly until her lips met mine, and kissed me languidly and tenderly. "You are still a beautiful woman," she whispered, "a very beautiful woman." Then she straightened and returned to her companion's side. They opened the door and, with a bustle of silken skirts, were gone.

Several days later, there was another knock on the door. It was Mademoiselle Édmonde's coachman. He delivered a sealed envelope, but I told him I could not read. He opened it and read it aloud: it was an invitation requesting the pleasure of my company at four o'clock the following afternoon at an address in the Lorette neighborhood. A coach would be sent to take me there and return me afterward. It was signed Ma-demoiselle Édmonde de Bressy.

The following day I arrived in front of a *hôtel particulier*. The coachman assisted me from the buggy and set me in a chair on wheels, which, with the help of a butler, was carried through the doorway and into an entrance hall decorated and furnished in a splendor I had not seen since my youth. I waited in silence, studying my surrounds. Every surface was exquisitely decorated. Every wall bore a work of art. Every object sparkled. Mademoiselle Édmonde and Mademoiselle Adélaïde appeared shortly after, walking side by side, the silks of their dresses whispering conspiratorially as they approached. As on the previous occasion, Mademoiselle Édmonde's face was veiled. After the usual exchange of formalities, they asked that I join them on a tour of the residence.

With Mademoiselle Adélaïde pushing the chair, we set off to inspect the ground floor of the building, room after room, each one decorated in its own style, each as richly ornamented as its predecessor. As we proceeded, Mademoiselle Édmonde described what it was we were seeing, the rooms on the levels above us and what they contained, as well as the other properties she owned, and a brief description of them. By the time the tour was over we had made a full circle—the residence was built around a courtyard in its center—without having seen the same room twice. I had been given the description of a fortune that included several more buildings like this one, in Paris and in the provinces. Mademoiselle Édmonde's mother had died in childbirth; her father had inherited a banking fortune and added to it railway interests. He had died only the previous year. There were no other heirs. The fortune was large enough that three men dedicated their lives to overseeing it, leaving Mademoiselle Édmonde free to live as she pleased.

"Madame Jeanne," she said, "you are no doubt curious as to why we invited you to visit, and why I am telling you about my affairs in such detail. Mademoiselle Adélaïde and I were greatly touched by the story you told us last time we met. In fact, it is fair to say we have spoken of little else since. We would like to make a proposal to you, but in order to do so there is something you ought to see first."

She put her hands to her veil and lifted it. When the countenance behind was at last revealed, I was frightened by what

I saw. Her face was grotesquely disfigured. No sooner had I seen it than she once again lowered the veil. "You can see," she continued, "why I keep it concealed. It is the result of an accident involving a candle in my bedroom when I was a child. There have been many times when I wish I had been altogether consumed by that fire, but had that happened I would never have had the joy of meeting Adélaïde." The two women turned to each other and clasped hands. "This is not a decision that we have undertaken lightly. The past week has been spent, for the most part, in earnest discussion. But by now we are of a common mind, and both of us speak to you today as one. It has always been a dream, nay, an obsession of mine to imagine what it would be like to be in another body, above all in another face. This explains my devotion to painting and literature. Character is destiny, according to Shakespeare. And yet our bodies, above all our faces, are so bound up with how others perceive us, one might say that, especially for a woman, they are just as powerful an influence over our destinies. Our faces influence the perceptions others hold of us, and those perceptions influence, in turn, our character. Wealth shapes our lives too, as does social position. But while character is malleable, and one's wealth and social position can change for good or ill, one's body is a fait accompli. One must accept its limitations, one must age with it, one cannot exchange it for another. Not, at least, under normal circumstances.

"Madame Jeanne, the beauties of your body have been immortalized in verse and in paintings. You have been a muse to great works of art. Men who knew you still dream of you today. Though no longer the body it once was, it is a desirable body all the same, a jewel whose tarnish only adds to its rarity. Your face is still the face of a great beauty, one who has lived a singular life. My proposal is simple. Perhaps you have guessed it already. I would like to offer you my body, and half of my fortune, in exchange for yours. If I had a choice, I would no doubt choose a younger body, a healthier body, but I don't have a choice. A crossing into your body is the only crossing I will ever be able to make. I would like to take that chance, even if it means I will not live as long. I am not in love with life itself. I don't desire to live a long life. I would rather live a life of sensuality and pleasure. I would gladly give up this body and half the fortune it was born into to be kissed by Mademoiselle Adélaïde the way she kissed you last week, even if it is only for a few short years."

I could scarcely believe my ears. "You would like to cross with me?"

"Yes. On one condition. I do not wish it to be a blind crossing. I must be able to remember my previous body, and bring across with me all my memories. I must be able to remember who I am, who we are, after the crossing. Can you promise me that?"

I assured her that such a crossing was indeed possible, even when crossing for the first time.

By the time the coach left, several hours later, it was loaded with luggage, and there were two women in the carriage: Madame Jeanne and Mademoiselle Adélaïde.

☞ *{31}*

Édmonde de Bressy

Born 1845
First crossing 1864
Second crossing 1900
Died 1900

"Do you believe in metempsychosis?"

It was mid-afternoon on a bright day in late March 1900, and I was in the parlor car of Union Pacific's *Overland Limited*, hurtling across the American Midwest. Through the window, a snow-dusted prairie sparkled under a wintry noonday sun. I was lost in a daydream, seated in a leather armchair with a book in my lap, selected at random from the car's library shelf, when I heard those words repeated in French in a deep, beguiling voice:

"Madame, do you believe in metempsychosis?"

I looked up and beheld a handsome, olive-skinned man seated in the armchair opposite mine, sporting a thick walrus mustache for which he was much too young, wearing a purple smoking jacket and a carmine turban, gazing at me intently with eyes of Japanese lacquer. It was odd, I thought, that he should address me thus in French.

"I beg your pardon?" I said.

"Metempsychosis—do you believe in the existence of such a thing?"

"The transmigration of souls after death? Young man, I'm quite sure it is none of your business."

"On the contrary, it is more than my business, it is my living! Behold, my name is Hippolyte Balthazar," he said, extending his hand across the aisle of the carriage and holding it there a few seconds until I could not help but shake it. "Delighted to make your acquaintance."

"Madame Édmonde Duchesne de Bressy," I said, and instantly regretted it.

"I am an Orientalist," he said.

"What is that?"

"Why, a scholar of the Oriental races! I have an especial interest in the question of metempsychosis, and have just completed a lecture tour of the United States and Canada, during which I spoke at length on the subject." A part of me had taken an instant dislike to Monsieur Balthazar. Another was already in his thrall. My natural instinct was to stand and leave the buffet–library car at once, but in the confinement of journeys by rail or sea it is necessary to be diplomatic with one's fellow passengers. It is no small inconvenience to avoid a passenger for the entirety of a long voyage all because of a slight or a cross word. "Madame de Bressy," he continued, "as a student of the Oriental arts of meditation I have become adept at the perception of aura. Do you believe in such a thing, madame?"

"Monsieur, you keep asking me questions on subjects to which I have never given a moment's thought."

He leaped out of his chair and came to sit beside mine. "Madame," he said, "I noticed your aura at once. Behold! It is a most remarkable aura, perhaps the most remarkable aura I have ever come across, more so even than that of President William McKinley, with whom I dined only a few months ago, and who really has a most magnificent aura." And so he continued in this way for some time longer, and offered to read my aura—at no charge, of course—an offer that I refused with more firmness than politeness. But he continued all the same, despite my entreaties, until I determined to leave the buffet–library car, at which time, just as I was leaning forward to stand, he said something that arrested me.

"Madame," he said, "there is a way out of the hall of mirrors in which you are imprisoned."

I sat in that chair for some time looking at the young man, lost for words, before I lifted my veil and said to him, very slowly and low enough so that only he could hear: "Monsieur Balthazar, as you can clearly see, mirrors are of no use to me. If you speak to me again, I will see to it that you are ejected from this train." I stood and, simulating an unhurried determination, walked off in the direction of my compartment, where I spent an agitated day and a restless night. *A way out of the hall of mirrors* . . . The phrase ricocheted in my mind.

I did not venture from my compartment the following morning, but had breakfast delivered to me. After breakfast, a steward came to the door holding a silver bucket, inside of which were a bottle of champagne and a champagne glass.

"Compliments of Monsieur Balthazar, who requests the pleasure of your company in the dining car for luncheon."

I sent the steward away with the unopened bottle and the glass, but all the same, all morning I hesitated about accepting Balthazar's invitation. By midday my resistance was beginning to wilt. This strange young man was possessed of an equally strange power, compelling me to do things I did not wish to do. At one o'clock, I made my way to the dining car. I found Balthazar sitting alone at a table for two, a contented little smile playing on his full lips.

"Behold!" he exclaimed, beaming with pleasure. He stood to greet me, kissed my hand, and helped me into my seat before returning to his. "I'm honored you decided to take up my invitation, madame."

"My curiosity got the better of me. You seem to be able to make me do things no one else can. How is that?"

"In the course of my studies, I learned the art of mesmerism from a Sufi dervish in Cairo. I am an expert in the technique, madame. I have hypnotized the great and the good across the world, not to mention certain members of Europe's most illustrious royal households."

"I see." It was impossible not to be charmed by the man. "And so is it with mesmerism that you make people do what they don't want to do?"

"No mesmerist is capable of such a thing, madame. It is not the mesmerist who mesmerizes, it is his subject who wishes to be mesmerized."

"Are you saying I wanted to come to dinner all along?"

"Of course you wanted to come. You said it yourself. Curiosity got the better of you. Perhaps other urges too, which are more deeply buried within you. We are all conflicted creatures. There are things we want that we don't want to want. Yet we want them all the same."

"And what do I want from you?"

"At a guess, solace. It's what most people want."

"If I am like most people, why take a particular interest in me?"

"You are not like most people. On the contrary, madame," he said, "you are most interesting. You have a unique presence. You conduct yourself with the dignity and grace of an ancient soul."

"And I suppose you consider yourself an expert on the matter?"

"Most assuredly! I have devoted my career to it. I have made it my life's work."

I admit I was more than a little amused that so young a man could refer to his life's work. Despite my veil, I felt more than usually exposed by the candlepower of his gaze. "So let me ask you this," I finally ventured, "*is* there such a thing?"

"As a soul? Most decidedly."

"The work of a certain Englishman concludes against it."

"Monsieur Darwin? I completely concur with all his ideas. The man is a genius. But on the subject of the soul he has nothing to say."

"What do *you* have to say about it?"

He stroked his walrus mustache for a moment as he considered his reply. "I myself have nothing to add to the body of knowledge that already exists. But I concur with the Persian poet who said, *A soul is more than the sum of intellect and emotions, more than the sum of experiences, though it runs like veins of brilliant metal through all three.*" He leaned forward, holding up an index finger for emphasis. "*It is an inner faculty that recognizes the animating mysteries of the world because it is made of the same substance.*"

And so Balthazar began to tell me about his life, which, though young, overflowed with event and variety. It was a pleasure to listen to his tales, following each other like brightly painted carousel horses. He told stories with all the skill of a coffee-house raconteur. His brief but complicated existence could be summarized thus: he was the son of a Hungarian duchess, a famous beauty who had fallen in love with an Armenian maritime painter. His mother died giving birth, when Balthazar was eight. In his childhood he had been given, in his words, the finest education possible, consisting of Sufi poetry, the *Arabian Nights*, the writings of the ancient Greeks, and the algebra of the great Muslim mathematicians. He was a polymath: right now, he said, he was writing the music to a ballet that would represent the synthesis of all his teachings. He spoke seven languages: French, Russian, Magyar, English, Italian, Armenian, and Ancient Greek. He had learned hypnotism and mesmerism at the hands of French neurologists and Oriental mystics and claimed to be a master of the yogic and tantric arts. It was impossible to tell if he was an ingenious fraud or if he truly believed his preposterous claims.

And now, said Balthazar, he was returning to Europe, and then to Alexandria, traveling up the Nile to Khartoum, where he would attend the marriage of his sister to an Ethiopian prince. After that, he declared, he intended to settle in Paris, where he was determined to establish himself as a mesmerist. It was his life's work, he said, to help others.

"And how may I assist you, madame?" he asked, leaning forward with his great brown eyes wide open, chewing on candied chestnut pudding.

"Give me peace," I said, once again finding myself ceding to unknown desires I could not control. "Give me consolation. Take away this burden I carry within me, I beseech you."

"What is the nature of this burden?"

"Its name is heartbreak."

That evening, I dined with my traveling companion, Lucien, who had a cabin of his own. It was a bittersweet affair for me because I suspected it would be the last time I would see him, and I was very fond of him indeed.

After breakfasting alone in my compartment the following morning, there was a knock at my door. It was Balthazar. He entered my compartment with a smile, locked the door, and sat in the armchair. I was already lying on the narrow bed, sitting up on a pile of cushions.

"Shall we begin?" he asked after we had exchanged pleasantries. I nodded. "By the time I count backward from ten to one," he said, "you will be asleep. Then, when I ask you a question, you will open your eyes and look into mine. You will answer it as honestly as you can." He counted slowly, looking me directly in the eyes. When he had finished counting, he asked, with the softest imaginable voice, "Tell me about the happiest day of your life."

"The happiest day of my life was the twenty-second of March, 1881, almost nineteen years ago to the day. It was the day I was finally able to return home."

"And where is home?"

"The island of Oaeetee. It is a small island in the eastern Pacific Ocean, between the Sandwich Islands and the Marquesas archipelago."

"This is where you were born?"

"In a manner of speaking, yes."

"And you left there when you were young?"

"I did, not realizing how long it would take to return home."

"How long did it take you?"

"Lifetimes."

Balthazar hesitated. "How many lifetimes?"

"I am now at the end of my fifth."

He leaned back. "We are not playing a parlor game, Madame Édmonde," he said with a look of poorly concealed annoyance. "Mesmerism is not something to be undertaken lightly or frivolously."

"I am not being frivolous," I replied. "I am utterly sincere. It took me ninety years to return to my island."

He narrowed his brown eyes, cocked his head sideways, and clicked his tongue, lost in thought. "What is this strangeness? Yesterday you told me you didn't believe in metempsychosis."

"Metempsychosis is the transmigration of souls after death. As such, what I am talking about is not metempsychosis, because there is no death. I call it 'crossing.'"

He considered what I'd said a moment before his face lit up with epiphanic joy. He knelt by my side and took my hands in his. "Behold!" he said. "I was certain that your soul is uncommon—and this is the proof!" He kissed my fingers rapturously. "Please, madame, do me the honor of telling me about your lifetimes. All of them."

I knew I was within striking distance of my prey. But I also knew that outwitting the trickster would not be easy. I would need to lull him into dismantling his defenses, and there is no better way to lull a professional charlatan than with feigned guilelessness. "Very well," I said. "But the story will take all day to tell, and I will brook no interruptions." I began at the beginning, with Alula and Koahu.

On the twenty-second of March of the year 1881, standing on the deck of the *Equator*, a trading schooner that plied the waters between Tahiti, the Marquesas Islands, and Oaeetee, I truly believed my long journey of several lifetimes was finally nearing its end. For this was the day I returned to the place I'd abandoned so thoughtlessly, a place to which I'd dreamed of returning ever since. The veil I wore in public concealed more than a disfigured face—it hid more than a century of memories. At thirty-six years old and still unmarried, I was considered an old maid. Thankfully, my considerable fortune shielded me from ostracism, for the merest whiff of a fortune can magically transform a defect into an idiosyncrasy and impudence into eccentricity. But money does not soothe every distress.

Hours before the lookout's call of *Land ahoy*, I had sensed signs of our approach all around: I recognized the shape of the clouds and the scent of the winds. The night stars, the breezes, the way waves played on the water's surface—all of these were signs to me that my return was nigh. I recognized those carmine-red flying fish, the ones with two sets of fins that leap out of and into the water with the simple joy of being alive. When the island came into view at last, no more than a blue smudge on the horizon, my heart began to beat wildly. When I caught sight of terns up ahead, diving repeatedly into the sea in search of food, it almost leaped out of its cavity altogether. The more we neared the island the more of its forms I recognized: the obelisk-shaped rock at the southern tip called the Black Crane, the countless forested valleys and hills, the waterfall known as the Silver Tear, the belltower-shaped pilasters, and, looming above it all, the mountains.

My joy was mixed with trepidation, for along the way I had seen enough of other islands to fear the worst for my own, and its people. I had learned that the island was ruled by a king called Mehevi, but it was the French who had made him king, and he was a king in name only. The island had, for almost half of my absence, been a part of the French empire.

As the ship moored at a jetty extending from the same beach where I had left the island all those years ago, I was grateful to be wearing a veil, for I did not wish anyone else to guess at the tears that fell behind it.

Upon disembarking, I was immediately mobbed by a throng of young children and infants. Evidently these children were unused to the sight of a woman in a black riding habit, top hat, and veil. I cursed myself that I had not thought to pack toffees to offer them. An official brushed the children aside and ushered me into the customs building, one of several dockside tin sheds. Inside, it was intolerably hot. The official sat himself behind a rickety desk and introduced himself as Lieutenant Perrault. Perspiring profusely, he hunched over a large ledger, murmuring the words he scrawled under his breath as he wrote. I was questioned on my background and my intentions. I replied, truthfully, that I was a wealthy woman dedicated to the instruction of native children, and that I intended to establish a school. This gave him a start. He sat back as if he had just been given troubling news. As a frown of disapproval congealed on his forehead, I took from my purse several letters of introduction from important personages in the colony of New Caledonia, recommending me to King Mehevi and the island's Resident-General. The official, with the immaculate instinct of self-preservation universal among colonial officers, refused them, instead advising me to take a room at the only hotel on the island, the Hôtel Hibiscus, to await further instructions. In the meantime, he said, I was to stay within the confines of Louisville under all circumstances. "This is no place for an unmarried woman," he added, "of any age or description."

I stepped out of the customs building, crossed a wide expanse of vacant land, and walked into Louisville, followed by a Chinese porter carting my luggage on a trolley. To call Louisville a town would be an embellishment. In 1881, it was barely a village, a forlorn cluster of tin sheds and whitewashed wooden cottages linked by dirt tracks, better described by that vague term, "settlement," although the most settled aspect of the scene was the fine, dry-season dust that covered everything. Behind Louisville rose the hill where I had first seen Marchand's ship, ninety years before. Behind the hill, clad in violet shade, were the mountains.

Louisville boasted a population of fewer than a hundred foreigners, most of whom were French—soldiers, gendarmes, functionaries, priests, merchants, a handful of wives, a dozen children, a couple of beachcombers, and some farmers. Among them were smatterings of Englishmen, Germans, and Americans who monopolized the few shops and businesses, as well as some Chinese laborers and merchants. As for the islanders themselves, they'd converted to Christianity and were settled in a mission near the beach outside of Louisville.

I began walking down a main street flanked by modest commercial buildings: a general store, a post office, a tavern, and a bank, next to which was the Hibiscus. Behind the hotel was a school and a little mudbrick church with a steeple. Further up the hill stood residences with whitewashed timber walls, pitched pandanus roofs, and dusty little gardens bordered by white picket fences. The Hibiscus itself was an unassuming two-storied inn, whose upstairs rooms were rented.

That night, I was kept awake not just by a flood of remembrances of my youth, but also by the noises from the corridor and neighboring rooms, as men trudged up and down the stairs to pay their respects, judging by the noises emanating through the walls, to women who occupied the adjacent rooms. Having finally fallen asleep as the eastern sky lightened, I was woken only two or three hours later by a heavy knock at the door. It was Lieutenant Perrault delivering a letter bearing the letterhead of His Majesty Mehevi, King of Oaeetee. Mehevi was inviting me to the Royal Palace that very afternoon. The lieutenant offered to accompany me there.

That morning, I wandered the streets of Louisville, a promenade that did not last more than a quarter-hour before I had walked every path. After luncheon, Perrault took me to the Royal Palace in a horse-drawn buggy. I asked him where all the islanders were, as there were few to be seen in the street. He replied that natives were permitted in Louisville by permission, and that after sunset a strict curfew was enforced. Other than the King and his retinue in the palace, they were not permitted to stay overnight in Louisville. We passed a modest church flanked by a hut that doubled as a presbytery and a school for a dozen European children. The Oaeetian children, Perrault told me, attended the mission school. I asked if I could visit the mission. He replied that it was outside the confines of the town, and thus off-limits to me without the King's consent.

Located on a hill overlooking Louisville, the palace was hardly palatial. It was, rather, a two-storied wooden structure, not much larger than the Hibiscus, also whitewashed, and, as its only sign of distinction, was surrounded by columns on all sides. It occupied the summit of a hill that overlooked the settlement and a stately garden with a neatly trimmed lawn, adorned with breadfruit trees, mimosas, guava trees, and delicate touch-me-nots. Within a watchful distance of the palace, slightly higher up the hill, was another building in the same vein, more modestly proportioned and featuring columns only on the front facade. This was the Residence-General, where lived the chief representative of the French empire.

We alighted from the buggy. A servant opened the grand carved entrance doors that led inside the palace, and we were guided to an antechamber. Once I had taken a seat, Lieutenant Perrault requested that I remove my veil out of respect for His Royal Majesty. I refused.

"The King will consider it an impertinence," said Perrault without further protest, and left.

There were half a dozen islander people with me in that antechamber, waiting to petition the King. Presently Perrault reappeared and invited me into the Royal Hall. I pointed to the petitioners who had been waiting longer than I, but the lieutenant shook his head. "They're used to waiting," he said. The teak doors opened and I followed him into a long, white, high-ceilinged room with wide, open windows, through which the plants of the palace garden extended their tendrils. At the end of this great hall sat three men, the one in the middle seated higher than those at his sides. I approached them, the silks of my dress rustling and the leather soles of my shoes clacking ostentatiously on the parquetry.

The man sitting in the middle seat was King Mehevi. His Royal Majesty's military uniform, stiff with gold lace and embroidery, decorated a great and powerful chest, and where his heart beat all kinds of silks, ribbons, and medals were proudly arrayed. His neck seemed broader than his head, while his shaven crown was concealed by a wide *chapeau-bras*, waving with peacock plumes. A dark ribbon of tattoos stretched across his face, in line with his eyes, which shone all the whiter in their frame of blue ink. The throne he sat in was burnished with silver and gold and carved with biblical scenes. On Mehevi's right-hand side was Colonel Mirabelle, the Resident-General, sporting gray mutton-chops and dressed in the iridescent uniform of a senior officer of the French Navy. On the King's left-hand side was a bald, round-shouldered man in a clerical collar, a long black cassock, and a purple skullcap. Perrault announced him as the Archbishop of Oaeetee, Monsignor Fabien.

Colonel Mirabelle asked why I had come to the island. I described at length my vocation to spread the gospel among the pagan natives. Monsignor Fabien asked what experience I had in education. I described my years spent teaching the native children of New Caledonia. Colonel Mirabelle asked how I had come to be in New Caledonia. I replied that, though not a radical, I had once become embroiled in the Commune, but that my time as an exiled convict had impressed upon me that only Christ's salvation can bring true happiness. I held out my letters of recommendation, which were taken, at a sign from the King, by Lieutenant Perrault, who was standing by my side. Monsignor Fabien asked if I was aware of the activities of the missionaries, and I replied that their mission was renowned, and that I did not wish to encroach on their work but rather teach those children still living in a state of savagery.

Colonel Mirabelle asked me how I intended, as a woman, to communicate with heathens who had yet to repudiate their primitive language, manners, and customs and whom even the most dedicated of Christ's servants had been unable to bring into the bosom of civilization. I replied that I had learned to speak the islander tongue in New Caledonia, and had also become acquainted with native manners and customs. At this point, King Mehevi, who for all this time had said nothing, merely observing and listening to the conversation, emitted a sort of contemptuous snort. Colonel Mirabelle asked how I would finance my work, and I replied that I was the heiress to a substantial fortune and intended to spend it on spreading the message of Christ to the remotest corners of the world.

At length the questions came to an end and both the Resident-General and the archbishop fell silent. King Mehevi still had not said a word. Finally he spoke, in as mellifluous and charming a voice as I have ever heard, in as pure a French as was spoken in any Parisian salon: "Madame, why do you wear a veil before the King? Were you not informed that it is forbidden?"

"Your Majesty," I replied, "my veil is not intended to slight you but to protect you."

"How so?"

"It masks a deformity best left unseen."

"Surely I am the best judge of what I should see or not see."

"In all other matters I would agree with you, Your Majesty."

"In that case, remove that thing at once."

"Very well, Your Majesty." I lifted my veil and watched the faces of the Resident-General and the archbishop crease with disgust. The face of the King, on the other hand, did not change. He watched me from above, on his throne, with an inscrutable expression. Then, from the depths of his magnificent throat, I heard a chuckle rise. It grew louder, transformed into a cruel laugh, an open, extravagant derision that did not stop as most laughs do but continued to echo throughout the halls of the palace and into the gardens outside. He turned to his fellows as if expecting them to join in the revelry, and, sure enough, they picked up on the cue and also began to laugh, hesitantly at first but, before long, heartily. When the laughter had died down at last, the King's expression resumed its customary coolness.

"Lower your veil, madame," said Colonel Mirabelle. "And pray keep it lowered in our presence in the future."

Mehevi leaned over to whisper something to Colonel Mirabelle, who whispered a reply. He did the same with Monsignor Fabien, with the same result. Then I was addressed by Colonel Mirabelle: "His Royal Highness King Mehevi, Sovereign of Oaeetee, will consider your petition. You will remain within the limits of Louisville until you receive his royal assent. Good day, madame." With that, I curtsied and left the room, and indeed the palace, without anyone saying another word to me, or I to anyone, and returned to the Hibiscus on foot.

Thus I set out to wait for the King's decree. Day after day, as I waited, I remained in my room, staring at the lumpy whitewashed walls, or else took short walks around the settlement, beyond which I was not permitted to stray. Day and night I heard the clomping of heavy boots in the stairwell outside my room as men marched up and down from the tavern below, visiting the four island girls in the neighboring rooms. Smiling at one of them in the corridor one morning, I ventured to speak with her. Her name was Rahama. She barely spoke French, I quickly gathered, and so, after making sure we could not be overheard, I began to speak in the island language. I realized, when she replied, that the language had much changed since I had last spoken it ninety years earlier, but not so much that I could not understand her. When they learned that the strange new Frenchwoman could somehow speak their native tongue, the other women who worked in the adjoining rooms began to approach me. They asked how it was that I knew their language. I repeated the lie I had told at the palace—that I had learned it in New Caledonia, where a different form of it was spoken.

The days passed at a crawl. I yearned to be free of the strictures I'd been placed under, to walk barefoot on my land, to swim in the waters unimpeded by the encumbrances of a white woman's dress, to be with my people, to learn what had become of them and the Law. But on the threshold of my heart's satisfaction I'd been shackled. Even if there were no chains around my ankles, I was a prisoner all the same. I took the silence of the palace not as a sign that I'd been forgotten but that I was being watched and scrutinized. I imagined the King, the Resident-General, and the cleric hesitating about what to do with me. Knowing I must prove my trustworthiness, I did not venture beyond the limits set for me.

After several days of this pacing to and fro, I sat at the writing desk in my room to write a letter to Mathilde. But no sooner had I had inked the words, *My dear Mathilde*, than my mind's eye was flooded by remembrances that halted my letter-writing altogether.

Sixteen years earlier, after Charles had crossed with Mathilde, she and I had returned to live in Paris. I resumed running the

affairs of my businesses as well as those of the Baudelaire Society. For a brief time, Mathilde appeared delighted by her new
surrounds, and smiled at me with a semblance of affection.
Now that we were finally reunited, I took such moments as
an occasion to mention a return to Oaeetee. Although I knew
the Law was long since beyond repair, I felt, over and above
my yearning for our home, a duty to return, if only to observe
what havoc our actions might have wreaked, and what restitution might be possible. But as soon as the topic of a return
was broached Mathilde's smile would vanish, and her usual
sullen expression would take its place. She claimed, when
I gently interrogated her about it, to remember nothing of her
crossing, nor of her previous incarnation as Charles. There
was no doubt in my mind that they had actually crossed, despite her denials. I had evidence enough: after the crossing,
she began to have nightmares every night, as had Charles
before her.

After several months, Mathilde brought a son into the
world. She called him Lucien. I waited several months more
to raise once again the subject of our return. "Lucien is too
young to undertake such a journey," Mathilde replied. But
I never could bring her around to the idea of the crossing. Her
mind was too practical to entertain its possibility, despite my
convictions. Over time she came to consider me and my tales
as a kind of lunacy, just as Charles had. I gave her the story
Charles had written before the crossing, which he'd entitled,
"The Education of a Monster," but she could read only a little
and she resisted every attempt I made to read it aloud to her.
Like Charles before her, she dismissed my offers to cross with
her and then cross back to prove that I was telling the truth.
It was all sorcery to her, black magic, the devil's work. There

is no way of forcing someone to look you in the eye, after all—I have spent enough time trying to find a way to do it. It wasn't long before the mere mention of the subject incited an expression of contempt, and I began to avoid it. I decided I ought to be patient with her. As much as my own veil, her face was a blank surface behind which she lived a life that was carefully hidden from me.

As for Charles, he never fully recovered from the crossing. The doctors diagnosed a neuralgic attack brought on by advanced syphilis, but I knew it was the crossing that had caused it. Sometimes the shock of the new soul is too much for a body weakened by age and disease to withstand. His mother brought him back to Paris and placed him in a clinic. I arranged for one of the nurses there to report back to me on his condition. He spent his last days sitting in a big armchair, his skin pale, eyes searching and fixed. He was incapable of walking, of even sitting at a writing desk, and was ill-tempered and frequently driven to paroxysms of rage. Somehow in the crossing he had lost his powers of speech. His vocabulary was reduced to one solitary word that he repeated over and again: "*Crénom! Crénom!*" No matter how hard he tried, no matter how many doctors and experts were consulted, it was the limit of his self-expression. *Crénom*. Now he moaned it, he sneered it, and, with little cries of anger and pleasure, used it to translate his every need and thought.

He continued in this state for more than a year, slowly deteriorating until only one eye remained open a fraction, and his head hung down too heavily on the shoulder. In this eye, like a fading gleam, memory kept watch. His last days, in the summer of 1867, were cruel, and he was buried in the family crypt at the Montparnasse cemetery with his stepfather, where, years later, his mother would join them.

As I waited for Mathilde to decide that Lucien was old enough to travel, I continued to occupy myself with the Baudelaire Society. It now served the dual purpose of library for safekeeping Charles's writings and charity for young poets in need. I purchased the Hôtel Pimodan, where as Jeanne I'd lived with Charles, to serve as the Society's headquarters. The three of us lived upstairs. Meanwhile, I also began preparations for our forthcoming voyage to the South Seas. I became the first woman to join the Société de Géographie on the Boulevard Saint-Germain. In that little reading room, I read every book and magazine article I could find on the subject of Oaeetee and the nearby South Sea Islands. I devoured the descriptions of the islanders and their habits, studied the illustrations, and pored over the missionaries' reports and newspaper accounts.

And so we settled into our parallel lives, Mathilde and I, together but separate, each as stubborn as the other. She raised Lucien with utter devotion while I, equally devoted, prepared for our eventual return. Every time I raised the subject of the voyage, Mathilde would evade it. Lucien was still too young, she'd say, and we should wait at the very least until he had learned to walk, then talk, then read. And in the meantime I conceived an entire imaginary expedition, with a chartered boat and crew and provisions to last several years.

Lucien was the bridge that kept us connected. I ensured, from a polite distance, that he lacked for nothing. From the earliest, he considered us his two mothers. He addressed Mathilde as *Maman*, naturally, but for some reason he took to calling me *Mère*. At first, we accepted it as a natural childish confusion. Each time he did so, Mathilde would correct him: I was his aunt, she told him, not his mother. But on this subject the boy was not to be corrected, even when Mathilde scolded him. As soon as Mathilde disappeared into another room, he would come to me, and ask me to take him in my arms, finishing the supplication with that magical word, *Mère*, which I could never resist, and I would cradle him as he sucked his thumb.

But this domestic scene, the closest I had known to peace and family for generations, was not to last. In the summer of 1870, when Lucien was only three years old, the Prussians, who wished to make a modern German nation out of the ancient Holy Roman Empire, baited the emperor of France, the second Napoleon, who called himself the Third, into declaring war. The French Emperor was humiliated, the Empire capitulated, and a new republic—the Third—was declared. The Prussians continued their advance to Paris and, in the winter of 1870, the coldest in memory, laid siege to the city. I never saw such deprivation. On my way to or from the Société de Géographie, I would step around barely living corpses shivering in the gutter, or see starving children chasing rats to take home to eat. So Mathilde and I opened our house to all who needed shelter, turning it into a makeshift canteen at first, and soon thereafter an infirmary, a nursery, and a school.

Finally, the government decided to capitulate to the Prussians. Parisians refused to go along with the capitulation and revolted, and the siege turned into the Commune. Throughout these upheavals, our doors remained open. The makeshift canteen, infirmary, school, and nursery now tended to wounded Communards and their families. At the end of spring, at the time of the cherry blossoms, the soldiers of the Third Republic, fighting the Communards now rather than the Prussians, finally breached the city walls. Over the next week, Paris's finest monuments were set ablaze and its walls were reddened with rebel blood. Tens of thousands of Communards were shot on sight, and tens of thousands more were taken prisoner. I was among them.

Like so many others, I was sentenced to twenty years of hard labor and exiled to New Caledonia, leaving Mathilde in charge of my affairs. I departed for my exile convinced I would never see her, or Lucien, or Paris, or Oaeetee, again. My exile in the penal colony of New Caledonia comprised years of want and cruelty. But there were unexpected mercies too. Those female convicts who were literate became teachers, instructing the native children in reading, writing, and arithmetic. In order to better forget my sufferings, I plunged myself into my work.

Three years into our exile, we were given permission to bring our families to New Caledonia to be with us. I sent a letter to Mathilde inviting her to join me. From here, I wrote, we might sail on to Oaeetee, rather than return to France. Her reply arrived several months later. She had decided to decline my invitation, offering instead to stay in Paris and continue to manage my affairs in my absence. She never learned to read or write fluently, but through all those years she managed my business affairs with unfailing competence all the same. Later, when he was old enough, Lucien would stand in as her amanuensis.

After ten years of exile, the Communards were granted amnesty. I was free to return to France. But I felt I was too close to Oaeetee not to continue onward, so once again I wrote to

Mathilde to urge her to join me. Once again, she declined. And so I set off alone from Noumea bound first for Sydney and then for Auckland, from where I would, at long last, set sail for my final destination. It seems I was, as ever, destined for solitude.

After a week of voluntary captivity at the Hibiscus, I could suffer my confinement at the King's behest no longer. On the morning of the following Sunday, April 3, 1881, I finally summoned the courage to disobey His Majesty's orders. Knowing it was within walking distance of the settlement, I determined to visit the mission. I left the Hibiscus at a time I knew most people would be at church, using the back entrance reserved for the hotel staff. Soon, I entered into bedraggled fields pocked with coconut and breadfruit trees, goats, pigs, and an occasional buffalo. I approached a squat stone building that I supposed was the prison. It had few windows and from the inside emanated sorrowful groans. Next, I came upon a little wooden church, inside of which I heard the incantations of a priest and, in reply, the singing of a congregation in harmonies so rich and consoling I stopped awhile to listen, and was reduced to tears.

Soon thereafter I stepped through the mission's entrance and looked about. It had been built on the very location of the graveyard where, a century before, our sages had been buried. I had only ever set foot upon this once-sacred ground a handful of times, always at the express invitation of Fetu for some ritual. Our holiest and most secret ceremonies had been conducted here, hidden by the lush forest. But where trees had teemed, there were now four rows of six two-roomed, open-windowed cabins. In the center of the mission village, deserted other than for some mangy dogs sitting in the shade, was a planting of great breadfruit trees growing around a belltower.

I approached the nearest of these cabins and peered through an open window. At first, with my eyes habituated to the dazzling sun, I saw only darkness. I raised my veil to better see inside. The hut had an earthen floor, with straw mats overlaid upon it. Lengths of tapa cloth were stretched out to mark the place where the hut's residents slept at night. I peered into several huts until, through the window of one such cabin, I breathed in a fetid stench I recognized as that of a body long unwashed. As my eyes adjusted to the gloom, I noticed, stirring from a corner, a silhouette of a body lying on its side, its back facing me, under a length of cloth on the ground. Stepping through a doorway, I entered the hut. I approached the body and knelt over it. It was a very old man. I could not see his face but, as he was not moving, I presumed he was asleep. Only his limbs, sticking out from under the tapa cloth, were visible. I gently lifted the cloth and saw that he was in a state of advanced decrepitude, his muscles wasted, his joints swollen, his skin covered in sores. He appeared to be at death's threshold. I heard him whisper something. Unable to make out what he was saying, I lowered my head to hear him better and realized he was repeating the following words as if they were an incantation: "I welcome you, spirit, and beg you to guide me to the spirit world."

"I am no spirit," I said in the island language, unable to tell if he was talking to me or to an imagined being. "I am a creature of the real world."

The old man's eyes blinked open. The whites of his eyes

were yellowed, while the irises, once brown, seemed covered over with a graying hue. "I cannot see you," he said after a pause. I realized he was blind. "But I can hear you, and I know you are a spirit."

"And yet I have a body, just like you." I took his hand in mine by way of evidence.

"Then you are a spirit in disguise. You have taken on bodily form, but you are not of this world."

"Why do you accuse me of such deception?"

"Because you speak the language of the ancestors."

The dying man before me recognized my speech from his youth. "It is true," I said, "I speak the language of our ancestors."

"Where have you come from?" he asked.

I considered my reply for some time. Where had I come from? "I have come from the spirit world," I said at length, "just as you said."

"Ha!" He chuckled almost imperceptibly. "I knew it. About such things I am never wrong." He slipped into a paroxysm of coughing. When it had passed, he whispered, even more softly than before, so softly I had to raise my veil and lower my ear so that it was next to his lips. He repeated his question. "And have you come to avenge us?"

"Avenge whom?"

"My people—*your* people. The People of the Albatross."

"Against the foreigners?" I gave him the answer I presumed he wanted to hear. "Yes," I said, taking his hand and squeezing it. "Yes, I have."

"What is your name?" he asked.

I paused. "My name is Alula."

The old man's eyes opened fully with surprise, and his

mouth widened into an astonished smile. "So you have returned!" he said, instantly revived by the news. "Fetu was right after all!"

"He was," I replied, my eyes welling up with tears. "And what is your name?"

"My name is Koroli."

"Koroli, the son of Nani?"

"Yes, that was my mother's name."

The hand I was holding I had held once before, when the wizened man before me was but a newborn child, ninety years earlier.

At that moment, we were interrupted by the tolling of bells from the nearby tower and, soon after, the laughter of liberated children could be heard pealing across the mission as congregants spilled from the church. Mass had just ended.

"Go," Koroli hissed. "Go quickly. Don't let anyone see you here. There are enemies all around us."

"But I must talk with you more."

"Yes, yes," he said, "we will talk, but not now. Come back tonight, late, after dark. I will be waiting for you. We will talk then. But go now, while you can, and take care not to be seen."

As I made my way out of the mission, walking back in the direction of Louisville, every passerby stared at me as if they had never seen such a sight in their lives. Other than the priest in his black cassock, all were dressed identically—women in white muslin tunics and men in white muslin shirts and trousers.

I spent the rest of the day pacing to and fro in my room at the Hibiscus. Finally, well after dark, I returned to the mission. The entrance gate was shut, but a boy was waiting to greet me. He guided me to a hole in the fence hidden by a mimosa shrub. Once inside the compound, the boy took me by the hand and led me in the near-complete darkness to a clearing in a copse of breadfruit trees near the old man's cabin. All was dark and silent except for the soft light of candles burning in the cabins and, drifting from a distant place, the sound of voices singing in melancholic harmony.

The old man was waiting for me in the moonlight. He was lying on the same blanket as before and was somewhat revived from the near-cadaverous state I had witnessed earlier. He had been carried here on the pretext that it was time for his passage into the spirit world, and that he wished to die alone and in sight of the spirits in the sky. I told him I had held him in my arms once, only days before my departure. He replied that, although he could not remember me, he remembered the old people speaking of me in his childhood, awaiting my return.

"Why did you wait so long?" he asked. "All the old people are gone." I told him about what had happened at the time of the crossing, that there had been two crossings, that Alula had crossed with Joubert and Koahu had crossed with Roblet. He was not surprised by this, and he explained that the sage Fetu had guessed that this was what must have happened. Then I explained all that had happened to me as Joubert, how Koahu's crossing with the surgeon Roblet had been incomplete, and how I had become separated from Roblet. I told him about Jean-François Feuille and Jeanne Duval and finally I told him my story, and that of Charles and Mathilde. At the completion of my tale, Koroli shook his head in astonishment. "You have seen much and suffered much. But let me tell you what happened to us after you left." He proceeded, in his soft, rasping voice, to tell me his story.

"In the hours after you left, the old people did not suspect that there had been even one crossing, let alone two. Koahu was mortally injured. That was all they knew. No one noticed Alula was missing. It was only the following day that she was discovered, wandering along the beach, lost and confused. She was brought to Fetu, who spoke with her in his hut for an entire afternoon. When he finally emerged, he declared two crossings had taken place. You had committed a great crime against the Law, he declared, as had Koahu. It was futile to punish them, for the soul in their bodies had committed no crime. Alula was to be treated by all as if nothing had happened. There was no choice but to hope and wait for the return of those who had made the crossing. 'They know the Law,' said Fetu, 'and when they realize their mistake they will return. Of that I am certain.' Fetu was greatly wounded by your betrayal as you had been his favorite, but he resolved to look after the new Alula, to nurse her to health, to teach her the ways of the people, to explain what had happened to her, and to wait patiently for your return, when you would restore the world to its natural order.

"Alas, the body of Koahu never recovered from the blast of the musket. Several days after the feast, Koahu died of his injuries. This caused great sadness among us, as we understood what his death meant: there would be no return crossing. The Law had been irretrievably broken.

"Still we waited for your return. Over the years, more ships arrived, but you were on none of them. Some simply sailed on without stopping. Others traded with us. Soon enough, only the children considered these ships a novelty. When the strangers came ashore, they, too, carried muskets. Now that we knew the power of the musket we were more careful not to startle them. They traded with us: for water, meat, and fruit, they gave us nails and hammers, mirrors and beads. They told us with gestures that they were hunting seals and asked where they were to be found.

"The incident that had killed Koahu was soon forgotten. The people welcomed the arrival of every ship. New worlds appeared to open up for us. It seemed anything was possible, and everything that was new was desirable. The people became emboldened. The women began to disregard Otahu's orders and brazenly swam to the ship to trade for mirrors, beads, and cloth. The men paddled to the ships in their pirogues filled with pigs, fowl, breadfruit, and coconuts. The sailors taught them to smoke tobacco and drink rum. But of all their possessions, none was more highly prized by the people than the strangers' muskets. They could kill and maim better than any spear, and from a great distance. And whereas the crossing was a discipline that required many years of training from the youngest age, the foreigners' magic simply resided in an object.

"It was a woman who first traded for such a thing, holding it above the water like a trophy as she swam one-armed back to shore. It was coveted among the people and studied among the elders, but no matter how closely they imitated the strangers it would not explode with thunder and lightning. They could not understand how to make the magic work. So Fetu crossed with Alula to explore Joubert's memories, and learned that, in order to make the musket's magic work, a musket ball and gunpowder are necessary. From that day on, whenever a ship arrived, Fetu sent the women with the instruction to bring back more than trinkets with which to adorn themselves. They were to trade for ammunition.

"One woman swam to a ship and never returned. On another occasion, one of the men joined the ship and sailed away with it. With every ship the authority of Otahu and Fetu, of the Law itself, was weakened. Children were born who could not be conjoined by blood with the other children. Soon, like a stone under a waterfall, the Law was gradually reduced to a grain of sand, until even that grain was washed away.

"Then the tide began to turn. First the visitors hunted the seals until none were left alive. Then sickness came upon us. People would find wounds on their skin that would not heal. Day after day Fetu would apply ointments and tinctures, but the sores grew larger, and opened like a flower, and wept tears of their own, and multiplied in number, and when the sick finally died it was a blessing that their suffering was over.

"Others noticed a cough that would not go away. Over time the coughs grew broader and deeper and began to rattle, and their lungs seemed to be slowly filling up with water. Eventually, they drowned from all the water that had filled up inside them. Fetu nursed the sick as well as he could, without saying what was on his mind, but his thoughts could be read in the frown on his face: this was the Law's retribution for our sacrilege.

"Fetu lived a long life, longer than most. Each time another ship was sighted, he welcomed all who visited the island in the hope that one of them was the one he was waiting for. But there was no return. Eventually he died one morning, in the company only of Alula. She came back to the village in tears, telling us Fetu had died of one of the mysterious new illnesses, before they could make a crossing. The line of succession was broken once and for all. As Fetu's favorite, Alula appointed herself the new sage.

"By this time, I was a youth, on the cusp of manhood. I had been studying the crossing for some years. Fetu had taught me well, and he died just as I was preparing for my first unassisted crossing. Out of respect for Fetu, Alula said, there were to be no more crossings for twelve moons. This was not in our tradition, but as she was the new sage, the people respected her decision. Alula had become feared for her temper. Any perceived slight would send her into a rage that lasted days. By the time twelve moons had passed, the young people, having lost their appetite for the rigors of its instruction, never sought to resume their education. Thus the teaching of the crossing fell away, and I never made an unassisted crossing.

"After the sealers, other ships came in search of whale oil or sandalwood. Sometimes they stayed a day or two, when they were in a hurry, and sometimes they stayed for weeks, when rest and repairs were needed. They cavorted with the women, and traded with us; sometimes they would get drunk and occasionally a musket would be fired and cause heartbreak among us. Every once in a while, one of the people would leave with a ship, only to return years later, or never at all. Sometimes, one among us would cross with a stranger and thus leave the island. Whenever such a thing occurred, Alula's reaction was different from Fetu's. She insisted that, after such a crossing, the old body be sacrificed. After the sacrifice, she ostracised the family of the one who had crossed, banishing them to live on the far side of the island, where the breadfruit trees are fewer. And so we learned to keep the crossing to ourselves.

"The next calamity to befall us was the death of Otahu, whose lungs, like those of so many others among us, slowly filled with water, until he, too, drowned from the inside out. Before he died, Otahu designated his favorite child, his daughter Fayawaye, to be the new chief, as was the tradition.

"The first foreigner to stay and live among us arrived at the time when I was a father of my own young family. Much taken with the easy life here compared with that of a sailor, he jumped from the ship as it began to leave and swam to shore. We welcomed him as one of our own. He married and begat children, but several years later he joined the crew of another ship and returned to his faraway place. After him, there were others. They introduced us to their ways, and we became accustomed to them.

"Next to arrive were the missionaries—a dozen French priests. By this time, I was a grandfather already. They took possession of this place, our sacred ground, and destroyed the old, sacred statues that stood upon the graves. In its place, they raised this mission, and built walls around it. They taught us how to dress, how to plant vegetables, and how to read their sacred book. Again and again, they urged us to abandon our Law, promising their heaven in exchange. Several among us were persuaded, especially those who were afflicted with the foreigners' new diseases. They went to live on the mission. But the strange clothes they were made to wear chafed, the vegetables they planted wilted, and their sacred book made no sense. What's more, at the mission it was forbidden to sing our songs and dance our dances. So these people came back to be among their own, and we waited for the missionaries to leave.

"By now, Alula was a very old woman, an ancient. All these years, she had preached to us about her crossing with Joubert, and that of Koahu with Roblet. With every sermon, her anger became more vehement: she blamed all of our misfortunes on your impetuousness. Meanwhile, the people continued to waste away and die of strange new illnesses, for which we had no cures.

"The knowledge of the crossing was disappearing with the death of each of the old people. By now, Alula spent her days lying down. All the people knew that her death would be the death of the last teacher of the crossing. The people implored Alula to make one more crossing before she died. Finally, in a whisper, she called for a child to be brought to her—the strongest, healthiest child on the island. At that time, Mehevi was only five years old. He was an impertinent and imperious boy, but he was strong and never sick. When he was taken to her, Alula pointed to a tapa cloth that contained a sacred object. Inside, Mehevi found a whalebone knife, with fine engravings showing scenes from the old stories of the gods. On her command, all the people except Alula and Mehevi left the hut. Finally, Mehevi emerged from the hut and into the daylight, his hands slick and red. There was an expression of terrible triumph on his face that I shall never forget. He was holding the knife in one hand. It dripped with blood. In the other hand, he held Alula's eyes, which he had gouged out according to the custom. The new chief Fayawaye went and knelt before him out of respect, and the other people present followed her example. Mehevi was our new sage.

"It was now generally agreed that the Law was irreparably broken. And so the people naturally divided into two camps. On one side were those who still feared the Law, and insisted we reject the foreigners and all their ways, and return to the Law with increased devotion. They remembered the prophecies of the old people, and when they looked about at the sickness that afflicted so many of us they believed these prophecies were now being fulfilled. On the other side were those who believed that the Law was now outmoded, that it was time to leave the old ways behind and adapt to the new ways. The foreigners had shown us how isolated and backward we were. We had to embrace the new life offered us, turn our backs on the past, and look toward the future with hope.

"Then the French navy arrived. Three boats made of stone and puffing out smoke reached our shores. They seemed like nightmare visions, nothing like the ships the foreigners had sailed before. Sailors rowed to our shore and the admiral declared the island a possession of Louis Philippe, King of the French. Enormous muskets aboard the ships exploded in celebration of the occasion. Later we learned that they were called cannons, not muskets, and that the weapons the French soldiers carried were no longer called muskets but rifles.

"Swarms of soldiers came upon the island and began to build a wharf, a barracks, and a prison. The ships sailed away several months later, but some of the soldiers remained. Ever since, the ships have come and gone but the soldiers are always here, building, always building: cutting down trees, digging up stones, laying down foundations. They went on to build an infirmary, a prison, a courthouse, a customs building, houses to live in, sheds to store things in, gardens to grow vegetables in, shops to sell things in, and above all they built roads. After the French navy came, more foreigners arrived: officials and workers, farmers and businessmen, teachers and storekeepers, wives and children. They built a village, called it Louisville, and settled there. They took possession of the low-lying land and cleared it of trees. They built wooden fences around it and when the people climbed over the fences or took one of their animals they would shoot at us, or else soldiers would come looking for us and take us to the prison. The breadfruit and banana and coconut trees were fenced off in this way, and the foreigners planted new plants like sugarcane and cotton and rice. Chief Fayawaye went to complain to the French about the sufferings of the people. The French insulted her, threatening her with prison if more animals were stolen or any of the French property damaged. She returned to the people and told them that the land the French had claimed for themselves no longer belonged to everyone. The people had never thought of things this way before. It was a strange idea to them that the land could be divided into little pieces, and that these pieces would then be the property of one person or another, who could do as they wished with it, including keeping other people from using it.

"The people talked for a long time, over many moons, about the new ways the French had brought with them, and considered how to make the French compromise, or even go away altogether. Between us we had six rusty old muskets and precious little gunpowder, whereas the French had rifles and pistols and cannons, and could put the people in windowless cells with iron doors that could only be opened with keys.

"When the French learned of the plotting by some of the people, they approached Mehevi, who had grown to be an impetuous youth. Mehevi was fascinated by the foreigners' ways. He in turn fascinated them, partly because he spoke the language as if it were his native tongue, although he never spoke of Alula or the Law. The French told Mehevi that Oaeetee needed a king, a great and mighty warrior. They offered to make him king, and build him a palace, and respect him as the lord of all the island and its people. Mehevi agreed, and told them that he was in fact Oaeetee's rightful monarch, that his throne had been usurped by Fayawaye, and for proof he showed them the plaque that Marchand had left on the island all those years before, which he had received from Alula, who herself had received it from Fetu. The French were pleased by this, and saw it as evidence that their scheme was righteous and just.

"And so the division in the people widened: those who valued the Law and wished to restore it gathered around Fayawaye, whereas those who valued the new ways and wished to abandon the Law gathered around Mehevi. Over the years, the Fayaysaye people left the lowlands and retreated ever higher into the mountains, where life was colder and harsher, and to the far side of the island, where they could continue to practice the old ways in peace. They came to be known simply as the highland people. The others, those who wished to live in the new ways, came to be known as the lowland people. Their leader was King Mehevi who, from his palace, became known for his ruthlessness and terrible anger.

"Other than Mehevi in his palace, the mission was the only place the French would allow the lowland people to settle. In time, they were joined by those who could not abide the cold of the mountains or the hunger of the far side of the island. The sick went to the mission hospital in search of a cure. Everyone was welcome to stay on the mission for as long as they liked, and eat the food of the priests, on the condition that they set aside their nakedness, abandon their songs and dancing, and toil in the field from dawn to dusk every day except Sunday, when they were expected to attend Mass.

"The sickness among us continued to spread. There were fewer and fewer highland people, and the French were always complaining about them, accusing them of stealing from the farms. They are still there, and Fayawaye is still their queen, but she is an old woman now.

"I myself lived with the highland people for many years. As I watched others leave, I was determined never to join them. But as I grew old and became sick, I could not continue to live in the mountains. So with shame in my heart I, too, came to the mission. But now that I know you have returned, now that I have told you my story, now that I know the People of the Albatross will be avenged, I can die in peace. I am weary of this life, and ready to join with the divine breath."

The morning after my reunion with Koroli, I heard three sharp knocks at the door of my hotel room. When I opened it, Lieutenant Perrault stood before me, holding an envelope in his hand. It was a summons from the palace.

Once more I was ushered into the Great Hall, only this time King Mehevi sat alone on his throne. He beckoned me forward. I approached and curtsied.

"Madame Édmonde," he said in a soothing tone.

"Your Majesty," I replied, bowing my head.

Mehevi smiled. "Please raise your veil."

"But—"

"Please, madame, indulge me."

I lifted the black tulle over my head and looked the King directly in the eyes, trying to maintain my composure, for despite his calming demeanor I sensed a tension in him straining to be released. He stood from his throne and stepped down from the dais, hands clasped behind his back. "I have it on good authority that you have disobeyed my orders."

"How, Your Majesty?"

"Yesterday, you went to the mission."

"Yes. I thought it would be useful to familiarize myself with the conditions in which the natives live."

"Useful?"

"For pedagogical purposes."

A mirthless chuckle rose from deep within him, as if he were indulging a child. "So much so that you decided to visit a second time, after dark?"

It seems I had been followed. "I couldn't sleep. I needed to walk."

"And you had a long conversation with the old imbecile Koroli."

"Yes."

"What did he say to you?"

"I didn't understand very much. His dialect was near impossible to make out."

"Alula, let's drop the pretense." I was doubly startled—not just by the name he called me, but also because he addressed me in the islander language. "I know who you are. I know why you have come here." Now I understood why he'd wanted to see my face—to scrutinize my reactions. I remained mute. "Do you know who I am?"

"You are King Mehevi," I replied in French.

"I am the King, it is true. But I am also someone else. Can you guess who?"

"No, I cannot." We continued to speak in two different languages.

"Yes, you can. Think."

"Forgive me, Your Majesty."

He paused a moment and then tried a different approach, giving me a hollow smile. "It's me, Joubert," he said.

"Joubert—you're very familiar with that name, aren't you?" His words were tinged with menace. "There's no point hiding, Alula. I spoke with Koroli myself earlier this morning. He told me everything—what he told you, what you told him. He was under the impression you've come to avenge the people. Surely you're not so foolish as to believe that?"

I told myself to remain as still as possible, but my mind was racing with calculation. Was he bluffing? Did he subject every newcomer to the same treatment? It was intuition, and the memory of what Koroli had told me about Mehevi, that prevented me from unveiling the truth of my identity.

"And so I'm left wondering—why is it that you have returned? Surely you don't believe the Law can be mended, do you?"

"Your Majesty," I said, finally, in Oaeetian, speaking slowly and haltingly, as if the language was difficult for me to speak, disguising my words with an accent, "with respect, I know not of what you speak."

He reached out and put a hand on my shoulder, his fingers curled around my neck. "Drop the pretense. I know everything. So do you." By this time he was near enough that I felt a gust of hot breath with every word.

"The poor fellow was so close to death, he was hallucinating," I said, slipping back into French. "I merely consoled him as best I could."

"Why have you come back?" he snarled, his fingers tightening around my neck. I gasped, as much with surprise as with pain. He was now so near to me I could see the reflection in his eyes. I realized with a shot of panic that he was searching out my gaze. Was he attempting to cross with me? I fixed my sight on the bridge of his nose, between his eyes. "Are you not the very cause of your people's misery? Are you not the one who destroyed the Law with your recklessness? So why are you *really* here? To wreak more havoc? To destroy what little hope they have left? Haven't you done enough harm?" He paused, awaiting my reply.

His grip hardened. I gasped. "Please," I sobbed, "Your Majesty . . ."

His mouth was curled in a terrible grimace. "Did you really think you could hide behind that loathsome face? Did you really believe it would protect you?" He turned my face this way and that, studying it. "You are truly a hideous creature. Just like me." He pulled me closer to try to catch my gaze, but I kept it locked on that spot between his eyes. "Look at what you have done to your people, and the horror of their lives. Did your actions not bring this on them? Look what you have done to *me*! Yes, I am a monster, it is true what the old man told you. I *am* cruel and I *am* vengeful. But I am *your* monster. You created me! And every cruelty I commit is the offspring of *your* cruelty!" Our bodies were now conjoined. "You stole my life from me, and all this time I have waited for you to return. Shall we undo now what you did ninety years ago?" My entire body trembled. "Shall I administer the penance for your sin?" His lips curled into a vicious smile. "Vengeance is not yours to take—vengeance is *mine*!"

"Your Majesty," I gurgled.

"Admit it," he whispered as he loomed above me. "You are Alula. Your refusal to look me in the eye simply confirms it. Just nod your head, and I'll let you go at once." I kept my gaze resolutely locked in between his eyes. "*Look at me!*" he shouted, convulsing with the pleasure of his rage. I felt my life force drain out of me. If it had not been for a commanding knock at the door I might have perished at that very instant. Mehevi suddenly withdrew and, turning his back to me and the door, retreated to a more seemly distance. I lowered my veil and smoothed my dress.

Through the door stepped Colonel Mirabelle, the Resident-General, holding his pith helmet under his arm. Mehevi sat back on his throne. "What is it, Colonel?"

"Your Majesty summoned me?"

"I did no such thing, but no matter. The woman will leave the island on the next departing ship. Until then, she is to remain under confinement in her quarters." He turned his head away from me with an expression of disgust. No sooner had I begun to mouth a protestation than he erupted. "How *dare* you speak without my permission!" He gestured to Mirabelle. "Get her out of my sight at once." As Mirabelle ushered me out, Mehevi began rubbing his forehead vigorously, as if greatly troubled. I myself was clutching my throat and trembling with a violence I could barely control.

Outside, Lieutenant Perrault was waiting for me in the buggy. We made it most of the way back to the Hibiscus in silence. I was still shaking when he finally spoke. "Don't be too disappointed," he said as we neared the hotel. "He's like that with all the newcomers." I glanced at him with disbelief. "Oh, yes. Everyone who arrives on the island receives the same interrogation—*I know who you are, I know why you came here*, and so forth." The officer gave a wan smile. "And you're not the first to have been kicked off the island. The last Resident-General had barely set foot on dry land before Mehevi sent him back. The man is a lunatic."

He was interrupted by a strange and melancholic sound: choral music like the singing I'd heard the previous day at the mission. At the top end of the main street, a crowd of island-ers, dressed in white muslin, were shuffling toward Louisville's cemetery.

"Mourners," said Perrault.

"Who died?"

"An old man at the mission, an ancient fellow by the name of Koroli. The last of the old-timers. They found his body this morning. In the tropics, the dead are quickly buried." As we observed the funeral procession, he tut-tutted. "It's most strange," he said. "It seems when the old man's body was found, his eyes were missing."

I was to be kept under guard in my hotel room until the de-parture of a ship bound for Valparaíso two weeks hence. But my encounter with Mehevi left me doubtful that I would last that long. I feared the King would have me murdered before then. I spent a sleepless night devising a means of escape. The next morning, when Rahama came to visit, I gave her a note to take to Fayaway. *Alula has finally returned to the island*, it read. *She is being held captive by Mehevi at the Hibiscus Hotel and wishes to escape and join with your people.* "It is very impor-tant that Fayaway receives this note quickly," I said. "Bring me back her reply. And above all make sure no one knows about any of this."

Two young gendarmes took it in turns to sit on a wooden chair outside the entrance to my room at the Hibiscus, and for twelve hours at a time they would doze or flirt with the women. Three days later, I received Fayaway's reply urging me to flee immediately, promising to meet me in the moun-tains the following day. In the dead of night, I made my silent escape, taking the stairwell at the back of the building, which was left unguarded, accompanied by Rahama, with only what could be carried on our backs. We ran as far as we could in the moonlight, and when we could run no longer we walked. By the time the sun rose we were halfway up the mountain.

The sun was at its zenith when we stopped to rest by a stream gathered in the hollow of a rock. There, Fayawaye awaited us with her most trusted highland people. The daughter of Otahu, she was now an old woman, and nearing death. "Now I can die with a tranquil heart," she said when she approached me. After we had embraced, a young woman approached us and knelt before me. Fayawaye introduced her as Faïmana, her granddaughter, the great-granddaughter of Otahu. This young woman before me was to be the next chief of the highland people. Kneeling before me, Faïmana welcomed me and called me Ne'Alula: the second Alula. "The people have long awaited your return," she said. As I was introduced to the gathering of people, many a tear was shed, until Fayawaye warned it was time to continue our journey, lest the French discover us. We continued our march higher still into the mountains with happiness in our hearts. At long last, I was among my people. There I would remain for the next nineteen years.

One sunny morning early in the year 1900, I was bathing in a mountain cascade when I was overcome by the intuition that I was being observed. I looked around and saw by the water's edge a white, very white, almost spectrally white man in his early thirties, wearing a khaki suit and a pith helmet. On his face he sported a monocle and a curled ginger mustache, expertly waxed. Behind him a mule swayed under the weight of an enormous pack. We blinked at each other for a moment before the man uttered the last word I expected to hear.

"*Mère.*"

And then he blushed.

Only one person had ever called me by that name.

"Lucien?" And then I recognized him—the face of the child burst through the face of the adult, through his pale green eyes above all, and thirty years of separation evaporated in an instant.

That evening, we sat around a large bonfire lit in Lucien's honor, in a clearing deep in the woods surrounded by my beloved people. They watched and listened, wide-eyed with wonder, as we talked long into the night. The occasion was distinguished at first only by the bliss of our reunion. I told Lucien about my years living in the highlands, and how I had devoted them to teaching my people about the Law and trying to revive the crossing among the children. Lucien explained that he was now a writer employed by the Société de Géographie to travel throughout the world. He wrote articles that he would send back to France to be published in magazines and newspapers. He had come to Oaeetee specifically to find me. In France, he said, I had become somewhat notorious for my exploits.

"What exploits?" I asked.

"Why, your life as a savage, evading the police, and fomenting rebellion." I was aghast to learn of this. "In Paris, you are known in certain circles as the Queen of the Cannibals."

When they heard this, the people laughed. "But I am no such thing," I said. "And my people are not cannibals." I began to describe the pleasures and the rigors of mountain life.

"The truth of the matter is not important," he replied. "It is the legend that counts. And according to the legend, you are the leader of the oldest, most stubborn colonial rebellion in the empire. Even old King Mehevi is curious about you."

Curiosity was not a quality I readily associated with the King, who had launched several punitive expeditions upon my people over the years, as a result of which we had endured great hardships. These, combined with disease and the natural scarcity of our surrounds, had depleted our numbers. "What does Mehevi have to do with it?"

Lucien explained that, upon his arrival on the island, he had been granted an audience with the King, during which the monarch had, as was customary, inquired about his intentions for visiting the island. "I know why you are here," the King had said. "I know why you have come."

"So you know about Madame de Bressy," Lucien had replied.

At this point, Lucien said, the King's demeanor had changed. "Of course," said Mehevi. "I've known all along."

"You know about Alula? And Koahu?"

"Yes!" the King exclaimed. "Yes, yes, I know, of course I know. But there are aspects to the story that remain confused for me. Tell me everything you know, young man."

At this point, Lucien told me, he proceeded to tell the King the story of how I had known his mother, about Charles and Jeanne and the Baudelaire Society, and the stories I had told her about Koahu and Alula.

"You told him everything?"

"Should I not have?" He discerned the distress on my face, which even my scars could not hide. "But you don't believe those primitive superstitions, do you?" I realized that his mother had taught him to be as skeptical as she was.

"It's not a matter of belief, but of fact. All of these things did happen."

"Well," Lucien replied, "you needn't worry about Mehevi any longer. He has fallen gravely ill." The day after their exchange, he said, the King appeared to have descended into a mania and was confined to bedrest. His malady was unknown to the doctor. The news about the King's illness took the people by surprise, for he was famous for his strong constitution, but they were even more surprised by the next revelation: the French had taken immediate advantage of the King's illness to declare him unfit to rule and—pointing to the treaty Mehevi had signed with them all those years ago—annexed the island. The new Governor, who was none other than the old Resident-General, took up residence in the former Royal Palace, which was now called Government House, while the King was confined to the old Residence-General, now called the Royal Palace, where he lay in his regal bed, a king in name only.

"What was the nature of the illness that befell the King?" I asked. Lucien replied that he seemed to have lapsed into a kind of trance from which he would not be awoken. The only thing Mehevi could say was a single word, an exclamation that he repeated over and over, much to the discomfort of his attending priest: *Sacrilège!* He would shout it so loudly and so often that it had hastened his removal from power. The King now lived, in his enfeebled condition, shouting, "*Sacrilège! Sacrilège!*" over and over, day and night, from the comfort of the royal bedroom.

A shiver ran the length of my entire body. I thought of Charles shouting *Crénom!* over and again until the day he died.

"Tell me," I said to Lucien, "when you first met him, how did the King react to what you told him about the crossing and about me?"

"He was most fascinated, and deemed it a story worth telling in great detail."

"And—think back carefully before you answer me—how did his manner change upon hearing the story you had to tell?"

Lucien paused to remember the occasion. "Perhaps," he finally replied, "if there was a change, it was a subtle one. It wasn't anything he said so much as his bodily attitude. Yes, now that I think about it, there was a change in his demeanor. Especially in his eyes. His gaze became more inquisitive and searching, as if he was trying to hold my own. But I could not return it."

"Why not?"

"There was something about it that made me nervous, something terrible. And besides," he added, "Maman always taught me never to look too long in a stranger's eyes."

I asked Lucien to make a solemn vow not to repeat a shred of what he had just told me to another living soul. When we finally turned in for the night, I could barely close my eyes. I rose from my bed and went walking in the moonlight. I was deeply troubled by what Lucien had told me—by the prospect of Mehevi, of Joubert's soul, unleashed upon the world. For I knew that Mehevi must have crossed with someone— someone in the habit of peppering his speech with the word *sacrilège*. But why?

When I had arrived on the island, and for most of the two decades I had lived upon it, I had been quite certain that I would die there, that there would be no more crossings for me.

I had tasted enough of life's bitter fruit. I had caused too much harm. I had lost too much. But Lucien's appearance dashed all of these notions. More than dread, I felt a great mischief might be unleashed upon the world—a mischief for which I was responsible. What if the Law had been right after all—only not in the manner I had expected? What if, when I had crossed with Joubert more than a century ago, I had indeed planted the seed of the world's destruction, precisely as the Law had prophesied? What if Mehevi was the evil flower of my sin—a soul with no conscience, only rage, an adept of the most esoteric forms of crossing, roaming free in the world, motivated by terrible, unknowable desires? And what if I was the only person in the world with the power to curb his vengeance?

So it was that, several days after our encounter at the waterfall, after farewells marked by sorrow, we descended from the mountains to the lowlands and I returned to Louisville for the first time in nineteen years. As we journeyed, I turned the conversation back to the subject with which I was most preoccupied: Mehevi's crossing. I asked Lucien to cast his mind back to his arrival. Had he met anyone, in Oaeetee or on the ship on which he had sailed here, who habitually exclaimed *sacrilège*? After a moment of remembrance he replied: "I well remember the captain of the ship that brought me here. His blasphemies were a running joke among the ship's crew, and the passengers too. All day long one heard him shout, '*Sacrilège! Sacrilège!*'" Lucien looked at me. "Do you think this is related to the King's condition?"

"Perhaps," I replied, but of course my worst suspicions had been confirmed. I was convinced Mehevi had crossed with the man. "When we return to Louisville, I will no doubt be arrested and imprisoned. I fully expect to be banished from the island. While the wheel of justice turns, I'd like you to run an errand for me. See if you can learn where we can find this captain."

Word of my return spread quickly. On the outskirts of Louisville, greatly enlarged since my departure two decades earlier, a crowd had gathered, of islanders and foreigners both, lining the streets to witness the spectacle of the surrender of the Queen of the Cannibals. We marched, Lucien and I, all the way to the old palace, now Government House, accompanied for the last portion of the journey by an escort of mounted gendarmes. As soon as we arrived, I was handcuffed and placed in the charge of two gendarmes. In theory, I was under arrest, but as there was still no prison on the island for European women, I was detained instead, as I had been nineteen years earlier, in exactly the same room at the Hibiscus. The hotel had barely altered in all that time. Only the faces of the women working by the hour had changed.

The following day, I was to be taken to see the Governor, who was also the island magistrate. But when his aide-de-camp—no longer Lieutenant Perrault, who had left long ago, but a Lieutenant Thibault—knocked at the door and saw that I was dressed only in a tapa cloth, as islander women dress, he escorted me instead—by way of the bank, where a substantial sum of money was still deposited under my name—to the clothier. There, I purchased a set of clothes worthy of a European lady: a chemise, bloomers, a corset, a busk, a corset cover, a decency skirt, a bustle, an underskirt, a suit, a taille and garniture, leather shoes, a hat, gloves, a parasol, a nightdress, a veil, and a trunk in which to store it all.

The next morning I was marched once more to Government House. The Governor, no longer the Colonel Mirabelle of nineteen years earlier but Colonel Marie-Georges Duhamel, informed me that I was to be deported at my own expense, accompanied by Lucien, on a schooner leaving Oaeetee three days hence, bound for the Sandwich Islands, and then San Francisco. I asked to see Mehevi, the former king. The Governor refused. "His Royal Majesty, Mehevi, King of Oaeetee, is not receiving visitors."

I returned to my room at the Hibiscus and spent the next several days under lock and key. The girls working in the other rooms were banished. This time there would be no duping the guards.

Deprived of my liberty, I became like a wild animal caged in a zoo. Lucien finally came to visit on the second day of my incarceration, apologizing for my compromised condition and promising my freedom as soon as we had left the island.

"What did you learn about the ship's captain?"

"He left the island a week ago on the same ship that brought us here."

"And what is its destination?"

"Marseille."

My worst fears were realized. I would have to leave the island. I would have to make another crossing. I would have to return to France. I would have to attend to the monster of my making.

I opened my eyes in my sixth body and blinked several times. Through the window, the oceanic Iowa prairie through which the train was whistling was drenched in the golden light of dusk. Madame Édmonde sat before me, her body rocking with the motions of the train. Her face was marked with that stupefied expression I had come to know so well: the look of a fish that has just been taken out of the sea, no longer flopping about but simply wide-eyed and open-mouthed, as if it cannot quite grasp the strange turn of events that has befallen it. Only, with the scars on her face, it was a strange, monstrous fish she resembled, a fish from the darkest depths of the ocean.

No one is harder to mesmerize than a mesmerist. It was only near the end of my story that I felt the resistance in Balthazar loosen a fraction, and the possibility of a crossing finally open. The change was almost imperceptible, but there it was: as I recounted my story, looking him directly in the eye all the while, I felt that familiar swelling of desire, that peculiar wanderlust of a soul wishing to escape its prison, which we all feel at one time or another, especially when captivated by the charms of a storyteller.

Now, here she was, no longer me but rather inhabited by that young man's wonderstruck spirit. Édmonde's mouth opened and closed slowly. I leaned forward to try to catch what, if anything, she was saying. After a moment, I heard it. It was unmistakable. "Behold!" she whispered, "Behold! Behold! . . ."

{103}

Hippolyte Balthazar

Born 1876
First crossing 1900
Second crossing 1917
Died 1917

"HE TOLD ME he loved me and wanted to marry me."

Her words, hoarse as they were, seemed almost miraculous. They were the first words she had spoken in almost three weeks. We were twenty-three minutes into our first session. It had taken her all that time to answer the question I'd asked at the beginning of the session: *What seems to be the matter?* I'd been waiting patiently for her reply since. She looked down at her hands, which were fretting on her lap. Two tears hurried down her cheeks and softly plopped on the lap of her woolen skirt. In every other respect she was perfectly calm.

She cleared her throat. "He was one of the most mutilated men I've seen," she continued in a clearer voice. "A frightful mess." Another pause. "He had the most horrific burns and blisters all over his body. He was clearly not going to survive. The doctors and other nurses had left him for dead." The words were starting to flow now. "Sometimes, when a patient is a lost cause, there's nothing else to do but administer painkillers and concentrate on the men who still have a chance of making it.

But I took it upon myself to care for him all the same. He'd been in the ward for two days, on a lot of morphine, but in agonies. And, despite all that, whenever I was with him, dressing his wounds, he talked. The skin of his lips had been shredded and scorched in the mortar attack, but somehow despite the pain he managed to speak in a whisper. I had to put my ear close to his mouth to make out his words. He just needed to tell someone, anyone, what had happened to him. Not just how he was wounded, but who he was, where he came from. He was Australian, just a boy, really. He must have lied about his age when he volunteered. I couldn't understand why anyone on the other side of the world would volunteer for such a hell as this. I even remember the name of the place he was from: Ballarat. Sometimes, when I can't sleep at night, I try to imagine what kind of place Ballarat could be. I imagine it to be flat and bright and very quiet, with great trees swaying in the breeze."

"You speak English?"

"I speak four languages. My father was a diplomat."

I looked down at my notes. *Madeleine Pernety*, I read. *Volunteer nurse since May 1916. Born 1898, Saigon, Indochina. Father French, colonial official, deceased; mother Indochinese, deceased. Symptoms of shellshock and neuralgia. Admitted 10 February 1917.* "What did you say, when he declared his love to you?"

"I said, 'That's what they all say, when . . .' And I had to stop myself short. But it was too late. He guessed what I was going to say."

"What were you going to say?"

"I was going to say, *When they're about to die.* But he finished the sentence for me anyway."

She was reclining on the couch in front of me, but she wasn't really here at all. She was back by the soldier's bed, reliving the moment. Her recollection of an incident that had occurred weeks earlier was, at this moment, more real to her than the fact of her lying on a leather couch in a psychologist's consulting room in the Villejuif military asylum in the suburbs of Paris.

"Then what happened?"

"I left him to attend to another patient who'd begun making a lot of noise in the meantime." Another long pause. I said nothing. "Then we heard the whistles of the first mortars and all of a sudden everything was on fire. The casualty ward was in a converted barn, you see. I dived into a corner and curled up into a ball, thinking I was about to die myself. By the time it was all over there was barely a ward left. The barn was in ruins. But I came out unscathed. Not a scratch." She sat up and turned to look at me. "Not a scratch, doctor. I had some ringing in my ears that lasted a few hours, and that's it. The Australian died, as did the others—twelve soldiers, two nurses, and a surgeon. I was the only survivor. And then it was all over."

"And you had your first seizure that night."

"Yes."

I'd treated scores of men for shellshock since the start of the war, perhaps more than a hundred, but Madeleine Pernety was the first woman to have walked through my door. Women weren't supposed to suffer from shellshock, yet Madeleine exhibited all the classic signs: catatonia, insomnia, chronic nausea. And seizures—trembling that lasted a quarter-hour or more, trembling that became so violent she would have to be restrained.

"Surely," I said, "he's not the first soldier to have died on your watch. What was it about this particular soldier that you're having such a hard time forgetting?"

"I don't know."

"Is it that he told you he loved you?"

"No. That happens all the time." Her hands began fretting again.

"How often?"

"I suppose men have told me they love me about twenty or thirty times."

"What about you, Mademoiselle Pernety, have you ever told a man you love him?"

"Just once." Another long pause. I clocked it: four minutes. "We were engaged to be married. Then, when the war started, he was called up. He died in April 1915. At Ypres."

"And so, as soon as you were old enough, you volunteered yourself—as a tribute, I suppose, to the man you loved."

"Yes."

"Does it trouble you when a man tells you he loves you?"

"Very much."

"Why? Because he's dying?"

"Because I have no love to give him in return."

I waited to hear if she had anything else to say, but she seemed to have come to a kind of rest. Even her hands were in a state of repose. In clinical terms, it was a promising sign. We were near the end of the session.

"Mademoiselle, the method I use to treat patients is hypnosis. Do you know what that is?"

"Is it the same as mesmerism?"

"Mesmerism is what it used to be called, but these days it's only ever called mesmerism in circuses. The scientific name for it is hypnotism. It seems to have a therapeutic effect on my patients. In a minute, I'm going to put you into a hypnotic trance. It's while you are in this trance state that we're going to do all the hard work that is going to heal you. After, you won't remember a thing. Will you allow me to do that?"

I can only describe the expression on her face as one of imploring trust. I explained to her that, once hypnotized, she would remain in that state for a quarter of an hour before I ended the trance. Henceforth, she would undergo hypnosis at the beginning of our every session. The aim, I said, was for her to attain a state of deep relaxation that would relieve her neuroses.

And so the crossing began. For a quarter-hour I wandered the corridors of her mind: a joyous childhood in Saigon marred by the early deaths of her parents (her father of influenza, her mother, soon after, of grief), a solitary youth spent orbiting indifferent relatives in France, and falling passionately in love at the age of fifteen. In my years of clinical work, I'd encountered the charred remnants of many a love cut short. But the quality of Madeleine's love was different: here was a soul that had loved wholly and with abandon. It was so rare and so true that I found myself wishing I could stay there to be warmed in its afterglow. Yet I also sensed it with a certain awe: a love of this amplitude was powerful enough to burn everything in its wake, leaving nothing but ashes.

I was writing up the notes on the session with Madeleine when there was a knock at the door. It was the registrar. "Sorry to disturb, doctor, but there's been a change in this afternoon's schedule. An officer. Claims to know you." He looked down at his clipboard. "Aristide Artopoulos."

"Artopoulos! Yes, we're old friends." A pang of guilt pricked my heart. I'd received several letters from him since the beginning of the war, each of them urging me to see him. I'd set them all aside, unable to decide what to do about them, putting my response in a temporary but indefinite state of suspension. "Where is he now?"

"I told him your schedule is full, which he didn't take very well. He wouldn't be denied, so I've slotted him in for two o'clock. Sorry to cut your lunch short."

"Thank you, Julien."

"I must warn you, professor. Don't expect to recognize your old friend. He is a mess."

Not a day went by without a thought for Artopoulos. The word *friend* could barely contain the nature of our former bond. At one time, we had been more like brothers, with all the uneasiness brotherhood entails, but in the almost three years since the outbreak of war I'd only seen him a couple of times, by happenstance, while he was on leave. What had become of him? What had the war done to him? I took my coat and went for a walk in the park, my mind bursting with memories of a bygone friendship that stretched back seventeen years, to the time of my return to Paris.

Moments after my crossing with Madame Édmonde in the train seventeen years earlier, I decided I must vanish. She and I had been seen speaking at length in the parlor car, and in my velvet smoking jacket, turban, and walrus mustache, I attracted attention. I wished to avoid any suspicion that her sudden illness was attributable to our recent acquaintance. The last thing I wanted was to end up stuck in a Midwestern prison.

I began rummaging through Madame Édmonde's belongings, with which I was, of course, intimately familiar, having packed them myself. I knew where she kept her cash, her jewelry, and a promissory note for a rather sizeable sum of money she had written out in my name only the previous evening. I took almost all of it, leaving a little for Lucien to get himself and Édmonde back to Paris. With my hand on the doorknob, my conscience stung me like an angry wasp. I considered leaving a note for Lucien, but what was there to say? I was inflicting a terrible shock on the man, I knew that, but I could not risk being detained. After all, I hadn't left the island for his sake. I did not wish to return to Paris as Édmonde. Mehevi, or whoever he was now, would be looking out for her. He would not be looking out for Balthazar. I had no choice but to flee. I turned and stole a final glance at that contorted face, upon which the suffering of five lifetimes was etched. Her body had been the vessel that had allowed me to return home at last, but my attachment to her was far more profound. In patience, perseverance, and kindness, Édmonde had been my finest incarnation. Now she was in a sorry state—another blind crossing. I was overcome with shame. What had become of me? I was little better than an ordinary criminal, a mountebank stealing the lives of others—and to what end? I consoled myself with the notion that the soul I had stolen was that of a charlatan. But it was undeniable that I had, by now, become a kind of predator. I could blame Mehevi, but as I myself was to blame for him, it came to the same thing.

I had to remind myself, then, as I have countless times since, that there was a single and necessary purpose to my existence: if I had, as the Law prophesied, set in motion a cataclysm, no matter how slowly it unfolded, it was my duty to try to prevent it. My resolve thus stiffened, I fled the scene of the crime.

I returned to my own, second-class cabin, shared with an insurance agent and two youths. I took my seat and pretended to doze. In fact, I was undergoing that surge of memories that occurs upon the occupation of a new body, as every stimulus triggers a series of memories latent within it, which bubble to the surface of the mind from unsuspected depths. The sensation is overwhelming, staggering even, and best borne in stillness and solitude. Around dinnertime, a steward appeared to turn out the beds. I removed my valise and retreated to the water closet at the end of the carriage, as if I was doing nothing more than changing into a dinner suit. There, I discarded my velvet jacket and turban, shaved my mustache, and, in darkness, alighted from the train at the next stop. The following morning, at the post office in Junction City, Kansas, I dictated a telegram to Mathilde in Paris:

*AM RETURNING SOON AS HIPPOLYTE
BALTHAZAR STOP LUCIEN RETURNING
SEPARATELY WITH NEW EDMONDE STOP
DO NOT TRUST ANY NEW ARRIVAL STOP*

The consequence of this unforeseen detour was that it took me several more weeks to arrive in Paris than I had hoped. By that time, it was early June, and the city was now a heaving, dazzling city of two million souls. There was no finer place to be in the world than Paris in the summer of 1900. The streets teemed with people and were crisscrossed in every direction by telegraph wires, while the ground underfoot was riddled with quarries, Métro tunnels, and gas and sewage pipes. One could no longer saunter down the middle of the streets, for they were now cluttered with omnibuses, streetcars, carriages, rattletraps, velocipedes, deluxe coach-and-pairs, and, for well-heeled adventurists, horseless carriages.

The speed of existence had quickened: where life was once lived at walking or trotting pace, people now took underground trains to get from place to place. The arcades of yesteryear had been supplanted by giant department stores employing thousands of cashiers. The city's markets received produce transported on trains from across the country. If one wished to communicate with someone on the other side of town, it was no longer necessary to wait all day or overnight for a reply: a network of pneumatic pipes could deliver blue-papered messages almost instantly. In wealthy homes there were telephones and, in the best houses, one could even listen in on performances at the Opéra on a theatrophone.

The city had grown in size, too. The open fields that had once separated it from its walls were now filled in. More neighborhoods had been demolished and replaced with wide boulevards, sparkling with electric illumination. Thousands of chimneys belched smoke into the air, so that the streets were frequently shrouded in mist. Paris had become decidedly sootier, but also finer somehow, one of those grandes dames whose every wrinkle serves only to make her more resplendent. Women wore ostrich plumes, men wore monocles. Newspaper kiosks and Morris columns advertising the latest shows were dotted through the city. Men no longer relieved themselves in the gutter but in Moorish-inspired *vespasiennes*. At every corner, grimy street urchins were enveloped in some neighborhood conspiracy. And looming above it all was a great iron tower that seemed to have no purpose other than to proclaim the glory of the age.

Millions had come from every country to witness for themselves the wonders of the Exposition Universelle, a paean to the wonders of the whole world. They marveled at such modern miracles as an engine that ran on peanut oil, talking films, escalators, and a device that could record sound called the telegraphone. Intoxicated by the mood of frivolity and pleasure, they took river gondolas and electrified conveyor belts between carnivalesque palaces and specially built pavilions, panoramas of the world's great vistas, dioramas of life in the colonies, the world's largest Ferris wheel, a gigantic globe displaying the constellations of the night sky, and, in the Russian pavilion, a matryoshka doll as tall as a horse containing forty-nine identical versions of herself, each nested within the other, the smallest no bigger than a pea. On Sundays throughout summer and into the autumn, the crowds applauded athletes competing in the Olympic Games. More than just the Olympic motto, *Faster, higher, stronger* was the credo of a whole new century. And yet I could not help but be wistful for the slower, smaller, gentler Paris I had known decades earlier.

I took a modest room in a boarding house in the Sentier neighborhood and slipped into this human sea unnoticed. The Hippolyte Balthazar I'd crossed into was little more than a stage magician, a vaudevillian, a trickster preying on human frailty, but I was determined, with the resources I had inherited, to reinvent myself, even if I could not yet imagine what form my next metamorphosis would take.

While I waited for inspiration to befall me, I had a more pressing matter to attend to: I set out to find Mathilde,

Lucien, and Édmonde. On a fine morning soon after my arrival, I knocked on the door of the Baudelaire Society on the Quai d'Anjou. It had changed little in the three decades since I had left it as Édmonde de Bressy. The door was opened by an unfamiliar man. I asked after Mathilde.

"Madame Roeg is not in," he replied.

"What about Lucien?" I asked.

"Monsieur Roeg is not in either."

"Édmonde?"

"Madame de Bressy has not been in for some time."

"Well, is anyone in?"

"Monsieur Artopoulos."

"May I see him?"

"Whom may I say is calling?"

"Hippolyte Balthazar."

"What is the nature of your visit?"

I had a feeling, deep down in my stomach, that I ought to choose my words carefully. "I wish to join the Society."

He stepped back, opened the door wider, and admitted me into the building. "Please wait," he said before retreating down the hallway. It had been thirty years since I'd last been here. All was as I'd left it—the staircase, the drapes, the mosaic tiles, the rugs, the chandeliers, and the mahogany furniture. But I didn't have the luxury of wallowing in nostalgia. I was worried—worried for Mathilde and Lucien, of course, but also worried about Mehevi.

After a wait of several minutes a tall, rotund man dressed in a fine black suit and pressed white shirt and cravat barged into the room. He sported a curled mustache and a monocle over one eye. When he first laid eyes on me, for a moment that lasted no more than a heartbeat, his entire body froze, his facial expression—eyes widened, mouth agape—that of one beholding a vision, before he snapped back to reality. He approached me, enveloped my outstretched hand between both of his, and introduced himself to me as Aristide Artopoulos. He was, he said, the president of the Baudelaire Society.

"I'm on my way out the door to dine," he boomed. "Would you care to join me? It will give us a chance to discuss Baudelaire to our hearts' content."

My natural inclination was to refuse the invitation, but before I could speak he had taken me by the arm and marched me out with him. There was something compelling about the man. Besides, what harm could it do to luncheon with him if it allowed me to interrogate him? I followed him out the door and into his waiting buggy.

We trotted across town to La Maison Dorée, with Artopoulos talking the whole way, invariably about himself. I bided my time, waiting for an opportunity to turn the conversation to Mathilde and Lucien. At the restaurant, he asked for a private cabinet and, once we were seated, a swarm of waiters descended upon us. He ordered—without any consultation—lobster thermidor for us both, accompanied by a bottle of Les Clos Chablis.

The story of his life so far could be summarized thus: he'd been born in Alexandria into a Greek shipping dynasty. He'd attended boarding school in Switzerland and studied English and French letters at Cambridge. As the youngest of four boys, he'd been spared the duty of the family business and was free to dedicate his existence to the Muse, as he put it, adding that despite his passion for it he had no talent for literature whatsoever. "Like so many others," he said, "I developed an unhealthy obsession for Baudelaire, so naturally I decided to join the Society dedicated to the preservation of his work and legacy."

At last, here was my opportunity. "How was it that you took up the position of president?" I asked.

"It's rather a dismal tale, I'm afraid. You see, the previous president has vanished. Technically speaking, I'm currently the Society's only member—and thus its president by default." This news set my alarm bells ringing. Mathilde was perhaps the most sensible character I'd ever known. She was not the type to just vanish without good cause. I would have to proceed delicately. "How do you mean vanished—how does somebody vanish in this day and age, what with newspapers and telegrams and passports?"

"It happens more frequently than you would think. People disappear all the time." He chewed on his lobster thoughtfully. "I'm afraid I suspect the worst."

"Is that so," I replied, wishing to keep him talking on the subject without betraying my stake in the matter.

"My friend, you have arrived at the Baudelaire Society at a curious time in its history. At its height, around 1870, the Society had fifty-one members. They were the finest literary minds in Paris, all devoted to the work and memory of Baudelaire. Their patron saint was the Society's founder, Madame Édmonde de Bressy. Sadly, she became involved in the Commune, and was exiled, never to return. She left the Society in the care of her companion, Mathilde Roeg. Madame Mathilde's origins were, I understand, insalubrious. I knew her a little—she was practically illiterate. It's unclear to me quite how she came to preside over such a prestigious organization, but I was told she was the most trusted companion of Madame de Bressy." He leaned forward, confidentially. Again

I was struck by the charm of the man—in his mouth, my own story was as enthralling as a newspaper serial. "It was even rumored she'd been a prostitute before Madame Édmonde had taken it upon herself to raise the girl's station in society." He leaned back in his seat. "Madame Mathilde managed the Society's affairs until very recently, but I'm afraid she made a mess of things. We are in an awful state. As far as I can tell very little of Madame Édmonde's fortune is left. It has been entirely squandered."

My anger flared at the travesty of the notion that Mathilde was capable of such incompetence, but I kept my feelings to myself.

"When I joined the Society, only a few weeks ago, it had only three remaining members: Madame Roeg, her son, Monsieur Lucien, a professional vagabond, and the infamous Madame Édmonde, living among the savages in the South Seas. Lucien had gone to fetch her, as no one had seen her in twenty years. It seems he not only found her, he somehow persuaded her to return with him to France. Tragically, both Lucien and Édmonde perished during their journey back to Paris."

Needless to say, Artopoulos's news was a thunderbolt, but I was fortunate to be inhabiting the body of a vaudevillian. The scrutiny of the man sitting opposite me was palpable. Other than for a twitch of the eyebrows and a little, moderately interested grunt, I made sure to keep my face as still as possible. I picked up the glass before me, took a measured sip, set it down again, and tilted my head sideways as if I were merely listening to a curious story about people I'd never met. Inside, I was reeling.

"How terrible!"

"They were on a train from Nantes to Paris, sharing a

cabin. Madame de Bressy had recently suffered some sort of neuralgic attack, I'm led to believe. Lucien was supposed to be caring for her. It appears he killed her with a steak knife, and then he stabbed himself."

My heart was thudding. "Why would he do such a thing?" I managed to utter.

"That's what all of Parisian society would like to know. It is an incredible story, is it not? In my opinion, it should come as no surprise that a man reared by two women should be prone to hysterics."

The look on his face was hard to read. If I had known the man better, I might have called it triumph. Inside this body, I suspected, behind those startling eyes, lurked a familiar malevolence: Mehevi.

Artopoulos continued, apparently unaware of my discomfort. "Of course as the only member of the society, I had to take care of the burial myself. I even paid, out of my own pocket, for a plot in the Montparnasse cemetery. I took the liberty of interring them together in a crypt crowned by a fine pink-and-gray marble plinth under the name of the Baudelaire Society." Yes, all remaining doubts had by now vanished. I was certain this was Mehevi. My nemesis had laid his trap. Somehow he had crossed from the body of the sacrilegious sea captain into that of an exotic dandy—and now he was enjoying himself immensely. Had he guessed who I was? The turn of conversation suggested he harbored his own suspicions, at the very least.

"And what of Madame Roeg?" I asked as casually as I could muster.

"We have heard nothing. Disappeared for good I think. For all I know she simply abandoned her life and went wandering." Artopoulos looked reflective. "It happens from time to time. Someone will set off one day, and never come back. I've heard of some nomadic cultures whose religions revolve around this kind of peregrination. The alienists call it ambulatory automatism."

He turned his attention back to his lobster. He ate quickly, packing his mouth with food and then chewing like a rabbit. I, on the other hand, had lost my appetite altogether. Noticing this, Artopoulos stopped eating and looked up at me with his mouth open, his fully laden fork hovering near its entrance. "What is the matter?" he asked, putting down the fork. Again, I felt the intensity of his gaze.

"Pardon my ignorance, but what is an alienist?" I asked, deflecting the conversation to a safer subject.

Artopoulos was visibly surprised. He lifted his eyebrows so that they formed two perfect circumflexes. "Damnation, man, where have you been for the past twenty years?" I noticed there was a little morsel of lobster flesh spiked in his mustache.

"Forgive me." An alibi sprang unbidden to my mouth—the inherited talents of the born liar. "My education consists of four years at a seminary in Rome."

The eyebrows rose higher still into the middle of his forehead. "How extraordinary. And what finally drove you from the seminary?"

"A crisis of faith."

He laughed. "How charming! And pray tell, what was the nature of this crisis of faith?"

"I began to question the catechism. I began to doubt the existence of the soul."

He studied me with narrowed eyes for a moment before

resuming his feast. "Well, dear boy, it sounds like you would make a wonderful alienist yourself. But I can assure you I have no such doubts."

"Is that so? You believe you have a soul that will go to heaven, or hell, depending on your actions in this lifetime?"

"I didn't say I believe in an afterlife. I believe in the existence of the soul, which is quite a different matter."

"What makes you so certain that there is such a thing, if there is no afterlife?"

Once again, Artopoulos scrutinized me. He seemed to come to a decision. "Dear boy, I think we are going to be the best of friends." He gestured to a waiter to fill our glasses. When they were full, he took another sip, sloshing the wine in his mouth. Once he'd swallowed he resumed his speech—for even when one was alone with Artopoulos, he spoke mostly in speeches, each one delivered as if to a vast assembly. "There is no more exciting field in all the sciences than that of alienism. The alienists proclaim that society stands finally on the threshold of unravelling man's deepest mysteries. In the future, they say, there will be no suffering. There will be remedies for our moral torments as efficacious as those for our physical afflictions." He shoveled another forkful into his cavernous mouth, chewed, rabbit-like, several times, swallowed, and took up the thread once more. "I, for one, am not so convinced. If we have no soul, we are little better than animals. I am no different from this lobster here, for example," he said, pointing toward the crustacean's mutilated carcass. "But which of us is devouring the other?" He half smiled. "The simple fact that I am eating this lobster, in this restaurant, in this city, is proof enough for me that there is no moral equivalence between us. I have a soul, and as long as I am alive it is eternal. You really do drink far too slowly. We shall have to remedy that."

Before I could stop him he'd taken my glass and filled it. On that afternoon, as forever after, Artopoulos was one of the most entertaining men I'd ever known, and not without a certain guile. He asked me about my family, provenance, education, station, and knowledge of poetry. The picture I painted for him in reply was that of a young man of inherited means, a gentleman at large, newly arrived in Paris, with exotic origins and a taste for dilettantism.

As we ate and drank, Artopoulos elaborated his plans for the Society. He seemed to covet an elevated social station and believed the Society was his means of achieving it. But first, he said, the Society must be restored: as it was, its library was in disarray, its finances a mess, its popularity so diminished that the members could now be counted on a single finger—"Unless, old chap," he added, slowly lifting another finger, "I haven't altogether discouraged you, and you still wish to join?"

What choice did I have? "Of course."

"I'm delighted to hear it. I fully intend to return the Baudelaire Society to its rightful place as the most prestigious literary society in France. But currently, I am its only voting member. Without another member to second my motions, nothing can be done. The Society is in a state of complete paralysis."

So am I, I thought to myself. Despite my misgivings, he was so relentlessly compelling that he left me no opportunity to leave him without causing offense. As the afternoon progressed, I decided that perhaps this wasn't such a bad thing. I'd left the island to find him, after all, and now, apparently, here he was. And with the others gone, now that I'd found him, I had nowhere else to go.

After we had eaten, he persuaded me to return to the Society on the Île Saint-Louis. He wanted to show me something, he said. He led me to the library. I studied my surrounds discreetly as we went, once again astonished at how little things had changed in the three decades of my absence. Once at our destination, Artopoulos pulled out a slim volume bound in carmine leather and embossed in gold. He opened a page at random. I immediately recognized the long, sloping handwriting. "A short story by Charles Baudelaire, completely unknown to the world. 'The Education of a Monster.'" Artopoulos was testing my composure to its limits. I had to suppress the mnemonic torrent that came with the sight of it. Once again I felt myself under an especially perceptive scrutiny, and once again I felt compelled to dissemble my emotions and simulate a perfect ignorance. No easy task.

"Is it any good?"

"It is, perhaps, the truest thing he ever wrote."

I hesitated, unsure how to proceed. "I should very much like to read it."

"And you shall have your wish, old chap, once you are a member. We shall attend to that this very day."

From the Society, we proceeded to his apartment on Boulevard Haussmann. He kept me enthralled so long into the night that, at his invitation, I slept in his guest room. We had, somehow, become instantly inseparable. But below the surface, something far more sinister was afoot, and I had confirmation of it the following day, in the Labrouste Reading Room at the national library, when I found a newspaper article reporting on the recent deaths of Édmonde de Bressy and Lucien

Roeg. The account Artopoulos had given me was entirely accurate, other than the omission of a single, crucial detail: the two bodies had been found with their eyes gouged out. I wept hot, silent tears right there in the reading room. I thought of Koroli, the old man at the mission who, after speaking with me, had been murdered in the same way. The evidence wasn't conclusive, but all the clues pointed in the same direction: it seemed I had found my target. Mehevi, or rather Joubert, had positioned himself at the exact center of the web. And yet, having caught me, why hadn't he finished me off? It would become the enduring mystery of our friendship.

For the next several years, Artopoulos and I remained inseparable. We luncheoned at noon most days, mostly at La Maison Dorée, but occasionally at the Café Anglais or the Café de la Paix, and we often dined in the evening too. We sent each other several letters a day, either by post or by *pneumatique*, and as soon as it was possible we had telephones installed in our respective homes. We were regular guests at the Lemaire salon on Rue de Monceau and Laure Hayman's salon on Avenue Hoche. We shared a box at the Opéra and sponsored the same dancers at the Russian ballet. Artopoulos was fond of racing horses, and we were often seen together at the Hippodrome. With the help of connections, he eased my admission into the Jockey Club, despite my obscure origins. On Sundays we would go hunting, driving to his country estate in his Richard-Brasier, or riding along the shaded paths of the Bois de Boulogne, saluting the carriages of the grandes dames of Paris's demimonde. In the summer, we holidayed in Cabourg.

Artopoulos was the epitome of the modern gentleman. His cigars were banded with personalized gilt paper rings. His shirts were from Worth or Redfern and were sent to be washed and pressed in London. When he hosted a dinner, he made sure there was always one footman for every three guests. All year round, he filled his home with great bouquets of flowers— preferably chrysanthemums—ordered weekly from Lachaume or Lemaître. He only drank coffee bought from Maison Corcellet, served from a small silver coffee pot engraved with his initials, AA, and with piping hot milk in a porcelain jug. At tea, he served petits fours from Rebattet and brioches from Bourbonneux. And, without ever asking for anything in return, Artopoulos always made me feel a welcome and natural part of his world, a world of soirées and masquerade balls, hunts and boating expeditions, cabarets and casinos. His generosity to me had no bounds. His only complaint, which he used on many occasions to taunt me affectionately, was that I would never look him in the eye.

Throughout this time, the Baudelaire Society flourished, thanks mostly to Artopoulos's charisma and connections. He rebuilt it into the glittering social salon he'd described to me when first we met, using it to make his inexorable climb to the highest echelons of society. At its peak, around 1910, the Society boasted among its members such luminaries as the Comtesse de Chevigné, Robert de Montesquiou, Lucien Daudet, Comte Henri Greffulhe, Antoine Bibesco, and Anna de Noailles. The guestbook was pocked with such names as the Duc d'Orléans, the Empress Dowager, the King of Greece, the Serbian pretender Karageorgevich, Prince Karl Egon von Fürstenberg, and the banker Bischoffsheim. Even the Prince of Wales attended on one occasion, as the guest of Odile de Richelieu.

What did he see in me? What did I mean to him? What

did he want from me? He didn't say, and I didn't ask. Not once did we attempt to breach our respective alibis. The truth was suspended between us, binding us, unacknowledged and ever-present. It was sufficient to me to be near him, a friend and ally on the surface, but always keeping a watchful eye over him, like a guardian, looking out for a sign that he might once again wreak the havoc I knew he was capable of. I felt a responsibility for him. I never had a plan as such, and in the glow of our friendship, the violence I knew was in him never revealed itself. It seemed I might achieve my purpose simply by being by his side. In all our years of friendship, there were no murders, no eye-gougings. Did I need to wait for him to kill again to act? And, if so, what could I have done? I would surely have had to kill him in turn. I never felt even remotely capable of such an act. What would I have used for the purpose? A pistol? A knife? Poison? It was all unthinkable, and given how perfectly content we were in each other's company, I deemed it preferable to let things slide.

I'd decided I didn't wish to spend my life as a glorified vaudevillian preying on the credulity of the uneducated and broken-hearted. I wished a more respectable destiny for myself. Artopoulos had planted a seed in me, that day over lunch, a seed that grew, watered by my inherited skills in mesmerism, by his encouragement, and by my own interest in understanding the mechanism behind the act of crossing. I would become, I resolved, an alienist. I began to study psychology, at first as an observer of the lectures, for I had no formal qualifications. At the Sorbonne, I took meticulous notes in the lecture hall and, afterward, read everything I could in the libraries. I took tutors and volunteered to be a laboratory assistant. Artopoulos pulled some strings on my behalf and before long I was admitted as a student.

Within a year of my arrival, I had been accepted into the preparatory classes to study medicine. In 1908 I graduated as a doctor, and began higher studies in psychology. From the start, I'd resolved that my methods would be unorthodox: I would use hypnosis in the treatment of my patients. The idea was not new. It had already been entertained and, ultimately, rejected by the previous generation of alienists. But I had one advantage they didn't have.

Along the way I studied under Alfred Binet at the Laboratory of Physiological Psychology. Later, I researched retrograde amnesia under Théodule-Armand Ribot, assisted Théodore Flournoy in his study of cryptonmesia, and attended the lectures of Pierre Janet at the Collège de France on memory, trauma, neurotic dissociation, and the subconscious.

I established a private practice treating patients suffering from melancholia or neurosis with the aid of hypnosis. I benefited from Artopoulos's high-society connections and many of my habitués were members of the Baudelaire Society. My method was unique and controversial: first I would hypnotize, and only then would I analyze. My growing reputation began to attract the attention of the younger generation. Some of them courted my favors, intrigued by the reports of the breakthroughs my clients achieved, which they themselves could not replicate, no matter how closely they imitated me. Little could they guess the secret of my success—I was using the art of crossing to look inside the minds of those I treated. For my patients, there seemed to be something beneficial about it, something restorative and healing simply in the fact of, however briefly, no longer being held captive by an overactive imagination. And while visiting their bodies and minds, I would explore their memories, dreams, illusions, and delusions, their secrets, pretenses, and lies. This way, during the analysis that followed the crossing, I could detect every self-deceit, every avoidance, and every dissemblance. I came to know my patients better than they knew themselves. I knew when they were lying to me, and more importantly I knew when they were lying to themselves, an all-too-frequent occurrence.

Around this time, the profession of alienist was undergoing profound changes. It became fashionable, in certain high society circles, to seek the assistance of an altogether new kind of doctor. In March 1910, I attended the Second Congress for Freudian Psychology in Nuremberg and, upon my return to Paris, stopped calling myself an alienist and instead took up the title of psychoanalyst. My method, however, didn't change.

If it was a sham of a kind, it was a sham with indisputable results. I was invited to lecture at the Sorbonne, and later at the Institut de France. I published essays in medical journals and popular magazines, and occasionally my name was printed in the newspaper society pages, usually alongside that of Artopoulos. He would tease me about my progress—his favorite joke was to beg me to hypnotize him. In the spirit of the joke, I always refused him good-naturedly, telling him we were too close, that I knew him too well, that he wasn't suggestible enough. Joking aside, I never trusted him enough to hypnotize him. His friendship was akin to keeping a tiger for a pet: I never allowed myself to forget I might be mauled to death at any moment.

Perhaps inevitably, I developed a particular interest in the fugue state, which in those days went by several names: traveling fugue, psychogenic fugue, ambulatory automatism, dromomania. The fugue state is extremely rare, so rare it is at best a medical curiosity, hardly the kind of condition upon which a psychoanalyst might build a career. But over time, having published several articles on the disorder, I came to be recognized as its pre-eminent specialist. My interest was, of course, more than merely professional. I had witnessed a fugue state of sorts several times, after each of my blind crossings. On each occasion, I had been its cause. I was haunted by the faces of the bodies I'd just vacated, the physiological mark of the bewilderment that follows an unforeseen crossing. But there was also a practical dimension to my interest: it was a way of looking out for Mathilde. I hoped that, if she was still alive, Mathilde would remember what I'd told her, decades ago before I had gone into exile. If she did make a crossing, if her body was left flailing with bewilderment, and if some doctor somewhere diagnosed it as a fugue state, there was every chance that I, as the only specialist in the field, would be called upon to treat it. As schemes go, it may have been far-fetched, but it was my only hope of finding you.

Only I didn't find you. Rather, it was you who found me. I was looking out of a window at the Baudelaire Society one morning in the winter of 1911 when I saw a hunchbacked old woman laboring across the Pont Louis-Philippe and then up the Quai d'Anjou. She was dressed in rags, her face obscured by a hood, and was pushing a cart laden with old books. It was a remarkable sight, for she was bent over in two, and getting the wooden wheels over the cobbles of the street was no easy feat. As she neared the entrance to the Society, she was overtaken by the valet, Renand, carrying several loaves of bread that would be served at lunch. As he passed her, the old woman said something to him that I could not hear. He answered her briefly, shaking his head, and then entered the building. I made my way to the kitchen, where the valet had set about helping the cook, Carlotta. I asked Renand what the old woman had said to him.

"Which old woman?" he said.

"The book peddler you just spoke to outside on the street."

"Oh, her! She's a lunatic, not a book peddler. Her books are worthless. I often see her loitering about. She's always asking me the same thing."

"Are you talking about the old Belgian woman?" said Carlotta.

"Yes," Renand and I both said at once.

"She does the same thing with me! She's been asking me for years, the pet. I feel so sorry for her."

"What does she ask you?"

"Every time I see her," Renand said, "she asks if Madame Édmonde has returned."

"She asks me the same thing," added Carlotta.

My heart skipped a beat. "And what do you say?"

"I tell her Madame Édmonde is dead," said Renand, "but she never remembers. She's lost her wits."

I felt a charge like being plunged under cold water.

"I asked her once why she wanted to know," said Carlotta. "Hard to imagine it, but it seems she and Madame Édmonde were both Communards."

Excusing myself as politely as I could without drawing attention to myself, I dashed out of the building, grabbing my jacket and hat on the fly. I looked up and down the street. The woman was nowhere to be seen. I turned left and ran around the corner, to the end of the island, where the cathedral and the Île de la Cité come into view. I saw her from a distance: she had just stepped onto the Pont Saint-Louis, headed toward the cathedral. I ran after her.

"Madame!" I shouted as I neared her. The hunchbacked figure stopped and turned. It was some four decades since I'd last seen her. She had aged terribly, but she was still recognizably Mathilde. "Madame, I'm told you're looking for Édmonde de Bressy."

"Yes."

"Unfortunately, Édmonde passed away several years ago."

"I see. You're quite sure?"

"Quite sure, madame. You can stop looking for her."

"Thank you for letting me know." I could hear her familiar, sing-song accent.

"You're welcome," I said. Mathilde turned to continue her way along the bridge. "She did manage, however, to make a crossing before she died."

Mathilde froze for a moment and then straightened her back. She turned to face me. "What is your name, monsieur?"

"My name is Hippolyte Balthazar."

"And what is mine?"

"Your name is Mathilde Roeg."

"I've been waiting for you a long time."

We must have made a curious sight, she and I, beggar-woman and dandy, embracing on that bridge for so long.

I could not lodge Mathilde in my apartment on the Boulevard Haussmann, as it was too close to that of Artopoulos. I feared what he would do if he discovered I was harboring her. Instead, I found her a comfortable room in an out-of-the-way hotel where we might converse to our hearts' content. There we talked for the rest of the day. For eleven years, Mathilde told me, she had been in hiding, moving from boarding house to boarding house, making a living of sorts peddling books. She had never received the telegram I'd sent her from Kansas, or if she had, she'd never read it. Although a bookseller, she was still illiterate. Stubborn as she was, she had never even attempted to learn. When Lucien traveled, she told me, she would put all her correspondence in a pile on her desk at the Baudelaire Society, awaiting his return. When I heard this, I could not suppress a shiver of horror. Artopoulos must have read the telegram. It was the first definitive sign that he was who I'd suspected him to be, and that he had known who I was from the very beginning. He must have been expecting me, when I first appeared at the Baudelaire Society. And ever since, he had been toying with me, never once saying or doing anything that gave himself away, even though he must have known that I suspected him in return.

Why had he indulged me so? I have considered the matter many times since, and my only answer, unsatisfactory as it may be, is the memory of that first glance he gave me the day of our first encounter in the lobby of the Baudelaire Society. Perhaps he had found an unexpected solace in our friendship, a relief from what would otherwise have been a crushing loneliness. And as I was the only soul in the world who truly knew him and his secrets, he showed me something I would never have expected of him: he showed me mercy. That mercy mixed with solitude and became love. I in turn had found solace in him, I in turn had loved him, the way one loves a sparring partner, a cellmate, or an *enfant terrible*, knowing it to be dangerous, painful, wrong even, but doing it anyway, out of fatalism, defiance, or compulsion.

As for the mystery of Mathilde's disappearance, I never received a satisfactory explanation from her, but I suspect there was more to it than just grief. The double loss—and in such dreadful circumstances—of her son and Édmonde would have unhinged the sturdiest mind, but there was more to it even than that. Artopoulos had only just joined the Baudelaire Society, the first new member in more than a decade. I imagine, upon his arrival, he assumed his characteristic quasi-aristocratic entitlement over the place, as if Mathilde had merely been keeping the chair warm for him. Something had occurred between the two of them, soon after the news of the murders of Lucien and Édmonde, something that forced her to flee. Perhaps he'd attacked her, perhaps he'd admitted to his crime, perhaps it was something else altogether. Whatever it was, it was something vicious, something cruel, something unforgivable. Mathilde never told me the full story, and what little she revealed was only ever let slip or hinted at, but I remembered my encounter with Mehevi on the island decades earlier and no further explanation was required. Thereafter, my vigilance around Artopoulos was only heightened, and I began orchestrating an almost imperceptibly gradual cooling of our friendship.

I rented Mathilde an apartment on the Rue du Faubourg Saint-Denis and saw to it that she lived a life of ease. I was overjoyed that—despite everything—she had survived. I visited her every day. We shared our sorrows about Lucien. Other than Artopoulos, she was the only person in the world who knew me truly, but I kept them hidden from each other. On one occasion, I managed to smuggle the story Charles had written out of the Baudelaire Society library and read it aloud to her. She showed me none of her previous resistance. Time, memory, our reunion, the death of her son, perhaps even the shadow of her own mortality, all of these seemed to have softened her opinions on the subject of crossing. When I raised the possibility of undertaking another crossing, she didn't dismiss me as she once might have done, but rather listened with an open mind. Within a few months, she agreed that the time had come. She never gave up peddling books—it was her way of finding a new body. The only problem, she often complained, was that no one ever wanted to look an old woman in the eye.

In the spring of 1913, I was called one day to the Hôtel-Dieu hospital to attend to a woman who had suffered, that very morning at a café on the Boulevard Saint-Germain, a fugue state. There was Mathilde, her eyes wide open, her lips whispering something indecipherably Germanic, her head shaking as though in disbelief—all symptoms of that bewilderment that haunts the ambushed soul after a crossing. I asked the policeman who'd brought her there what he knew of what had occurred. Witnesses had reported, he said, that at the time of the incident she'd been telling the fortune of a German tourist. Precisely what had happened was a mystery—the young man had left the scene. That was all the policeman knew.

My relief that she had managed a crossing was tempered by the sorrow that whoever she'd crossed with was now somewhere far away. How much of his previous existences did he remember? What were the chances of our ever crossing paths again? I placed the shell of Mathilde in a home for the elderly. She never recovered from her fugue, and some time later she died in her sleep, a year before Europe began to tear itself apart. She was buried in a grave in a suburban cemetery marked only by her initials. I'd managed to keep our reunion a secret from Artopoulos, and I wanted to keep it that way.

Like so many others, the outbreak of war brought out a
bloodlust in Artopoulos hitherto disguised as a fondness for
hunting and social advancement. He enlisted at the declaration of hostilities and urged me to do the same. Having gone
through the horrors of the Commune, I was a little more cir-
cumspect, but I figured I might do some good in the Medical
Corps. Artopoulos pulled some strings and received a captain's
commission in the cavalry. The war only widened the distance
that had grown between us. As the conflict dragged on, its
barbarity seemed to shatter the artifice of our already dubious
friendship. I found my distance from him a relief. Our letters
became less frequent and more guarded until eventually we
stopped writing altogether.

The man who was wheeled into my office at two o'clock that
afternoon was unrecognizable as the man I'd once counted as
my closest friend. His body, face, and limbs were contorted,
distended, and racked with convulsions—one of the worst pre-
sentations of shellshock I'd seen. The war had wrecked him.

"Bonjour, Artopoulos," I said as the nurse handed me his
case notes.

"B-b-b-b-bon-j-j-jour," he labored as I skimmed the paperwork. The notes revealed his rank was second lieutenant. This
surprised me. The death rate of commissioned officers in battle
was such that promotion was almost guaranteed, and his bat-
talion, stationed in Champagne, had seen some of the worst
of the fighting. But Artopoulos had been demoted, twice.
The notes explained several of his men had complained of unwanted, forceful advances.

The nurse cleared her throat. I looked up from my reading
and sprang to my feet, pulling her by the arm until we were

both outside my office door. "Can you stay?" I asked in a low voice. "In case he takes a turn for the worse?"

"I'm sorry, doctor," she replied, "I must attend to my rounds. If you need me, just ring the bell."

As soon as I had closed the door behind me, Artopoulos jumped up, smiled, and, taking a cigarette from his shirt pocket, began to smoke as he sauntered to the couch and let himself plump happily into it.

"Sorry about the histrionics, but it isn't easy getting an audience with Your Highness these days."

"Is this one of your pranks, Artopoulos?"

"Not at all, old chap. In fact, this whole war is a little on the serious side, wouldn't you agree? Not that you would know it, from this island of tranquility." He flashed one of his trademark smirks, laced with irony.

"I know all about it through my patients. I was assigned this role because somebody thought I might make a difference here. And so far that has tended to be the case."

"You could have insisted on active combat, I suppose," said Artopoulos. "But I don't blame you for avoiding it. It's hell out there." He stood and began pacing the room. "Balthazar, you need to get me out of this war."

"Why would I do that?"

"Because we're friends," he said, turning toward me. He raised an eyebrow. "Are we not?" No, I thought to myself, we are most decidedly not friends.

"How do you suppose I might go about it?" I asked.

"I don't know. A medical discharge perhaps? Write me off as an incurable case."

"But you're not sick."

"*They* don't know it."

"I wish it were as easy as you presume, but I can't do that with a stroke of my pen. I don't have the authority. There are processes in place precisely to avoid that kind of . . ." I realized I could not finish the sentence politely.

"Of what?"

"Of cheating."

"Cheating?" Now it was his turn to be taken aback. "I'm sorry you feel that way after I've taken such trouble to find you." There was a hint of menace in his voice.

Artopoulos paused, standing at the windowsill, looking out at the park that surrounded the asylum. "Careful someone doesn't see you," I said. He returned to the couch. My mind was bursting with questions. Why had he come to me? Why had he not crossed with someone else?

"Well, since you're here, why don't you tell me something. A little talking cure could be very helpful."

"What would you like to know?"

"Tell me about your demotions."

Artopoulos froze, giving me a very serious look, as if deliberating on some thorny dilemma. "Ah, yes," he said. "Most unfortunate. I—I was . . . I was trying to . . ." His voice trailed off, his mouth open as if about to speak, but unable to articulate the words intended to pass through it. He was perfectly conflicted between two equal and opposite desires: the desire to reveal himself and the desire to remain hidden. At last, I thought, the veil of civility is about to fall away. At last, he is going to tell me who he really is. He is going to tell me what he can do. He is going to tell me that in fact he wasn't making advances on those men at all, that what he was actually doing to those men was holding their faces still so that he could look them in the eyes. He is going to tell me that it is impossible to force a man to look you in the eye, that an eyeball is a slippery and rubbery thing that cannot be controlled, that it is easier to pop it out of its socket than to keep it still, that it is simpler to blind a man than to make him look. Then finally he is going to tell me why he is here, and what he wants from me. He is going to tell me that he was responsible for the murders of Lucien, of Édmonde, for their eyeless bodies, for their lives cut short. And finally he is going to tell me that I am the one ultimately responsible for his crimes, that I started it all, all those generations ago, when I deprived him of his body, his friends, his world.

"There's something you should know," he said at last.

"What's that?"

"I know."

"What do you know?"

"I know that you know."

"And what do I know?"

"Everything. Everything there is to know."

"So why speak in circles, why not just say it?"

"I can't."

"Why not?"

"Because I don't want to push you away. Because you're the only friend I have. You're the only friend I've ever had."

"Nonsense. You have many friends. Many more than I have."

"No. Without you, I have no one. You're the only one who knows."

"Knows what?"

"Everything."

Evidently, that was all I was going to get out of him. I suppose it was a confession, of sorts, or as close to one as someone as secretive as Artopoulos could manage. I waited for him to say more, but by now he was just sitting on the couch opposite me, staring sadly into nothing.

"Well, your performance has earned you twelve weeks' respite here at the hospital," I said. "It's a start."

"What good will it have done if I have to go back? The war won't end in three months."

"But you're not sick. So technically you're on a holiday to which you're not entitled."

"Entitled? Do you think anyone is entitled to what is going on out there?"

"Of course not. Every day, I treat men—and now it seems also women—whose psyches have been destroyed by what they've endured out there. But I can't end the war."

"What *can* you do?"

"I can alleviate suffering."

"Alleviate mine!"

"You're not sick!"

"So you refuse to help me?"

"Oh, I'll help you, don't worry. I'll keep the secret of your charade to myself. But I can't get you out of the war. You see, I'm rather good at my job. My patients tend to get better. To get you a discharge, you would have to be too sick to go back. That's quite rare. It would require some first-rate acting on your part. And the decision is out of my hands. Of course, I can make a recommendation, but ultimately it's the Medical Review Board that decides. You'd have to convince them, and they don't like me very much."

"Why is that?"

"Because no one else can replicate my success rate."

"Your success rate!" he spat. "Tell me, how *do* you achieve your success rate?"

"The same way I've always done it. I hypnotize, and then I analyze."

"So hypnotize me. I've asked you often enough—dozens of times, probably, and you always fobbed me off."

"I didn't fob you off."

"Do it now. Don't you think you owe me that much?"

Of course I owed him. I owed him everything, in a way. But crossing with him was out of the question. Obviously I didn't want to cross with him only to be sent back to the trenches, who would? But equally I didn't want him in *my* position, occupying my life, colonizing it. "Well, for one thing, you're not sick. And for another, we know each other too well. As I've said to you many times, I don't think you're suggestible."

"Oh, that's nonsense."

"Not at all. It's a fact. Not everyone can be hypnotized."

"How do you know I can't? You've never even tried."

"Well, even if I could, there's another problem. You see, recently, treatment of shellshock has changed. When analysis doesn't work, they send you off to electric shock therapy."

"So they're torturing men back into the trenches?"

"Precisely."

"Ah," he huffed, "you're just making excuses." He slumped back despondently in the couch. "I think you're being most unreasonable. After all, I welcomed you when you were a nobody. I cared for you. I paid for your studies. I gave you your career. And the one time I ask you for help, you refuse me."

"I'm not refusing you. I'm telling you I can't give you a discharge."

"Then hypnotize me, at least!" he shouted, loud enough for someone in the corridor to hear. The menace had returned, this time as more than a hint.

"Please, keep your voice down," I said, placating him. Perhaps, I thought, there was a way I could squirm my way out of the corner I was backed into. "Very well. We'll try it. But if it doesn't work, don't blame me." With a sigh, I dragged my armchair closer to the couch and sat on its edge. I had no idea what to do. Improvising, I pulled out my pocket watch and opened it.

"What are you doing?" asked Artopoulos.

"I'm going to hypnotize you."

"Not with your watch! Do you take me for a fool? We're not in a circus. I know your methods. With your eyes! Hypnotize me with your eyes, damnation."

"Yes, yes, keep calm, I beg of you."

Until now, I'd never looked into someone's eyes for any length of time without *wanting* to cross. This situation—*not* wanting to cross—was completely unknown to me. Moreover it wasn't just anyone's eyes I was looking into. It was Artopoulos. There was nothing I knew about crossing that he didn't know.

Our gazes met and settled into each other. The key, I told myself, was to keep my soul completely still. I had to stop it from reaching out. I had to stop his, somehow, from reaching in. But almost as soon as our eyes met I felt the forward lurch, the tingling, the beginnings of dissipation. A tide of panic began to rise in me. I had to do something. I had to abandon ship. So I looked away.

"Just as I thought," I said. "Nothing's happening. It's no good."

"Try again," snapped Artopoulos.

"No. I don't think it's going to work."

"Try it again, damnation, and this time don't look away!"

"I'm sorry, Aristide, no."

Artopoulos rose, lunged toward me, and slapped me. "You fraud!" he snarled. "You liar! You snake! After all I have done for you!"

"How dare you!" I said, standing so that we were face to face. I slapped him in return.

He began pummeling me with both hands, fists clenched, over and again, cursing me as he did. "You are a monster!" he said. "You are evil!" I covered my head with my arms but I was no match for him. From under his blows, I fell back against the desk, reached behind me and somehow managed to grab the bell, ringing it vigorously before, with a swipe of his arm, Artopoulos knocked it from my hand. Now, consumed by a scarlet rage, he threw himself upon me until we were both writhing on the desk. He wrestled me onto my back. With one hand, he grabbed me by the throat and began to throttle me while, with the other, he reached his hooked fingers toward my eyes and began digging into them around their edges. At that same moment, the nurse entered the room, saw our imbroglio, and screamed. Soon, several orderlies had rushed in, lifted Artopoulos expertly off me, and strapped him into his wheelchair, where he continued, as they wheeled him out of the room and down the corridor, to shout, "You are *evil*! You are *evil*! You are *evil*!"

I was left breathless and trembling. I rubbed my eyes and my throat and straightened my collar. From my mouth and nose I felt a trickle of blood. The nurse sat me down and went to fetch some gauze and alcohol. Monsieur Julien the registrar rushed in and asked what had happened. As the nurse daubed my wounds, I assured him that no great damage had been done, that no disciplinary action was necessary, that the patient's outburst was merely the act of a troubled mind, that such things were a professional hazard, that if anything it was a good sign, an indication he would, sooner or later, make a full and complete recovery, only it would not be me treating him, needless to say, no, it would certainly not be me.

When, the following morning, I next saw Madeleine, I was still shaken by the events of the previous day. I'd barely eaten or slept and my mind was racing. That incantation, *You are evil*, was still ringing in my ears. Was it meant as an insult or a condemnation? I didn't know then and to this day I still don't know. It is a profoundly disturbing experience to be judged evil by someone upon whom one has delivered the same judgment.

My entire therapeutic method consisted in making a blind crossing with a patient—that is, a crossing of which the patient would afterward have no recollection, other than a faint, residual impression of psychic relief or alleviation. I had performed it hundreds, perhaps thousands, of times, and never had a patient ever expressed the slightest hint of awareness of what had just happened. But on this occasion, something went wrong. Perhaps it was inevitable that, sooner or later, I'd make a mistake. Perhaps I was run down, or distracted by my reunion with Artopoulos. Perhaps it was subconsciously intended, or provoked by something about Madeleine herself. Whatever the case, it was my intention, as always, that after the return crossing she should have no recollection of what had occurred. But as soon as the initial crossing was complete, I felt something was amiss. I must have overlooked something, or been careless somehow in my method. All the same, I proceeded in my exploration of the patient's body and mind when she, in my own body sitting in the chair opposite me, spoke.

"Please," she said, in my own voice, "I don't want to go back."

"Excuse me?"

"I don't want to go back," she repeated with more emphasis.

"Go back where?"

"To my body. To Madeleine. Don't make me. Please."

"You want to stay in that old man's body?"

"Yes."

"I can't let you do that."

I watched in horror as Madeleine-in-Balthazar rose from the chair and leaned over me, whispering the following words very slowly: "You cannot make me go back to that body."

"I would remind you that you are under hypnosis, which you entered into voluntarily. When I command it, you will look again into my eyes and you will return to the body that is rightfully yours."

Balthazar paused, as if considering mutiny, but after a long moment he sat back in his chair and we began the return crossing. I was more determined than ever to leave in Madeleine not a trace of a memory of what had just occurred, but naturally I was also perturbed. My confidence in my abilities was shaken. The technique of crossing is based on a kind of mental purity. Obstructions, distractions, hindrances can tilt the entire process off-kilter. When the return crossing was complete, Madeleine didn't say anything untoward, but there was something about her expression that suggested her state of mind was not how it was supposed to be. She beheld me with an expression somewhere between wonder and suspicion, markedly different from that depressed countenance that had characterized her demeanor before the crossing.

"What just happened?" she asked finally.

"You were under hypnosis."

"How long did it last?"

"A little under thirty minutes, as we discussed."

"And what happened in that time?"

"You were in a state of deep relaxation the entire time."

She mentioned nothing more of it, but when we launched into the analysis I found her to be distant and standoffish, and nothing was achieved. I ended the session early.

A fraud lives in perpetual fear of the cataclysm of his unmasking. Days later, I received a letter from the Medical Review Board. I was under investigation, it said, after a patient had made a complaint against me. My methods were to be reviewed by a panel of three specialists the following week: Gustave Roussy, André Léri, and Jacques Jean Lhermitte. Until then, I was suspended from my duties. The board had been stacked against me, as if handpicked specifically for the purpose of discrediting me. I knew I had enemies in both the military and medical hierarchies, all of whom considered my methods suspect. Léri, in particular, was my professional nemesis, a champion of electric shock treatment, hostile to any doctor who advocated analysis as treatment for shellshock. He thought hypnosis was quackery. The letter didn't name the complainant, but I guessed it was Artopoulos. He was going to force me to hypnotize him in front of the review panel.

I would be his ticket out of the war after all: he would make a crossing, and I would be the one to return to the trenches, only in his body. In the seventeen years of our friendship, he'd never shown me the slightest enmity. There had never been any question of violence. If one of us had wished to harm the other, we'd forsaken countless opportunities to do so. As his creator, his only link to the past, I'd always been exempted from his vengeful nature. No longer.

The morning of the review, I was pacing up and down in my office when there was a knock at the door. It was Madeleine.

"Madame," I said, "I didn't expect to see you here this morning."

"Why not?"

"My appointments have all been canceled. Surely you were told. I've been suspended. Someone's made a complaint about me. I'm supposed to meet with the Medical Review Board in the Great Hall this afternoon. I have to defend my methods before a panel of three doctors."

She looked at me with a confused expression. "It wasn't me," she said. "I have no complaints about your methods, professor."

"I wasn't suggesting it," I said with a smile, "but I'm glad to hear it all the same."

"My only complaint," she continued hesitantly, "although it's not a complaint at all really, is the one I expressed last time, while I was under hypnosis."

I played dumb. "Remind me?"

"That if there is the possibility of passing over into another body, I wish to take it."

I considered my predicament briefly before concluding I

had nothing to gain by insisting on the pretense. "Madame, I must be honest with you. Something went wrong. You're not supposed to remember that."

"But I do. I remember everything about it. Most of all, I remember thinking, I don't want to go back. I meant what I said, professor. I still do."

I tried to reason with her. "I'm sorry, madame, I can't accept your proposition. It would be a travesty. Do you really want to forsake your youth, health, and beauty to live the rest of your days in the body of a middle-aged bachelor?"

"I want to live someone else's life. I don't want to live mine. It's too painful. Don't you understand? When I look in the mirror, I look at myself with someone else's eyes—the eyes of the man who loved me, the man I lost, the only man I will ever love. It is painful for me to look at myself. I cannot extinguish the love that is in me, and every time I see myself I am reminded of it. In order for me to be fully alive I need to leave this body—or I shall have to take my own life."

"But you have so much to look forward to, so much still in front of you."

"Do I? I'm a widow and an orphan. I'm penniless. I have only a basic education. What do you imagine I have to look forward to if love is out of the question? An empty marriage? Raising the children of a husband I don't love? A convent? Praying to a god I don't believe in?"

"You could be a nurse—you're obviously very good at it."

"There'll be little need for nurses when the war is over. No, I see nothing in front of me. A long, vast stretch of nothing." She turned and looked around the room, and as she looked around it I looked too, following her gaze across the bookshelves and the paintings and the certificates on the walls.

"Whereas," she continued, "if I were to spend the rest of my days in *your* body, even if there were fewer days to live, they'd be better days. I'd be surrounded by books and luxuries. I'd be educated and never want for anything. I'd heal people and move in high circles. If ever I was bored I would simply go back through your memories, and relive for myself one of your many adventures. I imagine there are enough memories in you to last me a lifetime. And of course there is the not inconsiderable advantage that I would be a man." She turned to me, took my hands in hers, and gave me an imploring look. "What do you say, Professor Balthazar? Please, won't you set me free?"

I looked into her dark sparkling eyes and wondered if I should warn her about Artopoulos, about what had happened to Édmonde and Lucien, about the Baudelaire Society and Charles's manuscript. If I did so, would she change her mind? Would she decide that her own body, her own life, were not so insufferable after all? But as I wondered these thoughts, I felt that familiar flicker of pleasure as the first stirrings of the crossing began, and I decided that she already knew everything she needed to know.

{124}

Madeleine Blanc

Born 1898
First crossing 1917

BALTHAZAR SAT IN his chair very close to me, staring vacantly at nothing in particular. For a moment, I thought I'd made a blind crossing. "How are you feeling?" I asked.

Balthazar shook his head a little as if recovering from a blow. "Fine, I think."

"No regrets?" I asked. "No second thoughts? Once I walk out that door, there'll be no turning back." For the sake of my own conscience, I needed to make one last gesture of goodwill before making my escape forever.

"No," he replied, "you have granted me my wish. I'm grateful to you."

To be certain he was fully lucid, I questioned him about his current name, his former name, where we were, the day of the week, the name of the President of the Republic—he remembered everything. "You're not in a fugue state, which is a good sign," I said. "But I should warn you: you are going to need all your wits about you. This very day, you will face a tribunal inquiring into your clinical methods." As I spoke, I saw that memories of the matter came to him, and he nodded with recognition. "They will ask you to hypnotize a man called

Aristide Artopoulos. I urge you to reflect a moment upon the history of your acquaintance with him." Balthazar nodded as memories of Artopoulos rushed to the surface of his mind. "The critical thing is that you must not look him in the eye, or he will cross with you. And, believe me, you don't want that."

As I shook Balthazar's hand, I suppressed a shudder at the thought of what might happen if Artopoulos were to divine that this was not the man he was after. I knew I must once again vanish. I didn't want to lose the advantage I had over Artopoulos—he didn't know what I looked like. I fled the Villejuif military asylum with nothing more than the clothes on my back. I caught a suburban train to the center of Paris and went to a shirtmaker's workshop in the Arts et Métiers neighborhood run by a Saigonese family I knew from my childhood. They did not turn me away. I stayed with them until after the war. I burned my identity papers and took on the surname Blanc.

From that day on, I lived in hiding—and with good cause. Two weeks later, I learned that Hippolyte Balthazar had been murdered in his own bed. According to the newspapers, his body was found with the eyes removed. My grief was compounded by guilt. There could be no doubt about his killer. As with Édmonde and Lucien, Artopoulos had either had Balthazar murdered by proxy or done the deed himself. I could not know if he had discovered my deception, but I assumed the worst. Either way, the removal of the eyes felt more than just a message or a demonstration of power, I interpreted it as a kind of macabre vow. From now on, the price I would have to pay for my freedom was the torture and murder of innocents.

In ordinary circumstances, such a murder would have scandalized Paris. But the relentless slaughter occurring only a day's drive away had inoculated Parisians to individual acts of violence. Balthazar's death was soon forgotten. Artopoulos had him buried with Édmonde and Lucien in the Baudelaire Society crypt at the Montparnasse cemetery—yes, at the very spot we were to meet, you and I, twenty-three years later. It isn't every day one has the occasion to attend one's own funeral. It was a modest affair held on a rain-soaked morning. I stood at the back of the small gathering, my identity vouchsafed by my veil. There were barely more than a dozen mourners, all of whom I recognized: clients of Balthazar's and members of the Baudelaire Society. Artopoulos was there, of course, standing by the graveside. He had given up feigning the tremors of shellshock. Beside him was a striking, square-jawed woman I'd never seen before. Later, I would learn that her name was Gabrielle Chanel, better known by her nickname Coco.

Shortly before Christmas 1920 at the Saint-Quentin market, I spied Renand, the Baudelaire Society's valet, from across a crowd. We locked eyes momentarily before I managed to duck out of the way. Thankfully, the Christmas throng was thick enough for me to make my getaway before he could catch me. I'd been shopping there since my flight from the asylum, knowing Renand normally went to the Place Maubert market on the other side of the river to buy provisions for Artopoulos and the Baudelaire Society. The encounter rattled me for months. I could not be sure that Renand had been there looking specifically for me—he'd never seen me, after all, and I'd taken care to avoid all cameras in the intervening years—but I haven't been back to the Saint-Quentin market since.

I resolved to leave the family I'd been boarding with and vanish more completely. I took to living underground, as generations of Parisian fugitives had done before me. For many years I have made my home in the labyrinth of quarries, sewers, tunnels, and catacombs below the city's surface. The subterranean life is easy enough to enter into: all one needs is a belt buckle with which to lift the grates that lead below and a map of the maze of old limestone quarries and abandoned Métro tunnels under the city. Dry, spacious, and temperate, they make excellent habitations. I have made a home of several such places, moving only when another fugitive discovers my hideout or when some above-ground construction work makes it unsafe to remain there.

For the last few years, I have resided in the quarry below the Montparnasse cemetery—the grate is very near the crypt of the Baudelaire Society. An iron ladder leads into the quarry. Every afternoon, toward closing time, I stand in front of Baudelaire's grave until the guardian blows his whistle. That's what I was doing when we met. When I'm certain I can't be seen, I hide among the gravestones until the guardian, having locked all the gates, returns to the gatehouse. When I am alone, I take my belt buckle, lift the lid of the grate, and slip into my abode. There are other grates outside the cemetery walls that I can use if, for one reason or another, I cannot be sure that I am alone in the cemetery, but as they are on the street I can only ever do so in the dead of night, and even then, between the homeless men and the streetsweepers, I am courting danger each time.

By far the most joyous occasion of this lifetime has been to find you again, dear Koahu, and to love you again. I never abandoned the hope that somehow we might be reunited, you and I. I never entirely lost faith that your nightmares would lead you back to me somehow. Like a spider in a dark corner, I waited for you. My faith in you has been vindicated. You came to me, even if you don't know it. Something in you sought me out—how else could you possibly explain it? And though, with your little round glasses and funny mustache, you are much changed, the spirit of Koahu still lives in you.

All this time, I have tried to keep a watchful eye on the happenings at the Baudelaire Society. I have spent my days doing the rounds of booksellers and bouquinistes, keeping up with book gossip, which is always rife with scandal and conspiracy, or when the weather was inclement holing up in a library to browse the newspapers and magazines, study auction catalogues, and dissect the annual *Gazette de la Société Baudelaire*. This is how I learned, several years after the war, about the death of a bookseller who was said to be selling an unpublished short story manuscript by Baudelaire called "The Education of a Monster." When I read that his eyes had been removed by the murderer, there was no mistaking the culprit. Artopoulos was baiting me, hoping to flush me out of hiding. Whether he had committed the act himself or through some third party mattered little. It was a coded message intended only for me: *Here I am*, the monster I had created seemed to say. *Come and get me if you dare. The longer you wait the more harm I will do. Only you will be to blame.*

It was also in the newspapers, the following year, 1923, that I learned of the death of that same monster. He too was buried in the Baudelaire Society crypt, although this time there was no question of my attending the burial. I knew he would not have died without crossing, so when, soon after, I learned that Gabrielle Chanel was the new president of the Society, I naturally assumed he'd crossed with her. Still I had to wait a decade for definitive confirmation. It came when the body of a Belgian industrialist was found, eyeless, in the Bois de Vincennes. A book collector, he'd come to Paris to buy the same previously unknown manuscript by Baudelaire. The soul of Joubert lived in that woman, I knew, and was mocking me still.

Nowadays, locked in my stalemate, I lead a quiet life. I prefer the dark to the light, night to day, underground to above ground. I shun society and have only one friend, the singer you met at the Shéhérazade. I work as a waitress there. Never in my previous lives have I been as alone as I am now. Sometimes I watch people passing by, yearning to live as they do, in the certainty of their mortality.

Since my last crossing, I am beset as never before by a surfeit of memory. Every place I go reminds me of another place, or of the same place at another time, or of several places at once. Every scent reminds me of other scents, every melody of other songs. I take a bite or a sip of something and I am instantly transported to another time and place. A word, a face, a birdcall, a cloud, and I am plunged into other worlds. Perhaps there is a natural limit to remembering, beyond which it is simply impossible to bear the weight of all that remembrance.

Sometimes, I wish I was more like you, Koahu. I wish I, too, could forget. This is my seventh body. I hope it will be my last. Every crossing adds a lifetime of memories to the hoard. As Chanel, Joubert is in his sixth lifetime, and you are in your fifth—but he has his rage and you have your forgetting. I only have my guilt to sustain me. I have lost all desire for making another crossing. All of my lifetimes, combined with the hundreds, perhaps thousands of crossings I undertook as Balthazar, seem to have taken a toll. I find myself living in a constant state of exhaustion. Perhaps there is something in Madeleine that contributed to it too—the fatalism I noted before our crossing.

Time and again I ask myself why I am still alive. I'm not proud of myself. I've been a thief. I've made a mess of things. I've tried to undo something that cannot be undone. I only seem to have made things worse. The world we came from is gone forever and nothing can bring it back. *There can be no crossing without a return crossing.* I think about that often. It torments me day and night. Perhaps the world doesn't end all at once, but slowly, imperceptibly, as a chain of seemingly innocuous events measured across generations.

If it wasn't for Joubert, I would already be dead—and once I no longer have to worry about him and what he might do, I look forward to my ultimate release. I have yearned for death long enough. Chanel is getting closer, I know it—sometimes I imagine I can feel her hot breath on my neck. She has a network of informants looking out for me, I'm sure of it. Perhaps Massu, your friend at the Quai des Orfèvres, is one of them.

Whenever a murdered corpse is found with its eyes missing, like Vennet the bookseller, it is Joubert playing on my guilt, taunting me, luring me, daring me. One day I will take up the dare. One day I will finish this story once and for all. You, Koahu, may be my beloved, but he is my destiny. I hold myself responsible for him and all his acts of cruelty. Now that I have seen you, now that you know all you need to know, now that you've written it down, perhaps my story is finally approaching its end. Perhaps you can take on the legacy of our sin, all those lifetimes ago. Chanel doesn't know about you. She doesn't know for sure if you are even still alive. But if she finds out, she will want to destroy you just as surely as she wishes to destroy me.

You have the manuscript now, but it alone is not enough. You must write down your own story—the story of our meeting at the cemetery and everything that has happened since. You must write down my story too, the story of my seven lives. Add to it the story you wrote as Charles Baudelaire. The true tale of the albatross is all of these stories, together. They unite us. Keep them close to you so that, next time you cross, they will be the first thing you see. It is the only way to ensure you won't have to piece together your true self over a lifetime of nightmares. Let the stories be your guide.

Perhaps you still don't entirely believe me. Perhaps you never will. I've become accustomed to your skepticism. But when we met your nightmares stopped. And when we crossed you saw yourself staring back at you. When the opportunity to make a crossing comes, I know you will take it. You always have. Choose your inheritor wisely. Choose someone who wishes to die, and if you cannot, choose someone who deserves to. A crossing is no small thing. Every crossing is a theft of a life, and all that goes with it.

When this war is over, we'll meet again. I'll be waiting in my usual place: in the cemetery, standing by Baudelaire's grave, in the late afternoon, smoking a cigarette just before closing time. Until then, all that is left for me to say is farewell, my beloved. Farewell, good luck, and bon voyage.

{141}

Cast of Characters

Alula	Madeleine Pernety/Blanc
Pierre Joubert	Koahu
Jean-François Feuille	Claude Roblet
Jeanne Duval	Charles Baudelaire
Édmonde de Bressy	Mathilde Roeg
Hippolyte Balthazar	Walter Benjamin

Acknowledgments

THE AUTHOR WISHES to thank the following for their assistance in the publication of this novel: Mathilda Imlah and staff at Picador Australia, Geordie Williamson, Chris Womersley, Susan Golomb, and Mariah Stovall. For support given during the writing of the novel: Anna Landragin, Marie Landragin, Armen Landragin, Odin Ozdil, Maxime Kurkdjian, Jane Rawson, Andy Maurer, John Ryan, Stuart McDonald, Jeremy Dole, and Gwenola Naudin. I am indebted to all my readers, especially the encouragement and feedback of the following: Bruce Melendy, Rachael Antony, Lucie Thorne, Simon Bailey, Rose Mulready, Josiane Behmoiras-Smith, Patrick Witton, Rachel Blake, Hilary Ericksen, Emily Aspland, the Bro Book Club, Sally O'Brien, Piers Kelly, Luke Savage, Leon Terrill, David Carroll, Laurence Billiet, Julia Lehmann, and Katrina Gill. Apologies to anyone I've left off the list. Thanks to all the librarians who helped me along the way. Special thanks to Melissa Cranenburgh. This novel was inspired by a story told to me long ago by Chris Wallace-Crabbe. In memory of Naomi.

ALEX LANDRAGIN is a French Armenian Australian writer. Currently based in Melbourne, Australia, he has also resided in Paris, Marseille, Los Angeles, New Orleans, and Charlottesville. He has previously worked as a librarian, an indigenous community worker, and an author of Lonely Planet travel guides in Australia, Europe, and Africa. Alex holds an MA in creative writing from the University of Melbourne and occasionally performs early jazz piano under the moniker Tenderloin Stomp. *Crossings* is his debut novel.